The
BRIDE WHO
GOT LUCKY

JANNA
MACGREGOR

St. Martin's Paperbacks

THE BRIDE WHO GOT LUCKY

For information address St. Martin's Press, 175 Fifth Avenue, New York, NY 10010.

ISBN: 978-1-250-11614-7

Our books may be purchased in bulk for promotional, educational, or business use. Please contact your local bookseller or the Macmillan Corporate and Premium Sales Department at 1-800-221-7945, ext. 5442, or by e-mail at MacmillanSpecialMarkets@macmillan.com.

Printed in the United States of America

St. Martin's Paperbacks edition /November 2017

St. Martin's Paperbacks are published by St. Martin's Press, 175 Fifth Avenue, New York, NY 10010.

10 9 8 7 6 5 4 3 2 1

To Willie,
Others have said it before, but it is a universal
truth—you are the best mom ever.

Acknowledgments

M y incredible publishing journey would never have
progressed very far without the unwavering support of my family. My sisters, Sandy and Pam, have been
my constant supporters and gladly read the pages I
pushed under their noses. They helped me brush the neg-
atives away so I could write another day. Thank you for
everything.

My lovely children, Nicholas, Anthony, and Rachel
have helped me immensely. Nicholas, the ballroom
scene in *Madame Bovary* will always be a favorite
memory. Thank you for critiquing the first page of every
book. Anthony, your guidance and unwavering patience
with me over Socrates and logic will forever be appreciated. Rachel, thank you for all your inspiration. You
made me believe. I feel the same way about you all as
Ginny does with Emma. I'm *so* lucky to have you as my
children.

My biggest supporter is my darling husband, Greg.
When I announced I wanted to write a romance, he
thought it a marvelous idea. That week, he purchased a

keepsake so I could always hold the memory of that day near. He was the first one to read my book—his very first romance. Of course, he is the author of my romantic life. *Lucky me.*

Prologue

◦～◦

For most, the opportunity to see one's father visiting the esteemed halls of Eton College would be far more preferable than cleaning chamber pots.

Unless your father was Drake St. Mauer, the Duke of Renton.

Alone in his room, Nicholas St. Mauer, the Earl of Somerton, tried to ignore the tremble of his hand, a sign of weakness, as he held the muslin drape aside. His sticky palms were another matter. Another swipe down the side of his breeches did little to stem his nervous energy. He wasn't a coward. No matter how downcast, he'd meet his father.

Refusing to blink in case he missed the duke, he locked his gaze below on the black-lacquered ducal carriage emblazoned with a coat of arms as familiar as his name. Two lions holding shields that bore the family heralds reared on hind legs, back-to-back, ready to attack any foe. As a small boy, he'd developed a strong sense of familial pride and awe whenever he saw the crest. Today, it brought an immediate sense of censure.

His father had arrived on the grounds over an hour

ago. The expected summons from the provost hadn't yet materialized. Nick relaxed his vigilance and pressed his eyes shut for a moment to relieve the dryness. An undeniable foreboding continued its relentless march through his thoughts. He cleared his throat in a poor attempt to lessen the panic that squeezed his chest.

He was currently missing a Latin exam. Normally he'd have been eager to prove his adeptness. Now, he could not have cared less since it mattered little. His father was here.

The fact his father deigned to grace the hallowed halls of Eton should have been marked in the annuals of the school's history books—an event rarer than a total solar eclipse and just as ominous. His father never came to see him.

Ever.

In the ten years he'd attended school, Nick had never had a visitor—until today. No one cared. During the school break for the holidays, he was always the last to leave. As if an afterthought, one of the ducal carriages would lumber into the school's driveway and bring him home.

At fifteen, school was the only constant in his life. Gifted with figures, he'd been shuffled from one elite boarding school to another. After he'd mastered a school's offered mathematics curriculum, which inevitably occurred, the headmaster would politely suggest another institution might be more of a challenge to his analytical prowess. The routine of changing schools had repeated ad nauseam until Nick had learned it was far easier to become a recluse. There was no pain if you didn't leave behind any friendships. It made life less complicated.

That had changed once he attended Eton. His instructors had taken a special interest in him and his talents. For the first time in his life, he belonged somewhere.

It wasn't a secret that his father despised him. Never allowed to call him "Father" or "Papa," Nick had learned at an early age to address his sire as "Your Grace." Even the servants at Renton Hall cleared a wide berth around him, the heir and the one and only child of the duke. No doubt, they feared his loss of favored status could be contagious.

The familiar tightness around his throat grew stronger. The first time he'd experienced it, the ducal carriage had deposited him at a school close to the Scottish border. No one said a word or offered comfort as the carriage pulled away. He didn't leave his watch until the vehicle disappeared from sight.

Bloody hell, he had only been five years old.

Over the years, he'd trained himself not to feel or acknowledge the pain. He exhaled, and the suffocating shackles of disquiet loosened.

Muffled voices broke the quiet in the courtyard. The provost, Mr. Davies, was practically running after the duke and speaking in a raised voice. Nick rested his forehead against the cool glass of the window, desperate to hear every word. Waiting to assist, a Renton footman had opened the carriage door at the first sight of the duke.

Fate was in his own hands, so Nick flew to the door and flung it open. He ran to the dormitory steps and collided with two philosophy students several years his senior.

"Pardon me." His voice cracked in a high pitch that closely resembled a pig's squeal. The two young men fell against the wall and uttered curses his way. By then, he was halfway down the steps. His ungainly legs and feet tangled in a hopeless knot causing him to miss the last three steps. Pain screamed through his legs as his knees took the brunt of the fall. The skinned palms of his hands burned as if on fire. He paid little heed as his only concern was reaching his father and showing him the man he'd become.

Throughout the course of his years, he'd watched and learned the rituals and intricacies of being a gentleman. Perchance, his father would see the results of his work and find some pride in his actions.

Nick threw open the door, causing it to bounce against the stone wall. The crash reverberated in the courtyard. He stopped, willing his father to turn in his direction—waiting for an acknowledgment.

The duke half-glanced in his direction and lifted a foot to step into the carriage.

If he didn't do something, the carriage would leave. "Your Grace."

The provost stepped aside as Nick reached his father.

"Your Grace?" Nick lifted a hand, but a stern footman stepped between them to keep Nick away. He'd quickly squelched the faint hope his father would invite him home for a visit. Nevertheless, he expected the duke would speak to him, at least for a moment or two. "Please, Your Grace," Nick begged.

His father turned. In his early forties, strength and vitality emanated from his body. Simply put, the duke was a force to be reckoned with. The yellow hair and patrician features were similar to his own, but the duke's hardened expression was one Nick would never grow accustomed to.

"What is it?" the duke snapped.

Nick swallowed the searing pain clogging his throat. He hadn't cried since he'd left Renton House at the age of five and would be damned if he gave the old man the pleasure of seeing his weakness, the desire to be wanted or simply accepted. "Sir, did you need to see me? I hope we could perhaps . . . I could have a few minutes of your company."

God, Nick hated the desperation that leaked from his throat. His father didn't give a damn about him or his accomplishments. He shouldn't have bothered. The duke didn't waste time on his only son or the letter he'd painstakingly written seeking two hundred pounds. He'd retched after posting the missive seeking such a large sum, but he had no other choice.

His only friend, Lord Paul Bartstowe, was also a duke's son. Full of bravado that others envied, Lord Paul had entered a card game at the local tavern with some unsavory men and lost. Thrilled to have been invited by the powerful Duke of Southart's second son, Nick had foolishly accompanied him.

Holding the game-winning hand, a giant of a man had threatened Lord Paul's life if he didn't pay. The look of desperation in his friend's eyes triggered something within Nick. Stepping in as any gentleman would, he signed the notes to keep Lord Paul from harm. It was what any friend would do for another. They left the tavern together, safe from the ruffians with the understanding Lord Paul would have the funds within a week.

Repeatedly, Lord Paul had assured Nick he'd pay his debt, but the monies never materialized. Two weeks ago, the man who'd won the game ventured to the dormitory and paid Nick a visit. He demanded payment with a convincing fist to Nick's stomach and explained the dire consequences for both Nick and Lord Paul if the money wasn't forthcoming. The threats had been quite graphic with gruesome descriptions of rearranged facial parts and broken appendages. Nick had no recourse but to ask his father for the funds.

"You're asking if I need to see you?" The duke's voice sounded so familiar to Nick's ears, but yet so foreign. "Why would I ever ask for *you*, a debauched wastrel with gambling debts? You bring shame—" The duke's mouth thinned into a line. He tugged his beaver hat securely onto his head while his steely gaze burrowed into Nick's own.

Several windows creaked opened in succession, and a few of the students leaned out the casements to watch the scene unfold. Nick glanced around the courtyard in a futile effort to gain his composure. With a sniff, he quickly swiped his left eye. The duke stared at the tell-tale wetness against Nick's hand. They both knew his words had wounded.

The duke shook his head. "You're weak and unfit to be my heir. You're not even worthy to be called the Earl of Somerton. The courtesy title would be better bestowed on a stable boy."

An unleashed defiance that came from years of living on his own broke free, and Nick took a step closer. He'd not suffer another insult. Even though his father had at least a five-stone advantage, Nick was almost tall enough to stare straight into the duke's eyes.

"I don't like you much." The duke lowered his voice. "You're like one of those vain, ostentatious race horses that can't win a race, all looks but worth nothing."

Involuntarily, Nick took a step back. A few of his classmates had gathered at the edge of the courtyard. Like vultures ready to feast on carrion, they drew his attention away from his father. Some of the well-known bullies mocked and snickered at the duke's retort. Others simply stared in horror. One young man, the Marquess of Pembrooke, stepped forward but must have thought better of it and retreated. Something akin to pity crossed his face. Lord St. John Howell, the biggest tormentor of all, stood front and center. He stood a half-foot taller than Nick, but his most remarkable feature was his chest. Thick and muscled, it resembled a barrel.

Nick sneered at them all to hide the blistering shame

he suffered at his father's cruel words. "At least I had one loving parent," he whispered.

"Well, that's debatable as your mother never made mention to me," the duke scoffed. He tapped his finger against one cheek as if contemplating a mathematical theorem. "Come to think of it, how could she? You killed her when she gave birth to you."

A fiery heat bludgeoned Nick's face. At that precise moment, he couldn't have cared less whether any of his classmates witnessed the tears that coursed down his cheeks. Irate, his fists clenched, he focused on the man in front of him.

"Don't even consider lifting a hand against me," the duke growled.

"Go ahead, old man, hit me first," Nick challenged. It wasn't hatred that spewed from the blue-green depths of his father's eyes, but something else. It resembled bitterness or maybe resentment.

The duke was the first to break away. He spat on the ground as if to rid himself of a foul taste. "We're done. Perhaps it's best if you not cross the threshold of Renton Hall again in the near future and don't ask for anything. I'm finished."

"Finished with what?" Nick was incredulous at the statement. The duke was the only family he had.

"You. Find your own way. If you're man enough to take on someone else's foolish debts, you can take care of yourself." The duke turned on his heel and entered the carriage. He tapped the roof once, and the team of four perfectly matched bays jerked the carriage into motion.

Numb, Nick stood rooted in place, grasping to comprehend what had happened as the carriage lumbered off the grounds. His ears rang, and in that moment, all he could do was concentrate on the tinny sound.

"Well, that didn't go well, did it?" Lord Paul slapped

him across the shoulder. "What a bloody bugger. I'll ask for the funds today. I apologize."

"You haven't asked for the money? It's been weeks." The words echoed in his brain as if he were speaking into a well. He shook his head to clear the haze that threatened to drown him.

"I'm waiting on my monthly allowance. It'd be easier—"

"For whom?" Nick swallowed the nausea that threatened to overtake his last ounce of control. "You selfish bastard."

"This is not the time or the place for a discussion." Alex Hallworth, the Marquess of Pembrooke, had recently inherited his father's title. Somehow, he'd joined their conversation.

With a shrug of his shoulders, Lord Paul returned to the dormitory.

Nick dismissed the interruption by turning his back on Pembrooke. The pain refused to leave him.

"Even your own family doesn't waste time in your company," Howell jeered. "Seems the duke has finally dropped the leading strings."

Others laughed at the taunt, but their unease hung in the air like a thick London fog. Howell was known for his cruelty, and no one wanted to be his next target.

"Enough." Pembrooke's menacing tone scattered most of the students, including Howell, back into the dormitory.

Pembrooke was nothing more than an acquaintance, someone Nick nodded to when they passed in the hall, yet the marquess sidled next to Nick as if an ally. Pembrooke stared in the direction the duke's carriage had taken. "If there's anything—"

"Leave." Nick managed to ground out the single word.

Pembrooke didn't answer. After a moment, he pivoted on his heel and left Nick's side.

The bitter sting of humiliation seeped into his conscience, little by little. He tried to ignore it, but it grew stronger and threatened to take him to his knees. He spared a quick glance, enough time to see the remaining students leave the courtyard and the provost's quiet exodus while shaking his head.

This was his reward for trying to be a man his father would be proud to claim as his son.

The duke had exiled him.

Fat cold drops of rain had started to fall. He let it soak through his clothing until his skin was wet and chilled. If heaven was crying for him, it was a wasted effort. He'd already decided what to do.

Every ugly moment of this day would be locked into a safe and reliable cage, one that would insulate his heart. Strong and unbreakable, it could be opened only by him.

He'd abide by his father's decree. He'd never again step foot on any Renton property. Nor would the duke be allowed anywhere near him. As important, Nick vowed never to acknowledge any student who had laughed and mocked him while his father cast him aside.

They could all rot in hell.

Nick made one more promise. Whatever he had to surrender, whatever he had to endure, whatever sacrifice, he'd amass a fortune greater than his father's wealth.

Moreover, he'd do it on his own. He needed no one.

Chapter One

Fourteen years later
London

Lady Emma Cavensham opened her beaded reticule and checked it twice. The fifty pounds she'd saved from her pin money lay folded neatly inside. As the carriage accelerated through Mayfair, she exhaled the tension that had been building all night. In its place, pure unencumbered joy burst free like fireworks in the night sky over Vauxhall.

It had taken meticulous planning, but her efforts would pay off. Tonight, she'd purchase the rare first edition of *Bentham's Essays* at the Black Falstaff Inn. She'd arrive within forty-five minutes, make the purchase, and return to Lady Dalton's ball all within two hours. Moreover, she'd celebrate with a defiant glass of ale in the public taproom like any other person. Well, more specifically, like a man.

Why should it make any difference she was young, unmarried, and a female? Why should it make any difference she was a duke's daughter? Even if society thought such action ruinous, she didn't see the harm. Society's strictures for appropriate behavior wouldn't keep her from attaining her goal tonight.

No one, not even her cousin Claire, who had escorted her to Lady Dalton's ball, had an inkling that she was on her way to meet Lord Paul Barstowe at an inn outside of London. After discovering he owned a rare copy of the coveted book, Emma had sent him a note earlier in the evening inviting him to the inn so she could make the acquisition. It was the perfect place to meet, as no one would recognize her.

Every piece of Emma's brilliant plan fit perfectly together. She'd pat herself on the back if she could reach it. She'd have the adventure under her proverbial belt along with *Bentham's Essays* and be back at the ball hopefully before Claire or anyone else knew she was missing. The groomsmen and driver who had picked her up from Lady Dalton's would keep her secrets.

"Whoa!" The loud command came from the driving box. The sudden stop practically threw Emma to the floor as the ducal carriage with its team of four came to an abrupt halt.

Quickly, she peeked outside the window. At the intersection of the street perpendicular to their route, a carriage similar to hers had stopped. Odd place to leave a vehicle, and there was no one milling around it. Not a single groomsman or coachman to be found. It was as if someone had abandoned it.

"What is it, Russell?" she called to one of the Duke of Langham's groomsmen.

Russell leaned down from the driving box. "I'm not certain, Lady Emma."

"Can we go around it?"

"No, my lady," he answered.

A man with a deep voice, one she didn't recognize, started to speak. Russell turned his attention to the stranger. Disaster loomed if she stuck her head out the carriage window and someone discovered her alone. Tamping down the urge to peek, she strained to hear the conversation. The even cadence and the rhythm of the stranger's words thrummed like a drumbeat, one that suddenly caused goose bumps to skate down her arms. Precious time was slipping through her fingers, and she couldn't afford any delays.

"Russell—" Before she could say more, the carriage door sprang open and a tall man dressed in black entered. When he closed the door, the carriage lurched forward, continuing the path they'd taken earlier.

"Who are you?" Her heart beat so hard she feared it'd explode from her chest.

With his back to her, the stranger blew out the sole carriage lantern that lit the interior. Then with a stealthy grace, he sat on the bench opposite of her.

Trouble had found her.

"Why did you extinguish the light?" Her voice quavered, betraying her unease.

Hidden in the shadows, he resembled some type of phantom, one who had settled into position ready to attack. He didn't waste a glance as he removed his hat and threw it on the bench next to him.

"Who are you?" she repeated as a hint of hysteria nipped at her reserve.

"Lady Emma," the man chided. "The light is out to lessen the chance someone might recognize you."

The stranger's rich but dark whisper intrigued her. Who was this mystery man who had taken control of her carriage? Short-lived, her curiosity faded when they passed by a streetlight.

"Lord Somerton," she hissed. The night she wanted to stay hidden, the elusive earl who rarely ever showed his face in society found her. This wasn't bad luck. This was fate playing a cruel joke and then laughing hysterically.

There was no denying he was breathtakingly hand-some with his turquoise eyes and lithe stature. However, she couldn't be bothered with his looks or with him—not tonight. The earl's best friend just happened to be Claire's husband. Her parents would know of her adventure before the night was over.

Her goose was cooked.

"I'm at your service, Lady Emma," he drawled.

"I didn't ask for your service. What do you want?" With a deep breath, she subdued the petulance in her voice. She had to save the evening and her book. All she needed was a little charm. "Lord Somerton, I apologize for my manners. You've taken me by surprise."

Instead of heading straight, the carriage barreled through a sharp right turn causing her to slide across the leather seat. Certain a tumble to the floor was in her future, she braced for the fall.

With a gentle strength, he grabbed her around the waist, causing her to gasp. As if she were a fragile por-celain doll, he settled her on the bench.

"Thank you," she whispered.

"There's no need. I promised I'd bring you home safe and sound, and I plan on accomplishing it." He pulled the curtain aside for a moment. When he released it, he leaned back against the squab.

"Who asked you to bring me home?" She dreaded the answer but asked anyway.

"Your cousin and her husband," he offered.

She released the breath she'd been holding. It'd be dif-ficult, but she could convince Claire not to tell her par-ents. The unknown was whether she could trust Claire's husband Pembrooke and the enigma sitting across from her.

She *would* salvage her evening. Somerton's presence

was nothing more than a slight hindrance, much like an annoying gnat.

"My lord, I appreciate the escort, but I've other plans. Is there some place I could have the coachman drop you? White's perhaps?" Lud, her calm demeanor was astounding.

"No, thank you."

Bold action called for bold moves. If she told him her purpose, perhaps he'd leave her be. Surely, a man would understand the desire for a book. If he thought her a bluestocking, a woman who constantly had her nose in a book, it made little difference. She was going to capture her prize.

"I'm on my way to buy *Bentham's Essays*, first edition. For over a year, I've been hunting for it." In the darkness, she couldn't see his expression, making it difficult to gage his response. If only he hadn't extinguished the lantern.

"Have you thought of securing your book someplace else . . . more respectable? I've heard there are *these* shops called bookstores," he teased.

She bit her lip to keep from lashing him with a verbal blistering. That would seal her doom. "Please, this is my only chance to make the purchase. I've sent inquiries to every bookstore within London to no avail. No one has it. Mr. Goodwin at Goodwin's Book Emporium thought he had found a seller ready to part with their copy, but unfortunately, the seller changed his mind."

"Goodwin?" he scoffed. "What the devil are you doing shopping at Goodwin's? That's not an acceptable shop for a young woman."

Though she couldn't see him, she sensed Somerton towered over her, his presence pushing her back into the squabs.

"Goodwin isn't known for his selection of books." He enunciated every word in a husky manner designed to frighten her. "His real business is selling information—he's a snitch, and a very successful one at that."

The impertinent Earl of Somerton would not intimidate her. She pulled herself forward to give him an appropriate setdown. Without warning, the carriage lurched, causing her forehead to bump his chin.

"Careful." His hand cupped the back of her head as he pulled her close. His scent—clean, spicy, and male, one so different from the other men of the *ton*—wrapped itself around her like a binding. She didn't move.

Neither did he.

"You can't kidnap me," she whispered and forced herself to lean back. He was so close, his breath brushed against her cheek like a kiss. Without thinking, she ran her fingers over his lips. She'd never noticed before, but his mouth was perfect. Perfectly kissable. She jerked her hand away and mumbled, "Pardon me."

This was pure madness.

A streetlamp cast enough light that she saw his face clearly along with the dangerous flare in his eyes.

"I'm not your responsibility," she demanded softly. "Please, I beg of you. Let me go."

"For your assignation?" he whispered. "With Lord Paul Barstowe?"

"What? *No*." She shook her head hoping she'd wake from this nightmare. "How do you know I'm meeting him to purchase the book?"

"One of the guests at Lady Dalton's informed me after overhearing your plans."

"Of all the rotten luck," she muttered. She shouldn't have told her friends Lena and Daphne in public, as there were too many ears at a ball. Determined, she'd persevere.

"Come with me if you don't believe I'm speaking the truth. Please, I *need* that book."

Again, silence reigned between them except for the trotting of the horses' hooves. Even that sound drifted to nothing as the carriage slowed to a halt. A glance outside confirmed they'd arrived at her home. Soft light flooded the carriage from the lanterns that surrounded the courtyard.

With her last chance looming before her, Emma swallowed her pride, nearly choking. Lacing her fingers together to keep from fidgeting, she stared into his eyes. "Please, my lord, I'm begging you. Come with me if you're concerned for my safety. I'll prove to you I only want the book." She opened her reticule and pulled out the fifty pounds. "I'll pay you. If this isn't enough, I'll get more. . . ."

He released a deep breath and studied his clasped hands.

Dare she hope she'd convinced him? Indeed, he seemed truly conflicted. She sat on the edge of the bench waiting for his agreement. To nudge him a little, she made her final plea. "Please?"

"I'm truly sorry." He covered her hand with his and squeezed. "Let me escort you inside."

His effort offered little comfort. For an eternity, she sat unable to move and stared at nothing. There was little doubt she'd face a harsh reprimand from her parents and some fitting punishment to accompany the lecture. Her heavy heart slid to the floor. It mattered little as she'd already been punished. *Bentham's Essays* was again out of her reach.

"Lady Emma?" Somerton squeezed her hand again—his gentle touch still a betrayal. "Come."

He helped her from the carriage and walked her to

the door. As if she were being lead to the gallows, she held her head high masking her stinging disappointment.

"Good night," Somerton whispered. "I apologize I've caused you such distress." He bowed over her hand in farewell.

"My lord?" Her question caused his gaze to capture hers. The sincerity in his eyes stole her breath. Briefly, she turned away until her emotions were somewhat under control. "I can't offer my thanks for your assistance. I'm sure you understand." She turned and entered Langham Hall.

Intact, her pride was still stuck in her throat.

The next day
Banished.

She'd been eradicated like an infestation of kitchen vermin.

The only difference was her parents were dispatching Emma for her own good, and no one bothered to offer condescending explanations to mice.

As of tomorrow, she'd reside at Falmont, the family seat, for the remainder of the Season. Her father and mother had stood together united in their decision, a bulwark designed to protect her from last night's indiscretion.

All because she desired a book.

The tome in question wasn't a lewd collection of Elizabethan bawdy, or a frothy romance of thwarted lovers, or even a tirade by revolutionaries threatening to overrun the government.

It was a book of essays about individual freedom.

Hidden in the shade of the trees, Emma leaned her head back against her favorite bench in Langham Park and stared at the cloudless blue sky. Completely enclosed, the private park, famous for its groomed gardens and orangeries, surrounded her home and was her own private refuge. She could wander for hours to her heart's content. The gardeners and other servants were always respectful of her privacy. Heaven knew she needed solitude today.

A plump red squirrel skidded into view with a cache of food stuffed in his cheeks. The creature examined her as if she was an intruder in *his* private garden before he swooshed his thick red tail and started to chatter.

She was receiving yet another proper scolding. He paused as if waiting for a response.

"After tomorrow, the park is all yours." At least someone would benefit from her ostracism. "If you were a true gentleman, you'd cease your prattling rant."

"Shall I slay the impertinent beast?" A low, sensual voice spoke softly in her ear. "Before I go into battle, I must ask, how does the lovely Lady Emma fare today?"

"As one would expect after being informed of my upcoming sojourn to the country." A slight breeze caressed Emma's face, but she refused to turn around. There was no mistaking that silken smooth voice. She didn't need to see him to know it was the killjoy from last night. "Lord Somerton, imagine you finding me, *again*. Whatever are you doing here?"

"The duke and duchess asked if I would meet them today. Lord and Lady Pembrooke were in attendance," he said. "They wanted to know how far you'd traveled before I caught you."

"Oh, you mean my cousin Claire, *the paragon of perfection*, the Marchioness of Pembrooke, and her *utterly flawless husband*, the Marquess of Pembrooke, otherwise known as *the happy couple*." She hadn't intended to sound so sarcastic, but really, what could Somerton expect?

A blindfolded fox had a better chance of escaping the hounds than she had to escape him. The thought made her swallow hard. It was just so humiliating, and the fact *he* had found her made it worse. The traitor.

"I'm to be sent to Falmont tomorrow," she said dully.

The squirrel sat on his haunches as if finding her situation riveting and cracked a nut.

"I'm sorry for my part in it." He was close enough that his warm breath tickled her earlobe. If she wasn't mistaken, his lips brushed her cheek.

Emma didn't have a qualm of disgust for him, which he deserved—definitely. Instead, something strange and new formed inside her chest. A shiver skated down her spine that made her sit straighter. "Don't apologize. I was aware of the consequences."

His breath stroked her cheek. Emma clenched her eyes to concentrate on his smell. He had to be leaning adjacent to her. The scent of bay rum with undertones of saddle leather and male wafted toward her. She wanted to swim in it.

"I would hate for last evening to have a negative impact on your ties to Lady Pembrooke," said Somerton. "She's really quite fond of you."

"Don't worry." She stood and faced him. "I consider Claire my sister, and sisters don't hold grudges. At least that's what my mother would say. You'll discover that about my family if you keep our company. But if you and your friend, Pembrooke, think you'll dictate my behavior—"

"Easy, Lady Emma." He held his gloved hands in front of his chest as if to ward her off. "No one, least of all me, shall be giving you deportment lessons."

Granted, he was handsome in his morning coat, but his tone reminded her of one that the Langham head groomsman always used to soothe a spooked horse. That was a first. Normally, men would walk away without a glance back if she made it clear how she expected to be treated.

Really, all of this was beyond the pale.

"With Pembrooke marrying your cousin, we'll be in each other's company a fair amount," he said. "It'd be regrettable if you were uncomfortable with me."

He'd lost the timbre of a groomsman only to replace it with a rich tone that would have charmed a howling banshee.

"In a twisted view of fate, I suppose I should thank you," she added nonchalantly.

"I knew you possessed great intelligence," he teased as he rounded the bench that separated them. "Never mind all your reading."

His actions last night were honorable, and he'd treated her with respect. She couldn't hold him accountable for her circumstances. Nevertheless, she couldn't help but blame him.

"I'd much rather you stay here," he offered. "London will be a dreary place without you."

If she wasn't mistaken, the rumble of his words and the slight hesitation hinted at his remorse. *What a bouncer.* Except for her friend Lena, she doubted anyone would notice her absence.

"London and the Season have little to offer." In fact, she hated high society with a passion comparable to her disgust of Brussels sprouts. She'd had her fill of self-important fobs and fortune hunters examining her much like a hothouse peach.

"Were the duke and duchess harsh with your punishment?" His simple question floated like a piece of silk over her body.

"Yes, it was dreadful. I'm forbidden from saying goodbye to my friend, Lady Lena Eaton. We'd planned to attend Lady Farold's ball tonight." Even though she hated balls, Lena loved them and she loved Lena. For her friend, Emma suffered through the miserable affairs. "Since our debut, we've never missed attending together."

The fact she couldn't see Lena hurt more than the lecture or the bitter humiliation of being sent away. It was akin to being cut in two. She and Lena were inseparable.

Emma stopped the incessant twiddling of her fingers. "You'll be happy to hear I've learned an important lesson from last evening. Never take your father's carriage with the coat of arms adorned on the sides when you want to travel incognito. Hire a hackney."

"I would have found you, whatever carriage you were in. You could have been ruined if word got out about last night." His voice was light, but the threat was obvious. "Aren't you concerned about making a match with some bold and gallant gentleman ready to sweep you off your feet?"

"Not in the least." As a duke's daughter, she was still a prime catch even at the advanced age of twenty-two. She had plenty of time to find a husband if she so desired. She just wasn't at all certain she wanted one. At Falmont, she could read to her heart's content without the interruption of insufferable social calls. However, without Lena by her side, she had many lonely nights ahead of her at the family's ancestral home.

"To make up for my part in last night, I have something for you," Somerton said.

"You shouldn't be giving me anything." *Where had that come from?* The paradox of her sudden concern for propriety was laughable.

He smiled and retrieved something from his morning coat inner pocket.

Tentatively, with her heart pounding in her ears, she accepted the package and unwrapped the paper. The earl was a magician. He'd found the book she wanted, the one she'd searched for last night. "*Bentham's Essays*," she whispered.

"First edition."

"Where did you find it?" To her utmost regret, common sense barged into her thoughts. The book was rare and too expensive for her to receive as a gift—particularly from him. "Somerton, I can't accept—"

"Nonsense. It's from my library. I've read it. You're more than welcome to it." He stood close and peered down as she opened the cover.

Was he serious? This was a treasure.

"I'd like for you to have it." He grinned at her, and his face transformed from slightly forbidding to irresistible. "Come now, my best friend and your cousin are married. That makes us practically—"

"Friends," she finished for him.

Truly, he was unique from other men she'd met. He'd actually paid attention to the book she'd coveted. Discreetly, she raised her gaze and appraised him. Last night, his full bottom lip fascinated her. In the light of day, it was magnificent. The curve of his top lip deserved no less than a full evaluation. What would it feel like to touch lip to lip? How would he taste? There was only one way to find out.

She should offer a kiss for payment. Emma clasped the book tightly to her chest for courage. "I must pay you. You prefer fair exchanges, value for value, so to speak?"

He cocked an eyebrow.

"I'll take it in exchange for a kiss." The breathy softness in her voice surprised her. She was flirting! She'd never done anything like this before, but to leave for Falmont with the experience of her first kiss would make the trip tolerable.

The hint of laughter rumbling through his chest startled her. "A kiss?"

Before he could say another word, she stood on tiptoes and pressed her lips to his. Her face burned from the touch, and a pleasurable tingling slowly started in her toes and moved to her legs. It continued its upward path to her chest until he moved.

He pulled away, the shock evident on his face, and mumbled something.

Did he say she tasted sweet, or was it he'd make a fast retreat?

With her bad luck, why did she even try? He was the most gorgeous man she'd ever seen, and she'd just stolen a kiss. Stung, she turned away to hide her embarrassment. This whole encounter was horrifying, and she'd just made it doubly so. Whatever his response, it made little difference at this point. He found her kiss disgusting.

Suddenly, he spun her around, and the unmistakable warm softness of his lips met hers. His hands cupped her face. Gently, but firmly, he tilted her head and moved his mouth back and forth along the curve of her own. All thought drifted to oblivion. His kiss became everything, the only thing she craved.

An uncontrollable need to touch him in return caused her to twist her hands in his hair. Silky strands, a lighter gold than hers, slipped through her fingers. Her hands settled on his wide shoulders, and his muscles bunched under her tentative touch.

"Is this the first time you've been kissed?" His low voice mesmerized her. A ripple of excitement swept through her, but a sting of mortification soon replaced it.

Was it that obvious? "Yes. . . ."

"Good." His tongue lightly pressed against her lips. Her willpower floated away, and with a sigh, she opened to him. It was heaven. He gentled his movements and enticed her tongue to play with his. This time it was deeper, wetter, and hotter. She could barely believe he was kissing her this way. Exploring her. Teaching her. His teeth grazed her lower lip as if feasting on it. She gripped tighter in an effort to get closer to him.

All too soon, the pleasure stopped.

Emma opened her eyes to discover his brilliant turquoise ones assessing her. His lips, full and wet, drew her attention and made it more difficult to calm the riot of emotions surging through her. However, it didn't stop her from memorizing every feature. A square jaw line and sharply angled cheekbones framed his face. He resembled a Viking king with his tall build.

However, his most striking feature was his captivating blue-green eyes. Whenever his gaze captured hers, she understood the power he held. Women of the *ton* vied for his attention whenever he made a rare appearance at some society event, but it hadn't escaped her notice that he preferred his own company. He never seemed to crave female companionship.

He blinked and shook his head gently, then stared as if she were a strange creature he'd discovered on a jungle expedition. "Last night when I intercepted your coach, you possessed a passion that I'd never seen in anyone before."

"My family would refer to it as recklessness."

"Perhaps from their vantage point. But from mine? It's a thing of rare beauty." He cleared his throat.

She responded as taught when receiving a polite compliment. "Thank you, Lord Somerton."

"For the kiss or the book?"

Her gaze shot to his. The playfulness he'd exhibited when he first approached her on the bench had returned along with the sparkle in his blue eyes.

"Both," she whispered.

"No thanks needed. The pleasure was all mine." He extended his palm.

Unsure, she reached for his hand. Instead of the perfunctory bow over her clasped fingers, he shook hands, as a gentleman would take his leave of another.

Her heart skipped a beat at the gesture. His eyes were full of hope, and he smiled with a candor she'd never seen on his face before. Emma bit her lower lip to keep from laughing. It was a perfect way for them to part—equals, not adversaries.

"All of this for a book." He bent and whispered into her ear. "It was your good fortune I stopped you last night. No telling what trouble you'd have found."

Emma squared her shoulders. Under no circumstance would she suffer through another lecture from a squirrel or an English lord—particularly one she'd just kissed. "Thank you for your concern, but there was no need. I know how to handle awkward situations."

Somerton glanced over his shoulder, then delivered another blinding smile. "I might have other books that will interest you."

Was he trifling with her? The man had never taken any notice of her before, and she'd been out in society for four and a half years. Emma drew a shaky breath. "It would depend upon the subject matter."

"Trust me, I have exquisite tastes." His sensual drawl made her heart speed up again.

"As do I," she replied. His voice was too exciting for her own good.

"Well . . ." Somerton glanced down at his boots as if he didn't want to leave. "When you return to London, perhaps you'll give me a tour of the park?"

The slight uncertainty in his voice surprised her. "That'd be lovely."

"I enjoyed your company. Until the next time, sweet Emma."

As the words drifted away, he was gone. She turned for one last glance at her park. How she'd miss its beauty during her banishment.

With a decisive swirl of his tail, the squirrel rotated his tufted ears and dropped an empty walnut shell. He darted to the nearby oak. There was nothing else to see.

Emma strolled to the house. It was time to pack every book and memoire she'd collected over the years for her trip to Falmont. She'd have more than ample time to read them again as she suffered through her expulsion. *Bentham's Essays* and *Angela Tarte's Memoire of a Courtesan* would travel with her in the carriage.

Books could take you on the grandest of adventures.

Chapter Two

Emma rolled the leaded crystal paperweight between her hands, the rub of the cut edges soothing in her palms. With each movement, reflected light bounced from the crystal and cast rainbows that darted from one end of the library to another. She wasn't certain how long she'd been sitting at the mahogany table, but long enough for the hall clock to have struck the hour at least three times.

Papers and favorite books covered every inch of the surface. Today's issue of *The Midnight Cryer*, the most popular gossip rag in all of London, lay open before her. Two lines on the second page had stopped her cold. Keith Mahon, the Earl of Aulton, sought a new countess after three months of mourning.

The words lit a blaze of loathing inside of her.

She ignored the clutter surrounding her and concentrated on the letter she'd received from Lena's lady's maid, Mary Butler, three months ago after Lena's death.

Dated July 8, 1813, the letter was from Lady Lena Aulton, the previous Countess of Aulton, to her unborn child. She had written every conceivable piece of wisdom and life lesson she thought would protect her child from the harsh reality of life as a woman.

And certain she was delivering a baby girl, she'd named the child Audra.

My dearest Audra,

Our time together may be measured in minutes or years. Fate never reveals her hand. However, over the course of months as my belly has swelled, you've become a part of me that is as vital as the air I breathe. If I never have the chance to hold you in my arms, know that you're loved.

If I'm robbed of that joy, there are things I must share with you. Lessons designed to teach you that a life lived to its fullest is a life worth living. With a determined mind and an uncompromised spirit, you can rule the world.

Tired of the grief, Emma skipped to the second page before she lost her battle against the barrage of tears that threatened.

I have a dear friend who epitomizes this spirit. She inspired and taught me about the joy and glory of womanhood. Lady Emma Cavensham is my inspiration. Try to find your Emma, too.

As you travel through life, you will need a purpose. Help women who need protection, or perhaps friendship. You'll receive great rewards for your efforts.

Carefully choose a husband. Otherwise, you risk all freedom. A wife's position is tenuous in this world. The truth is harsh. If a husband tires of his chosen bride, he can cast her aside in some

remote cottage on the edge of the Outer Hebrides
without any repercussions. If he doesn't want to
feed and clothe her, that's his prerogative. A
rabid dog receives more respect than an English
wife. Remember, only you have your best inter-
ests at heart. I've set money aside so you can
more easily live the life you are destined.

The only disgrace in fear is not facing it. It's a
strong ally, for it whittles down wants to needs.

Raising her head, Emma stared blindly at the wall. Her
friend's haunted words echoed her own thoughts. Why
should she marry—ever? Why be subjected to a life where
she might be considered nothing more than a piece of
property or a nuisance, or worse yet a punching bag?
She'd seen enough in her life, even before Lena's death,
to confirm the truth. A woman subjected to a hard-hearted
husband was a fate worse than spinsterhood.

Today's announcement that Aulton wanted a new
bride demanded immediate action. Emma couldn't wait
anymore and neither could Lena. Her friend would receive retribution, and who better to serve it up than a
woman like herself, a woman who planned to never
marry. Over the months, she'd sought information and
made plans. Several years ago, Lord Somerton had informed her Mr. Goodwin's real profession was selling
information. The revelation had been invaluable. Over
the last month, with Goodwin's help, she had discovered
that Mary Butler, Lena's maid, still worked for the Earl
of Aulton. Once Emma brought Mary to London to testify against him, no other woman would suffer at his
hands.

"Mind if I join you?" Emma's cousin, Claire, stood before her with a book clasped to her chest. With auburn hair

and dark green eyes, she favored her late Scottish mother, the previous Duchess of Langham. To Emma, Claire was more than a cousin. The word didn't adequately describe their relationship since they were as close as sisters.

"Please." Emma moved some journals and books from the chair closest to her. Relief at having company, particularly Claire's, lifted Emma's mood—a little.

Increasing for the second time, her cousin sat gingerly. The baby would be Claire's third child. She and her husband Alex were the proud parents of twins.

Precious and perfect, the children could do no wrong in Emma's eyes. Of course, as their godmother, her ability to notice any misdeeds or wrongdoings was severely hampered. The rest of the family shared the same affliction, too.

Emma reached over and squeezed Claire's hand. "How are you feeling?"

"Besides wonderfully happy and quite large? My life is perfect." Claire caught Emma's hand and pressed it against her belly. "The baby just kicked. Do you feel anything?"

She shook her head. How do you politely tell a mother-to-be that her baby feels like a round rock?

With an innate sense of humor, Claire grinned. "I suppose it doesn't feel like much to you, but to me? It's nothing less than a miracle."

"I'm thrilled for you and Alex. You're marvelous parents."

Claire laid her book down and surveyed the table.

Letting out a silent but long-suffering sigh, Emma waited. Her cousin's ability to ferret out problems was uncanny, particularly when it came to her. Her Bentham exploit three years ago was proof. Claire had been the one to discover she'd gone to buy the book.

"How are *you*?" Claire asked. She picked up the paperweight and carefully put it out of Emma's reach. "That's to keep you from fidgeting. I understand you've been sitting here for hours."

She nodded, fearful if she disclosed anything, she'd collapse into a watershed of sobs that would have them both crying. But it was unlikely. She'd hardly cried at all over Lena's death. What kind of a friend didn't shed tears at such a loss?

One who found it hard to look in the mirror every day.

"Darling, don't you think it would help to talk about it?" Claire had leaned so close, the worry lines etched around her eyes were clearly visible.

Perhaps it was time to share a little. Or a lot. She wasn't certain what, if anything, could lift the constant cloud of melancholy and guilt that followed her. She suffered as much now, if not more, than when she first heard of her friend's death.

Emma took a deep breath for fortitude. This wouldn't be easy, but when she discussed Lena's death and her own duplicity, she deserved the pain.

"I . . . I don't know where to start." Without the paperweight, all she could rely on were her fingers. Before she tangled them into knots, Claire took her hand and laced their fingers together.

"Use me for strength?"

Emma nodded. Claire would help her get through this and steer her in the right direction. "Whatever I say to you stays between us. I must have your word, or I can't start."

The open honesty of Claire's face almost blinded Emma in its purity. "Em, not even Alex?"

"Will he tell Father or Mother?" she whispered. Though Claire was trustworthy, she would always take the path she thought right. Her actions the night of the Bentham fiasco proved that point clearly.

Claire shook her head. "Alex won't say a word if I ask him. I won't know if I'll need his advice until I hear what you have to say."

"Fair enough." She took in the view of Langham Park out the library windows. It always provided succor, a peacefulness Emma found nowhere else. Today, it stood as her support, a fortress she desperately needed. "I suppose it's best just to lance the wound as they say."

Claire smiled affectionately as if she knew how excruciatingly painful this was for her.

"Lena directed her maid to send me all her correspondence before she passed." Emma waved at the pile of letters in front of her. "There's one for her brother, my letter, and one to her unborn child, Audra. When Mary Butler, Lena's maid, posted them to me, she included her own note. She didn't say it per se, but I could read between the lines."

She glanced at Claire, who nodded for her continue.

"Aulton murdered Lena. I don't know the how or why, but I know he did it. He'd been beating her, Claire. I saw the bruises myself when I visited."

"I thought Lena fell down the steps and the baby was stillborn?" Claire squeezed their hands together, encouraging her.

"She was the most graceful person I've ever known. I can't believe she'd have lost her balance." Instead of lessening, the pain increased with each word she spoke. Still, she couldn't cry.

Maybe she never would. That's how empty she'd become.

"A week before she died, she invited me to visit. By then, she was close to delivering. I received her letter three days before the Langham annual garden soiree. When I asked mother if I could go, she said 'after the party.' She needed me here." Emma found enough courage to look Claire in the eye as she confessed her sin. "Lena never said outright, but I think she feared Aulton. She wrote that she needed me by her side. I believe she knew he was going to hurt her. She was in fear for herself and probably terrified for the baby."

"Oh, Emma." Claire's shock was evident, but she didn't let go of Emma's hand.

She needed her cousin's strength as she tried to purge the rest of her misery.

"I didn't go. I stayed here. I had a chance to save her, and I didn't." She stole one last glance at the park. "Mother's party was on a Wednesday. The next morning, we received word of her death."

Claire gently pulled her into her arms. Still, the tears refused to come.

"It's perfectly reasonable you'd feel that way, but I don't agree with it." Claire's voice held no judgment. "It wasn't your responsibility."

Emma shook her head emphatically. "She couldn't leave him without me. Where would she go? Her brother Jonathan is in France fighting the war. If she left by herself, Aulton would have hunted her down."

Pensive, Claire studied her. "What could you have done if you'd been there? You could have been his next victim."

"I don't know. Nothing maybe. Nevertheless, perhaps I could have stopped him or brought her here. Father would have protected Lena." Her father and Claire's uncle, the Duke of Langham was renowned for his political acumen. No one, not even Aulton, would dare challenge him.

"I don't know if it would have made any difference." Claire examined their entwined hands and took a breath. "You're not going to like what I have to say—"

"Please, just say it." She closed her eyes, ready for the

condemnation that was surely forthcoming. She deserved it and so much more.

"I'm glad you weren't there to experience any of that. It leaves scars." Claire lifted her chin. "My own grief over the carriage accident that caused my parents' death . . . even though I survived, paralyzed me on so many levels. But one thing I found is that if you can channel your grief into something beneficial for others, it helps relieve the heaviness."

Emma nodded. "Over the last several months, I've been toying with an idea. I'm thinking of an institution that would allow women a means of creating financial independence. Allowing them a freedom so many are denied. A place where people like Aulton could never breach the walls."

"What are you thinking?" Claire scooted up to the edge of her chair as best she could.

"A bank for women run by women. Based upon my research, I believe it'll be wildly successful. I've prepared a prospectus including plans for repayment of the money I'll need. Would you read it and give me your thoughts?"

"How remarkable. Of course I'll review it."

Emma nodded and let out her breath. An heiress in her own right, Claire possessed an acute business sense. If she thought the idea had merit, a tremendous weight would be taken off Emma's shoulders.

Working hours on the plan had been a pleasant task as she considered the details. The population of London was experiencing a rapid growth, based upon her research from the 1811 census. She'd even attended "hiring fairs" where servants tried to find new employment. It helped gauge the need for such a bank. It wasn't surprising to discover working-class women had little resources for escape when subjected to violence in the workplace or at home.

Emma couldn't expect to be taken seriously unless she could present a precise and detailed proposal of its operation and the expected impact. The hardest task had been thinking of the possible objections her parents would have and her own counterarguments when she presented the idea.

"Perhaps, I'll contribute to your bank. Truly, I love the idea." Claire leaned over and kissed her on the cheek.

"Your time and thoughts mean the world to me." Though the sentiment was unoriginal and timeworn, her family's support could help her through this grief. She'd bear the onus of the hardest part, the guilt, then find a way to learn how to work through her own culpability.

Her first step to healing required she visit Lena's maid, Mary Butler. If Mary confirmed her suspicions, Emma would bring her to London under her father's protection to testify against Aulton. With Mary's testimony and her father's influence, Aulton would answer for Lena's murder.

Her bank would be the next step to healing. She'd help others escape from brutal men. What she didn't do for Lena, she would do for other women.

"Now, I want to discuss something else," Claire said.

For the first time today, Emma found herself grinning. "You've listened to me all morning. It'd be my honor to return the favor."

"Aunt Ginny and Uncle Sebastian are considering a marriage proposal for you from the Earl of LaTourell." Her cousin blurted the news in an uncharacteristically hurried manner. "Next week—"

"Stop." She held up her hand. Couldn't she find any peace in her own home? "I refuse to discuss it. My feelings haven't changed."

"Emma . . . it's best to be prepared," Claire chided.

"My, it's stuffy in here." Ignoring her cousin, Emma

rose from the chair and opened the French doors into the courtyard. The chill of the autumn wind swept around her, and she tilted her face to the sky. The sun refused to give up its warmth to autumn, a gentle reminder she never forget Lena or her own hopes and dreams to make a difference in this world. She'd not waste her time on marriage nonsense.

At the sound of deep masculine voices, Emma turned. Her oldest brother, Michael Cavensham, the Marquess of McCalpin and her father's heir, strode into her personal domain, the family library. Behind him came Claire's husband, Alex.

"Em, we're going for—" McCalpin's words stopped abruptly. He stood by the table and studied the letters she'd been reading. An undeniable pity darkened his gaze, but when he directed his attention to her, it was gone.

"Come with us on a walk with the twins." Alex delivered a slight smile. His gray eyes flashed silver as he clasped an arm around Claire's waist and drew her close.

After a rocky start to their marriage, Alex and Claire had to be one of the happiest couples in all of England. Proof miracles did exist if only under the rarest and most auspicious occasions—much like a Rose Moon.

"My son and daughter will revolt if their favorite godmother isn't beside them after we promised them your company," Alex prompted.

"I'm their *only* godmother." Emma regarded Alex with a tentative smile. "Thank you, but I'd rather stay here."

Claire took her hand in hers and squeezed. "A little air would be good for you."

"Come with us, Em," McCalpin coaxed. "I'm leaving in a couple of days for Falmont."

She cast one last glace at the letter to Audra. Emma owed it to Lena to enjoy her freedom and as much of life as she could. "Let me get my coat and gloves."

But more, she owed it to Lena to bring Mary back to London. Now, after discovering that Aulton hunted for a new wife, it was more important than ever. Goodwin's Book Emporium would be Emma's first stop tomorrow. The bookshop's owner, Mr. Goodwin, had sent a note. He'd found Lena's maid in Portsmouth.

Chapter Three

〜

"Come, Arial." With her maid falling in step, Emma crossed the distance from the carriage to Goodwin's Book Emporium.

The autumn sun broke through the gray clouds over London, a positive omen for her success. Emma grasped the shiny brass doorknob and stepped into the shabby little bookshop. The tinkle of a bell heralded her arrival. She stopped beside a towering stack of leather-bound books, but her skirts continued the forward motion as if coaxing her farther inside the mysterious worlds each volume offered.

A thin, middle-aged shopkeeper sprang from behind the counter much like a jack-in-the-box. He sketched a bow. What little remained of his hair fell forward revealing the bald crown of his head. "Good morning, my lady."

"Truly a glorious morning, isn't it, Mr. Goodwin?" She couldn't hide the hope that colored her voice.

Carefully stepping around a stack of boxes in the middle of the aisle, Goodwin smiled, then walked the short distance to the back of the shop. He swept a ragtag curtain aside, creating an opening to the back storage room. "My lady, after you."

"Wait here, Arial. I'm not certain how long we'll stay," Emma said.

"My lady, this is highly improper. There aren't any other customers." Her maid's normally pleasant voice turned guttural, much like the growl of a cat when irritated—or fearful. Her sharp foot taps echoed through the shop and added a unique rhythm to the room's acoustics. "What if the duchess finds out?"

"Shh! No one will discover we're here. I'll hurry." She left her maid at the shop entrance and dared not dwell on the disapproving frown. The woman's gift to inflict an air of censure was a true tribute to her Welsh upbringing. However, the effort would not dissuade Emma from today's business. Failure was not an option.

At the doorway to the back room, she stilled. Her stomach dropped as if trying to find a way to escape. She had never ventured beyond the visible shop area. Drawing a deep breath and relying on her bold confidence—unfortunately, a trait declared unbecoming throughout the *ton*—Emma brushed the unease away much like a piece of lint on her sleeve and followed Mr. Goodwin. She was close to success. No amount of trepidation would ruin the day.

The musty smell of books hung heavy in the air while shadows loomed like highwaymen waiting for their next victim. She expected to hear the cry "Stand and deliver" any moment. With a tight tug of her gloves, she banished the image from her mind. Her insatiable habit of reading gothic novels late at night had to stop.

"Your assumptions were correct. I sent an inquiry to friends of mine. Mr. and Mrs. Parker own a bookshop in Portsmouth. They've connections in that part of England similar to mine in London. They've verified Mary Butler recently returned to Lady Aulton's childhood home. Her brother, the Earl of Sykeston, is still abroad fighting in France." Mr. Goodwin's forehead shone with little pebbled beads of perspiration, making the pockmarks on his face prominent.

"And your colleagues? Will they help me?" Emma ignored the dust motes that floated through a lone sunbeam's path and focused on the shopkeeper.

"Indeed." When he smiled, the effort narrowed his eyes until he resembled a mole. "They're looking forward to meeting you. I have your lodging secured at the Ruby Crown Inn. The innkeeper, who's also a friend of mine, has reserved a room for your stay. He's expecting you the day after tomorrow."

"Perfect," Emma said. Truly, she couldn't have asked for better timing as her parents and brothers were due to travel within the next several days.

A twitch appeared underneath Goodwin's left eye. It gave the appearance he was repeatedly winking at her. "While Lord Sykeston is away, his library is undergoing a renovation. Mr. and Mrs. Parker have access to the house as they inventory the library's collection. The Parkers are perfectly situated to watch the house, and Mary's comings and goings. They'll also secure a copy of the coroner's inquest findings. Since Lady Aulton died at her husband's home, it was relatively easy to acquire the information since Aulton Court is within four miles of Portsmouth."

"I don't know what I would have done without your help." Emma searched her reticule for coins. "Thank you. Allow me—"

"Please, my lady, no thanks needed." Mr. Goodwin actually blushed. "It's a delightful task to help a fine young lady as yourself." He leaned toward her as if sharing a great confidence. "You remind me of my missus.

Always ready for an adventure and willing to help others."

Emma's heart fluttered at the kind words. "An adventure" was a mild understatement. It was only natural she'd approach Mr. Goodwin. His connections throughout England were legendary. Within weeks of her request, he'd verified Mary's location.

"You're too kind, Mr. Goodwin," she said. She searched his face for any hint of disapproval or doubt, but found understanding.

"One other thing. The innkeeper, Mr. Fenton, has made arrangements for your trip to the cliffs at sunset." Mr. Goodwin picked up a package. "It's a wonderful way to remember your friend. She was lucky to have you."

"She was special in so many ways." Emma had promised herself she'd not become maudlin. Lena would have hated it. "Please arrange the remaining details."

"Yes, my lady. I'll send word." The shopkeeper beamed as he held out a wrapped package tied with twine. "I think you'll enjoy these novels on the trip down."

"Thank you." Little took her by surprise anymore, but today marked one of those rare occasions. Mr. Goodwin was truly a thoughtful and very sweet man. "I must be going."

The chime of a bell joined the noise of Arial's perpetual foot taps. The package in her hands would be the perfect peace treaty to diffuse her maid's ire. Arial loved to borrow her books and would have something to while away her time as Emma finished her plans for travel.

She made her way to the front of the shop between the narrow aisles while thoughts of her journey percolated. She bowed her head and traced the creases of the neatly folded brown paper surrounding the package in her hands.

"Arial, I have news—" Before another word escaped, she rammed headfirst into a brick wall.

"Ow!" She raised her hand to soothe the pain radiating from her poor nose and tried to take a step back, but an iron grip thwarted her effort. Instinctively, she pushed against the obstacle. Her fingers collided with a warm, felt waistcoat accompanied by a rich scent of bay rum cologne and leather.

Somerton.

Her eyes watered, but Emma lifted her head to ascertain if her suspicions were correct.

Blast it. She gritted her teeth to keep from swearing aloud. Never for one second did she think this catastrophe would happen. Now, she'd never make it to Portsmouth in this lifetime or the next. She shook her head in annoyance at her own negativity. *She was going to Portsmouth.*

"Are you all right?" A familiar, low rumble greeted her. The concerned look from an exquisite pair of turquoise eyes made Emma stop her retreat. His large hands slid down her arms to steady her.

"Yes, I believe so." Her eyes still teared in rebellion from the lingering sting.

Of all the people to run into, she was mortified to find Lord Somerton before her. She bristled as the earl's look of concern transformed into curiosity.

If the floor wasn't so filthy, she'd have melted into the wooden planks. Somerton would want to know her business. Then he'd tell Pembrooke, who would tell Claire. If her parents got a whiff of her plans, she'd have a greater chance of wearing the crown as the next queen of England than of making it to Portsmouth. It was humiliating. She was twenty-five years old and still subject to her parents' whims and concerns for proper chaperones.

Bother.

Emma might as well take out a full-page advertisement in tomorrow's *The Midnight Cryer.* It would have the same effect.

She should be used to his presence by now. As godparents to Alex and Claire's twins, they interacted quite frequently. At family events, he always seemed to be included. After their infamous kiss three years ago, he hardly gave her any notice, which was fine, as she hardly gave him any either.

Liar.

Her traitorous gaze quickly surveyed the length of his body. What was a woman to do when a golden-haired Adonis stood before her? Dressed in a tight-fitting black morning coat that framed his broad shoulders and gray breeches that molded every well-toned muscle of his long legs, he was perfection incarnate.

If she *were* the Queen of England, maybe she'd command the handsome earl to follow her to the royal yacht in Portsmouth. She'd make him strip to his lawn shirt and work the rigging while she watched his muscles swell and flex. . . .

With a deep sigh, Emma imagined Lena laughing at her antics. A grin tugged at her lips. Somerton leaned close, and a hint of mischief blazed from his eyes, layered with an unwelcomed inquisitiveness.

She *wasn't* a queen and had better think of a plausible reason why she was in a back-alley bookshop with only Arial as her escort. Perhaps she could borrow a portion of a queen's majestic bravado, though.

She boldly surveyed his body again. There was no padding in his clothing, much to her delight. The view was quite spectacular.

"Are you finished with your examination, or shall I turn around so you can study my backside?" Somerton challenged her with a raised eyebrow.

"If it wouldn't be a bother? I've had my fill of the front." She dared to stare straight into his eyes. It was madness to bait him this way, but she had to protect her travel plans from becoming public knowledge. Any sign of discomposure on his part would help shift their conversation away from her reasons for being at the bookshop.

He wasn't offended as evidenced by his sudden slight grin. "Lady Emma, what a surprise to find you at Mr. Goodwin's this morning. Did anyone accompany you besides your maid?"

"I won't trouble you with the boring, banal details." The situation had turned into one she fervently hoped to manage, but it was doubtful. Designed to strip away her defenses, his sudden infectious smile turned blinding. She enhanced her grin into what she prayed was an enchanting smile. Somerton clasped his hands behind his back and slowly scrutinized her. A tingle crept up her spine like a slow, meandering spider, but she refused to succumb to her unease. She raised her chin and straightened to her full height.

The earl stepped closer and motioned to an isolated corner in the bookshop. "I'd like a private word."

Somerton's demand for a tête-à-tête did not bode well for a quick exit. With shoulders squared, she was determined to meet her fate with as much aplomb as a ship's captain walking the plank.

He maneuvered her into a corner with a natural grace. "You shouldn't be in this part of town"—he closed the distance between them—"or a shop of dubious repute such as Goodwin's. When I walked in, you spoke to Arial about news. Whatever is this *news* you wanted to share with your maid?"

Her grin melted as she juggled the package of books in her hands. Her smile hadn't had any impact.

He towered over her with an expression she couldn't quite identify. Clearly, he was immune to her charms—what little she possessed. Perhaps he was irritated she'd discovered *him* at Goodwin's.

"I'm merely shopping. Arial is always interested in my books." She presented the parcel in her hands as if evidence to clear her of any wrongdoing. With a quarter turn, she took a step, but he blocked any means of escape with his long, lean body and one arm resting on a bookshelf. Trapped and forced to make conversation, Emma met his gaze. "I understand you'll be at Langham Hall next week for my mother's dinner party."

"Don't change the subject." His breath caressed her cheek. The delicious scent of cinnamon and coffee wrapped around her. "What are you doing here?"

She leaned forward until she was less than an inch from his warm body. If his words weren't so bothersome, she'd stay in this spot all day. Nonetheless, she was close to accomplishing everything she needed for Portsmouth, and no random meeting would stop her. "Let's not mention we saw each other here."

His chiseled cheeks and brow remained frozen much like the marble statue of Apollo that lorded over the entry hall of her home. His lack of agreement left her little choice but to raise the stakes.

"Otherwise, I'd hate to start the rumor you're showing interest in me. You visit my home often enough." When he flinched at the words, she didn't ignore the opportunity. "Good day, Somerton."

With a quick movement she had mastered years ago when she needed to escape from her two older brothers, she ducked under his arm and walked to her maid. The fiery heat of his gaze bored into her back. "Come along, Arial."

Her threat would have the intended effect. Somerton

avoided the *ton* and its social events for fear they'd think he wanted to wed. She experienced no shame in using every weapon in her arsenal to win an advantage.

Before she reached the door, Somerton was by her side and gently clasped her arm. "One more thing, Lady Emma." A devilish gleam flared in his eyes as he commanded Arial, "Wait for your mistress outside."

The maid hesitated. "My lady?"

Emma nodded her assent. It was better to end this dreadful conversation sooner rather than later. Her derring-do won out over her fluttering heartbeat. When the shop door closed, she stepped closer him. Two could play at his game. "Hmm, yes, my lord?"

His left brow raised a mocking fraction of an inch while his gloved hand reached for hers. In an even motion, he traced his thumb back and forth across her knuckles. The silken touch was a shot-across-the-bow attack on her composure. She swallowed the cannonball lodged in her throat. His audacious move left her unbalanced, and she couldn't pull away—nor was she certain she wanted to.

That was the problem with Somerton. He possessed an uncanny knack for turning her insides upside down. He was like a ride on the fastest horse in a steeplechase—thrilling but dangerous.

"Please, what more can I say to convince you?" If she told him her business, she'd most likely find herself on a permanent hiatus at Falmont.

"Make no mistake. I'll discover your purpose for *shopping* here from Goodwin." His rich cadence was soothing like a cup of hot buttered rum, but his eyes flashed with a quick jolt of humor. The beginning of a smile tipped the corners of his mouth. "When I do, I shall not be averse to sharing my newfound knowledge with others."

His threat broke whatever spell he'd cast over her. She snatched her hand from his.

"Somerton, we share family, friends, and our joint responsibility as godparents. However, that doesn't mean we share everything." She'd had enough and didn't wait for his reply. "Are my private matters worth starting a war between the two of us?" She dismissed him with a terse nod. "Good day."

His laughter followed her all the way to her carriage. *Insufferable cur.*

Humored by the whirlwind in front of him, Nick chuckled at the first volley of attack in her declared war. Lady Emma, the one and only daughter of the powerful Duke of Langham, sashayed her way to the carriage. Even in this rank part of London, her demeanor never changed. She acted as if she owned the very city itself.

He couldn't remember when he'd had this much pleasure in a conversation with a woman. Quite possibly, the last time he'd seen *her.*

She'd always been comely when she was younger. Now, she could strike a man mute. Her plump red lips demanded to be kissed, and the glow of her pink cheeks was irresistible. Not to mention, her lush curves and graceful movements demanded he pay attention, which was never an issue. He could watch her for hours.

Something about her was different. When his gaze lingered on hers, her normal brilliance and incomparable confidence seemed shaded by a hint of reticence. The relaxed ease in her stance was missing, replaced by a stiffness, almost a wariness. He shook his head. Clearly, he was overthinking her reasons for being here. From all their interactions, Nick had firsthand knowledge of Emma's first love—books. She'd already confessed that she shopped here occasionally. That fact alone should make it reasonable he'd find her at Goodwin's.

With a deep breath, he turned from the shop window. Word had it that the Earl of LaTourell was boasting he'd gotten the official nod from the Duke of Langham to court her. The earl had spouted some nonsense that the duke and duchess had grown weary of their daughter's perennial unwed status.

The news rankled Nick's normally calm reserve and caused an unexplainable tightening in his chest. The cad wasn't good enough for Emma. Besides, the earl was a known fop who overindulged in sweetmeats and blancmange.

Perhaps he should throw his hat into the ring. One day, he'd need an heir.

Damnation, where had that come from? He blew out a breath and squelched the wayward thought.

Marriage wasn't in his future. His work was a most demanding mistress, leaving him little time for others. He kept his evenings free to scour the streets of London for information about ships, sailing routes, and treasures. With the gathered facts, he'd pick his investments, decide which merchant ship in his fleet to send abroad for the most lucrative trades, and buy cargo shares from the Orient. He enjoyed his life and planned to keep it simple without the added complication of a woman, even one as lovely as Lady Emma. He was so close to surpassing his father's wealth, he could taste victory.

As her carriage pulled away, he couldn't quash the nag that demanded attention. What possible reason would she have to visit Goodwin? His instincts warned that it couldn't be just books. The titles Goodwin carried were old, but certainly not rare. Why would she purchase books here without checking other more reputable establishments closer to her home in Mayfair? What about Nick's own library? He'd made the offer to her before and encouraged her to borrow anything that caught her interest.

He made his way to the counter and rang the bell. Before it stopped vibrating, the shopkeeper emerged from behind the filthy curtain.

"Good morning, my lord," the shopkeeper crooned as he wiped his sweaty forehead with his arm. "Always a delight to help my favorite customer."

He nodded in acknowledgment. "What have you discovered?"

Goodwin cleared his throat. "The ship landed last night, and the crew unloaded part of the cargo. At the captain's direction, the rest tomorrow."

"Anyone take inventory?"

Goodwin displayed his front teeth in a smile that made his round cheeks look like red moons. "The captain hired my brother, Rodney, on recommendation of the portmaster. *Her Splendor* enjoyed quite a successful voyage. Rodney will provide a full accounting shortly." The man leaned over the counter and lowered his voice to a whisper. "The routes were safe with no sign of enemy ships. With favorable winds, *Her Splendor* arrived weeks ahead of schedule."

"Excellent." Nick thrummed his fingers on the counter. The little tidbit was the final piece he needed to make the decision to purchase *Her Splendor*. It would make a profitable addition to his fleet. Pleased with the news, he reached into his pocket and withdrew a purse heavy with coins. "There's an extra guinea if you provide some additional information."

A look reminiscent of a hungry dog waiting for a butcher's bone spread across the shopkeeper's face.

Nick studied the bag and came to the sobering conclusion he wasn't much different from Goodwin. They both craved money and its alluring promise of power—a grim thought that left an unpleasant taste in his mouth.

"Why did Lady Emma come to see you?"

The change in Goodwin's expression from a warm, friendly face to one of feigned innocence was immediate. "She's a customer looking for a book."

He had little patience for Goodwin's false acts of sincerity. This interlude kept him from work. "Might two guineas help your memory?"

The shopkeeper's words tumbled like a waterfall. "There's a book in Portsmouth she seeks to acquire."

"Why does she want it?"

The shopkeeper winced. "I don't know. She collects private journals. Please, she's fascinated by the pirate queen Anne Readington's history."

"A pirate queen?" Every inch of his skin prickled in awareness. "Who has the journal?"

The shopkeeper's whisper wheezed into a hoarse gasp. "A private collector who owns a bookshop in Portsmouth."

Claire and Alex couldn't be aware of her latest whim, or he'd have heard mention in passing. Where were her brothers in all of this? "Is anyone else interested in the acquisition?"

The shopkeeper's eyes grew wary. "Not that I'm aware of."

"Anyone else accompany her when she visits?"

"Only her maid," Goodwin replied.

"How much is she paying you? Perhaps I'll double it." As in incentive, Nick juggled the bag, causing the coins to jangle.

Goodwin's dubious glare wasn't the expected response. "My lord, sometimes helping a lovely lady is payment in itself."

"You certainly charge me for everything," Nick challenged.

"We have a business relationship." Goodwin didn't even blink. "Besides, I have a reputation to maintain."

"Which is?" Nick asked.

"I'm somewhat of a favorite among the ladies."

Nick rolled his eyes and threw the purse in the air. "Inform me of her plans. It'll be worth your while."

Goodwin caught the purse in one hand. "Of course, my lord." With a wink, he sketched an elaborate bow.

Nick paid little heed to the rest of Goodwin's hijinks. With quick steps, he made his way out the door. He could hardly fathom why Emma would be brazen enough to attempt such a trip.

As he inhaled the cool morning air, it cleared the tangle of revolving thoughts in his mind. He must remember this was Emma. The same woman who had risked her safety and her family's wrath to acquire a book of essays several years ago. He'd never seen a woman so resolute in her actions or convictions. Whatever she deemed important, she went after with an enthusiasm that made most gentlemen appear cowardly.

Just like the kiss she gave him in Langham Park. Over the years, he'd fondly reminisced about that event. He always found a lightness in his step for hours afterward.

Lady Emma Cavensham was simply the most magnificent creature he'd ever laid eyes on.

There was only one solution. He'd acquire the diary and then present it to her. With one transaction, he'd put her pirate-queen-seeking nonsense to a stop. It would eliminate her need for travel to Portsmouth, and keep her safe and her reputation intact.

Perhaps, he'd find a little entertainment along the way and tease her about a bloodthirsty pirate queen's diary.

Her rose-colored cheeks deepened to the reddest scarlet when she was agitated.

A tinge of doubt took ahold and wouldn't let go. What right did he have to intrude upon her business?

He dismissed the thought. He was saving her from herself.

Maybe he'd get another kiss for his efforts.

Chapter Four

After her unfortunate meeting with Somerton earlier, Emma along with Arial had joined Lady Daphne Hallworth, Alex's sister, for what her friend promised was a short shopping excursion. Emma pushed the curtain aside and peeked out the carriage window. The entire street was empty of horses, carriages and, more importantly, people.

It was too early for members of the *ton* to drag themselves out of bed. Why couldn't Somerton have followed their lead? Why did he always have to be the one to find her when she wanted to stay hidden? Nothing, not even the annoying Earl of Somerton, would keep her from escorting Mary to London—she was the key to bringing Aulton to justice. Nor would anyone interfere in her efforts to create a bank. If Emma could help even one woman have a better life or escape a fate similar to Lena's, then her life would have purpose.

She sighed. "How did I ever allow you to convince me to go shopping? I must be a true friend. If it was a bookstore or the library, at least there would be something of interest." Emma stole another glance as the carriage came to a gentle halt. Beside her, Daphne was a vision in a pale plum gown that emphasized her striking silver eyes and jet-black hair.

She and Daphne had been close friends since her brother had married Claire. Over the years at various family holidays and celebrations, they had shared their secrets and desires for their respective futures. They entertained one another at the insufferable balls and other social events they attended. Like Lena, Daphne relished such events, and no matter what Emma confided, she trusted Daphne would never judge or divulge any secret.

"Grigby's has a new selection of gloves and several pairs of pink silk stockings that promise to be the latest fashion." Daphne settled her hand over Emma's to stop the incessant fidgeting. "Claire said it's the most delightful shade of pink she's ever seen, and the silk stockings are as delicate as a butterfly's wings."

Skeptical, Emma scowled. "That's why we're here at this time of the morning, so you can have first selection?"

"I need a pair for Lady Emory's ball." Daphne leaned a little closer. "A fashionable lady must always be prepared to show a little ankle for that someone special when the opportunity presents itself. Wouldn't you agree?"

Emma's maid sat silently in the backward-facing seat as Daphne lectured on how to beguile a man. With a smirk tugging at Arial's lips, she let it be known she preferred Daphne's idea of shopping to Emma's. "Lady Daphne makes the most astute observations. Bookstores won't help in the department of enticing men, my lady."

The obvious feigned look of wide-eyed innocence on Arial's face made Emma laugh. Arial was more than her lady's maid. She was Emma's confidante and sounding board, hence the familiarity. They might share books, but Emma's ideas of how she envisioned her life without a husband sometimes shocked Arial. Yet, since Lena's death, Arial had patiently listened to Emma rail against Aulton as she declared she'd never suffer such agony with a husband. Trustworthy, her maid never passed judgment. She was worth her weight in gold.

"Shall we stroll?" Daphne asked.

As if on command, the carriage door opened. The trio made their way to Grigby's, a fashionable haberdashery and women's shop. Mr. and Mrs. Grigby ran the store and were excellent purveyors of the finest accessories for women in all of London.

"You've not kept your displeasure a secret," Daphne hummed in Emma's ear. "Tell me what's caused your somber mood."

"It's been a difficult week." Emma glanced at the shop windows unwilling to let her emotions flood the sidewalks.

Daphne took her hand and squeezed. "How could I have forgotten Lena? I'm such a wretched friend."

"No, you're wonderful," Emma answered. "I've just preferred my own company over the last several days. This morning didn't help matters."

Daphne linked her arm with Emma's. "What happened?"

"Somerton happened to be at Goodwin's this morning while I was there. He kept pressing for answers, so I told him to stay out of my business. Tell me if he mentions my visit to your brother."

Before Daphne could comment, a young woman with her head held high strolled out of the famous Garrard's jewelry shop. Once she was past the shop's windows, she collapsed with her back against a brick wall, her arms outstretched. The woman's posture gave the appearance she was holding up the wall much like Atlas holding the world.

Emma rushed forward. "Miss, are you all right?"

"Yes." The woman cleared her throat and straightened away from the wall. "I'm just out of breath."

Proud and tall, she wore a serviceable brown cloak several seasons out of fashion, but her bearing indicated she was familiar with the elite shops in Mayfair.

"Do you need assistance to your carriage?" Daphne asked.

"No, thank you. It's really nothing. A transaction I'd hoped to complete today was unfortunately delayed." The woman's crimson cheeks and fluttering hands betrayed her agitation. She pocketed a small antique jewelry box. "The disappointment must show on my face."

There was no use standing on ceremonies when the woman was in dire need of something. Emma made the necessary introductions. "My name is Lady Emma Cavensham and this is my friend, Lady Daphne Hallworth. My maid, Arial Harris."

The tall woman gracefully took a step back and dipped a curtsy. "Miss March Lawson. It's a pleasure to make your acquaintance. If you'll excuse me, Lady Emma and Lady Daphne?" The woman didn't wait for responses. She nodded to Arial and was soon out of sight when she made an abrupt turn at the corner.

A sinking sensation settled deep into Emma's chest. Miss Lawson's acute sense of desperation was written all over her face. She'd tried valiantly to hide it, but it was there for all to see. It reminded Emma of the helplessness Lena assuredly experienced in her marriage. A piece of paper danced against the wall, the wind flirting with it. Before it took flight, Emma caught it.

"What is it?" Daphne's brow furrowed in a manner that mimicked her brother's expression.

"It's a repair bill in the amount of twenty pounds for roof work. It's marked overdue." This explained Miss

Lawson's evident distress. "She needed money. No doubt she was trying to sell a piece of jewelry."

"Are you positive it's Miss Lawson's?" Arial asked.

Emma nodded. "It says the services were rendered on Lord Lawson's Leyton estate six months ago. Who is he?"

Daphne peered over Emma's shoulder to read the paper. "I thought her name sounded familiar. She must be one of his sisters. Lord Lawson is a viscount. He's a young lad of about eight or ten. Claire has friends in Leyton, and they were discussing the family's plight. Apparently, the viscount's estate is in shambles. Their guardian and the trustee in control of their fortunes have completely ignored the young viscount and his sisters." Daphne's gaze drifted down the street in the direction that Miss Lawson had taken. "Poor woman. She looked frightened, lost even."

"Her distress is all too common for most women." Emma stared at the corner where Miss Lawson had turned and disappeared from their sight.

"She needs to visit a banker. Perhaps he'd find a solution to their unfortunate situation," Daphne whispered.

"What man would lend money to a penniless woman, even if her father or brother held the title of viscount?" Emma countered.

"I suppose you're correct. No one would."

"I would," said Emma defiantly.

Somehow, she'd find the means to gather the necessary funds for her lending institution. It would first provide security for Mary when she came to London and testified against Aulton. Then, Emma planned to help other women find their own peace and safety in the world so they wouldn't face the same fate as Lena.

Perhaps it was time to approach her parents for the money.

Emma stuffed the bill in her pocket. "Opportunity is

missed by people in our society because they undervalue a person in skirts."

Emma swept into the Duchess of Langham's salon, ready to discuss her plans of creating a bank with her mother. With a glance, she stopped. "What's happened?"

Her mother's normally vibrant face was pale, while her cerulean-blue eyes shimmered with unshed tears. Her father placed his teacup on the table beside him and shifted to his feet. His forehead crinkled into neat rows of lines.

"Hello, Puss. How's my prettiest daughter today?" Her father delivered a hint of a smile.

"Wonderful." She reached up on tiptoes and kissed his cheek, then crouched in front of her mother. She wouldn't move from this spot until she discovered what trouble plagued her parents. Taking her mother's cold hands in hers, Emma leaned forward and delivered another kiss. "What is it?"

"Oh, sweetheart, there's no reason for alarm. I received a note from Blanche this morning." Her mother tried to smile as if nothing was amiss. Her effort failed miserably.

"Is she all right?" Her mother's best friend from childhood had married a beast of a man who refused to let her come to London. The Earl of Chelston chose to keep his wife at his ancestral seat while he openly flaunted his mistress in London. If allowed to make an appearance in town, the countess was forced to sleep in a guest bedroom while his mistress occupied the Countess of Chelston's suites.

Some men were nothing more than selfish beasts, concerned only with their own pleasure. Lord Chelston, the perfect example of a horrid fiend, provided another reason to escape the marriage trap.

Her mother pressed her eyes closed as if trying to erase what she'd read. "Blanche is looking forward to our visit. Apparently, Chelston was drunk and . . ."

"Is she hurt?" Emma stood with clenched fists and faced her father. This was further proof that every woman deserved—and required—security from a husband's irrational binges.

"No, sweetheart. He said some hateful things, and Blanche is naturally quite upset. Tell us of your morning." Her mother tried to appear interested, but her eyes told another story.

Emma scrunched her nose. "I went shopping with Daphne for pink stockings, but that can wait until later. How long will you stay at Lady Chelston's?"

Her father scooped her mother's hand in his and pressed a gentle kiss across her knuckles. He took the seat beside her. "Three days, then we'll return to London before we head to Falmont. The soonest we can leave is the day after tomorrow. I want the family to gather tomorrow for dinner."

"I look forward to it." A shot of excitement quickened the beating of her heart. "Should you cancel next week's party?"

"We'll only be gone a few days. Next week's entertainment schedule is too important to cancel." Her mother swallowed. The effort cleared some of the worry from her face. "Your father and I have something important we want to discuss with you."

"Lord LaTourell will join us before Lady Session's soirée next week," he announced. "He wants to discuss your future."

The air escaped from her lungs faster than an elephant's stomp on her chest.

Precisely what she wanted to do with his

proclamation—stomp on it. She struggled to take a deep breath. Control was the key to surviving this skirmish, and she fought to remain calm. "I don't want to marry."

She couldn't think of marriage now. She'd readily agree LaTourell was nice enough, though somewhat turgid. His redeeming grace was his three sisters, who were everything lovely. However, the inevitable state of holy matrimony with anyone reminded her of a dose of cod liver oil. Her skin crawled with the notion that she'd be saddled with a husband for a lifetime, or heaven help her, eternity.

No question, eternity with any man was entirely too long.

"I'll never want to marry." Her heartbeat sped into a rhythm that rivaled a rabbit's jagged sprint through a forest.

"Your mother and I were under a different presumption."

As were the majority of people in London. The betting books at the exclusive gentlemen's club, White's, favored the Earl of LaTourell as most likely to win her hand. Fools disguised as gentlemen would soon part ways with their money.

"Emma, we've been lenient. It's past time." Her father softened his voice. "Come now, a marriage to Lord LaTourell would be the match of the Season."

"We've already extended the invitation." Her mother chimed in her agreement. "Dearest, this isn't unexpected."

She pressed her lips together and walked to the window overlooking the grounds of Langham Park. She shuttered inwardly. She knew what was coming next.

"Emma," her mother scolded in the voice she *always* used when they discussed this topic. "Many couples aren't comfortable with each other at the beginning.

You could learn a great deal about marriage if you'd observe Claire and Pembrooke. Their marriage had an inauspicious start, but now, they're ideal partners for each other."

She forced a demure smile to her face, then pivoted on one heel. Marriage left a woman vulnerable. "I have observed the lessons well. Most married women lose the ability to move, think, and act once the signatures are dry in the marriage register."

Her father's jaw tightened. "Your mother and I don't have that type of marriage. Do you think I'd allow you to enter into such a union?" He was practically shouting. "It's time to give serious thought about your future."

Her mother placed her hand on his forearm in an attempt to calm the storm. "Sebastian."

"I don't want the decision made for me." She crossed her arms over her chest in a move to convince them her reasoning was sound. "It should be my choice."

Prudence dictated she keep her opinion to herself, but she highly doubted there was a man out there she'd be willing to sacrifice her freedom for.

"Choosing a husband isn't like a visit to the circulating library and browsing the selections." Her father's face flushed with a color reminiscent of a bullfinch's breast. "You shall marry. Sooner rather than later."

Her mother tried again to diffuse his temper. "This is not the time to bring up the subject. I should have never mentioned Blanche."

"I have other aspirations." Emma's voice was courteous, but she didn't hide the strength in her convictions. Absolute silence descended around the room. "I've thought about how I want to live my life and what would make me happy. I want to start a bank for women run by women, a financial institution that recognizes the distinct circumstances that women face."

"What?" Her mother's soft gasp shattered the tenuous peace in the room.

"Emma." Her father sighed and shook his head. "Why am I not surprised?" He exhaled and then strolled to the tea tray and selected a raspberry tart. "I grant you this. It's an interesting concept. But, why?"

That one simple question represented far more than his interest in what she proposed. It was the first volley in their engagement. Tall, with chestnut hair streaked gray at the temples, he could be intimidating. She recognized his easy posture and the slight hint of indifference he exuded when he was about to obliterate an argument.

Emma was prepared. She'd observed and learned from the best—her father. She mimicked his stance. "Think of it. How progressive would it be if the Duchy of Langham backed an enterprise designed to help women better their lives?"

"Would you allow men to conduct their business there if they requested it?" Her father gracefully sat beside her mother. Nonchalantly, he placed his arm on the back of the sofa. He reached for one of her mother's blond curls and twirled it in his finger. Immediately, her mother leaned against him, a move designed to exhibit they were a united force.

Emma matched her father's dissembled ease and sat across from her parents. "No. This would be an exclusive establishment. Think along the lines of a gentlemen's club—a private bank for the women of London."

"Intriguing concept." He rested his ankle across the other leg and contemplated her.

"Would you manage it yourself?" her mother asked. "I suppose Claire and I could lend some assistance."

Emma inhaled at her mother's acquiescence. The offer to help meant she thought the idea had merit. With her mother on her side, her father would capitulate in no time.

Her father drummed the fingers of one hand against his knee. "Before we go any further, let's discuss capital. How much and where would you acquire the funds?"

The startling blue of his eyes pierced her gaze, signaling the inevitable paring of the argument into layers. Her brothers, McCalpin and William, referred to them as "shreds," but Emma had confidence she'd survive the skirmish.

She clasped her hands in her lap in the perfect pose to demonstrate nonchalance, as if her father queried the weather. "I'd hoped that I might borrow ten thousand pounds from you or from my dowry since it won't be needed. I've estimated I'd be able to repay the loan within—"

"Your dowry," her mother exclaimed as she sat on the edge of the sofa. "Those monies are for your financial security later on."

Her father uncrossed his legs and rested his elbows on his knees as he considered Emma. "You'd rather operate this business in lieu of marriage I take it?"

"Yes," she answered without any hesitation.

"Puss, I can't help but think this is tied directly to your grief for Lena." All his earlier detachment dissolved in a vat of disquiet.

Emma straightened in her seat. "Well . . . yes and no. Certainly, I want to help other women escape the same circumstances. When hardworking women find their luck fickle, I want to provide resources to help them reestablish their lives. Just today, I met a young viscount's sister who was desperately seeking funds for the maintenance of their estate."

"Really, who?" her father asked.

"Miss March Lawson. Her brother is a boy, and Miss

Lawson has taken all the responsibility of his viscountcy. But another reason for the bank is that I plan to use part of the profits to pay you back and the other to bring Aulton to justice."

Suddenly, her father and mother stood.

"Absolutely not," her mother cried.

"I forbid it," her father bellowed.

They both spoke in unison. Their harsh reprimands reverberated throughout the room, even making the tea in her china cup quake.

But she wasn't as delicate as a cup of tea and stood in answer. "If not me, then who?"

Her father studied the rug as if he could divine the appropriate response in the red and blue oriental patterns. Tenderly, he took her mother's hand in his.

Emma expected her father to speak, but it was her mother. "My love, this is not your responsibility. It's Lord Sykeston's."

"He's fighting in France. How can Lena's brother accomplish anything from there?" Emma paced in an effort to stem her outrage at the injustice of it all. Jonathan Eaton, the Earl of Sykeston, was her brother Will's age and had left for France shortly after Lena married.

Her father stepped forward and took her hands in his, effectively halting her strides. "Your mother's correct. It's Sykeston's concern. For us to step in is an insult."

"Insult?" She did nothing to hide the amazement in her voice.

"Emma, no." Her father's hand cut through the air as if he'd brook no more opposition. "Your mother and I are aware you're hurting, but this isn't your fight."

"What if the husband you choose for me is unkind or cruel? What would you do?" Emma didn't hide the challenge in her voice.

"I'd tear the bastard apart." Her father's answer was a promise, bluntly spoken.

"What if it was too late?" she pressed.

Her father exhaled, the redness in his face receding. "Sweetheart—"

"I'm not a woman who wants to marry." At one time, she'd dreamed of having a marriage like her parents' union. The love they held for each other was obvious. They listened to each other's opinions on everything from agriculture, estate management, even politics.

However, her fantasy had dwindled quickly with her disappointing Seasons. Year after year, the eligible men of the *ton* proved their conventionality. They all adhered to the provincial concept of how a proper wife should conduct herself. Not one seemed able or willing to accept a woman as an equal partner. But the truth of Lena's marriage was the final blow. She vowed to live on her own terms without answering to anyone. She had too many important things to accomplish, namely, helping women flourish and prosper in lives that were safe. Only then could they pursue their dreams and succeed. Her own personal goal was to find a way to make Aulton pay. With what she'd seen of Miss March Lawson today, her business would be a resounding success.

"Emma, love, we won't force you into making any uncomfortable decision. But we want you happy and secure in your life." Her mother's voice had returned to its normal soothing tone. "Promise me you'll keep an open mind about next week's party."

"I agree with your mother. Don't make any rash judgments." Her father's tone deemed the subject closed. "We only want what's best for you."

She groaned under the weight of her frustration.

She didn't have time for marriage. Nor did she have time for Somerton and his threat to discover her plans from Mr. Goodwin. She turned all her focus to Portsmouth, but Somerton invaded her thoughts once again.

It would be her luck he'd stick his perfect nose in her business once again. If he thought to stop her from traveling south, she'd squash him like a rotten apple on the road.

Chapter Five

~

After finishing at Goodwin's, Nick started his morning as he did every day when in London. He reviewed correspondence, read the information provided by his long list of informants, and studied ships' manifests against his warehouse inventories. The fire chased away the morning chill, and a cozy warmth filled his study. He hadn't moved in over four hours and rose to stretch his legs.

"Pardon me, my lord. The Marquess of Pembrooke to see you." His butler Hamm clucked his familiar disapproval. "You failed to eat last night. I'll prepare a tray."

"Thank you." Who needed a wife when there was Hamm? "Go ahead and send him in."

He stole a quick glance at the ever-increasing pile of correspondence and reports on his desk. Another unopened note from his father, the Duke of Renton, protruded from the stack as if begging for his attention. Nick picked it up and threw it into the blazing fire like he'd done with all the rest. It wasn't worth the effort to watch it burn—or read it. Normally, the missives from his father arrived monthly. Now, their frequency had increased to weekly.

"Good morning, Somerton." Alex strolled into the room. The marquess was Nick's business partner, but more importantly, he held the distinction of being Nick's closest friend. After his father had cut him off, Nick had struggled financially to complete his university studies, but the provost had allowed him to tutor in lieu of tuition. One evening, Alex had discovered him weak with a raging fever in the dormitory stairwell. After helping him to bed, Pembrooke had summoned a doctor, then insisted Nick take a small sum of money. They'd been friends since.

Alex sat and propped one leg over the arm of a chair.

"Tell me, what do I owe for the pleasure of your company?" Nick broke away from his desk and poured the customary two cups of coffee.

"I'm here to extend an invitation to dinner at Langham Hall tomorrow. It's the family. Emerge from your dark vault and enjoy yourself for a couple of hours."

Nick flinched as he brought over the coffee.

"Both Claire and I worry about you constantly hiding in this house." Alex paused before continuing the often-repeated lecture. "You hardly ever seek company except for us. You've got to leave this haunt. You deserve a little comfort, a partner."

Nick turned from Alex and stared into the fire. To contain his ire, he counted to five. He had his whole life planned, and it didn't include needing anyone, particularly a wife. The companionship he received from Alex and his family was enough.

His attention reverted to his friend. "I'm elated you've found true happiness with your marchioness, but don't mistake your road to marital bliss as the only way to find fulfillment. I'm a different beast."

Alex took a sip, then drained the rest and set his cup down. "Don't let your father's vitriol color your actions now."

"Pembrooke," Nick warned. He stiffened at the suggestion his father still mattered in his life. "He has no influence."

"We both know different. When he cut you off without a shilling, it changed your life." Alex shook his head.

"I'm satisfied. I have everything I need." Nick picked up a prospectus and sat down. He hoped the subtle hint would convince Pembrooke to depart or at least to change subjects.

Alex drew a deep breath. "I've never understood your father. You did what any honorable man would have done. You signed for a gambling debt to keep a man, a friend no less, from getting killed."

"Unfortunately, Lord Paul never repaid me. In my father's eyes, I was and still am a spendthrift. That's my sin." Nick waited for the inevitable bitterness to bite him at the mention of his father. He wasn't disappointed. Even this many years later, dwelling on the betrayal shot anger through Nick. He tightened his hands on the prospectus and longed for an extended session at Gentleman Jackson's boxing salon. The fact his father blamed him for Lord Paul's gambling loss and accused Nick of wasting two hundred pounds only added suffocating layers to the betrayal. After Lord Paul's perfidy, Nick wouldn't allow anyone to take advantage of him ever again. And after his father's desertion, Nick had learned to count on no one but himself. Alex was the exception. His friend had proved himself loyal time and again as evidenced by today's stalwart defense of Nick's actions.

"What you've done with your life is remarkable. You're a regular Midas." Alex stood and refilled his cup. "It's time to move on."

Nick threw the now-wrinkled prospectus back on the desk. "It gives me great pleasure to be *in trade*. Whenever I'm on the wharf or in a coffeehouse conducting business, I think of Renton. I hope his skin crawls knowing his one and only ducal heir is in the philistine world of commerce." Nick twisted his mouth in a false smile. "Besides, can one ever have enough money?"

"You need more than money." Alex leveled a look that would frighten a weaker person to do his bidding. "Don't look back years from now and discover you've turned into a bitter replica of your father."

"I'm content."

"You already sound like an eighty-year-old man." Alex quirked an eyebrow but was earnest. "Come with us tonight to Lady Emory's ball. Lady Emma is joining us."

Nick let Pembrooke's words fade into silence. When would the man realize he was a hopeless cause? "I'm not interested."

In one swallow, Alex finished the second cup. "You always seem a little more, how shall I say, *animated* when she's present."

"Lady Emma?" Nick hid his unease by pretending to study another prospectus. A prickly heat crept up his neck when he realized the document was upside down. He let it fall from his hands and considered sharing his discovery of Emma at Goodwin's, but decided against it. Her coy reserve intrigued him enough to keep her secret, at least for another day or so.

"She's highly entertaining at a social event." Alex reclaimed his chair. "With a simple exchange, she can have any man tied up in knots. Her political acuity reminds me of her father."

"Your ideas of amusement are questionable," Nick reprimanded. Suddenly, "tied up in knots" summoned all sorts of salacious images—neck clothes, silk ties, and Emma tied to his bed with her skin flushed the same lovely pink shade that colored her cheeks when she'd studied his stature at Goodwin's. He picked up the prospectus again to sweep the picture from his mind.

"Seek her out." Pembrooke grinned. "You'd learn a great deal from her. Speaking of which, take a look at this for me, will you?" He pulled a document from his morning coat and threw it on Nick's desk. "Tell me what you think. Emma presented a plan to create a bank for women to Claire. My wife's enthralled with the idea and wants to invest in it."

"I'd be happy to." This plan of hers would be the perfect excuse for a visit. After what he'd discovered at Goodwin's, it would be an excellent investment of his time to have a little chat with the minx. Emma didn't disclose she was looking for a particular book. If she thought she'd go gavotting to Portsmouth for a damned pirate queen's diary, he'd do his damnedest to end her merry dance. He'd already sent word to Goodwin he wanted the pirate's diary for her.

The mathematical tie of his cravat started to squeeze like a boa constrictor around his neck. In a predictable manner, the tightness occurred every time he discussed Emma. "She'll be there tonight?"

"Yes, with Daphne." Pembrooke appeared oblivious to the tumult playing havoc in Nick's mind. "It's no secret Emma's struggling with her friend Lady Aulton's death. She'll be mortified when she hears the latest. Apparently, Aulton's seeking another engagement." Pembrooke exhaled. "Well, if you're not interested in Emma, then let other society ladies get a glimpse of you."

"Thank you, as always, for your unsolicited advice." Nick affected a look of boredom. It was torture to go to society affairs. His skin turned clammy when every unmarried and even some married women examined him as if he were a sweet-going stallion on the Tattersalls' auction block. He'd decide who and what he'd go after. No one controlled him.

Of course, a golden-haired, green-eyed enchantress came to mind. Pathetically, a groan escaped and drew a grin from his friend.

"I only want you to experience happiness." Apparently satisfied with his efforts, Alex smirked in a manner that most men would take exception to, but not Nick. After their long friendship, he was accustomed to such ribbing.

He could never imagine himself in Pembrooke's position—blissfully happy, married to the woman he loved with two children and another on the way to dote upon.

"It would give Claire and me great pleasure to see you settled."

"For all that's sacred, stop." Nick took a deep breath. "I'll attend just to satisfy you and your wife's meddling. However, it changes nothing. I'll be my own master."

A picture of Emma surrounded by a gaggle of golden-haired children, laughing and playing at her feet, slipped past his defenses and into his thoughts. The emerald-eyed girls favored their mother while the boys bore a striking resemblance to him.

Damn Pembrooke and his description of ties.

Emma fanned herself, fighting the evening's warmth. It kept the inane conversations floating around her at bay. The Earl of LaTourell, Lord Honeycutt, Lord Greyston, and a throng of others, including Daphne, surrounded her.

Her boredom didn't derive specifically from the men attending her. Emma liked most men. She had a true fondness for footmen with their powdered wigs, laborers with their thick cockney accents, bakers, shopkeepers, even aristocrats with their big noses and round bellies.

What she despised were the so-called gentlemen who hunted the ballrooms for some female prey they could capture in their claws. Men who sought perverse pleasure at stealing the virtue of some debutante or wallflower and forcing marriage were the vilest. Emma's well-honed avoidance of marriage was never in danger, but some of the innocents in the room were lambs for the wolves who wore suffocating sweet cologne and too-tight breeches.

To keep her sanity, she had to leave the ballroom.

Daphne came to her rescue, and not a moment too soon. She was the only reason Emma attended this evening. Her friend gushed about how much she enjoyed these *ton* events. Why she loved the crowded affairs and routs was something Emma had never understood.

"Gentlemen, I apologize, but I must have Lady Emma's counsel on a topic of the upmost importance." Daphne's pewter-colored eyes sparkled from the glow of the candlelight and added to her striking beauty. She took Emma's arm and walked briskly to the side entrance where a full view of the ballroom stood before them.

Billowy drapes of white silk framed each window, making the entire room soft and radiant. Hothouse flowers of red and pink in large silver urns dominated every available tabletop. It was lovely, but mundane at the same time. The room, the guests, and the flowers were a well-worn ritual, the redundancy as stifling as the warmth in the room.

"Em, look there. Wonder what forced him out of hiding?" Daphne whisked her fan in a direction across the dance floor. "The she-wolves will soon be circling."

Emma followed the motion of the mother-of-pearl fan. Across the sea of elegant dresses and their black-suited partners, her gaze rested on the steps leading down to the ballroom. A tall man dressed in a gray evening coat trimmed with black cord to match his black silk breeches captured her attention with his perfect presentation. The woven silver thread in his moss-green waistcoat caught the light from the candles spread throughout the ballroom. With his golden hair, it appeared a halo encircled his head. If only angels were that gorgeous.

Making a rare appearance at a *ton* event, Lord Somerton graced the ballroom in all his glory. She moved slightly to gain an unfettered view of his progress. Somerton's manner and movement resembled a tiger—assured, dangerous, but utterly breathtaking.

She'd do well to remember this was the same tiger that practically pounced on her at Goodwin's that morning.

Without wasting a glance, he gracefully maneuvered his way through the ballroom until he reached their side. With a subdued flourish, he sketched a perfect bow.

"Emma and I are all agog you're here," Daphne said. "Have pigs flown over the Thames?"

"Lady Daphne, I'm honored by your lovely greeting." With an assured ease, he settled his gaze on Emma while he continued to address Daphne. "Would you mind terribly if I steal Lady Emma away?"

His words confirmed her worst fears. Somerton meant to dog her about Goodwin's. She'd made a tactical error not scurrying from sight when she first saw him. Immediately, she straightened her shoulders. She did not scurry from *anyone*.

Her friend's smile broadened. "No. Enjoy yourself. She's the best dancer here."

Somerton's grin brought an immediate softening to his features. It was pure sin a man could be that handsome.

"I agree. She's the best. Lady Emma, may I have this dance?"

Her cheeks were on fire. "I might have promised this one to George—Lord LaTourell." *Lud.* She'd never been this tongue-tied, and schooled herself to calm down. Somerton was a constant in her life, nothing more than a frequent visitor to her home.

At the mention of LaTourell's name, the muscles in Somerton's jaw tensed and caused his chiseled cheekbones to become even more prominent. "He's not here, but I am." His eyes roamed over her figure before settling on her face. He leaned close enough to whisper. "You and I have much to discuss, don't you think?"

His invitation was a challenge, and she never resisted a dare. What did he seek by tormenting her? All her secrets? All her plans? All her confessions? He couldn't have any of them.

Somerton bowed to Daphne, then placed Emma's hand in the crook of his arm. The air between them practically crackled as if charged with electricity. She flexed her gloved fingers against the muscle. If his forearm was this firm, she'd give her monthly allowance to see the rest of him. A view of Somerton without his shirt would be worth a year's worth of pin money.

What was the matter with her tonight? She had to put such thoughts out of her mind. Her Portsmouth trip was at stake. For this dance, she needed a level head and sharp wits. Besides, she did not drool over men. Period.

Deep down, she couldn't deny the truth. Every time he was near, she was drawn to him. He was like an exotic nectar, akin to the juice of a passionflower rather than your average hothouse rose. One no bee could resist.

What utter twattle.

Best to get the blasted waltz over with. She admired his form and manners, but that was all. She'd not allow him to sway her from her plans. She'd have him eating out of her hand or running for cover before the last note of the music faded to nothing.

He artfully escorted her around the waltzing couples. Still visible but away from the crowd, they stopped at the far end of the ballroom.

With a deep breath for fortitude, she meant to tame the tiger in front of her. "My lord, what matters shall we discuss?" She kept her voice light.

"Come now, Emma. We're way beyond 'my lord' and 'my lady.'" He twirled her around the dance floor, his gaze never wavering from hers. "Nick."

A flutter took flight in her chest, and she dropped her gaze. His effort to unsettle her could not succeed. Determined, she tried to move her body away from his, a simple gesture to create distance and keep him at arm's length, but his hand tightened on her waist. When she lifted her gaze to his, her stomach tingled almost as if she'd had a glass of her favorite champagne.

Her dress, a heavy ivory silk embroidered throughout with seed pearls, followed their movements. Thankfully, its sheer weight kept her grounded since her instincts made her want to lean closer. He rubbed the pad of his thumb over her waist, branding her skin through the gown. The penetrating blue of his eyes held her captive.

"Nick . . . why are you doing this?"

"Why does anyone dance at these events? Relieve boredom. Enjoy the company of a beautiful woman. Stake a claim. Give warning." He raised an eyebrow and delivered a slow grin. "Which one do you suppose applies here?"

The sensual web he spun split in two. She'd seen the same expression a thousand times from her brother, Will, before he dropped the ax on one of her misdeeds. "Pray tell, and put me out of my misery."

"Emma, sarcasm? Such an inelegant emotion from

such a bewitching lady. What have I done to deserve your rebuff? I simply wanted a dance." The twinkle in his eyes was wicked and forbidden in design. "Any man here would risk a flogging for a chance to dance with you in that dress."

Her reservation melted at his obvious teasing. "That's quite an extreme. Would you risk a flogging?"

"Repeatedly," he quickly answered with a squeeze about her waist again. "I'm here about something else."

She blinked slowly to stay focused.

"I know your game." His declaration cracked the air like a well-oiled cat-o'-nine-tails.

Her gaze whipped to his. "Game?" He definitely resembled a seraph—Lucifer to be exact.

He whirled her around in a move that made her dizzy. "I know about Portsmouth."

Emma tripped when her feet failed to lead her body.

His hold tightened and prevented her fall. With a smile, he continued the pretense all was well, while his words gouged a hole in her confidence. "I know about your little escapade to retrieve the diary. Are you mad? You'll cause your family the scandal of the century if you try another madcap travel escapade for a book. Portsmouth is not some little seaside spa for young ladies."

"Diary? What are you talking about?" Truly, his inordinate preoccupation with numbers and investments must be making him addlebrained.

With his gloved hand on her back, he pulled her closer. "Goodwin told me all about your obsession with the pirate queen's diary." His lips barely touched the tip of her ear, but it was enough that her body tensed as his whisper tickled her skin.

She'd play his game for as long as necessary until she ascertained what he meant. "I fail to see how it could be any of your concern what type of books I seek."

His low rumble of laughter vibrated against her chest. When he pressed her closer, she didn't resist. She glanced at the other dancers and caught Lady Swaledale staring.

"Pembrooke gave me a copy of your prospectus for a bank. I'll be more than happy to help you with it, but in exchange, you'll stop this ridiculous plan of yours. I'll not help if you're planning some idle, illogical odyssey that has disaster written all over it. Besides, I've already directed Goodwin to purchase the dairy for you. There's no need for travel to Portsmouth."

As the waltz was ending, the explanation for Goodwin's behavior crystalized before her eyes. Instead of Goodwin revealing the real reason for her visit, he'd led Nick down a merry path. Relieved, she exhaled a breath. Now was her chance to put the arrogant earl in his place for trying to dictate her actions.

She lowered her eyelashes in a manner designed to give the audience a show of modesty. "My lord, am I to understand you're instructing me on appropriate behavior?"

"It's a naval town brimming with British officers, sailors, and others not so savory."

"I'm flattered you're concerned for my welfare. Rest assured those who have need of my social calendar are fully informed of my daily activities." Her body simmered with a mixture of peevishness and amusement at the idea that he actually believed he could dictate her actions. "You, sir, are not one of those individuals."

The music had stopped, but Somerton pulled her closer, almost as if embracing her. Emma prayed Lady Swaledale had found something else to watch. If not, they'd be married before the morning.

With his lips a hairsbreadth from her ear, he whispered, "I saved you from ruin once. Remember when you set off alone to retrieve a book without thought to the consequences? I kept your secrets then, and I'll keep them now. No one will know of your trips to Goodwin's, but I demand you forget Portsmouth."

Emma stepped back and stood before him as determined as David in front of Goliath. She bit her lip with enough force she could taste blood. Her aggravation threatened to ignite an uncontrollable ire that would consume them both.

She raised her chin to prove to him and, more importantly, herself that she wouldn't yield or grovel before him. "I'll not agree to any of your dictates. Nor will I accept your meddlesome interference. Certainly not for a book. I'm not that young lady from years ago who is easily enchanted by a kiss."

"You were the one who demanded a kiss that day. Besides, it wasn't just any kiss." The deep timbre of his voice resonated through her capricious body like a tuning fork. "Need I remind you, it was your first." His voice softened to a silky whisper. "I'm not seeking your kisses, delightful as they are, just asking for your acquiescence. However, if you prefer the same trade, who am I to argue with a beautiful lady? My only condition is I say where and when I receive my kiss."

She stepped away to increase the distance between them. Heat blanketed every inch of her skin. Her fury grew until it threatened to burst in a string of curses that would make a ship's captain blush. Somerton's high-handed dictate burned, and his overbearing ideas of how a woman should behave made her want to scream. She forced herself to take a calming breath. She would not allow herself to be at the mercy of his outrageous demands.

"Explain to me why I am any of your interest? You're not my keeper."

He stiffened, and a muscle clenched in his jaw. She'd

shocked him, and it delighted her he failed to have a ready answer.

Slowly, one of his devastating, incandescent smiles—the ones designed to melt a woman's heart—transformed his face. "Because you're one of the very few people in this world I enjoy."

Now, her treasonous heart skipped a beat. Was nothing in her control anymore? She swallowed to gain her composure.

Suddenly, the muddle instantly cleared from her brain. Why didn't she think of this before? There was a perfect way to handle him. She delivered her best dazzling smile, the one she used only for the most special occasions. A feat so rare in appearance, she could recall each and every one bestowed. The first was her seventh birthday when she received Robert, a gorgeous piebald pony; the second when she found the gold ring in her serving of the Christmas pudding; and the third when she'd met the queen. It had worked like magic. Her Majesty had chatted with her for almost twenty minutes.

Tonight, her smile held a special meaning reserved only for him.

In response, his eyes widened and then his own incandescent smile grew more scorching in effect. Good heavens, this man was dangerous in so many different ways.

She forced herself to remain calm. "What a fright! For a brief moment, I thought you were going to say something important." She waited for her comment to register. "May I share something?" This time she didn't wait for his agreement but whipped open her fan to move the stuffy air between them. "You may go to the devil."

She turned and with a glide, increased the distance between them. She kept her smile to bestow on anyone lucky enough to be in her way and went in search of Daphne. Emma found her at the mezzanine terrace doors, a discreet viewing area that overlooked the entire ballroom.

"Why do you have that look on your face?" Daphne asked.

"It's nothing to worry about." Still reeling from her confrontation with Somerton, Emma let out a sigh.

The most beguiling grin broke across Daphne's face. "I didn't realize Somerton was such an unpleasant partner. He doesn't attend many events, but he should have grasped the basics of conversation with a lady. He darted out of here like there was a fire to attend."

"Forget Somerton. I certainly have." She whipped her fan open. She'd not allow him to affect her mood any longer, nor would she allow him to interfere with her plans. "We didn't have an opportunity to finish our conversation this morning. I have news. Mary Butler is in Portsmouth."

Daphne eyes held a hint of tears. "Oh, Em." With one quick movement, her friend grasped her hand and squeezed. "I know how much this means to you."

"You're the only one who does, and the only one I've told." Emma squeezed her friend's hand in return.

"Claire doesn't know?"

"I couldn't risk her worrying. Not with the baby coming. She'd tell Alex or my parents," Emma explained. Claire loved her dearly, but her cousin was still too protective of her, especially after Lena's death.

"What about your parents' demands you not pursue Mary?"

"I've thought of that. They're the type of people who wouldn't send a servant away if she needed their help. I must bring her back to London. Perhaps she's desperate."

"I have Claire's carriage ready for travel. Shall I go

with you?" Daphne asked. She'd do anything for her, and Emma would do the same for Daphne.

"No, it's too risky. I need you to send it to the smithy's on the pretense of repair work. Have it prepared for travel tomorrow night. Arial and I will meet it there the next day and leave for Portsmouth. My parents are taking a trip out of town."

"What if your cousin asks for her carriage?"

"Claire hasn't used it since she married your brother. Besides, I can't take one of my father's carriages. I've learned my lesson the hard way. With outriders and the ducal seal on the carriage doors, it all but announces itself as the Duke of Langham. Word would reach my father before I'm five miles out of town."

"That is a dilemma." Daphne tapped her finger against her chin.

"The only missing piece is who will drive me to Portsmouth. Is your old driver, Harry, still in London?"

"Emma, this is madness." Daphne shook her head. "Harry is trustworthy. You're one of his favorites, but you can't go with only one attendant. Who will help drive?"

"I'm sure he's fit enough to handle a day's travel. If need be, I'll hire someone to assist." A look of disbelief crossed her friend's face, but Emma pressed on. "Hear me out. We'll meet the next morning, then he can drive through London. We'll stop at the first inn and engage another coachman for the trip down and back."

Daphne's face darkened with doubt. "Em, no. Have you asked McCalpin or William to take you?"

"McCalpin's out of town for two weeks. William would never agree. My window of opportunity is closing fast. Besides, what could possibly go wrong?" Emma widened her eyes in a desperate plea. "I can't bear another ball without taking some action. If I ever meet Aulton at one of these blasted things, I won't be responsible for my actions.

Soon, we'll hear an announcement of his betrothal. I have to stop him, and Mary will help me, I'm sure of it."

Daphne studied her without saying a word.

"Besides, I'll never find any peace in this gilded cage we live in with all these men."

"Oh, come now. It's not *that* horrid of a life." Daphne waved her fan around the room. "Look at all these fine specimens. There must be a hidden treasure among the lot you'd be satisfied with."

"There are no hidden treasures. Every man here looks at you, me, and all the other women as steppingstones." Determined to bridle her frustration, Emma shook her head. "We should all list our dowry amounts on our calling cards and pin them to our bodice. It would make our lives so much easier."

"I don't agree with your opinion of courtship, but I'll help." Daphne's faint smile still held a hint of uncertainty. "I'll see Harry accompanies you, but nothing else. I'm honored you trust me with your secrets. Be forewarned. If there's as much as a hiccup, I'll go straight to Pembrooke. I want you safe."

Emma closed her eyes in relief. "Thank you."

This was the perfect opportunity to show Somerton never to cross her.

The next morning Emma found several posies and nosegays arranged on the entry hall table. All sent from the few smattering of men she'd danced with last night—in appreciation, they had sent flowers. None held any special interest.

Her stomach grumbled to remind her there were more important matters that needed attention—toast and jam. When she made her way to the breakfast room, a large bouquet stole her breath away. Dozens of deep yellow roses majestically reigned over the table with what looked like hundreds of black-eyed Susans as subjects. A package addressed to her rested against the vase. When she opened it, a note and a small painting of a bumble-bee were enclosed.

> *Lady Emma,*
> *Your sting was sharp. Let us start anew.*
> *Somerton*

Emma inhaled the sweet fragrance of the roses and caressed the prickly black center of the wild flowers. Many used the flower to calm a bee sting.

What an exasperating but clever man.

A soft sigh escaped. She should forgive Somerton's boorish and, even worse, authoritarian manner from last evening. Anyone who put that much thought into a gift deserved a reward, even if his motives were still questionable.

Truly, it was a shame he would not get what he wanted. She was leaving for Portsmouth first thing in the morning.

She supposedly had a fictitious pirate queen's diary waiting for her.

More importantly, Mary was there, and Emma wouldn't take no for an answer.

Chapter Six

That evening Emma entered the library where the family and a few close friends had already assembled before dinner. Even though the group was small, the noise from the collective conversations hinted at the comfort and love shared by her family.

She started toward the group that included Daphne and Pembrooke. When Daphne shifted, she revealed . . . Somerton. Emma stopped as if she'd stepped in knee-deep mud. What in the devil was *he* doing here? Dread threatened to chase away her good spirits.

Her reverie broke when his arresting eyes, accompanied by a slight indention in a square chin, focused on her. Somerton immediately separated from the others and came her way. In a silent prayer, she begged he'd not introduce the mythical pirate queen's diary or Portsmouth as a topic of conversation. If anyone overheard a peep, all would be lost.

"Lady Emma, I wondered when you'd join us." In his elegant but subtle manner, he took her hand and bowed.

"Thank you for the flowers and the painting. I've

enjoyed them immensely." Remarkably, it was easier than she imagined feigning a nonchalant casualness.

He rewarded her with a wink and a sly smile that intimated he wasn't through with Portsmouth. The scoundrel thought to unsettle her with such an intimate gesture. She wouldn't give him the satisfaction.

If she kept repeating that thought, tonight would be bearable.

"You accept my apology?" His eyes glowed with a touch of humor and something else, regret maybe.

"We shall see how you behave as the evening progresses." She playfully tapped him on the arm with her closed fan. "You were a horrid rogue last night. How do I know you're sincere in your claim to be remorseful?"

As they spoke, the rest of the dinner party drifted past to the door. Soon everyone, including the servants, had vacated the library. It was the perfect opportunity to set the mood for the evening. She would chase him away before he brought up Portsmouth again. With a step, she closed the distance between them. His maddening scent wrapped itself around her as if to force her to succumb to his allure.

Years ago, she'd acquired a famous eighteenth-century courtesan's memoire that described the best way to shake off a clingy and demanding paramour. The author advised stealing a kiss and then suggesting marriage. Within hours, the potential beau would part company.

Besides the woman's erotic adventures—an education in and of itself—her instructions on how to get rid of a man were scintillating. If Somerton fought against her charms, she'd double her efforts—anything to make him lose interest and stay out of her business.

"Shall I claim the kiss we discussed last night?" Her heart pounded with her forwardness, but she forced herself not to flee.

He stiffened and seemed incapable of speech. Finally, he relaxed and leaned close. "The door is wide open. Have you taken leave of your senses?" The underlying sensuality of his whisper floated between them.

"On the contrary, I'm using all of them." With a deep breath, she closed her eyes and waited. Waited for his mouth to touch hers. Waited for the softness of his lips to caress hers.

Waited . . . for nothing.

With an exhale, her brief surge of triumph turned into confusion and emptiness. It wasn't a surprise he didn't want the kiss, but it hurt nonetheless. She hadn't kissed another since their first kiss. She sighed at the sudden sadness and pushed her disappointment aside, though her heart protested. His departure was her goal—not his kiss. He must have taken heed and silently bolted from the room.

When she opened her eyes, he had shifted closer. Startled, she took a step back, and he smiled as if he were the cat that ate the last canary in the cage. If a feather fell from his lips, she wouldn't be at all surprised.

A fiery heat marched up from her neck to conquer every inch of her face.

"You little minx. You want to play?" He lightly brushed the knuckle of his forefinger down her inflamed cheek, the touch soft and seductive. His sinfully dark whisper caressed her with a promise of something forbidden. "It'll be a pleasure for both of us when I claim your kiss. But, sweetheart, *I* say when and where. Not you. This isn't a game you will win."

Without a look back, he walked from the room.

Stunned by his words, she snapped her mouth shut. It wasn't a game. It was a declaration to stay away.

She made her way to the dining room—unaccompanied. Somerton's revelation about the kiss left her unbalanced and truthfully bewildered. The best way to prove he hadn't set her world spinning was to act as if nothing had happened. The only way to do that was to concentrate on her surroundings. She'd take the comfort she always found in Langham Hall's informal dining room and settle her runaway nerves. She loved to dine here with her family. It served as their lodestone. All celebrations, gatherings, and remembrances occurred in this small room. Her family drew strength from these events. Moreover, unbeknownst to the others, tomorrow morning would mark another milestone—her trip to Portsmouth and the hope that the singularity of women would be recognized throughout England.

She joined the others around the table. Somerton sidled up next to her. Without a glance, he held her chair as he answered her father's questions. With little movement to draw attention, he slid into his chair and caught her gaze. She was in danger of drowning in the ocean blue of his eyes. Her heart rattled and tumbled in her chest as if in a free fall. He shifted closer—surely closer than propriety allowed. She struggled with the urge to change places, with someone as far from him as possible. Even the next room might be too close.

What a bloody blunder. She wanted to slip under the table and flee. It should have been simple to convince him to cease showing up at her home and everywhere else. Trapped, she sat beside him without any plausible means of escape.

Somehow, she made it through the seven courses without completely ignoring the family. By the time the footmen presented the dessert, she'd found her bearings. A fabulous assortment of sliced fruits, cheeses, and exotic nuts decorated the table. The pièce de résistance was a decadent orange torte soaked in brandy.

With the first bite, she closed her eyes and savored the

fusion of flavors that melted in her mouth. Her older brother Will, garnered her attention when he cleared his throat. The gleam of deviltry in his eyes meant his topic of conversation would not be to her liking. She didn't move an inch. She half-expected it to be a lecture on Portsmouth, but the first shot fired was a surprise attack.

"I'm curious about the consensus of the room. Does anyone believe women will ever have the right to vote? If so, does anyone believe they'll understand the issues?" Her brother discreetly waggled his eyebrows at her.

Her father's gaze shot to Will. The previous conversation had been light with little political comment, a perfect start to a casual evening. Her brother leaned back in his chair. If she wasn't mistaken, little red demon horns had popped out of his head, a definite improvement to his looks.

She swept her gaze the length of the table to gauge the other's reactions. The majority gave their full attention to their desserts. Only her father, Pembrooke, and Daphne appeared interested. If it had just been the immediate family, the conversation would have started at once with all taking sides until everyone exhausted their arguments. Her father had a fondness for throwing out controversial topics at family dinners and leading a raucous debate. But with Somerton and Daphne present, he played the perfect host.

Emma glanced at her mother who, with the slightest shake of her head, warned her not to engage Will. She cleared her throat, another sign to let Will hang in the wind.

With a deep breath, Emma tried her best to control her tongue. In all honesty, Will's taunts caused her blood to boil, which wouldn't take much tonight since her whole body felt primed to explode from the earlier debacle with Somerton.

"Emma? Cat got your tongue?" Will prodded.

Someone needed to issue a challenge and put her pretentious buffoon of a brother in his place.

But not her. Not tonight. She kept her focus on her plate.

"You prove my point." Will's words hung in the air like a putrid smell.

Enough was enough. How could her parents expect her not to challenge him? If the rest of the family wouldn't take umbrage at Will's histrionics, she would.

"You've managed to insult over half the people at this table." She broke the lull in conversation and threw her serviette to the table like a gauntlet. "To answer your question, it's long past due. Surely, the most intelligent people would welcome it. Women deserve the right to have their voices heard on all issues that affect the country, their compatriots, and their families. Only when each and every person accepts a woman's right to education, the inherent right to make her own decisions, and an equal place in society will true freedom to think and act prevail for all."

The delighted glee on her brother's face reminded her of a jack-o-lantern.

"Emma, please." He shifted his attention to Daphne and Somerton. "Our family, I'm afraid, is at fault. We've encouraged her to the point she gives her opinion on all subjects whether she has the experience or capacity to address such complicated matters or not."

"Lord William." Her father's voice had dropped to a low baritone, a clear warning he'd reached his limit for her brother's pranks.

A flash of heat blistered her cheeks, fueled by the fact that more and more eyes came to rest upon her. They wouldn't have long to wait for her response. She planned to string him up like a haunch of venison.

With the slightest twist in her chair, her gaze pierced Will's. "You should have paid more attention at Oxford. Proof of the intelligence and acumen of women is rife throughout the centuries. Boudicca, Cartimandua, Queen Elizabeth, and even Mary Wollstonecraft are just a few examples. They all cherished freedom and, in their own way, brought it to the men and women of England. Of course, a woman's privilege is still much less than a man's in our current society and should be changed for the greater good of all."

Emma waited, hoping for someone, anyone, to join the discussion. The only sounds around the table consisted of forks tinkling against the plates as her family scrambled to ensure their mouths were full.

"Emma, darling, you're correct. But perhaps we should leave this discussion for another time." Her mother's voice was soft, but her heated gaze indicated she wanted to throttle Will.

"Allow me one more point." She didn't wait for her mother's reply, as her time to answer was short. Her father was bound to change the topic of conversation.

Somerton shifted until one leg rested against hers. The heat from his body caused another flush to wash across her cheeks. She chanced a glance in his direction only to discover his lips pressed together in a grimace. Surely, he didn't judge her or discount her beliefs. *Damn William and him, too.* She didn't have to answer to either of them. Ever.

"Mary Wollstonecraft was maligned for her beliefs. The others had the right to voice their ideas and make decisions because of their royal blood. Every one of these women deserves our praise for their bravery in their speech and actions." Her gaze settled on Will. "Someday a woman will serve as prime minister."

"Would you send women to war, too? If they have the right to vote, then shouldn't they have the duty to defend the country?" Will asked. He popped a slice of apple in his mouth and chewed. The effort did little to hide his smugness.

"Of course, women have always gone to war in defense of their countries. Queen Elizabeth's brilliance as a soldier and leader during the Spanish Armada's invasion is one of England's proudest moments. Consider all the women who've followed the drums in support of the troops."

After her impassioned speech, the sound of a single person clapping rang through the dining room, followed by a masculine chuckle. Will's laughter grew until he was practically bent in half from his guffaws. Her father cracked a smile. Even Pembrooke found the comments amusing, and he never laughed at her.

Anger hotter than a fire in a smithy's forge shot through her. "Imagine how different England would be if there was no right of primogeniture. Firstborn males might have to work for a living if their birth order falls after the firstborn female."

Every one turned to her with a wide-eyed gaze as if a parliament of owls had taken up residence in the dining room.

"Under the right circumstances, Claire would be the Duchess of Langham." She'd see this through to the end, no matter the repercussions. "Her daughter, Lady Margaret who was born five minutes before Pembroke's heir, would bear the courtesy title Marchioness of McCalpin."

No one said a word. Silence hung heavy in the air. Finally, the longcase clock chimed the quarter hour, breaking the eerie quiet.

"Lady Emma and Lord William, need I remind you we are entertaining guests?" Her father had practically growled the words.

"Your Grace, I find this most enlightening." Daphne trained her gaze on Will. "Lady Emma, correct me if I'm wrong. Under your scenario, if my brother was still the Marquess of Pembrooke, wouldn't Lady Margaret also bear, by courtesy, the Pembrooke title, Countess of Truesdale?"

"Indeed." A sudden sting burned Emma's eyes, and she blinked to clear the offensive intrusion. All she could manage was a nod. Daphne's loyalty was worth far more than the Crown Jewels.

"Emmy, I was teasing." Will's voice hinted at contriteness. "But what you suggest is beyond ridiculous—"

"Oh, this is rich coming from the debauched genius who placed a one-hundred-pound wager that Mr. Clayton's pet leopard would change its spots overnight when it rained." Those words would cost her, but it was money well spent. "If you believed that dubious hoax, is it so difficult to accept that women deserve freedom and autonomy in life?"

"The wager was whether his spots would fade in winter." Her brother leaned back in his chair and regarded her. Nervous laughter echoed throughout the room. "Watch your step, little sister. With your chosen course of spinsterhood, you may in the future beg me to let you live in my home. How would you describe that freedom?"

She swallowed and pressed her eyes shut. As if an inferno had landed on her lap, heat blazed from her chest to her face. William had eviscerated her with the sharp truth of his words.

Under the table, something warm grasped her right palm. Fingers entwined with hers before delivering a gentle squeeze. She settled for a moment. What was Somerton doing? Surely, he wasn't trying to comfort her in front of her family?

"Lady Emma makes an excellent point." The laughter died when Somerton spoke. "Unrest is sweeping into our country and its territories. The Ludd riots are just an example. We only have to study France and America to see the results if we ignore it. We'd all be better served if we took others' ideas seriously and welcomed an open debate."

Her father rubbed the bridge of his nose.

The duchess stood to lead the women out of the dining room for tea. The men would stay to enjoy a glass of port and finish their discussions.

The bitter taste of humiliation squeezed her throat. This everyday ritual made her point exactly. Women left the table while men dissected into minute-detail politics, the nation's economy, war, and anything else of importance. All under the guise that such a ritual was sacred.

Irritation over her circumstances singed her hard-fought control. Why couldn't they stay and join in the discussions? Women's perceptions and observations provided a completely different lens through which the men could better understand the issues.

The harsh truth?

She lied to herself. She was furious over more than some silly ritual. No one gave a fig about a woman's role in the world, or her right to safety in her own home. Her own family thought what happened to Lena was a travesty best swept under the table for others to handle.

Without realizing, she'd squeezed Somerton's hand so tightly that hers throbbed. "Forgive me," she whispered.

Somerton traced the edge of her thumb with his in answer and then slid his hand from hers. With a dignified air, she hid the restiveness that bucked like a wild horse inside her and rose from the table.

Pitts, the Langham family butler, stood nearby and gave her two apples from the side buffet table on her way out. "In case you're hungry later, my lady. They arrived this afternoon from Falmont."

"Thank you," she said softly.

With a resigned breath, she grabbed her shawl for a walk to her bench in Langham Park. It was the perfect place for the night air to cool her temper.

With perfect timing, Mr. Goodwin had sent a note earlier that afternoon. Everything was arranged for her arrival tomorrow at the Ruby Crown. It was fortuitous the distance was only a day's journey if the weather held.

For her own sanity, she'd might just move to Portsmouth.

Chapter Seven

Nick stood next to the window and ignored the deep thrum of conversation behind him. It was black as ink outside with nothing to see except the reflection of the duke and Lord William behind him enjoying their port.

When he moved closer to the window, the glow of a brilliant harvest moon caught his attention, and slowly his gut unclenched. His anger fueled by Lord William's confrontation with Emma slowly dissipated.

The entire dinner had been delightful until dessert. The duchess, Emma, and Claire were gifted conversationalists. Whenever there had been a lull in the conversation, one of them had picked it up without obvious effort. After he left Emma in the library this evening, he had little doubt she could entertain him for days.

"You're a million miles away." Alex stood beside him with two glasses of port and gave one to him. "Care for a game of billiards?"

"You never cease to amaze me with your boorish behavior." Nick bit out the bitter rebuke. "Bad form to find amusement through your wife's cousins."

He turned to the window and caught the glow of a small lantern cutting through the darkness. He needed to get out of this room. It was stifling hot, and the conversation too loud and boisterous. He'd follow the light and wager it was Emma walking in her park.

Alex followed Somerton's gaze to the lantern outside. "You're right. I do owe her an apology. It's no excuse, but the scamp was so serious. When she suggested the idea that Margaret could be the Marchioness of McCalpin—" Nick's friend stopped abruptly, and his brow furrowed into neat rows of lines. "Did Daphne say Countess of Truesdale or Earl of Truesdale?" He shook his head as if to clear the confusion. "Either way, I couldn't hold it in. Even Langham found it amusing."

Nick held up his hand to stop Alex from continuing. "Did you happen to see the expression on your wife or sister's faces or catch a glimpse of the duchess? If not, I suggest you seek them out and apologize."

"Come now, my behavior wasn't that offensive." Alex drew silent for a moment before his forehead wrinkled again as if presented with an unsolvable puzzle.

"If you don't apologize, I'd not be surprised if you're locked out of your room tonight. If you'll excuse me, I need some air." With a brisk nod, he made his way into the night. He had business in Langham Park.

He crossed the grounds in long strides. The evening dew had made an early appearance, accompanied by the cool dampness of the autumn air. The moon's orange cast reminded him of tonight's cake. Its glow bathed the land with a light bright enough to follow Emma's path through the formal gardens.

A stone archway and a copse of trees hid a granite bench, the place he'd first kissed her. Tonight, he found a far different woman from the girl he met years ago.

A missile sailed through the air, and he caught it in his right hand before it hit him square between the eyes.

"You bloody oaf!" Emma stood on the bench and hurled another apple his way.

He caught it in the other hand. "Is your arsenal empty? Otherwise, I'll need to fetch a basket."

She braced a hand on the back of the bench and gracefully hopped down. "I . . . I thought you were Will."

"I figured as much." The moss between the cobbled bricks of the walkway softened the sound of his boots as he approached.

"I'm not good company at the moment." Her voice was low and cracked with emotion. She tilted her face to the moon.

He slowed his approach. "That's a pity."

Emma continued her study of the sky.

He tried to think of a way to ease her back into conversation, but instead observed her without saying a word. Normally, he didn't mind the silence, but tonight, it felt awkward. He didn't have a clue what was appropriate to say or do.

Seemingly nonplussed, Emma started a conversation without any self-consciousness on her part. "I apologize for throwing the apples and . . . dinner. Sometimes, I allow Will to goad me to the point I say things without thinking of others."

"There's no need." The moonlight kissed her skin and seemed to transform her into an ethereal creature.

"Since I turned seven, my mother has allowed me to wander the park. Whenever I seek my own counsel, I come here." She finally looked at him with a small smile and whispered as if sharing a great confidence, "I enjoy it as much now as I did then."

"We should discuss Portsmouth before I say good

night." As soon as he got her promise not to travel, he'd apologize for interrupting her evening, then leave.

"Portsmouth again?" Her voice grew soft. "Stay. Please. Let's find something to talk about that pleases both of us. We could discuss business or banking or anything else you'd like . . ."

He smiled, no doubt like a bloody fool. She wanted his company. Surprising, since her behavior at dinner indicated his teasing in the library had displeased her. He sat and placed her arsenal, namely the apples, beside her.

Another luminous moonbeam caught the sheen of her hair. With little provocation, he'd pull the hairpins one by one until her hair tumbled free, then he'd run his hands through the golden waves. How he wanted to gently spear his fingers through her tresses and tilt her head for a kiss that would consume them both. She shifted, and the silvery light fell across her face. She resembled a faery considering which spell to cast on him.

A chill ran down his spine as reality hit him. He faced real danger of succumbing to her if he wasn't careful. He wanted to see if she was all right, apologize, tell her to forget Portsmouth, and then leave. His study possessed a mountain of work demanding his company.

Now, all his thoughts focused on the softness of her skin. What was the chance one of her family members would find them? Not likely, as they all knew of her fondness for spending time here alone.

He needed a whip to tame such wild thoughts. He was in danger of seducing a duke's daughter and losing what little self-restraint he possessed. He was completely bewitched.

"It's late . . . I should return to the house." Privately, he cringed at his clumsiness as he stood. He stared at Langham Hall alight in a yellow glow paler than the moon. He sounded like a schoolboy with his first crush.

He'd never had a crush or a love or even an infatuation before. How did anyone even distinguish between such knotted messes?

Escape was the only possible solution, particularly prudent before he said something witless. He shouldn't confuse fondness for anything else. He found the chit fascinating and didn't want her smarting from the embarrassment caused by her beastly brother. That was his real reason for following her here, besides settling the issue of Portsmouth.

He was known for logical thinking, but tonight, he was at her mercy. Pembrooke was correct. She could tie men up into knots with just one word. In his case, just one look.

"Please stay." Emma looked straight ahead. "I'm happy you're here."

Once again, she drew him in with that simple request, so he reclaimed his seat.

Her hands played with her dress. "Thank you for supporting me at dinner. It provided an excellent opportunity to leave the room without engaging Will again. Sometimes, I don't think before I speak. I made everyone uncomfortable." After a sigh that seemed to restore her ability to look at him, she lifted her face. Her grin didn't hide the hurt. It made her appear drawn and waif-like. "It was the perfect escape. My only regret is . . . I didn't get to finish the orange cake, my favorite."

Probably the number of times Emma Cavensham suffered public humiliation could be counted on one hand. Her natural warmth made most people gravitate toward her. The men and women who ignored her were fools. It pleased him that it seemed to make little difference to her. She was completely unfazed by the trappings of the gossiping *ton* as she held court on the sidelines of a gathering. Laughter and smiles were freely given.

Somewhere within the past few moments his exasperated free will had gone home—alone. Beside her, he was unable to move as his rational mind sounded the alarm and cried "Retreat." He turned to take his final leave and got lost in the glimmering depth of her eyes while her familiar clean rosewater scent washed over him. He inhaled deeply and released a groan. The fragrance stole every reason to leave her side.

He raised the white flag, surrendered the fight, and leaned toward her.

Emma's heart pounded loud enough that everyone at Langham Hall must have heard it. When Nick leaned close, awareness rushed through her body with the force of an ocean wave. She matched his movements, but didn't wait for him to continue what he started.

Heedfully, she reached with one hand and cupped his face. The hint of bristles from his evening beard surprised her. It tickled her palm and made her realize what she had in her hand—a virile, vibrant man who she wanted to kiss.

Trying to appear composed, she slowly moved toward him, but her insides quivered like a fresh pudding. She closed her eyes and silenced all thoughts to concentrate on the sweet touch of his mouth. In sharp contrast to his evening beard, his lips were as soft as she remembered from years ago.

Their first kiss remained a secret locked deep inside; one she'd never shared with anyone—not even Lena. It was her first kiss ever—her first taste of him. From that day forward, she'd understood they were connected. She had replayed that kiss hundreds, thousands—no millions—of times in her mind.

As she swept her mouth over his, she took her tongue and caressed the seam of his lips, coaxing him to open as he'd taught her years ago. Without protest, he opened to let her in. She ran her tongue over his and he matched her movements. Her kiss was a conversation between them, and he listened. He allowed her to play for some time, and the raw power of seduction swept through her, but then it became apparent he tired of her gentle volleys and deepened the kiss. All thought surrendered to the pleasure of his potent lips on hers.

Growling, he crushed her body against his. It wasn't enough—she needed to get closer.

In a flash, Nick stood before her with his long legs spread apart ready to escape.

"What is it?" Since her mouth throbbed from his kisses, it was miracle she could whisper anything at all.

A rustling sound came from the direction of the main path.

"Someone is coming," he whispered. "I'll call tomorrow to discuss your bank proposal."

"I'll be out of town." *Why had she blurted that?* There was only one reason; his kisses were intoxicating.

"Portsmouth?" His gaze pierced hers with a strength that reminded her of a newly forged sword.

"Daphne and I . . . are visiting a friend." Completely flustered, she let the words tumble.

"No one mentioned this at dinner." One of Nick's perfect brows arched in disbelief. "Tell me," he demanded.

"Please, don't. This is important to me," Emma pleaded softly and placed her hand on his arm. "It's not what you think." She had to diffuse his anger while protecting her real reason for travel.

"Your mischief is at an end," he clipped. "You'll not go to Portsmouth."

"Emma, where are you?" Claire's soft voice carried to the shadows where they stood.

Fire flashed in his eyes. "*Damnation, tell me.*"

"Please," she meekly offered. "You must go."

"Emma?" Claire's voice was getting closer.

"Nick, please." She'd never had much luck pleading with him before, but as it was her only option, she'd try anything. She smoothed her hair before answering her cousin. "I'm here by the arch," she called out.

She studied his face, cold and hard, much like a frozen river in the dead of winter—such a contrast to his earlier blazing kiss.

He ignored the pathway and left through the park. She'd never witnessed his anger before, but it burned like a wildfire out of control.

There was little else she could do. Within seconds, Claire stood beside her.

"Your lips are swollen." Her cousin's voice was barely above a whisper as she carefully sat. "Your dress is askew."

Emma stiffened at the challenge in her words. "I couldn't stay in the house another minute with Will, and I came here to be alone." She drew a deep shuddering breath. "I've been crying. If my appearance is off, you have your reason."

"Don't make another mistake you'll regret. Your banishment to Falmont will look like child's play if your integrity is questioned again. Protect your reputation, as it's nigh impossible to repair. Take my word for it." She drew Emma into her arms and squeezed tight with a hug.

"Please, it's nothing."

Claire tucked several loose curls behind Emma's ear, then tugged on her dress sleeves. "He'd marry you without hesitation if he thought you were interested. My only concern would be you."

"What do you mean?" The idea Somerton would marry anyone was ludicrous. How could Claire even suggest such an idea?

"He's complicated and not accustomed to compromise. Neither are you." Her cousin playfully tapped the tip of her nose. "It's not your strong suit."

She let Claire's words fade into the night. Her appearance wasn't perfect, so Claire tugged and twisted the bodice until her breasts wouldn't make an uninvited appearance. In silence, they walked back to the house.

The warning tasted like bitter medicine. Putrid to swallow, but designed to protect. When Claire's own marital status, or lack thereof, became a favorite topic of the *ton's* fodder after four failed engagements, Emma had witnessed the cruel attacks. With Claire's string of broken engagements, most of the *ton* and several "close friends" delighted in spreading rumors she was cursed. Claire had walked through life wounded and convinced she'd never marry until Alex came and changed everything.

Tonight, Emma would have welcomed a little of Claire's curse coming her way, anything to keep Somerton from interfering in her life.

Chapter Eight

∽───∽

The cold added a damp bite everywhere. Emma leaned back against the plush squabs and stretched. If the horses kept the same pace, she'd reach Portsmouth within three hours.

After her parents left to visit Lady Chelston, Emma met the old Pembrooke coachman, Harry Johnson and Daphne at the smithy's business. Ever thoughtful, Daphne had provided a packed basket and a velvet coverlet for Emma's comfort.

Daphne had merely nodded when Emma had asked her to stay hidden for the day. Emma explained that she'd slipped last night and told Somerton that she and Daphne were visiting a friend today. It'd been a poor excuse, but it was all Emma could think of when Somerton had confronted her. If he discovered Daphne at home, he'd know Emma had traveled to Portsmouth.

However, Daphne didn't hide her dismay when she had discovered Arial hadn't accompanied Emma. However, with a fever and chills, Emma wouldn't risk Arial's health on such a short trip. Besides, with Goodwin's friends, she'd be perfectly safe.

Only one more stop before she'd arrive at the Ruby Crown Inn. Tomorrow, she'd go and meet the Parkers and examine the coroner's report. Then, she'd visit Mary. The Parkers had sent word to the maid that Emma wanted to see her.

She examined the silver locket in her hand. Warm from the heat of her hands, the simple necklace glistened with light and memories of Lena. Inside, was a carefully protected lock of Lena's soft brown hair and a few crushed petals from the first posy Lena had received from an admirer—ordinary items they'd shared as they embraced their first Season together.

She carefully placed the locket in her reticule. Needing to fidget, she caressed the soft dark navy velvet on the seat. Claire recently had the vehicle renovated to match the interior of her husband's carriage.

Such a waste in Emma's opinion. If it had been her vehicle, she'd have made the interior fit her own tastes. Cream-colored leather with a green-blue velvet would be perfect. She imagined a handsome man sitting across from her with a playful teasing smile, his eyes matching the interior.

Her vision of perfect transformed into Nick. After their second kiss in Langham Park, she could only think of him as Nick. With a start, she sat up straighter. The man wouldn't leave her alone even in her daydreams.

The morning had brought Claire's warning into a new light. With surprising speed, Nick had left her last night to face Claire alone. He couldn't wait to escape her company and didn't give her a proper leave. What would a proper good-bye consist of in their situation? How do you say good night after leaving a lady with her mind muddled from kisses?

He'd been masterful at dinner when he took up the proverbial arms and had come to fight beside her against

Will. Never would she have imagined Nick willing to assist her as she'd argued vehemently for her belief in a woman's right to participate equally in politics—all without a hint of criticism or chastisement for her convictions.

He relished his isolation and encouraged society's opinion of him as an enigma. Granted, his looks were near perfect and his manners gentle and kind, but there was so much more to him than what he allowed others to see. Some considered him nothing more than an avaricious man of trade who raided and plundered others' inability to make a fair bargain. But his talent to ferret out opportunity while others saw nothing was a true gift. London had ridiculed his purchase of merchant ships to set up trade routes to the States and Lower Canada as the height of foolishness. Yet he had turned it into one of the most profitable businesses ever to sail from London.

Others, particularly women, regarded him as a mystery that begged to be solved.

She saw him for what he was—a treacherous man.

She had always prided herself on the ability to resist the charms of any gentleman. Yet whenever his heated gaze settled on her, she became lost, and her thoughts would scatter like leaves in a fall gust. There was a promise of something in his eyes, as if he held a secret that could shatter her world and highly organized convictions.

When his bold attention focused solely on her, it was deeper than a glance or a look. It reached somewhere hidden inside her heart and mind. He was like a gravitational force, and she was helpless, caught in his orbit. Dangerous was too tame to describe him.

Sweet kisses and gentle caresses were one thing. Without much effort on his part, he could bend her willpower and break it in pieces with one rapacious look. She'd do well to remember that simple fact.

Emma embraced the bright sunshine and closed her eyes. Time to put her thoughts of the Earl of Somerton to rest. She wanted to savor every single moment of her day without any distractions. Everything she hoped to accomplish in Portsmouth was before her.

The irresistible smell of apples, cinnamon, and butter wafted through the breakfast room of Pembrooke's town house, and Nick inhaled deeply. Tarts were his weakness. "Are those apple tarts? I didn't see them on the buffet."

Alex looked up from his paper. "Daphne's not here, so there aren't any. She and Emma left this morning to visit a friend. They'll return tomorrow."

A young maid passed by the doorway holding a plate of the hot, fragrant confections. She took the stairs to the family's quarters, an odd destination since Claire and the nurse had taken Lord Truesdale, Alex's heir, and Lady Margaret, for a walk.

Nick's gut tightened. No one else should have been upstairs in the family quarters. Besides, the tarts were Daphne's favorite.

"I found the pies." Nick motioned for Alex to follow.

"Your hunt for sweets is a little obsessive." With a sigh, Alex stood.

Both silently followed the maid upstairs. Oblivious, she entered Daphne's room briefly, murmured a greeting, and then closed the door sans tarts without passing a glance in their direction.

Alex took the lead and silently opened Daphne's door. She had her back to the them and sat at her desk with a full breakfast tray and a tower of steaming tarts. Before she brought one to her mouth, Alex intercepted her wrist with his hand.

"What—" Her gaze snapped to her brother's. "What are you doing here?" Daphne's face grew deathly pale.

"That's my question." Alex elevated one eyebrow. "Think of something else to ask."

"I'm a little under the weather." She sniffed.

"I'd not realized tarts were a cure for colds," huffed Alex.

Her silence screamed things were awry.

"Let's continue this in my library, *now*. Somerton, join us?" As he escorted her through the house, Alex held Daphne's forearm much the same way he grasped his son's and daughter's arms to insure they didn't flee. He released his grip once they reached the library door. With a wave of his hand, Alex invited his sister to enter first. The skirt of her silk dress brushed against her brother's leg and a spark of static electricity snapped like a portent of the blaze that would surely erupt once the door was shut.

After he clicked the lock, Nick turned and faced the interior of the room. The silent communication between the two siblings held the drama of a well-played card game. Alex raised a haughty eyebrow and stared at his sister, daring her to speak. Daphne matched him, tapped her foot, and added a smirk for effect.

At an impasse, Alex broke the silence. "Does Mother know you're not where you said you'd be? If she did, I doubt she'd have traveled to Bath today to take the waters. You told us all you were spending the next two days at Miss Cassandra Fuller's house with Emma."

As Daphne's resistance crumbled like last week's biscuits, she lifted her face to the ceiling and closed her eyes. After a moment, her gray eyes, identical in their piercing color to her brother's, opened to glare at both of them.

"As a ruse to protect Emma's travel plans, I was going to stay in my room for two days." With a heavy sigh, she started her negotiations. "Promise not to inform Mother? Otherwise, I'll not say another word. She'll tell the duchess."

After a tense moment, Alex nodded.

"Emma is on her way to Portsmouth in Claire's carriage." With a defiant throw of her head, Daphne crossed her arms. "She plans to spend two nights and be back the day after tomorrow."

Nick's unease ignited into a full blaze of anger. "To get the pirate's diary? When did she leave?"

Alex gave a bewildered look first to Somerton, then to Daphne. "Pirate's diary?"

"Calm down, Somerton," Daphne scolded. "What pirate's diary?"

"The bookshop owner, Mr. Goodwin, told me she was after some diary of a pirate queen named Anne Readington." His heartbeat drummed in an uneasy staccato rhythm. How could Emma do this after he'd specifically warned her not to try such a folly? "I directed Goodwin to buy it for me. I planned to give it to her in lieu of her traveling to Portsmouth."

"Somerton . . ." Daphne's voice softened as she shook her head. "She's gone to convince Lady Aulton's maid to return to London with her."

"Lady Lena Aulton?" Alex blew out a breath. "That explains some things."

"Why the maid?" Nick was well aware of the rumors surrounding Aulton and the recent death of his wife, but he'd never given much thought to it after Alex suggested Aulton was ready to marry again.

Daphne clasped her arms around her waist and exhaled. "Emma wants a witness to Lena's death to come forward. She believes the lady's maid saw everything. The maid was so distraught after Lena's death she sent

all the countess's unposted correspondence to Emma as
a safe measure. The countess was convinced her husband would likely kill her before the baby was born."

Nick tilted his head to the ceiling to keep from roaring like a beast. Why didn't Emma confide in him? If he
hadn't been such an arse about Portsmouth, perhaps she
would have trusted him enough to tell him her plans.

Alex pursed his brows. "Does McCalpin know where
she is?"

"She wrote to him." Daphne's piercing gray eyes narrowed. "Somerton, how do you know about it? She only
told me of her plans a couple of days ago."

"She was at Goodwin's with only her maid in attendance. When she wouldn't tell me her purpose, it took
little persuasion on my part for Goodwin to spill. Apparently, he thought a fib would lead me off her trail. Our
Lady Emma is quite cozy with Mr. Goodwin."

Alex's mouth tilted upward in a half smile. "Did I hear
correctly? *Our Lady Emma?*"

Nick waved him off. His ridiculous badgering could
wait.

"When did you see her at Goodwin's?" Alex asked
Nick.

Nick propped a hip against the massive oak table that
commanded the center of the room. "The day of Lady
Emory's ball. I told her to forget Portsmouth and went
so far as to threaten I'd tell the duke."

In his typical headstrong manner, Alex's anger erupted
like a volcano, always later than expected. "Daphne, you
didn't stop her or tell anyone? My God, Aulton's home is
within thirty minutes of Portsmouth. If he catches wind
of her real purpose, he'll likely do anything to her."

Daphne threw back her head in defiance. "What could
Aulton possibly do to Emma?"

Alex, smooth as a panther stalking his prey, approached

his sister, never taking his eyes from hers. Daphne was taller than most women, but Alex towered over her. "In a major thoroughfare of London six months ago, he beat his horse until the poor creature had to be destroyed," he whispered. "The wretched beast's only crime? It lost a shoe and stumbled, causing Aulton to fall to the ground. Can you now imagine what could happen if he feels threatened by Emma?"

Daphne paced in front of them. "Don't lecture me. She's . . . alone at the Ruby Crown Inn. Her maid woke extremely ill this morning. Emma wouldn't hear of taking Arial with her. She said the poor woman looked like death. She wouldn't take me or anyone else. Just Harry. She thought the fewer people who knew, the less chance of discovery."

Emma was on her way to Portsmouth, and he needed to make sense of Daphne's explanation. What if she found herself stranded? What if some disreputable dandy, or worse, Aulton, stopped to offer his help? The instinct to pound his chest and roar his displeasure detonated with a force he could barely contain. He focused on his breathing. Succumbing to such primitive antics would not help now. Later was another story.

"Do you mean she only has that old man for protection?" Alex had moved to the front of the fireplace, and his voice boomed across the room. "He should have retired years ago."

Daphne retreated to the window. "Harry will protect her. She's always been a favorite."

Alex wiped his hand over his face. "Go to the family salon. We're not finished yet."

"You're not my keeper." Daphne tilted her head and stared out the window.

"As head of this family, what I say is law." His words echoed off the walls and surrounded them. "Don't tempt me to find a husband for you this upcoming Season. I promise my choice will not be to your liking."

"I now understand Emma's point entirely. I should have escaped with her." She held her head high and her back straight as she left the room.

The door closed, and Nick broke the tension that blanketed the room. "That was harsh even by your standards. She's your sister, for God's sake."

"Yes, and I plan to keep her and Emma safe. Both believe they're above all rebuke. Someone has to go to Portsmouth before she finds real trouble and *before* her father finds out." Alex continued, "I promised Claire I'd take her to a charity function tonight. Would you mind escorting her? If I leave now, I'll arrive in Portsmouth before night falls."

"Let me go after Emma. It would appear odd if you're not with Claire tonight. Besides, I feel responsible. I should have told you or Langham what I suspected."

Alex nodded. "I appreciate you jumping into the middle of this. If there's anything I can do, just name it."

"Are you going to inform the duke and duchess?" Nick exhaled. Emma's parents would be livid over her actions. After everything she'd suffered over the last several months, he didn't want her punished. Yet he feared that would be the case, and he'd be the cause once again.

Alex paused. "No. I'll send word to McCalpin and see if I can find William with the news. I'll ask they not get the duke and duchess involved."

Relieved, Nick would do his damnedest to get her back to London before her parents discovered what she'd done. "I expect to leave within the hour. I'll keep you informed."

Alex escorted Nick to the entry hall where a footman gave Nick assistance with his greatcoat. With two steps,

Nick was outside, and a groomsman held the reins of his mount.

Impatient to depart, Nick's black stallion Proteus stomped the ground. When Nick mounted the horse and settled into the saddle, the beast's gait turned into a full gallop before given a command. Time became a demanding mistress. He couldn't afford to spend a night from his work, let alone two days chasing Emma. If all went as planned, he'd make it to Portsmouth before nightfall. He'd find her, and they'd return early tomorrow. Then he should brush his hands of the whole affair and the Duke of Langham's troublesome daughter.

Much to his dismay, the thought brought little or no comfort. The fault of Emma's travel to Portsmouth lay at his door—all of it. He shouldn't have left her alone last night until he'd gotten her promise. Her entire travel could've been circumvented. More importantly, if anything happened to her, he'd never forgive himself.

Of all the damn things he'd seen in his life, this one topped them all—Emma, alone in Portsmouth, determined to secure a lady's maid's testimony to bring a murderer to justice. She was a danger unto herself.

In addition, a danger to his self-control. Claire had almost caught them kissing last night. Strange . . . instead of the usual prickles of unease at the thought of matrimony, something else had taken up residence, but he wasn't certain what it was.

Marriage to Emma wouldn't ruin his life. He'd always found he'd preferred her company to the other Cavenshams, or any woman for that matter. Her gentle laugh and wit drew him to her as if she was a light or a compass designed to help him, and only him, find his way back.

But back from what? He had no idea what the journey was. He sounded like a lovesick fool with his musings.

He had everything he needed in life, but he forced himself to face the truth. He wanted her.

The truth was he didn't think he'd be able to keep her and make her happy.

His father had assured him of that certainty all those years ago.

After Emma had settled into her suite, a clean and neat sitting room and bedroom, she was ready for her evening. At precisely eight, Harry escorted her across the threshold of the Ruby Crown's public dining room. Completely mesmerized, her gaze swept over the planked walls. The entire room was crowded with mementos and souvenirs from ships the sea had allowed into port.

She could spend hours studying the intriguing sights and learning more of the inn's history, but the noise demanded her attention. Boisterous masculine singing rose into a final swell, then quickly dissolved into robust laughter. Shouts for another round filled the dining room.

Crowded with locals, the entire room fell silent when the patrons' attention fell to her and Harry. Slowly, one by one, all of the men, the few women in attendance, plus the servers turned toward them. Half-full mugs of ale littered the tables, and not a single person uttered a peep. In a moment that felt like years, every single person stared at them.

She had a gift for stopping conversation, but normally it was in a ballroom after she'd shared her views on a woman's right to invest her own dowry. Not in a public tavern swimming with people she didn't know.

Harry stood two steps behind her. In a loud whisper, his rough voice carried through the room. "Something don't smell right here, my lady."

Two burly men with matching lecherous smiles pushed their stools back and stood next to her. The fetor of week-old sweat and grime wafted toward her, causing her protesting stomach to lurch. Her pulse raced, and the blood pounded in her ears, but she delivered her best haughty look. She would not cower in front of them.

"Well, what do we have here, Jasper? The little lady looks lonely, doesn't she?" The man identified as Jasper attempted a smile, but all she saw was a mouthful of rotten teeth.

"Ay, Murray. The little dove looks like she could use some consoling." Jasper leaned close. "She smells good, too."

Harry swallowed and shuffled forward. "Move along. She's not for either of you."

Murray's beady eyes shifted to Harry. "Old man, we decide who and what we want." In a flash of movement that defied his hulky size, Murray pushed Harry aside as if he weighed nothing. He and his barrel-chested companion stood side by side and blocked Emma's path.

Wisdom required she pivot one foot and flee as she considered the chances of successfully escaping the taproom. She stared at the two men while attempting to find the courage to run. It became difficult to judge the passage of time, but finally, the silence broke when the innkeeper, Mr. Fenton, stood by her side.

"That's enough. Let her and the gentleman through," he said. "My lady, please join me. There's room at my table."

"Fenton, we're just havin' fun," Jasper growled.

"Not at the expense of my guests," he said in an even tone. Middle-aged, the innkeeper boasted a solid build. Along with his massive size, the crook in his nose and his large hands indicated a man not afraid to toss unruly patrons from his establishment. A veiled expression fell across his face, but his eyes warned of an anger that once released would be difficult to control.

Emma stayed glued to the floor unable to move. Finding ease with Mr. Fenton's direction, the crowd relaxed in unison and waited to see what Jasper and Murray would do.

"Come on, she ain't worth it." Murray tried to pull the other man away. "I can't afford trouble."

Jasper stood planted like a thick elm tree. After several moments, he stood down and looked away from Mr. Fenton. With a spit to the floor, he joined Murray and walked to the door. He took one last look at Emma. With a smile that would make the devil cringe, he left the room.

As if it were an intermission between acts of a play, the crowd exhaled in relief and went back to their whoops and roars of conversation.

Emma swallowed her choking knot of fear and turned to Harry. "Are you all right?"

Harry's complexion resembled a ripe apple revealing his distress at the unsuccessful attempt to convince the brutes to leave. "Yes, my lady. It's best we eat and retire early."

"Please follow me." Fenton waved a hand, then escorted her to his table in the back.

"May Mr. Johnson, my man of affairs, join us?" she asked.

"Of course." Mr. Fenton held the chair out for Emma and then assisted Harry, who at the pronouncement of "man of affairs" stood tall. With a nod to the serving girl, the innkeeper held up two fingers, signaling the need for more ales and food.

"Don't mind the locals, they're a superstitious lot. When some of the men have too much to drink, particularly if they've just come to shore, they have a tendency to forget their manners. Not many out-of-towners take their dinner in the ale room." As if the last several minutes hadn't happened, he continued genuinely interested, "Mr. Goodwin told me you have business in Portsmouth."

Emma's earlier fear began to recede. "Yes, but I have a few places I'd like to visit for pleasure."

"In my estimation, that's a perfect combination." Mr. Fenton studied her, and a smile curved his lips. "I've known Goodwin for years. When he asked for my assistance, I was delighted to help. He's a great admirer of yours, and any friend of Goodwin's is a friend of mine."

"That's very kind. I wouldn't be here without Mr. Goodwin," she said. "Thank you for your earlier aid dispatching those two men." Emma stole a glance at the door the two brutes exited. She'd always considered herself a woman capable of handling any situation, but now she wasn't so sure. What would have happened if the innkeeper hadn't come to her assistance? Harry's age and feeble stature were no match for the two men. "I'm not certain what I would have—"

"My lady, it's over." Fenton smiled briefly and turned his attention to Harry.

An easy conversation ebbed and flowed among the three of them. She and Harry erased their gnawing hunger with fresh oysters, haddock, and a delicious potato stew. They devoured the freshly baked bread with home-made jam and butter. The meal ended with hot tea for her and another round of ale for the gentleman.

"Sir, I need to make arrangements for our return." Harry stood and crushed his well-worn cap between his fingers. "I'd be most grateful if you'd stay with Lady Emma until I finish."

"My pleasure. She'll be perfectly safe." Mr. Fenton nodded as if giving a solemn oath.

The promise was all Harry needed. Quickly, he exited the taproom and left the two of them to finish their conversation.

"The booksellers Mr. and Mrs. Parker are expecting you tomorrow. I have a serving girl, Bess, who is more than happy to act as your lady's maid. She's not fancy, but an honest hardworking girl who'll look after you."

"Thank you." A gentle breeze blew through the window's cracked opening. Emma glanced around the room and inhaled the combination of salt and sea. Lena had described the smell to her millions of times, but Emma never understood the power of it until now. There was a magical quality in Portsmouth almost as if Lena was there—greeting her.

"My lady, if you'll excuse me for a moment?" The innkeeper stood in response to his wife's appearance in the public dining area. "The missus must have need of me."

"Certainly, sir."

With a nod, Mr. Fenton strode across the room to his wife.

Her disquiet from the earlier confrontation with the two ruffians abated. Like a complicated dance, the servers wove their way through the crowd with trays of food and returned with empty platters. Emma let her attention drift back to the window as the conversations around her melted into a pleasant hum.

"May I join you, Lady Emma?" A familiar masculine tenor swept across the table and stole her newly acquired ease.

Without a glance at the speaker, she gripped the edge of her chair. Otherwise, she wouldn't stay upright. Every instinct told her to duck for cover.

Without waiting for permission, Keith Mahon, the Earl of Aulton, slid his frame in the chair opposite her. He wasn't as large as Nick or her brothers, but he towered over her. Emma forced herself to meet his gaze. It was difficult to tell what was darker, his black hair or his midnight-blue eyes. Both reminded her of a murky loch on a Scottish moor.

Aulton surveyed the room as if he were the king and the inn's customers his loyal subjects. "In this very room, I shared a marvelous meal with my countess shortly after we married. She was always partial to the Ruby Crown's oyster stew. Did you find the food to your liking, my lady?"

"My lord." Her voice quavered slightly. "What a surprise to find you here."

"Really?" he asked. The upward curl of his mouth, more like a sneer, destroyed his serene expression. "Your room is where we spent our wedding night. I do miss my wife." He sighed as if to convince her he was still mourning.

Emma discreetly glanced toward the door in hopes Mr. Fenton or Harry had entered the room.

"Imagine my surprise when I learned you were visiting Mr. Goodwin. I assigned one of my footmen to follow you. Hiding the carriage at the smithy was clever, but not clever enough." Aulton leaned across the table as if sharing a secret with her. Entranced with the pine tabletop, he traced a crack in the wood with his forefinger. "My lady, your business in Portsmouth?"

"Is no concern of yours, my lord." By then, Emma's heart rate had slowed down to a gallop. She leaned back in her chair hoping to appear unconcerned.

One of the serving girls stood watching their conversation. She whispered something to the man collecting the dirty dishes, then walked out of the room.

Aulton cocked a half grin, though they both knew he wasn't amused. "Perhaps you might have business with Mary Butler, my late countess's maid? If so, I should inform you the girl isn't in Portsmouth anymore. She's run off to God knows where with some sailor."

"Politeness requires I thank you for your assistance." However, the reality she'd ever say thank you to this animal was nil. She'd never suspected that such dark depravity could exist in a man, so dangerously hidden, yet so easily exposed when threatened.

"Well, my lady, I'll not interrupt any more of your evening." Without warning, he reached across the table and took one of her hands.

She tried to pull away from him, but his grip tightened.

"After Mary Butler left my house, I discovered most of my late wife's personal effects missing, letters and jewelry to be precise." His hand slid across hers until he held her wrist. "I'd hate if you were involved in the theft."

His fingers tightened, crushing her skin against bone. The pain became acute when he found a sensitive area, causing her to wince.

"What are you implying?" she whispered as she twisted her wrist in an effort to escape the pain. Aulton released her hand, but her bones throbbed in response to his grip.

"Nothing really," he drawled. "It'd be a shame if your good name was sullied any more than it already is."

"Are you threatening me? My father is not the type of man who allows threats to his family without a sharp reprisal," she challenged.

Aulton stood. "Consider it constructive advice"—he tilted his head as if giving the matter great thought—"or perhaps personal instruction. If you're not inclined, then perhaps my employees, Murray or Jasper, possess better persuasion skills than me. I bid you good night, Lady Emma."

He delivered a mocking bow and tipped his hat. He strolled toward the exit as if threatening a person with bodily harm was of no concern and a part of his everyday routine.

Before Aulton reached the door, her body instinctively released the tight coil of tension in her chest. She started to shake involuntarily from the shock of the encounter. Through her glove, the skin around her wrist had started to swell.

"My lady, Bess fetched me with word that another customer was frightening you?" Mr. Fenton's eyes were pinched with worry.

"A man thought he'd made my acquaintance, but was mistaken. I'm perfectly fine." Of course, she didn't dwell on the fact that Aulton did indeed know her but had underestimated her dedication to having him brought to justice. Composing her appearance, Emma rose from the table. "I'll retire now, Mr. Fenton. It's been an exhausting day. I have business at the bookstore first thing in the morning."

"Bess will accompany you upstairs," Fenton answered.

She agreed with a stoic nod. The more the merrier in her opinion. Such a dark evening would be best put behind her. She could concentrate on her day tomorrow.

Bess stood next to the table with a glass of brandy in her hand. The smoke-scented fumes invaded Emma's nose. "My lady, I thought you might need this. Was there anything else I can get you?"

The idea of a pistol, knife, or sword plus a broadax came to mind.

Chapter Nine

Within minutes of his arrival at the inn, Nick discovered Emma's suite. He'd tread lightly since she would resist his efforts if her tenacity with her brother, William, was any indication of her likely response.

At the top of the staircase, two men, clearly inebriated, stood directly outside Emma's room. One held several strips of cloth and a soiled rag.

"Murray, while I gag her, you tie her hands. Together, we'll wrap her up like a Christmas goose."

"I'm . . . I'm not so sure, Jasper. Where would we take her? I'm not risking the innkeeper's wrath again." A loud hiccup echoed down the hallway. "He's not the sort to go along with this."

"Neither am I." Both men turned at Nick's harsh warning. "Back away from that door."

Jasper dropped the cloths and held his hands in front of him. "Easy, my friend, no harm done."

Murray assumed the same position. "We must be at the wrong door."

Slowly, they inched their way from the door and slid along the wall like snakes.

Once they reached Nick's side, Jasper slurred an apology. "Honest mistake, sir."

Nick blocked their exit. He checked the men's hands for any weapons, then took a step forward. Murray quickly moved behind Jasper. Nick stared until both men dropped their gazes.

"One more thing." He didn't hide the venom in his voice. "Just so we're clear, if I ever see you near her again, or if you spare her a glance, I'll kill you without question."

Both nodded without raising their heads. Nick stepped aside and let them pass. He waited until their steps melted into the boisterous calls and jeers from below. After a quick knock, Nick waited outside her door. When a slow shuffle approached from the other side, he called out, "It's Somerton."

The door creaked opened.

"My lord, is it you?" Not waiting for an answer, Harry continued, "Thank the merciful heavens. Come in quick, sir!"

Nick swept through the threshold and inspected the room. A quick survey indicated a clean sitting room with a cot in the corner and a door on the opposite wall. "Where's Lady Emma? Is she all right?"

The old man shook his head back and forth.

Nick battled the weariness that had seeped into his bones from the daylong pounding ride. His only concern was Emma. "Harry, answer *now*."

"I'm sorry, my lord. It's been a long night. She made me promise to stay with her." He leaned forward as if divulging a great secret. "The lass is afraid of staying by herself. She's in there. Every once in a while, I hear the floor creak as if she's pacing. I've knocked on the door to see if she's all right, but she won't let me in. Two men frightened her at dinner this evening."

"There were two men outside her door just now." Nick shot a glance at the door. His fury returned with a vengeance as he considered what those two animals wanted with her. He exhaled. Whatever it took, he'd protect her.

Harry gasped. "I didn't hear them. What if they'd—"

"Go and make arrangements for my horse, if you wouldn't mind." The last thing he needed was to console a panicked coachman. "I'll keep her safe. We'll leave at first light."

Harry shook his head. "With all due respect, that's not likely, my lord. Lady Emma is adamant about staying for a few days. You see—"

Nick didn't wait for the explanation. "We're leaving tomorrow."

Harry nodded, then with a sprint that belied his age, left to attend his duties.

Nick made quick work of crossing to Emma's door. With a soft knock, he entered without an invitation. Decorum be damned. He needed to see her for his own assurance.

Light flooded the room from a dozen candles; each flickered in warning. Emma sat in the middle of the bed with a vacant look in her eyes that made her appear wild and feral. Her hair had cascaded down her waist into waves of soft honey-blond curls giving her a wanton appearance—if not for the cocked blunderbuss pistol aimed at him.

This was an Emma he'd never seen before and hoped never to see again. She was frightened beyond all reason. Her hands started to wobble as if the weight of the weapon was stealing all her strength.

"You throwing the apples at my head is one thing"—he gestured toward the pistol—"but that is completely unacceptable."

Her lips trembled as her eyes widened.

"Where did you get that?" He spoke slowly in a quiet and measured tone, much like the one he used to calm his horse when startled by an unexpected event.

It took about three seconds after he spoke for Emma to recognize him. She heaved a sigh, then lowered the weapon. Her hands fluttered to cover her face. When her shoulders began to shake, Nick closed the distance between them in two strides and then slowly removed the weapon from her hand. After setting it on the side table, he joined her on the mattress. She turned and scooted for the other edge.

"Emma." He pulled her into his arms. The warmth of her body was a balm to his weariness. She nuzzled as close as humanly possible with her hands trapped against his chest. His hands caressed the length of her back in a soft and sure rhythm as her silent sobs escaped in great gulps. Was this the proper protocol to deal with a crying woman? "You're safe. Look at me."

Eventually, she pulled away. He reached into his coat pocket and handed her a handkerchief.

She bent over the piece of cloth while her finger slowly trailed up and down the embroidered *S* on the ivory muslin. In some mysterious way, he found it comforting she concentrated on something that belonged to him and not on her fears.

"I have those custom-made." Whatever possessed him to share that fact aloud escaped him.

"It's beautiful." She wiped her eyes with her hands before continuing to caress the cloth. "My skills with a needle never progressed to what was expected of an accomplished lady."

Her normal creamy skin was white, and her nose was running. With a gentle pry, he took the handkerchief from her hands and wiped her nose much like he would do for

Lord Truesdale or Lady Margaret. "Are you hurt? Did someone—"

Emma shook her head. "I'm fine."

That was unlikely if she needed a pistol to sleep. Nick kept his voice friendlier this time. "After this charming interlude of having a gun pointed at me, you owe me answers."

"What—what are you doing here?" A stray curl begged for his touch. Gently, he tucked it behind her ear, the softness comparable to a rare ivory silk he'd recently acquired. He was selling it for a fortune, but it paled next to the silkiness of her tresses.

Her moss-green eyes liquefied into a molten pool, and the stillness of the room amplified into a profound silence between them. He couldn't decipher what power she held over him, but it left him ready to do something—leave and never look back or take her in his arms and never let go. Shocked, he stiffened, and as if she too shared the same thought, Emma looked away.

Timid. Never a word he'd have used to describe her. But they were both out of sorts this evening. There were dozens of questions that needed answers, but he'd allow her a chance to explain.

Selfishly, the truth was he wanted time with her. Alone. He wanted to see if he could make her laugh and take away her fear. He wanted to see her smile light up the room once more. With her so close, he found his vitality, a vigor even, renewed.

This was pure madness. He should be concerned with her safety, not wanting to kiss her and make her his in every way. He cleared his throat in a poor attempt to subdue the thoughts that were more wayward than a runaway coach and four. "Who frightened you?"

"There was a little scuffle downstairs in the taproom, but nothing I couldn't handle." Emma hesitated. "Two men were quite rude to me and Harry, but the innkeeper made them leave."

White-hot anger swept through him, firing a need to find the men and pulverize them for accosting her. He forced himself to regain control. To unleash his rage wouldn't calm her fears or relieve his pulsing drive for retribution against the two rogues. He exhaled a deep breath. "There were two men outside your room when I arrived. Harry didn't hear them."

Her fingers covered her lips, and she inhaled sharply. "Neither did I."

"Where did you get the pistol?"

"A serving girl." She swept her hand in the air as if finding a weapon, a pistol even, was an everyday occurrence.

"Why?" She was either downplaying her fright, or the chit didn't want to accept the danger she faced tonight. Either way he wasn't letting her off that easy.

"For caution."

Nick silenced his growl of exasperation at her reticence. "After finding two men attempting to break into your room and then you waving a pistol in the air, you owe me an explanation."

Emma closed her eyes and took a deep breath, then exhaled a sigh.

His hand traveled up and down her back, but he slowed the movement. He shouldn't touch her, but his need was too powerful to ignore. Each finger caressed the buttons down the back of her gown. "Are you going to tell me?"

She gazed at his face, and her lips pursed. Her pupils were large, and she took deep breaths causing her chest to rise and fall.

Caught in a gale of his own making, he fought against the undeniable magnetism that swirled between them. His body tensed, and his heartbeat thundered in his chest.

He had to change the subject. "Do you know how to shoot?"

"Of course." With a tilt of her head, a riot of blond tresses fell into a soft wave. "My father insisted both Claire and I learn how to handle a weapon." A frown creased her brow. "Speaking of Claire, is Alex . . . with you?"

"No, I traveled alone." He lowered his voice. "Tomorrow, I'll take you home."

She scrunched her pert nose. "I hate to disappoint you, but I'm occupied the next several days. I'm meeting Mr. and Mrs. Parker tomorrow morning at the bookstore. Harry is accompanying me." Her eyes searched his as if trying to divine some truth. "You're welcome to join us."

A primeval desire demanded he should shout she was his, then take her in his arms and never allow her out of his sight. "Who *exactly* are the Parkers?"

"The owners of the town's bookshop. I assure you it's perfectly safe." Her hands fluttered to her side, and she glanced away. "I—I'd very much enjoy your company."

There was no cause for such possessiveness, and he waited for the overwhelming upheaval of unease to subside. It wouldn't take much for him to roar his disapproval of how she planned to spend tomorrow, particularly after he found those two thugs outside her room. Why she would even consider staying in this town after tonight was beyond him.

She would try a bloody saint, but her unusual shyness wrapped itself around his chest, and bit by bit he relaxed. She was safe, and he'd do anything to keep her that way.

The extent of his exhaustion hit him with the force of a hurricane wind. He was dead tired after riding all day, which made it hard to concentrate—a perfect reason for his erratic thoughts this evening.

Nick pushed away from the bed at the same time

Emma grabbed his arm. With his balance upset, he fell, knocking them over until she lay beneath him. He studied her face before his renegade gaze rested on the stark contrast of the black velvet trim of her bodice against the creamy expanse of her chest.

He was by no means blind to her attraction—the sway of her hips, the color of her hair, the luscious swell of her chest, and the light in her green eyes—every part of her cast a spell over him. Every time she was near, it became harder not to touch her. She tempted him to throw his honor as a gentleman aside and take what he wanted.

Scorched by her heat, he pulled away. This was wrong. She was so vulnerable this evening.

His throat had thickened from his unease. It wasn't the only thing to have thickened this close to Emma. If she looked at the outline of his cock, he'd be lost. "I'm going to sleep in the other room."

"Wait! Somerton . . . Nick." She attempted to ease his embarrassment as well as hers. "I didn't mean . . . That was nothing." She wore her humiliation with a quiet dignity. "Please, I need . . . I'd prefer if you were close."

His own guilt rose from his gut and left a sour taste in his mouth. She was out of sorts. It was plainly visible and perfectly understandable. He nodded in agreement. "I'll be in the next room."

Harry returned in the company of a serving girl named Bess, who came to help Emma prepare for bed.

Within a few minutes, they left. Alone in the sitting room, Nick debated whether he should tell her good night or just leave her to her privacy. He knelt and prepared the fire for the night, then stood and lit a candle. The flame danced to life.

Was it his imagination, or had Emma's rosewater scent intensified in the small space? The flicker of the candlelight brought the fragrance closer to him—stronger and more vibrant than before.

He sensed her presence before he saw her. With barely anything on, she stood less than five feet away—close enough that her allure was within striking distance. With a minimum of movement, he could sweep her in his arms.

"I sent a note to McCalpin I was on my way here. I wanted someone to know my plans." Her eyes held a look of defeat, and her voice had softened until it sounded far away. She released a shuddered breath as if resigned to her fate. "I didn't just take off and run for Portsmouth. I've been planning my travel for several weeks. The reason you saw me at Mr. Goodwin's that morning? He was helping me with the arrangements."

Finally, he was getting some answers.

She tilted her head, causing another landslide of golden curls to fall about her shoulder. Her face clouded with uncertainty. "It doesn't feel right to withhold any of this from you."

"What else are you planning to do while you're here?" He knew damn well her plans, but he wanted to hear it from her.

"I'm going to visit Lord Sykeston's home after the bookshop." She shrugged her shoulders, but her attempt at indifference showcased how poor her acting talents were. "I'm visiting Lena's maid. I want to convince her to come home with me. It's my first attempt at my new business. I want to help women who are alone . . . teach them not to be financially dependent on a man. That's what I want—"

"Why do you need financial freedom?" She was the Duke of Langham's daughter. Why would she need anything?

"No, you misunderstand. It's something I dream of

doing. I want to work and find a purpose in life." She sighed in resignation. "I'm not like other women."

He almost howled at that statement. He'd been introduced to that truth the first time he'd met her. Defiant and proud, she'd used every argument available to convince him to let her go to a public inn and buy *Bentham's Essays*.

Nick was aware of how women viewed him—a wonderful steppingstone to money and the title of Duchess of Renton. None of that mattered to Emma, and he'd been immediately enchanted. Was it any wonder he'd allowed her to kiss him? That rash act—so out of his tightly controlled nature—had baffled him for weeks. He never chased women. He'd dreamed of kissing Emma, but he'd never acted upon the impulse.

Gentile young ladies were of no interest to him, but Emma Cavensham proved him a liar. The tug of her lower lip between her teeth made him doubt his own scruples once again.

"I-I promise not to disturb you, but will you stay in the other room with me?"

If she had possessed a feather duster, one swipe would have knocked him over. A tense silence filled the room, and the fact he stared at her wasn't helping matters. What possible answer could he give her? He'd relish holding her close until every speck of her worry dissolved, but Pembrooke would skin him alive. If he told her "no," which any sane man would do, she'd be terrified all night.

"Please." The softness in her voice soothed at the same time it stirred every inch of him. "Only until I fall asleep?"

She pushed the sleeve of her dressing gown up her arm. An angry black bruise that looked like a handprint encircled her delicate left wrist. In two steps, he stood before her. Not to frighten her, he slowly took her hand in his and then gently traced the swirl of greens, blues, and blacks that marked her perfect skin.

It was his undoing.

Only until I fall asleep? Begging was humiliating, but Emma didn't want to be alone, not tonight.

The last time she endured such agony she was nine and woke from a horrid nightmare. Her parents and Claire were out of town. After pleading and cajoling her brothers at length, they'd finally agreed to stay with her in what they declared was neutral territory, the nursery. In return, she had to give her solemn promise she wouldn't follow them when their friends visited for the school holidays.

Tonight's confrontation with the two men downstairs was a thousand times worse than any nightmare she'd ever experienced. But when Aulton had threatened her? There was no measure to his evilness. He and his henchmen could have done anything with her, and she would have been powerless. Tied in knots, her insides quaked again after remembering the two men outside her room. When Nick arrived she'd tried to gain control of her emotions, but it was hopeless. Her fright had inflated into pure terror.

"Who did this to you?" With a tender touch, he gently soothed the injury across her wrist.

The simple caress proved almost too much as she fought the onslaught of tears. Nevertheless, she succeeded in the epic battle, but all she could manage was a swallow. Her injury was minuscule when compared to the repeated trauma Lena had suffered throughout her years with Aulton.

"Sweetheart"—his mouth drew in a straight line—"answer me."

"You can sleep in the bed. I'll take the chair." She never had much talent at negotiating.

He raised an eyebrow. "Did those two men—"

"Aulton came to see me in the public dining room tonight. The two men were employed by him," she said thickly. Her words sounded foreign, and the extent of her exhaustion felt as if she were being dragged under by a vicious river current. She'd never survive sleeping in a chair. "Perhaps you wouldn't mind sharing the bed? I'll take the side closest to the window, and you can have the other. One of us will sleep under the covers and the other on top." His refusal was sure to be forthcoming if his eyes were any indication. The color had turned into a dark blue like his coat. She whispered one last pathetic plea. "Can we talk about this tomorrow? If you continue to ask me questions, I won't sleep."

"Whoever did this to you, I'll thrash them. Then for good measure, I'll kill them." He glanced at the injury, then his gaze pierced hers. "We're not done with this conversation. Just so you know."

She managed a single nod.

With precision, he unbuttoned his jacket and waistcoat. With one toss, both landed on the chair. He stepped to the porcelain basin and slushed cold water over his face. When finished, he raked his hands through his hair to tame the long blond strands.

Watching him do such ordinary things revealed an intimacy much like a familiar ritual a husband would perform in front of his wife. Her face heated at the movement of his large hands and long fingers. She shifted her focus to his back. His wide shoulders flexed and the muscles contracted as he accomplished his simple ablutions. He was pure male, and she was going to bed with him. Before her lungs burst, she exhaled the breath she had been holding and made her way into the bedroom.

He followed and blew out all the candles save one. She made short work of getting into the middle of the bed and under the covers. "Thank you."

He didn't answer, but his gaze swept across the bed. Whatever he thought important enough to examine must have met his satisfaction. He sat on the edge and made quick work of his boots. "What happened to each of us having our own sides? You're in the middle."

She nodded and then inched her way across the bed.

When he settled, his weight caused the mattress to dip. The movement tumbled her back to the center, and she didn't fight it. For whatever reason, he ignored her. With his back turned, he extinguished the lone candle. Though dark, a moonbeam stretched across the bed and lit the room with a soft blue glow. With a deep sigh, he lay on his back and draped an arm across his forehead. His other rested beside hers.

She dared to slide her hand over his, and he wove their fingers together. Her fear gradually receded little by little, like the outgoing tide. It helped to concentrate on their entwined fingers. "I don't scare easily, but you remind me of home and how far away I am. I've never been on my own like this without at least one family member—"

"Emma." The whisper of her name on his lips was as sweet as the taste of midsummer honey. He shifted and rested his weight on his side. The length of his body stretched alongside hers, and he brought her hand to his lips. "I'd never think you a coward. You're a bright, passionate woman who has more determination and will than anyone I've ever met."

Her whole body tingled at his charitable response. It was quite lovely resting next to him. The warmth of his body, the smell of leather and male, and the sound of his even breathing made her feel safe.

This close she couldn't resist a quick study of his form.

His stocking feet were at least twice as big as hers. In a courtesan's memoire she'd once read, the woman had described practically every part of a male anatomy, but never a man's toes or feet. His were rather elegant with high arches. Though ridiculous to notice, they were attractive.

Her gaze traveled up his body. Tight breeches framed his long legs. Well-developed calf and thigh muscles were a testament that he wasn't a stranger to exercise. The bulge behind the fall front of his breeches was obvious. If she wasn't mistaken, it started to thicken in front of her eyes. Of course, it was hard to tell in the dark, plus she'd never seen one before. What was the proper term? Penis, cock, shaft of delight, or her own personal favorite, Torch of Cupid? Or was something else more appropriate?

What *was* the cause of this physical response? Her attention to his body? Alert, her body tingled, and a subtle pulsing settled between her legs. Such thoughts destroyed any chance of her falling asleep.

She found no shame in her curiosity. Most of her friends probably had never heard of such a word as "cock" and would have suffered shock or disgust over such a sight. Not her. She wanted to trace its length and hold it in her hand. Discover the magnificence alluded to by poets. She should be mortified, but this was a step in her education of the male form. Really, it was a step in her own freedom, an experience she craved.

Her pulse quickened, and the throb in her lower belly increased in intensity. She wanted to nestle closer to him. See how their bodies would fit together. Like a barn cat, she wanted to rub against his whole body with abandon.

Her gaze traveled over his abdomen. Even with a lawn shirt covering his chest, it was evident he was fit everywhere with lean lines and a well-defined torso. Trim without any sign of excess—a body so different from her fleshy curves.

She continued her examination and found his riveting turquoise eyes studying her. No judgment or humor sullied his handsome face.

"Are you playing a game similar to the one at Goodwin's?" His smoky-dark baritone contained a silken thread of warning. "Or is this like the kiss you tried to win from me while we were alone in the Langham Hall library?"

She shrugged one shoulder in feigned indifference. Maybe it was the still night or the heat that radiated from his body, but she gathered the courage to pursue whatever was happening in the room. "You're beautiful."

He grimaced at her words. "I beg to differ."

His seriousness should have been frightening, but it wasn't. This perfect moment between them was something she'd remember all her life. His kindness at the discovery of her injury and his willingness to stay tonight proved he was a man worthy of her respect. Simply put, his presence soothed a restlessness that had dogged her for weeks, one she still couldn't define.

She leaned close. Without fear or hesitation, she brushed her lips against his. Made for kissing, his full mouth tempted her to nibble on his lips. She'd easily surrender everything for a simple smile or touch. When she drew away, he took her hand and brushed a kiss against her knuckles.

"Are we friends?" she whispered.

"Yes." His low voice vibrated in a husky timbre that filled the room.

"As friends, we're honest with each other." She didn't wait for his agreement. "Will you tell me what it's like when you're with a woman?" It was hard to believe she was asking such bold questions, but the moon's glow made it easy. Its gentle blue light kissed his face, and deep down, her resolve not to entrust her heart to this man weakened.

She'd do well not to fancy the whims of a moonbeam.

He blew out a breath. "I can't answer your question."

She rubbed her thumb over his and imagined his long fingers caressing her face and trailing down her neck. "What does it feel like to want someone? Like a man wants a woman."

"We really shouldn't be discussing such inappropriate matters." He straightened his legs. "I thought you didn't want to talk. If you're so anxious for a conversation, let's discuss your wrist."

"We agreed to have *that* conversation tomorrow." She shifted her body a little closer to his. Though separated by bed linens and a quilt, his warmth encompassed her, and she felt safe. "Tonight, I want to talk about something different. Tell me from a man's perspective."

He cursed under his breath. "I suppose it's nice if both people enjoy it."

"There has to be more to it than 'nice.' " She huffed a stray curl away from her eye. "Otherwise, why would ballads and sonnets wax and wane about it for centuries?"

His tight-lipped smile held a touch of sadness she longed to take away. The way Claire had described it, he lived an isolated existence. He had few close friends and spent all his holidays with Alex and Claire. If her cousin and Pembrooke joined her family at Falmont, then Nick received an invitation and usually tagged along.

With the room eerily quiet, his silence threatened to reveal the thunderous beat of her heart. "I want to experience it." Her words, though whispered, sliced the distance between them. No one knew that secret, not even Claire or Daphne.

He squeezed her hand. "Your first time should be with your husband."

"I won't have one." The shadows played along his cheekbones and enhanced the line of his jaw. "Strong and resolute" came to mind when she gazed upon his face. Poor thing, he'd met his match with her. "You and I share the same backgrounds, family, and societal expectations."

"Emma." He exhaled in a way that indicated his patience was at loose ends.

"You chose your first sexual partner." She scooted up the bed until they were eye to eye. "You weren't married. Shouldn't I be able to choose my first partner and not have to be married? Why should it be different for me?"

His blue eyes burned silver in the moonlight. He pulled her close into his embrace. "Go to sleep. While you're with me, you'll not suffer any harm."

Silence again filled the room, only this time it was peaceful—and pleasant. Outside, the wind moaned in sympathy with her plight to know more.

They shared no other words, but he rested his head on top of hers. If she wasn't mistaken, he touched his lips to the top of her head. His breath grew even, and the rise and fall of his chest against hers repeated in a comforting pattern. She closed her eyes. There were no judgments in his arms, just rest.

For the first time in ages, the world righted itself, and she was certain of her course.

Chapter Ten

The bright sun slipped through the window, hitting Nick full in the face. He turned to escape the rays, but the sun wouldn't retreat. Then it all came rushing back—last night holding Emma in his arms. If she'd asked him to make love to her last night, he had no idea what he would have done. He'd always prided himself on being a man of honor and proving his father's opinion of him wrong.

But Emma Cavensham made him forget. She'd tempted him from the first time they'd kissed in Langham Park. He inhaled deeply and caught her scent. No, she'd captivated him the night he'd found her on her way to the public inn.

He avoided any hint of scandal, purposely steering clear of women and men who found impropriety courted them. He'd worked too hard to allow gossip to jeopardize his business ventures. Yet with Emma, he'd gladly throw his convictions out the window. Whether her allure was his salvation or damnation, he couldn't decide, nor was he even sure it mattered. In her presence, Nick found his carefully crafted persona, not to mention his resolve, nipped away, bit by bit, like a fish teasing a baited hook.

The worse part? It didn't seem to matter to him.

It was heaven to hold her, a perfect fit of two bodies. Never had anything felt so natural. This morning, he'd gladly forgo everything for one more moment with her in his arms. Before he could talk himself out of it, he damned the consequences and reached for her.

The other side of the bed was cold, and the room stood still as if sworn to secrecy. His mind snapped fully awake. Where would she go this early in the morning?

His momentary panic receded. She was probably downstairs in the common room eating with Harry by her side. Nick rose and gathered his shaving kit. As he sharpened the straight edge against the leather, the normally calming sound of the *thwack, thwack* seemed to scream *fool, fool*.

What she asked last night would cause a saint to sin, and he was certainly no angel. In the wee hours of this morning, the image of possessing her had taken him hostage. Tormented by her soft body curled around his, he'd pulled her closer and caressed the curve of her hip. Instead of protesting, Emma had moaned as if in the midst of a sensual dream and nestled closer with her soft breasts pressed against his chest.

When he woke drenched in sweat, he couldn't dispute the truth any longer—he was fast losing his resistance to her charms.

He raised the sharpened blade for the first pass against his neck when a note on the washstand drew his attention.

Somerton,

> *I'm breaking my fast with Harry. I'm planning on taking a walk to the bookshop this morning,*

*then I'll find Lena's maid. I didn't want to wake
you as you slept so soundly. Tea and bread are
on the tray by the fire. I'm not certain how handy
you are with preparing a cup. Have a go. If I was
successful with the endeavor, I have complete
faith you'll succeed. Harry and Bess are escorting me through town as I go to my appointments.
Don't worry.*

*If you find yourself with free time on your
hands, I'd welcome your company. I'll watch for
you.*

*Thank you for last night. It meant the world
to me.*

E.

He let out a sharp breath. Who in holy hell had time
for tea and bread? He had to find her before she found
real danger. This was a naval seaport, one of the tough-
est, nastiest places in all of Britain. Harry would provide
little protection if the two ruffians found Emma during
her *appointments*. Everything within him stilled. What
if Aulton found her again?

Alex would kill him if she was hurt. Not to mention
Langham would flay him alive. He released a deep breath
and counted to five to subdue his exasperation.

If Emma's family couldn't control her, he would. He
was through with her shenanigans.

Who exactly was he fooling with that proclamation?
If anything happened to her, he'd never forgive himself.

She'd woven herself through every fiber of his being.
He didn't want the constant niggling need to hear her
voice. He didn't want the ache that took up residence in
his chest when she wasn't near him. He didn't want her—
period.

Perhaps if he repeated it enough, he'd start to believe it.

Customers and street venders selling their wares and goods littered the Portsmouth streets. You could purchase anything from pots to parrots. Emma's carefully chosen brown dress and matching pelisse blended nicely with the crowd and the late autumn day. She didn't look like a duke's daughter nor did she feel like one today.

Earlier, Emma had left the bed she shared with Nick, carefully untangling her limbs from his embrace. One final glance at his prone body had brought a heat to her cheeks, but his face had stolen her breath. In sleep, he looked younger. None of the usual wariness marred his fine looks. Instead, in a rare unguarded moment, he appeared at peace with the world and himself.

Even though she'd invited him with her, he'd never accepted. In hindsight, it was perfect. Emma couldn't risk him insisting they leave for London as she had too much to accomplish today. It was far safer to leave him to his sleep and venture out with Harry and Bess as her escorts.

She would have never dreamed of last night's events—Nick appearing in her room, her convincing him to stay, and then falling asleep in his arms. The thought of his embrace had consumed her this morning. Last night proved sleeping alone would forever be a desolate experience.

She couldn't continue to daydream as the morning slipped away. Her only stop prior to calling on Lord Sykeston's home was the single bookstore in town. Behind her, Bess and Harry dutifully followed her into the small shop. She'd verify Mary Butler's presence at Lord Sykeston's, gather the coroner's inquest findings, and then visit Mary.

The shopkeeper greeted them with a nod before turning back to his other customer. Surprisingly, the store stocked a great many books and novels. She could lose herself in such surroundings for hours and did just that until the customer's transaction was finished.

"Good morning, miss. How may I help you today?" The shopkeeper, a short middle-aged man, round in the middle with a full head of long, white hair, greeted her.

"Mr. Parker, good morning. Mr. Goodwin sent me. I'm Lady Em—"

The shopkeeper turned his attention to a staircase and shouted, "Mrs. Parker! Lady Emma Cavensham has arrived. Hurry, my dear!"

The boom of his voice across the small shop startled Bess. She took a step back and stumbled into Harry. Sheepishly, she apologized and moved beside Emma.

"Now, where were we? Ah, yes. Lady Emma." The shopkeeper examined her through gold spectacles. His beaming face immediately made her feel welcome. "The missus and I have been anxiously awaiting your arrival."

"I'm delighted to be here. I've been searching—"

"Mrs. Parker! Did you hear me?"

"I'm on my way, you old fool." A voice from above drifted down. "Don't keep the lady waiting. Ask her to sit."

His round countenance took on a quizzical expression before his warm brown eyes widened. "Oh, I'm sorry, my lady." His proffered hand indicated a sturdy oak chair next to the counter. "Would you care to sit?"

"Thank you, but no—" Before Emma could finish her answer, a woman descended the stairs.

"My lady, welcome to Portsmouth. I'm Mrs. Parker," she said with a respectable curtsy. Her command of the store was immediate as Mr. Parker took a step back to make way for his wife, a petite woman with gray hair and brown eyes that snapped with intelligence. "I have a lovely sitting room where we can visit."

Without waiting for Emma's acceptance, Mrs. Parker proceeded to a small door behind the counter. Emma followed and crossed the threshold. Before her was a beautifully decorated sitting room perfectly sized to accommodate two chairs and a small table in front of a welcoming fireplace.

Harry stood in the doorway and glanced around the room. "Lady Emma, I see you and Bess will be here a while. Down the street, there were meat pies for sale that made my mouth water. I'll go and get us some. Then I'll watch the bookshop entrance for you."

"Thank you, Harry," Emma answered.

After Harry left, Bess cautiously entered the room. "My lady, I'm not certain where I should go."

Mrs. Parker took the girl by the arm. "Why don't you have a cup of tea, my dear, while I put Mr. Parker to work? There's a lovely window overlooking the bay I think you might enjoy. I have a bright reading area that's comfortable. You take your time."

Whatever Mrs. Parker had to share, she didn't want anyone to overhear their conversation, and that suited Emma perfectly. The less people who knew her business, the quicker she could gather Mary and return to London.

"Do you read, Bess?" Emma asked the question softly so as not to embarrass the young woman.

"Yes, my lady. The local vicar's wife taught me."

"Would you like a book?" Emma offered.

The serving girl's face transformed into a vision of joy. "Oh, thank you, my lady." She immediately blushed. "I don't have any money—"

"Please, allow me. It would give me such pleasure to purchase a book for you." Emma leaned forward and confided in a conspiratorial whisper, "Reading gives a woman power."

Mrs. Parker nodded vigorously. "Lady Emma is a dashingly clever woman." She took Bess's hand and led her to her husband. "Mr. Parker, young Bess wants to find a new book."

"Miss, what are your interests?" Mr. Parker wiped his hands on his apron and escorted Bess down a row of books. "Have you read Hobbs' *Leviathan*? The man was literally born in fear. I myself prefer Locke's *Two Treatises of Government*. Oh, have you read Machiavelli's *The Prince*? Everyone misunderstands the text."

As the two wandered the shelves, Mrs. Parker closed the door and sat down next to Emma. The fire popped twice, much like the snapping of fingers, an omen that they needed to conduct their business before the shop got any busier.

"Now, my lady, let's proceed." Efficiently, Mrs. Parker poured two cups of tea and handed one to Emma.

Taking a sip of the perfectly brewed cup, Emma leaned back into the chair and relaxed for the first time since she rose this morning. "What can you tell me about Mary Butler? Is she safe?"

Neat and trim, the gray-haired woman moved with an assured confidence as she nodded. "Very much so." Her eyes grew pensive. "However, she never leaves Lord Sykeston's house. She's frightened."

"Of Lord Aulton?" Emma asked as she set the cup down on the table between them.

Mrs. Parker added cream to her tea. "He hasn't dismissed her per se and has allowed her to return to Lady Aulton's childhood home here in Portsmouth. The young woman is convinced he'll come and take her back to his ancestral seat one day."

"How many servants are there in the Sykeston house?" If there were prying eyes in the household, Emma needed to be aware it. "Anyone I should take special notice of?"

"No, my lady. It's a skeletal staff. Only the trusted servants who've been in employment for years. Some are from families who have served for generations. Every one of them is extremely trustworthy." Mrs. Parker handed a piece of paper to Emma. "Here's what we've discovered."

Emma sucked in her stomach, preparing for the horror of what was written on the summary of the coroner's findings.

It was worse than she'd imagined.

The coroner had described Lena as a twenty-five-year-old woman who had recently delivered a stillborn female child. For a moment, Emma's throat threatened to close, the words too sickening to read, but she forced herself to continue. The loss of both her friend and the baby made her heart break into a million sharp pieces, and each one gouged her conscience. The first wave of nausea exploded through her gut. She swallowed to keep from retching.

She forced herself to continue reading. The coroner listed Lena's cause of death as a severe trauma to her body due to a fall. There was added language that the smell of spirits was distinct on the countess's body. Not a single mention of Aulton or his responsibility for the two deaths.

She sighed and stared at the fire. There was no hope for justice in these words—only blame against Lena for her own death and the death of her child. She tightened her fists and welcomed the pain of her fingernails cutting into her palms. Emma forced a deep breath. She wouldn't collapse at the findings, or the lack there of—not today.

"The countess didn't even drink spirits. They made her ill," she whispered. Desperate for some warmth—

desperate for comfort, Emma walked to the fireplace and held out her hands.

Mrs. Parker gently nodded in understanding.

The fire offered little solace. Many battles loomed before her. For a moment, Emma considered shirking her promise and returning to London. It'd be so easy; she'd done it before when Lena needed her. But she wasn't a coward anymore, so she squared her shoulders and returned to sit by Mrs. Parker. "Was there a finding for the baby?"

Mrs. Parker shook her head. "I'm sorry, my lady, but the coroner in these parts . . . well, he can be influenced, you see. Whatever Lord Aulton says is law."

"I'm sure," she answered. A man's word is never challenged, particularly if they're a peer—no matter how black the heart.

Mrs. Parker shook her head. "The coroner is an old drunk about seventy give or take a year. But I must warn you to be careful, Lady Emma. Lord Aulton suffers from a horrid reputation, all of it deserved. He may have someone watching Lord Sykeston's house—"

"I don't care who you are." From the shop, Mr. Parker's voice rose in warning. "You can't barge through our private quarters." As if the bookstore suffered a sudden invasion from enemy troops, the door blasted opened with a racket.

Emma stood and turned to see the cause of the commotion. Mrs. Parker followed at a slower pace.

Handsome to a fault, a resolute Nick stood in all his glory. His stance revealed a sheer stubborn determination. Her heart stumbled in its regular rhythm, always the same effect when she saw him. However, today, the fierceness lining his face was breathtaking. He reminded Emma of an archangel prepared to slay every enemy in his path.

When his gaze fell to hers, the storm of fury that swirled around him immediately calmed to an unusual air of haughtiness. He inspected the room quickly before his attention once again returned to her. "Lady Emma, was there a misunderstanding? I believe we were to converse first thing this morning."

"My lord," Emma whispered. "I—"

"I informed Lord Somerton that the pirate's diary is wrapped and waiting for him." Mr. Parker wrinkled his nose with displeasure and a hint of smugness. "Apparently, he's not done browsing our selections."

"I'm not here for a *bloody* diary, or any other damn book," Nick growled.

"Mr. Parker, he's with me," Emma added quickly to diffuse the confrontation. "Thank you for your concern, but I invited Lord Somerton to join me this morning."

Mr. Parker waited until Mrs. Parker nodded her head. "It's fine, Henry."

At his wife's reassurance, Mr. Parker stood down, and everything seemed to calm at once.

"Are you ready, my lady?" Nick asked, his voice smooth but detached. The warmth and friendship they'd shared last night seemed a distant memory next to this imperious man and his frigid demeanor. With a hardened gaze, he inspected her.

At this point, it made little difference whether he found her lacking or not. Her own confidence had already plummeted. She nodded and gathered her things. She couldn't blame him for his bitter regard, but this distance between them hurt worse than she cared to admit.

"Mrs. Parker, your information has been beneficial." She grasped the woman's hand and squeezed. "Thank you for everything."

Mrs. Parker dipped her head in answer. "I hope to see you again, my lady."

Emma walked to Nick's side. He held his arm to escort her as if it was a command. No matter how difficult, they had to address his disturbing mood before they went to the Sykeston home. She couldn't let either of them alarm Mary Butler.

"Where's Bess and Harry?" Emma allowed Nick to lead her into the shop area.

"I sent them back to the inn." He bit out the words.

"I have to settle my bill with the Parkers." It was doubtful she could gracefully handle an obviously angry Earl of Somerton and keep the slim tether on her own composure. It was stretched to its limit from the revelations in the coroner's findings. She reached into her reticle and retrieved a coin.

"I've already taken care of it. Come, let's go," he demanded. He took her elbow and led her out toward the door.

"I'll reimburse you." Under no circumstances would she be beholden to him—not today. Her efforts had to be under her own resolve and resources. She owed that to Lena.

He shook his head. "No, consider it a redress for my behavior."

"It's obvious you were worried." She chanced a glance at his face. By the tight line of his lips, he was furious.

"No, you misunderstand," he answered. "It's for my *future* behavior."

Before she could ask what he meant, Mrs. Parker interrupted. "My lady, one more thing. Lord Aulton's housekeeper is Mary Butler's mother. She's still at his estate."

Emma clenched Nick's forearm to keep from falling to the floor.

Mary still had ties to Aulton.

Nick's relief at finding Emma had collapsed the anxiety that had built a fortress inside his chest. Finally, he could breathe easy. Every place he thought to find her this morning had turned up with nothing. The bookshop owner, Mr. Parker, had been deceptively helpful, but explained he hadn't seen her departure. Nick left the store and scoured the docks to see if she'd stopped there. He'd even knocked on Sykeston's door, but there had been no answer. He'd circled back to the bookshop. Once inside, he heard her dulcet tones through the door and realized she'd been there the entire time.

The *bloody* shopkeeper had sent him on a wild goose chase. The deception had sent his anger spiraling. Images of her hurt or accosted had caused him to suffer a blinding headache. When he saw her standing beside Mrs. Parker, his turbulent world settled, and magically, his headache had disappeared. However, his anger still smoldered.

The street crawled with venders selling everything from roasted chestnuts and wine to apples and tarts. His stomach growled at the lack of breakfast. They stopped before one vender's cart, and he purchased two cherry tarts, a fair consolation since the apple tarts had sold out hours before. When Nick offered Emma one of the pies, she shook her head politely.

With one bite, he demolished half of the first pastry. Emma rewarded him with a smile so uninhibited he would have sworn the entire street grew quiet at the sight. The only thing he heard was the blood swooshing through his ears. However, if Emma thought the gesture would insure she escaped his wrath, she'd underestimated him.

"You didn't dine on tea and toast this morning? I thought my note would encourage you to master the fine art of cooking for one's self," she quipped.

Nick swallowed the last bite of the first pie before he choked on her sweetness. Her innocent provocation piqued his already simmering anger. "I had more important matters on my mind. *Namely, finding you.*"

She bent her head, and a slight blush colored her cheeks. He steered them to a quiet alley away from the bustle of the people attending to their everyday business. He towered over her, forcing her to lean against the wall in retreat.

"You *promised* me we'd discuss what happened with Aulton last night. I wake up and you're out for the day? You could've found real danger, and I had no way of knowing what kind or who would be after you." He stepped closer until a hand's breadth separated them. "To me, a broken promise is akin to a breach of honor."

Her eyes narrowed, and a slight tick appeared below one eye.

"You slept so soundly. I asked you to come with me last night, and you didn't answer. I assumed you didn't want any part of my plans," she offered in protest.

"That was before I discovered you were hurt," he snapped. "You should have waited for me before you paraded and flitted your way across town."

The normal creamy pink of her cheeks darkened to a startling crimson color. "For your information, I don't flit, frolic, parade, or even gambol when I have important matters to attend. Can I help it you need your beauty sleep?" Her critical gaze perused his body from his boots to the top of his head. "Perhaps you should have stayed abed for another hour or so."

"Are you mocking me for trying to keep you safe? Your family sent me to bring you back." He'd laugh if he wasn't so angry. She was deliberately annoying him and, much to his chagrin, succeeding. "What are you trying to prove? You're the grand Lady Emma Cavensham who can have any man quaking in his boots? Well, your wiles won't work on me."

By now, their respective outrage had them both breathing hard. Almost nose to nose, she stared straight through him. Enhanced by flashes of her ire, Emma's eyes had darkened into an extraordinary color that reminded him of malachite.

"Fine. You want me to tell you about Aulton? Last night, Harry went to attend the horses and the carriage after dinner. I waited for him in the taproom. Aulton appeared out of nowhere after the innkeeper chased away his ruffians." Her fury high, she continued without a breath. "If I didn't stay away, he threatened to bring stealing charges against me and Mary for the letters she'd sent me after Lena's death. As a farewell, he grabbed my wrist and twisted, thus causing the bruises. Now, if you think I'll leave that poor maid vulnerable to that man, then you don't know me very well. Further, I'm not going home until I'm ready."

"*Fine*," he mimicked. "You don't have to go home to Langham Hall. Go to Pembrooke's. Either way, *you will not* stay here. Your little party is over. The inn is full, as they say. You can either walk or ride back to London. I don't care if you're seated on a horse or sitting in a carriage. You're going back to London. *Now*."

Without realizing it, he was pointing at her with the remaining tart, using it in lieu of his finger. She grabbed his hand and forcefully bit the tart in two. The act of defiance was so blatant he could only stare.

"It's still warm." The little vixen closed her eyes and moaned at the taste.

If in that moment, the heavens had opened up in a

rainstorm, he'd wouldn't have noticed. The expression on her face bewitched him. That simple joy from the taste of the tart transformed her from an angry, beautiful woman to a Greek goddess. Her moan invaded every part of him. As a mere mortal, he had no defense against her assault. It was the most sensual act he'd ever witnessed. As if he needed to suffer further, a spot of cherry filing clung to the beauty spot above her lip.

"Allow me." He took off his glove and with his bare thumb wiped the sweetness from above her mouth.

Her breath caught at his bold touch, and she eyed him warily. Then in typical Emma Cavensham fashion, she did the unexpected. She brought his thumb to her mouth and sucked the fresh fruit off his finger. Her tongue, hot and wet, slid against his skin. Immediately, every nerve in his body went on alert. Gently, she let him go while her eyes captured his. Her simple act caused an unwelcomed chain reaction as his throat tightened and his cock thickened to attention. This had to be what it felt like to be hit by a bolt of lightning—aware of your surroundings but completely unable to move or speak.

His mind wrestled enough control from the renegade response of his body to sweep a glance at their surroundings. Not a single person had frozen in shock or seemed aghast at her action. No one had given them any notice at all—a complete surprise since the volatile antipathy between them could have started a war.

"Well, I think we've accomplished quite a lot, don't you?" Her meek and docile tone would have disarmed most men to think the storm had passed.

He knew better.

"We've established you're a *proper*, not to mention *honorable*, unmitigated *arse*," she announced.

Without waiting for his reply, she executed a brisk turn, one that would have made any infantryman envious, and then marched away. Her brown wool pelisse snapped like a flag caught in a high wind on the battlefield. Nick couldn't help but admire the ramrod straightness of her posture and smiled at the feminine sway of her hips. It completely ruined her performance.

With a deep breath that flared his nostrils, he closed his eyes in an effort to gain control. It didn't calm matters when his mind reeled with thoughts of sex and Emma at the same time. Once back in London, he planned to carry her in his arms and dump her in the nearest chair once he entered Pembrooke's study. Let her family deal with her. He'd had enough of Emma Cavensham to last him a lifetime.

Once he grappled his comportment into a calm state, he followed. The furious pace of her stride was no match for his long legs, and he caught her before she turned the corner at the end of the street. With little surprise, the Ruby Crown was in the opposite direction.

"The inn is that way." He gently grasped her arm to turn her direction south.

"You may think me an addlepated virago, but I'm aware of the inn's location." With an evasive move, she stepped away from his reach. "I'm going to Lena's."

Again, he took her arm, but this time he turned her to the east. "Lord Sykeston's home is this way."

"Oh." She stumbled, apparently flustered. "Thank you."

All he could manage was a nod. With her mood, he'd follow her anywhere.

Just in case she found the shore, he had little doubt she'd walk to France under water.

Chapter Eleven

The urge to pace made Emma tap her feet in a synco-pated rhythm. She sat in a low coquelicot-colored brocade chair that reminded her of a field filled with red poppies. She'd purposely picked it since it was in the cen-ter of the neat sitting room. The low height would lend an easier position to look Mary Butler directly in the eyes since the maid was slight in stature and not as tall as Emma.

Nick stood a polite distance behind. With his height, the confounded man surrounded her with his presence.

The unencumbered truth was he gave her courage, something she sorely needed at this point. Even though this visit wasn't the only reason she came to Portsmouth, it was the most important. Whatever it took, she would succeed in convincing Mary to return to London with her. For some reason, with Nick by her side, it didn't seem like such a daunting task.

She made a quick half turn in her chair and caught his attention. He answered with a grin. It completely di-vested her of any remaining displeasure. She hoped his anger had melted too, as she hated it when they were at odds with each other. His fortitude inspired her, and she took it without reservation. With that strength, she wouldn't give way to tears, even if this was one of the most painful days of her life.

The door opened. The butler, Mr. North, and Mary entered together.

"Lady Emma, it's delightful to see you at Sykeston House." Mr. North, a man in his early seventies, peered down at her. His normal off-putting frown had transformed into a smile that lined his thin cheeks. His hazel eyes seemed to twinkle in amusement. "Lord Sykeston will be sorely distressed to have missed this visit."

"It's good to be back, Mr. North." She stood slowly. "Hello, Mary."

"Ma'am." Mary curtsied with her gaze lowered.

"May I introduce you both to the Earl of Somerton?" Emma asked.

The butler bowed and Mary bobbed another curtsey, this one deeper, causing the maid to flush and shrink into herself.

"Lord Somerton is my . . ." *Good heavens, how was she to introduce him? Her what?* There was no defining what he was to her. "Family friend" sounded too innocuous, and insulted them both. He was definitely more than a friend. Never before had she faced a dilemma of this sort. She'd witnessed her friends stumble much like she was now when they introduced their sweethearts or soon-to-be fiancés. He was nothing of the sort. Her gaze shot to Nick, and he smiled.

"I'm a good friend to Lady Emma," he added in a clear, compassionate voice. His rescue was perfect as both Mr. North and Mary visibly relaxed.

"Mary, do you want me to stay?" Mr. North discreetly asked.

The maid shook her head in response.

The butler nodded, then addressed Emma. "My lady, Lord Sykeston will be home in two to three weeks. He suffered an injury that dictates he forgo any further service to the crown." The loyal servant bowed his head. After a moment, he sniffed and drew to his full height. "I hope I'm not speaking out of turn, but I believe Lord Sykeston would greatly appreciate a visit at your convenience."

"I'd like that, too." Emma's chest tightened at the words. The poor Sykeston family had endured so much over the years. Lena's parents had passed away of an illness more than ten years ago, then Lena and her baby's deaths, and now her brother's injury. How much could a family take before every root in the proverbial tree was torn asunder?

"I'll take my leave. Ring if you need anything." The butler gave a brisk bow and left, closing the door softly behind him.

"Mary, come sit next to me," Emma coaxed.

The young girl made her way cautiously toward Emma in a route that kept her from going anywhere close to Nick. As if sensing the maid's distrust, he sat on the only sofa in the room, which put him a good distance away from her and Emma.

The maid took a seat next to Emma and neatly clasped her hands in her lap. "It's so good to see you, my lady. I've missed the times when you and Lady Lena would spend the days together. She was always so happy around you."

"Lady Aulton was everything lovely and a steadfast friend—"

"In this house, my lady, we refer to her as Lady Lena," the maid interrupted. Then, as if realizing she had misspoken, she bowed her head. "I apologize."

Emma reached over and clasped the girl's hands with

hers. "There's no need, Mary. To me, she'll always be Lena. That's the way I think—no, I'm sure—that's the way she would like for us to remember her."

Mary looked up and smiled with the telltale glisten of tears brightening her eyes. If she blinked, they would fall.

"Mary . . ." With her own ability to offer comfort completely unraveling, Emma hesitated. "Did . . . did she suffer?"

"Aye, ma'am." Mary bent her head once more, but gathered enough strength to look Emma in the eye. "She was badly injured. She survived the birth, but the blood . . ." The maid lost her fight, and her tears fell freely, streaking her pale skin. "He wouldn't allow anyone to call a doctor. My mum, his own housekeeper, went to his study and begged. He told her he'd dismiss her without references if she disobeyed."

Somehow, Nick had made his way to Mary's side and handed her his handkerchief. A solemn grin eased across Emma lips. Trust Nick to be duly equipped with the embroidered cloths. He was a man unabashedly ready to extend incredible kindness to others, and she'd been wicked to him earlier. Her own tears started to gather as she witnessed his gentleness with Mary.

If she wasn't careful, he would steal her heart, the very one she'd fought so hard to protect against all others. In answer, the unfaithful organ pounded its approval of his endearing offer of kindness to a woman unknown to him, but so obvious in need of his help.

"Lord Aulton had come to escort Lady Lena to dinner. I stayed in her bedroom. I heard her cry out, and I dashed to see what had happened." Mary pressed her eyes closed and clenched her fists. "He stood at the top looking over the balustrade. She'd fallen down the steps and landed on her belly." The maid took a deep breath.

"After her baby was delivered, she begged me to send her letters to you. She told me you'd know what to do with them. I think she understood she wouldn't survive. . . ."

Emma hadn't come prepared for the relentless assailment of heartache and pain that hit her. As it battered unyieldingly, wave upon wave, the intensity numbed every part of her. The carefully constructed wall of resolve and certainty she'd erected since Lena's death teetered, ready to collapse in a pile of unrelenting grief. Her throat burned with unshed tears as the reality of Lena's painful last days came crashing down.

"Did she get to hold the baby?" Emma gasped as the anguish lacerated her insides.

Mary stared at the floor and nodded. Big tears fell to her skirts.

Emma closed her eyes as her body shuddered with two sobs. She brought her hand to her mouth, but the powerful grief escaped into a landslide of tears.

"Did she name her Audra?" Emma choked out.

The maid nodded again.

Oh God, if she hadn't stayed in London. She should have defied her mother and left for Lena. Nothing important happened at the party, but Lena's whole world was destroyed that night.

It was pure torture, but she had to know. "Is the baby buried with her?"

"Yes," Mary whispered. "I prepared the bodies myself. They looked so peaceful. I tucked Lady Audra next to Lady Lena's side. Her Ladyship had the most gracious smile, as if happy she didn't have to suffer anymore."

Completely defeated, Emma dropped her head and allowed the burning tears to run free. A hand gripped her shoulder and squeezed. Without looking, she placed hers over Nick's. The firm grasp kept her grounded when it seemed as if she'd be swept away by the heartache. He didn't move, resolute by her side. His comfort forced the cascade of tears to lessen. After a few moments, he stepped away, but she felt him hover close by.

"Come to London with me. You can work at my house." Emma moved to the edge of her seat to squeeze Mary's hand. "Once you're stronger, I'd like for you to visit my father's solicitors. They're known as the best legal minds in London. They'll protect you and help us find justice for Lena."

The maid shook her head. "Please, my lady, don't think I'm not grateful or don't want to go. But don't ask. I can't."

"Mary, you'll be safe. No one will harm you." Emma wiped away her tears and gentled her voice. "I promise."

Mary was more adamant this time with her refusal. "My lady, I can't and I won't. My mum still works for Lord Aulton. Besides, he comes to check on me at the house every week. I expect that before Lord Sykeston returns, I'll be back in Lord Aulton's employment."

Nick had moved closer to Mary and sat in the chair next to her. "Mary, your mother could come work for me. I don't have a housekeeper, and my staff would welcome her."

Emma's chest constricted at the kindness in his voice. In response, the carefully crafted moorings broke free of her heart.

Enough! She could not fall in love with him.

For the first time since Mary had entered the room, her pale countenance flashed with a look of hope that shaded her cheeks with a hint of pink. With a gentle shake of her head, she quickly doused the smidge of optimism. "I can't, my lord. But thank you for the generous offer." She stood and took a step toward the door.

Emma grabbed her hand and held her in place. "Why, Mary?"

Mary drew herself to her full height. Her serviceable uniform of a dark gray dress and crisp white apron accentuated her steadfastness. "My lady, if I don't do as he says, he promised to have both me and my mum arrested for stealing. He has witnesses prepared to say I took Lady Lena's letters and her jewelry."

Lena's directive that Emma receive the letters would be a strong defense against those charges. And Emma was sure there was no truth to the charges of Mary stealing the jewelry. The girl had been with Lena for over ten years and was as trustworthy as they came. "I won't let that happen."

By now, Mary had opened the door. "I'm sorry, Lady Emma. It was truly a blessing to see you."

Before the maid escaped from the room, Emma ran and caught her in an embrace. "My door is always open. Please reconsider our offers. If you ever need anything, I'll be there for you. I'm at the Ruby Crown for the duration of my stay. If you change your mind after I leave, send for me and I'll come for you the next day. I won't let you face this alone."

Mary nodded once, but the evidence of doubt dulled her soulful brown eyes. "You can't help me, my lady. No one can."

Mary slipped from her grasp and disappeared out the door like an apparition.

Aulton's evil haunted them all.

Strong hands clasped her arms from behind, and she allowed herself to fall back against his chest. If he offered another tender gesture in comfort, she'd be inconsolable. She pressed her eyes closed and released the breath she'd been holding. "Do you see what he's done?"

Nick squeezed her arms. "There were rumors, but I had no idea."

Emma swallowed. "He's getting away with murder."

After she and Nick left Lord Sykeston's, they wandered the streets of Portsmouth aimlessly and ended up at the harbor. Emma stared out to sea, but she couldn't focus on anything but the sky. The wind had picked up, but she hardly noticed the cold as the sun started its elaborate performance of slipping into the western sky.

Astutely, Nick didn't make an attempt at conversation, proving he was a mind reader, or more probably, he couldn't decipher her mood. Frankly, neither could she. How could she have changed Mary's mind, or at least eased her concerns over Aulton's threats of arrest? Emma had replayed that conversation ten times since they'd left Lord Sykeston's home, and she still didn't have any answers.

Her hand rested on the railing before them. Nick's gloved hand covered hers, the breadth of his strength evident through the length of his fingers and the size of his palm. For one wild moment, she craved an escape and wanted him to take her in his embrace. She needed his hands against her back, pressing her close.

She shook her head at such dreamy thoughts and laughed in a mocking tone. "I've always thought myself strong with an intelligence that would rival any man's, a woman to conquer the world. Portsmouth has made me realize what a liar I am."

"Don't ever doubt yourself. You've given Mary an option if she chooses to change her mind. You can't force her to do anything she doesn't want." He tugged her hand. "Come, let me escort you back to the inn."

She didn't contradict him—there was no need. She was a fool who had pinned unrealistic hopes of redemption on this lark of a trip to Portsmouth. If anything, her actions today and the maid's recollections enlarged her guilt. The burden she carried was like an infection that slowly seeped into every crevice of her soul.

"I'm not ready to return to the inn. I'd like to see the water without any people or ships nearby. There's something I want to do before I go back to London." She pulled her hand away but didn't face him. His powers of observation would pierce what little composure she had. "If you're tired of my mood and want to go back to the inn, I can't blame you. I'll ask Harry to accompany—"

His fingers nudged her chin, and she closed her eyes to hide her vulnerability. All along, the hope this trip would cleanse her shame was a farce.

"I'll take you wherever you'd like to go," he answered.

A blast of wind lashed her skirts around her legs. She inhaled the salty scent of the sea and wished the pungent smell would clear the melancholy fog that enveloped her.

"I'd like to be with you." Nick took her gloved hand in his and led her away from the docks. Such contact might not be appropriate in public, but she needed his touch. It'd been a grueling day for both of them.

"Emma, look at me." His voice enfolded her like a rich brandy that burned before it soothed with a gentle warmth. "Your complicated and confounding mood is worrisome. Your grief is raw, too raw, for the time that's lapsed since Lena's death. Tell me what else troubles you."

How could she explain that no matter how hard she tried, she couldn't cleanse the blood from her hands?

Chapter Twelve

Nick and Emma made their way up a small hill that overlooked Portsmouth harbor. Ribbons of red, pink, and purple waved across the evening sky as the sun set over the sparse clouds.

Pure wonder and awe at her surroundings magnified her every thought, every sensation, and every vision. The trappings of a London ballroom could never compare to the beauty that encircled her this evening. With this journey, she prayed she'd find a little solace from the guilt and the grief.

The wind picked up speed, causing several loose strands of hair to whip across her face. Dust blew into her eyes. With a turn in the opposite direction, she tried to tame the disorder with little success. Nick must have seen the struggle and taken pity on her. He pulled her close to fend off the unrelenting gusts. He tucked the offending hair behind her ear and brushed her cheek with his thumb. The leather of his soft glove proved tender, like the most luxurious velvet to the touch.

"We're almost there." When he tilted his head close

to hers, his lips brushed across her ear. "Keep close to my side."

She did as directed until they reached the shore. A dark shale outcropping of rocks laid a pattern that made an uneven walkway to the shoreline. Isolated and distant from the bustle of Portsmouth, the view exposed the unfettered breadth of the sea. Close to the harbor entrance, two rowboats crept close to the shore. Each trailed a string of kegs that floated in the wake of their movements. The bobbing action mimicked a brood of ducklings following their mother.

"It's an amazing sight." Nick stood beside her in such a way his body blocked part of the wind's assault. Perfectly at ease, he clasped his hands in front of him and regarded the view. "Is that why you wanted to come up here?"

Emma shook her head and reached into her reticle. Her fingers traced the corner of Lena's letter to Audra, a remembrance she'd not possess much longer since she planned to give it to Sykeston. She found the locket and brought it out for his inspection. The chain draped across her fingers.

"What do you have, Em?" The wind immediately quieted, and his whispered endearment loosened the weary knots of distress that resided in her chest. His gaze paused at her hand, then captured hers, the bemusement in his eyes evident.

"It's a locket. Lena and I gave each other one to celebrate our entrance into society. We were such silly girls believing that such a superficial event warranted a commemoration." She didn't stop the tumble of words. "We gave each other a snippet of our hair and several petals of the first flowers we'd ever received from an admirer. I don't remember who gave me my flowers, but Lena would have. She had a memory for such events."

His face and eyes softened as if he knew this confession hurt her. He gently took the locket and examined it. "It's lovely."

"She always wanted us to sail from Portsmouth and visit Italy. For some reason, she thought the trip would be a grand adventure."

He chuckled. "Perhaps she thought the men parading up and down the docks in their crisp naval uniforms would be a sight worth seeing."

Emma made the mistake of gazing into his mesmerizing eyes. The blue color reflected the darkening sky, and for a moment, she was lost. She leaned close seeking the comfort of his embrace, then remembered where she was and returned her attention to the locket. "She'd always considered her home in Portsmouth the center of her universe—her personal North Star so to speak."

There was no use delaying as the setting sun threatened to disappear. She stepped to the water's edge where the waves lapped the rocky ledge. She closed her eyes and kissed the locket. Heartfelt, she prayed her love for her lost friend would seep into the silver and provide some warmth and consolation for all of life's moments that Lena had lost forever. With all the strength she possessed, Emma heaved the locket into the water. Wherever it landed, she hoped Lena enjoyed some freedom and peace from the simple gesture.

Slowly, like an incoming storm from the sea, hot tears and grief combined into a frenzy that stole her breath and made her gut twist. She bent at the waist, desperate to escape the pain. She was still a wretch who deserved no succor.

Suddenly, Nick swept her into his arms. His eyes searched hers. "Why?"

Shamefully, she turned away. Yet his question offered

her what no one ever had before—an opportunity to avow her duplicity in Lena's death. "Why" was such a simple word, an offer that tempted her to expose every black mark on her soul and wait for her richly deserved condemnation.

When she tilted her gaze to his, everything blurred and made her confession easier. "I had to set her free. She deserved so much more in life than Aulton."

He didn't press her for more. There was no need as she was ready to share the truth. Whatever judgment he passed on her inactions would hurt a thousand times less than her own silent perfidy.

"Do you remember when I was banished to Falmont and you gave me *Bentham's Essays*?"

"Yes." He pulled her close until her head rested against his chest. The steady beat of his heart assured her she could trust him.

"Lena became engaged to Aulton and married a month later. I only saw her one more time before she died. I was invited to stay for a week at their estate."

His hand played with the lose tendrils of her hair, a touch she wanted and needed but knew she didn't deserve.

"It was horrible. Every time Aulton attended us, he was so cruel with his mocking. He'd ridicule Lena's faults and mistakes to me, her friend. I never understood why a husband would torment his wife like that." Her thoughts clouded with images of the past. "Lena wore above-the-elbow-length gloves the entire week. I'd ask her why so formal, and she'd immediately come up with an excuse. Her day gloves were dirty, or she'd misplaced them. I actually thought Aulton suffered financially, and the gloves were a way to economize. I'd decided to send her a half dozen when I returned home." She shook her head at the idiotic reasoning. "At an afternoon tea, a glove slipped down her forearm, exposing a bruise in the shape of a handprint. Embarrassed, she immediately tugged it back in place."

"Did you ask her what happened?" He rubbed his lips across the top of her head.

"I did. She told me she was standing on a chair in her bedroom trying to straighten a picture. Aulton grabbed her when she lost her balance and fell." She found the courage to face him, ready for the disappointment she'd find in his eyes. "I didn't press her for more of an answer, but *I knew* she'd lied to me. When I left for London, I begged her to come with me. She said she could never leave him."

His arms tightened around her waist as if encouraging her to continue.

The agony became unbearable, but she perservered. "Every letter I received from her told of some clumsy accident." A sob tried to burst free, but she made herself finish. "*I knew*, Nick, and I didn't help her."

He gritted his teeth, causing a muscle to flinch in his jaw. "What could you have done? Even if you'd witnessed the violence, neither you nor anyone else could have stopped him. Have you ever heard the rule of thumb?"

Emma shook her head.

"Some men in society accept the convention that a man shouldn't hit his wife with anything that's wider than his thumb. Gillray had a cartoon of Sir Francis Buller titled 'Judge Thumb.' He carried a bundle of sticks, each the approximate thickness of his thumb. Behind him, a man beat his wife in the background with one of those sticks. It's heinous in the extreme, but some men advocate that type of discipline. Aulton adopted it to an unspeakable level. I'm not certain anyone could have stopped him."

"I should have made her leave with me or hidden her someplace. If I had to do it all over again, I—"

He tilted her head with a gentle tug of his hand. "Aulton would have found her. He's the type of man who'd have brought some legal suit. Not even your father could have stopped him."

When she searched his face, the vehemence in his eyes and the set of his jaw gave her hope. His strength might help her shed her sins. A fervent need for such redemption broke through her like a flash of fire. "Would you kiss me?"

His gaze never left hers as his fingers trailed across her skin. She didn't wait for his reply but stood on tiptoes. She twisted her arms around his neck for balance and touched her lips to his. A sweet shudder coursed through her.

He growled in response, but as if he knew she needed comfort, his kiss was gentle. She whimpered at his soft touch and the resulting relief from the pain. All too soon, he pulled away, yet the evident heat of their passion resided in his eyes.

"Come. Let's return to the inn before . . ." He stepped away and held his hand out for hers. The throb of desire in his voice was unmistakable.

"Before what?" she asked.

He grimaced. "Before I lay you down in that grass and make you mine."

"Oh," she whispered. It was the only answer she could muster.

The remnants of Emma's rose scent floated around him, and Nick leaned back in the cramped slipper tub. He'd ordered a bath for her on their return from the shore. After seeing the carriage and horses were ready for tomorrow's departure, he'd arrived back to their suite to find Emma behind the closed door of the bed-room.

Surprisingly, the water held a comfortable warmth after she'd finished. With a dip of his head, he rinsed, careful his movements didn't cause the water to overlap the edges of the copper tub. Relaxing for a few minutes, he realized he'd wear her fragrance as he slept.

He'd take more than her sweet scent with him to bed. What he'd witnessed this evening held him enthralled, and frankly, terrified. All his life, he'd been careful to guard against the type of heartache Emma had forced herself to suffer in Sykeston's home. He'd never allowed himself close enough to another human being that their loss would devastate him so. Because of his father's dismissal and the lack of friendships as a youth, he'd learned the lesson well. Granted, Pembrooke was as close as a brother to him, but the desolation he'd seen from Emma reminded him of his father's exodus from his life.

Every tear and sob she'd shed had lanced straight through his well-guarded reserve. When he couldn't take seeing her pain anymore, he'd reached for her at Sykeston's. Of course, with Mary Butler next to Emma, the only thing he could offer was a touch, a simple squeeze. The overwhelming urge to sweep her in his arms and carry her far away from that agony drove every prudent thought away.

When they reached the shore later, she'd been breath-takingly beautiful in her grief. When she'd kissed him, all his masterful evasion of anything unlocking his well-guarded heart had sailed out to sea. Since they'd returned to the inn, his erect cock had mutinied, ready to battle alongside his heart to thwart his best intentions.

He'd wanted her last night, and tonight . . . he wanted her more.

Damnation, if he was truthful with himself, he'd wanted her since he'd intercepted her carriage three years ago.

Awed by her, Nick doubted his sanity. His feelings for Emma were deepening. It wasn't lust. That could be satisfied. What she offered triggered an insatiable hunger. Indeed, her passion for life—all of it—happiness and sadness, overwhelmed him.

For the first time in years, he was circling around a desire that could devour him, and he wanted it. At least, a taste of it. Perhaps then, he'd be able to return home satisfied without any regrets.

Whatever magic she cast over him was deepening to a point he feared he was losing his control. God, for once, to let loose and unhinge the rules he'd bound himself to—his mind grappled with the promise of the liberation that awaited.

He stood and grabbed the neatly folded linen toweling Emma hadn't needed. With a deft hand, he dried his torso and left the remaining trails of water to slide down his arms and legs. He tied the sheet around his waist and stepped out of the cooling water.

The bedroom door stood open.

Emma reclined against one doorpost. Without any enticement or seduction in her regard, she studied him. Unused to such a direct examination, he felt a prickling heat slide up his neck. The wet toweling did little to hide his swelling arousal.

"You're wrong," she whispered.

How long had she studied him while he bathed? He'd received his share of seductive looks thrown hither by mistresses looking for a new benefactor, women desperate for marriage, and merry widows hungry for companionship. Yet, he'd never had a woman look at him like that before. Calm and collected, she observed him without a hint of shyness or unease, more importantly, without any titillating looks of promised pleasure.

With her lips parted and her hair trailing across her chest in gold waves of sunshine, she reminded him of innocence matured by the reality of life. He'd seen that look on her before at Goodwin's, but hadn't recognized it until now.

"Wrong about what?" He didn't want to frighten her, but his need for her pounded through him, bringing forth a desire he wasn't certain he could battle anymore.

"Last night, I said you were beautiful, and your answer was 'I beg to differ.' " Her eyes never left his. "I've seen every inch of you. You *are* beautiful."

He closed the distance between them. He inhaled the sweet scent of rosewater and her extraordinary fragrance that beckoned him closer. She stood still, her eyes wide, studying him without fear. He braced his arm across the door and leaned close.

As if she called to him, he brushed his knuckles over the smooth softness of her cheeks. Tonight he'd not forgo the opportunity to drink of her goodness, nor would he deny himself the taste of her glorious passion. It was a night made to feast and celebrate the marvel of her.

"Let me see your hand."

She gave it to him, and he saw that the angry bruise of last night had started to fade into a purple and green collar around her wrist. Gently, he brought the inside of her delicate skin to his mouth and reverently pressed his lips against her pulse. It jumped with a rapid fire, signaling his touch affected her.

Satisfaction exploded into a primordial need for her.

But she turned away.

"Look at me." He took her chin in hand and forced her

gaze to his. The candlelight enhanced her beauty and the vulnerability in her eyes.

She took a deep breath, and the movement caused her nipples to press against the thin silk dressing gown. His gaze slid down her body, appreciating the full curves of her feminine beauty.

Her eyes darkened to emerald pools.

In response, every muscle in his body tightened ready to claim her.

But then, a tear escaped.

He closed his eyes and exhaled. If she'd pierced him with a knife, it would have hurt less. His grip grew light, and he slowly drew her in his arms. "It was not my intent to frighten you. I . . ."

"I'm frightened . . . you'll no longer have a good opinion after what I shared tonight." Her whisper trailed to silence.

"Nothing you've done would change what I think of you. You're an incredible woman with an iron will softened by a generous heart." He drew back so she could see his sincerity.

She pressed her eyes closed. "I promised myself that your opinion didn't matter." Her breath caught. "But I broke that pledge."

Chapter Thirteen

Nick's left hand skated up and down her back. With his other hand curled around the nape of her neck, he pulled her tighter into his embrace. His lips captured hers in the sweetest of touches.

Her efforts to seduce him in London were nothing more than a tactic to free her of his presence, while now she'd give anything to have him. The comfort of his nearness and the gentle caress of his hand soothed, but his scent and the heat from his body made her own pulse with longing.

His lips followed a path from her throat to her ear. "All I've thought about yesterday and today was you. You're like an itch that's never satisfied. I may never let you go."

She found his lips with hers and ran her tongue lightly in a demand for more. When he complied, a whimper escaped her.

As if he understood her need, he took her hand and led her to the bed they'd shared last night. His hard thigh brushed against hers, and her whole body melted at the touch. He lowered them to the bed, his arm wrapped around her. This time, she was the one to break the kiss.

When his gaze pierced hers, she was lost. The only thing that kept her grounded was the pounding of her heart. The searing heat of his body warmed her, eliminating the chill that had possessed her.

Her silk dressing gown did little to conceal her body. Without a place to hide, Emma placed her arms around his neck and burrowed deep within his embrace. She tasted his skin as she caressed her lips up and down his jaw.

He captured her lips again as his arms formed a bracket around her head. He lifted his head and met her gaze. "I never thought you shy, but your body tells me differently. You've turned a glorious golden-pink."

Emma shivered and pressed closer. This was what she'd wanted from the first time he kissed her, to have him in her arms and in her bed. Now he was hers, and no one would tell her differently.

He was all sinew and defined muscles. Heaven help her, she was the recipient of all that magnificence. She settled her hand on his chest next to his heart. The strong beat caused her to close her eyes. She was lost. But the promise of something beautifully profound made her not care.

"Emma." His voice broke with a huskiness she'd never heard before. "We mustn't . . ." With a grimace, he placed his hand over hers.

"No, please . . . don't say anything. Don't put distance between us." With her pulse pounding, she needed a moment to reorient herself. But one thing was clear. It would take a team of plow horses to drag her away from his embrace. "After today . . ." She searched his eyes, and his uncompromising gaze demanded her honesty. "You're so sure in your path, and . . . I'm not sure about anything. Please, more than anything, I need you. I need this night."

He embraced her so tight she couldn't breathe. He kissed one side of her mouth before drawing his tongue over the seam of her lips. She opened without hesitation, and his tongue danced with hers as it explored in a deliberate, unhurried kiss.

With fingers entwined, he rose above her. "I'm not going anywhere."

He kissed her with a slow innocence as his hand cradled one of her breasts through the silk, his thumb teasing her nipple. Every rational thought escaped as her breasts grew heavy from the attention. She arched her back in a desperate attempt to get closer. He was a sorcerer who had enchanted her body. For once in her life, she had no qualms yielding to a man.

"How beautiful you are."

His words stole her breath, and she released a shuddering sigh. The simple act of responding became impossible. His tender words caused a vortex of fever and longing to collide. Hope and agony mingled to create the alluring promise of something so magnificent it'd change everything she believed.

He kissed her again, and she was adrift in a beautiful madness as he ravished her with his tongue. He moved to his side with his body in full contact with hers. She whimpered at the loss of his weight.

Burnished like fine gold, a light covering of chest hair caught her attention. Lower on his abdomen, the hair grew coarser and converged in a line that disappeared below the edge of the toweling. The outline of his erection was clearly visible against the soft linen.

"Like heaven." His hand moved to her waist and then crept upward and cupped her breast while he whispered, "I want you."

When his arousal pressed against her hip, her body flooded with desire. This feeling of bliss was what she'd asked about last night. Everything she wanted was this moment with him.

Before she could ask him what she was feeling, he straddled her hips and loomed over her. He tasted the hollow at her throat with his tongue. His lips moved to her shoulder before he concentrated on her chest. She cradled his head as he kissed and sucked the top then the side of her breast through the silk. Finally, he took her nipple in his mouth. The friction of his tongue against the silk drove her to fist his hair and hold him close. "Please."

He chuckled. "You want more?"

All she could manage was a moan.

She felt him smile against the tender skin of her breast as he stroked his thumb across her nipple. His caresses became a rhythm that caused a magnificent riot of pleasure to race through every inch of her body until it congregated low in her belly.

But he surprised her when he sucked her nipple, then gently nipped. The alternating sensation proved maddening as pain gave way to unspeakable pleasure. She cried out and bucked for relief from the overpowering sensitivity he created as he repeated the movements over and over. She thought she'd die from her need to crawl inside him.

She was panting out of her mind when he stopped.

He looked at her before he kissed her again. He brought his mouth to her ear. His hand gathered the material of her gown and slipped it up her leg in the most excruciating, languid movement. Every inch of her skin screamed for his touch. Finally, the material was above her waist, and his fingers stroked through her nether curls and repeated the pattern.

Emma tried to position herself so his touch would go deeper.

"Do you touch yourself here?" He growled low in his throat and lightly traced her ear with his tongue. "Tell me."

She waited for the shame to wash over her, but it didn't. This moment, perfect and intimate between them, made her want to share everything with him. She pressed her center against his hand. "Yes."

He stopped moving and rested his forehead on the pillow. With a deep breath, he pushed her hair aside and, this time, caressed her ear with his lips. "How did you learn?"

She searched his face for any hint of reproach, but there was none. His eyes had deepened to a dark blue. "I-I have the memoires of a French courtesan. She described how she touched herself. One night, I . . ." Finally, her embarrassment made a late, uninvited appearance. She'd never shared this with anyone either. Only he made her want to tell every secret of her desires.

His face softened as if he knew the turmoil running amok within her. "There's nothing wrong with finding pleasure by your own hands. How do you make yourself come?"

Emma froze. "I don't know . . . what that is . . . what are you asking? If you're talking about achieving a release, then . . . no. I've never—I like to touch myself when I think certain things, and it feels nice."

"What do you think about?" His nose nudged hers as if offering a different kind of kiss.

His simple caress stole her shame, and the words spilled free.

"Not what, but who." She closed her eyes and took a shuddering breath. "I think of you."

He lifted his body from hers and rested on his elbows. Their eyes locked, and their chests rose and lowered in unison. The silence between them grew until she felt as if she would go mad. His penetrating gaze pierced hers, and she was afraid she'd revealed too much.

Completely exposed, she waited for his response—his verdict of her worthiness as a woman. He had no idea how much power he wielded over her, and it was terrifying. She'd never allowed herself to become this vulnerable to a man.

Then, a glimpse of emotion flashed across his face. With a blink, he tried to hide it, but she sensed his own walls of defense rise to keep her away. Was it wariness? She'd not let him renounce what they were creating tonight.

Whatever battle he fought, his resistance conceded. His arms surrounded her, every movement slow and measured as if not to frighten her. He kissed her cheek and pushed his lower body against hers, his length hot and hard. "Do you have any idea what you've done to me?"

She shook her head.

His face grew serious, and he bent his head to his chest as if debating what to do. "I'll teach you how to find your pleasure."

She nodded. He shifted to his side once more. Her breath hitched when his hand caressed her hip, then meandered lower. Propped on one elbow, his eyes darkened dangerously.

His fingers danced across her skin and stopped when he found her folds. Gently, he pressed his finger against her center.

She bit her lip to stop from crying out. It took every ounce of strength not to beg him to continue.

"You're so precious." The warm roughness in his endearment enchanted her. "So wet. Where's your hand? Show me what you like." He placed his hand on top of hers and moved them both slowly to her center. "Touch yourself."

His pupils were huge, and the ring of blue-green in his eyes flashed with passion. She could not have heard him correctly. He brought his mouth to hers again and with his lips touching hers said, "I want to help you find your release."

She closed her eyes and moved her hand with his. In a slow and circular motion, she moved first up and down then around the swollen bud before repeating the pattern again. All the while his fingers gently followed hers.

"So sweet." He took a deep breath. "Soft." His large fingers interwove with hers. His body shuddered like a horse before a race.

Every part of her was splayed before him—not just her body, her desires, and every fault. Without much effort on his part, she'd spill all her fears and aspirations for life. All he had to do was ask. Who would have thought passion made a person so unguarded?

Soon, he swept her hand aside and took control of the caresses with a smooth and gentle touch. She was safe in his arms. An ache began to build inside. Nick kissed her again while his tongue caressed her mouth, slow and certain in his movements. She arched into his hand, hungry for more. Even though his touch was exquisite, it wasn't quite enough, and she whimpered, seeking more of him.

His manner told her there was no hurry. Whispers of tender, sensual words brushed her skin. She pushed nearer in an effort to get closer to him and satisfy this yearning he'd created. Crests of pleasure increased beyond anything she had ever felt before. It was if she were drowning in his touch. "Please . . . stop. This is too much."

"Don't fight it. Let go."

One finger entered her as he continued to stroke her.

The tension inside of her mounted, and she mewled in response.

"Shh," he whispered. "I'll take care of you." His tender promise only inflamed her more.

She closed her eyes as his name passed her lips. She barely heard him say her name in response as she pushed her center against his hand. She couldn't control anything anymore and felt as if she'd fallen over a cliff as waves of sensation crashed through her body. When the height of pleasure swallowed her, she was certain her heart would break through her chest. But the beat eventually slowed to its normal rhythm, and her gasps grew quiet.

Nick waited for her aftershocks to cease. He embraced her and claimed her mouth in a soul-scorching kiss as he pushed his cock against her abdomen. Her body melted against his as if it knew there was more for him to show her.

He never took his eyes from hers as he brought his fingers, the ones that touched her so intimately, to his mouth and sucked. He kissed her full on the mouth, and she tasted her own essence on his tongue.

She understood the power of the moment. What they had shared was beyond her comprehension just minutes ago.

She wanted every piece of him—body, mind, and soul.

He pulled their arms over her head, fingers entwined, all the while pleasuring her with his kisses, deliberately driving her mad. He rocked against her, mimicking the act of taking her. He placed sensitive kisses across her forehead, her brows, her cheeks, and the delicate skin behind her ears. It still wasn't enough. She arched to feel his chest rub against hers. Such wonder—such delightful torture.

Gentle as a breeze, his breath brushed her face. The

sensation burrowed deep. She was so befuddled from what they'd just shared.

Somehow within the last few minutes she'd lost the ability to speak. He must have seen her plight and taken mercy on her. His lips touched hers with a light sweep before he drew away. She moaned in protest. As if understanding her loss, his mouth covered hers again.

Her tongue met his in a caress that was at first gentle then grew bolder in its demands. She needed more, and he obliged. His mouth ravished hers while she tried to match his movements. He'd never kissed her like this before—fevered and desperate. He released her hands, and she tangled them in his soft hair. Never had she felt so reckless but exhilarated. She was in real danger. She could lose herself in him, and she didn't much care.

"Stop." He suddenly pulled away and shook his head. "We must stop."

"Why?" She reached to embrace him, but he gently pushed her arms away and escaped to stand beside the bed. Her body suddenly chilled.

"I shouldn't have touched you." He ran his fingers through his hair. The fire made the light color of his hair gleam. "I can't."

The haunted look on his face instantly seared her heart.

"Did I misunderstand? Didn't you enjoy it?" Bewildered, she clasped the sheet in a death grip and covered her chest. "Did I displease you?" She hated the weakness in her voice, but not as much as the pity in his eyes. Her heart wrenched in protest as she tried to understand what had just happened between them. "Tell me what I've done."

"You haven't done anything. I have." His rigid stance and clenched jaw didn't bode well for a discussion. "We both need a good night's rest. It's best if I sleep in the next room. We'll leave at the first break of light."

She tried to make sense of his reaction, but reason and emotion had scrambled together. Bending forward, she clutched her arms around her knees. She gasped as the fog in her brain finally cleared. His sudden need of distance made sense.

"You believe you'll have to marry me."

He tilted his head slightly to the right and narrowed his eyes. The stark intensity in his gaze ripped straight through her. Caught like a hare in a trap, she simply stared back. She'd rather attend thirty Wednesdays in a row of Almack's balls than go through this torture. Nevertheless, she was a Cavensham, so she collected every scrap of composure she possessed and confronted him with her own gaze.

"No." The word ricocheted off the wall, and she recoiled slightly. "I believe I *should* marry you."

Chapter Fourteen

Emma's every breath and small sighs tortured Nick with thoughts of her soft skin, her delicate lips, and the perfection of her curves. In all his life, leaving her had to be the most arduous ordeal he'd ever faced. His arousal was harder than a blacksmith's anvil and his sac just as heavy. His whole body ached for release. If she wasn't in the next room, he'd take himself in hand to relieve himself from this uncontrollable hunger.

Wide awake, he tried to settle for the night. The cot was lumpy, and he'd forgotten to attend the fire. Her confessing she had thought of him when aroused nearly killed him, but it had been her incendiary kisses and the sweet longing on her face that made him doubt his own sanity.

It was incomprehensible.

He'd never lived as a monk. When convenient, he'd taken a lover, someone unobtrusive who didn't make demands on his time. He'd always found it simple. He'd insure she was satisfied, then he'd find his release. Afterward, he'd leave. It'd been a simple physical act with no emotion.

Whether it was his dangerous thoughts or the blood pounding in his cock, something kept reminding him that Emma, thriving and lush, waited for him in the next room.

The simple truth? He couldn't have her.

What had he been thinking? He'd almost taken her because he selfishly wanted to experience her passion, taste her innocence, and comprehend her vivacity. All in hopes the emptiness of his own life would be forgotten—at least for one night. He considered himself an honorable man, and what he did tonight was unpardonable.

He shifted his legs and groaned. He'd never get to sleep like this. He wanted to leave the room. No, that wasn't far enough. He needed to leave this town. She tempted him to forget everything—his goals, his honor, and his promises.

His best friend had trusted him to bring her back unharmed. Nick had been welcomed into the duke and duchess' home when he had no one else. Yet he had dared to touch what was not his.

"Nick?" His name on her lips was like a siren's call, an allure too great to resist. If the end result was to lie shattered against the rocks, it'd bring sweet relief.

"What is it?" His throat felt raw from the strain of keeping his wits about him.

"Why?" She choked for a second. "Why did you leave?" Her voice sounded as if her heart was breaking. He was lower than a toadstool for making her doubt herself.

"I didn't leave. I'm here." He hesitated, then took a deep breath. It didn't calm his roaring blood for a moment.

"You're afraid." Her voice cracked as she gasped for breath. "Afraid you'll have to marry me. What if I don't want to marry you? Will you change your mind?" He heard the ropes of the mattress creak, then silence.

"Sweet Mother of God." He stood. "I don't want—" What could he say? That he didn't want her? They both knew that was a lie. He wanted to take her tonight and make her his in every way. "Think of the ramifications."

The outline of her body was several feet away. He lost the ability to move of his own free will. "Damnation, Emma! Go to bed."

Startled, she stopped. "You're truly angry with me."

"You want me in your bed? Then the consequence is marriage. I should go straight to your father and ask for your hand." Nick shook his head, then crossed his arms across his chest. "*Christ*, what have we done?"

She stumbled. Heaving for breath, she seemed to struggle for words. The truth was nothing she could say would change the outcome of tonight.

"Emma." Her name escaped like a prayer. He didn't want her to leave, but he didn't want her to stay. He waited for her to make the next move.

"I apologize. You needn't worry. I'll not bother you again."

Thankfully, he couldn't answer. Otherwise he'd have begged her to let him back in her bed.

The next morning, Nick had awoken early and informed Harry of their departure time. When he had returned to their room, Emma was already dressed for the day. His gaze settled on her lovely brown gown. The elegant line reminded him of what had happened last night. He closed his eyes. The image of her lush body and the feel of her fingers touching his skin ingrained itself in his thoughts. Hell, everything reminded him of her, from brushing his teeth to putting on his boots. He couldn't remember ever battling his desire for a woman like he had with her. She was delightful, but this was a dangerous game for both of them. Either way, he had to address what had happened between them.

They both had avoided disaster last night. She'd escaped the woeful mishap of marriage to him, and his complete lack of talent as a suitable husband would remain hidden. It was best for all concerned. He had his work and investments. It was all he needed.

From the sitting-room window, the sounds of the stable horses' jangling harnesses, the ostler's shouts of welcome, and the groans of carriages and carts drifted inside. Emma sat in front of the fire. When she looked up, her eyes were distant and filled with resistance.

"Before we leave, let's talk."

"No, thank you. I've detained you long enough. Please proceed with your own arrangements. I've decided to stay for at least another day, then Harry and I will return to Pembrooke's."

"Is this about last night?" He'd hurt her deeply. His head and heart jousted for supremacy, and the winner would take all. A wave of guilt joined the melee. "Em—"

"If you'd feel better, send word to Alex for an escort." With a smirk, she sent a volley his way. "I'd hate for you to suffer any further upset over me." She sat and twiddled her fingers together.

He walked to the fire and studied the lick of the flames. A mile-wide chasm lay between them, stretched even further by their mutual silence. He had little experience in mending the breach since he'd lived alone for so long. It would take little effort to toss out some pithy phrase or comment to make his point, but this was Emma. She deserved more from him. She was one of the few people in his life he was close to—even though she could infuriate a cow chewing its cud.

His disquiet faded, and the thinnest of threads held his

anger. Whether at her or himself was a question he didn't want to explore. "What on this vast earth is so important you'd stay in this town for another minute?"

Her tone and every curve of her body carried her defiance. "I must convince Mary to come to London." She glanced away. Her hesitation spoke volumes. She clearly wasn't impervious to the danger, but he'd not let her escape without understanding more.

"You'd risk everything? Your reputation, even your life?" He ran his hand through his hair. "Mary's situation isn't something easily fixed by a trip to London. Truly, I want to understand this obsession, but it's so far removed from anything I can comprehend."

A brief flash of pain or worry darkened her eyes in a color similar to the moss that covered the woodlands of his ancestral home, Renton Hall.

"This trip means I may find a way to bring Aulton to justice. I must see this through. Otherwise, I can't"—she spread her arms wide as if the room encapsulated her entire life—"I can't bear to let it go."

"Emma . . ." He gentled his voice and summoned enough patience to try to understand her meaning. "Surely you see this is Sykeston's cause, not yours."

"This may be the only chance to help Lena and clear my conscience. Besides, what's for me in London? I can't bear another ball or luncheon. It's like the same bad performance I must suffer through night after night." She pressed her eyes closed and straightened her shoulders. Her eyes fluttered open, and she inhaled deeply. "I don't want my life wasted. I want to help others like Mary. It's a chance to live a worthwhile life."

He took the seat directly across and studied her. She would not yield to his scrutiny, though he wanted to tear away her resolve, layer by layer. The stillness around them broke when he leaned his elbows on his knees and brought his face within inches of hers.

A raw need to prove her worth blasted through him with the force of a blizzard. "Your life is so promising. You're a treasure, and any man lucky enough to win your hand would be a fool if he didn't see that." He cupped her cheek in his hand. The soft warmth branded him. He fought to keep from taking her in his arms and promising her he'd give her the life she wanted.

"Treasure," she humphed. "Men gain power as they grow older, women lose what little they had in the first place. Why would I want that?"

"Your parents don't have such a marriage and neither do Claire and Pembrooke. How did you become so cynical with the world?" His thumb caressed a line from her mouth to her cheekbone. Finally, she leaned into his touch.

"Alex and Claire are the exception, particularly after the painful start of their union. It's a miracle they found any happiness." A bitter laugh escaped, and she pulled away. "My parents married for love before my father found himself the new Duke of Langham. He wouldn't have married my mother otherwise."

A sharp inhalation broke her façade of calm. "Duty would've required he make a match in the best interests of the duchy. My mother brought little financial worth or standing to their marriage." She turned her face away. "I sound so selfish. Look at Lena's life. There are scores of women just like her who face worse fates than mine every day. It's just that I—I want a chance to make something of my life. A chance to make a difference somehow."

His resigned sigh filled the quiet that flooded the room. "In what ways do you want to make a difference?"

"For instance, my bank."

"You're serious about starting a lending institution? You want to be a moneylender?" What could he say in response? "I've seen your plans, but it's a tremendous amount of work to make such an institution a success. Do you know anything about commerce?"

"Yes, is that so hard to believe?" She crossed her arms and tapped her foot. "I've read several books about banks. I'm a fast learner. Plus, I have a knowledge that can't be taught."

"What might that be?"

"I know women and how they think. What drives them. I can use that understanding to help better their lives and their community. You define yourself as an honorable man. Well, I want to define my life as a resource that women can turn to when they're in trouble."

The fact she wanted to be a moneylender made his business transactions look tame in comparison. Moneylenders were a despised lot. Her father would howl at such an idea. Really, it was rather daring—and so perfectly Emma.

"Your life has meaning," he offered. Her eyes flashed, warning him he had to tread carefully. She was getting angrier by the minute. "But there's more to running a banking institution than understanding women."

"I've the skills and intelligence to accomplish this and so much more. Things I've learned on my own. You have so many opportunities, such as university, financial independence, not to mention freedom to pursue any relationship you want. I'm denied such things because I'm a woman." She huffed out a breath.

He wouldn't be surprised if she jabbed her finger in his chest.

"I'll see Mary once more and then complete my travel without further inconvenience to you." She glanced at her intertwined fingers before placing her hands to the side as if to keep them under control. "Only then can I go home knowing that I did everything in my power to help her."

"You'd continue to risk your reputation and life on a servant who doesn't want your help?" He shouldn't have pushed her. He quickly got his temper under control.

"Don't you dare criticize." She never raised her voice, but her dictation was crisp and exact. "It's my life. I control it for now. Who knows how much longer I'll be free to make these decisions before I'm shackled in marriage. You made it abundantly clear your thoughts on marriage last night. If it's reassuring, I'm of the same mind. Only you have a choice, and I don't. But for now, I enjoy some independence."

The absurdity of the moment didn't escape him. She'd not control this situation any further. "I apologize. I had no right to speak to you in such a manner. Unfortunately, you have no other option. We leave for London within the hour."

By the time the words had left his mouth, her normally expressive face had altered into a mask of circumspect hauteur, a perfect subject for a portrait in some stuffy aristocrat's gallery. A tiny shimmer in her eyes told another story. He'd wounded her and that simple fact made him feel like dirt.

"You prove my point exactly. You believe you're entitled to make all the decisions. I'll make my own, thank you, even if they're mistakes. I revel in that power because it's *mine* for now." She pulled on her gloves with a defiant tug as powerful as any general readying to charge into battle.

She stood to exit, and he joined her.

"Somerton, you're afraid if you participate in life you'll experience it all, the happiness along with heartache." She shook her head as if expressing great sympathy

for him. "Sometimes, when I look at you, I see someone who'd cut off their hand to escape such heady emotions . . . just like last night. You tore yourself away
from the bed and left me with the carnage." She heaved
a sigh. "It must be a lonely existence. I hope you'll not
regret your decisions someday. I'm determined not to
waste mine."

All he wanted to do was kiss her until she gave up on
staying in Portsmouth, until she realized he didn't mean
to hurt her, until she accepted he was right. There was
no other choice for either of them, so he took her in his
arms.

The door flew open and bashed against the wall with
a resounding crash.

Nick pulled her behind him. The small mirror hang-
ing next to the door wobbled but managed not to fall.

Two men, dusty but elegantly dressed, entered the
room with pistols drawn.

As he should have expected, Emma wrenched her arm
out of his hand and stepped from behind to get a closer
glimpse.

Her brothers, McCalpin and Lord William, stood
shoulder to shoulder. Their probing gazes flew between
Nick and Emma, but their relief was immediate as smiles
broke across their faces.

"Good morning, Em," McCalpin said.

"Emmy, what have you done?" William drawled. "I
hope nothing I wouldn't do."

The room shrank in size when they directed their attention Nick's way. With his feet shoulder-width apart,
McCalpin, who had at least two stone on Nick, appeared
ready to pummel him to bits. It took little imagination to
know what he was facing. Repeatedly, he'd met McCalpin at Gentleman Jackson's for exercise and was familiar with his fighting technique. McCalpin had a deadly

left hook. But what Nick lacked in breadth, he made up for with speed. He'd get two swift punches in before McCalpin delivered his first.

Lord William was of similar stature as his brother. He fixed a stare designed to either peel Nick alive or peal his head like a church bell. He was clenching his fists so hard the white of his knuckles was clearly visible across the room.

"Somerton, fancy meeting you in my sister's room." McCalpin's voice was deceptively calm. "Was her fabulous set-down for you?"

At that moment, Nick knew the consequences. Caught like a river trout with the errant fly of a hook, he felt the line pull him deep. Pembrooke had expected both he and Emma in London last night. Who in the devil could have predicted both her brothers would storm into the room like two bulls ready to battle to the death?

"Indeed, it was." Nick raised an eyebrow and widened his own stance for balance *if* both charged at the same time. Blood pounded through his veins with every sense on alert. He'd not go down without a landing a blow to each brother. "How delightful you finally decided to join us."

"Good morning, McCalpin. William. What a lovely surprise." Emma's voice verged on a note between laughter and hysteria. She tried to behave as if nothing was amiss and it was perfectly natural she was alone with a man in her room. Any good luck she possessed had abandoned her in favor of the early coach back to London.

The pain in her chest, the result of her fight with Nick, hurt but was no match for the terror she experienced at the sight of her brothers. She needed time to come up with an explanation for why Nick was with her.

"Did he put you up to this?" McCalpin eyes roamed

over her face as if he sought the crack within her façade. "Tell me."

"No. It was all my idea. Lord Somerton is returning to London today. I'm not certain of my plans."

The weighted tension in the room had escalated to the point it felt as if a fifth person was present. Will and Nick glared at each other.

Nick's eyes flashed, but remarkably, his demeanor remained calm. "I assure you Lady Emma's welfare and safety were my only priorities during her stay."

Will bit out a bark of laughter. "We just saw your regard for her welfare."

Best to diffuse the situation if she started with Will. In two strides, she was beside him with her hand on his arm to draw attention away from Nick. "For my sake, leave it be."

Will focused on where she'd grasped his arm before he stared at her much like a kestrel before it spiraled into a strike. Calm and in complete control, he placed his hand over hers. "Only if you tell us what happened," he whispered. "Why are you alone and in his arms?"

Nick chose that moment to step forward and growled, "You're her brother. Why weren't you here? I'll tell—"

"All right, I'll tell you." Emma shot Nick a glance that was a plea to let her continue. If he said another word, the brawl of the century would break out. "I came to see Lena's maid and ask her to come work for me. Nick came after me to escort me home. What you witnessed was simple. I got lost in my emotions for a moment."

A crooked smile crept across McCalpin's face, and he turned his attention to Nick. "Not like you, *Nick*, to risk matrimony." He turned to her without a trace of animosity. "I don't see a way out of this. You'll have to marry him."

Time stood suspended as her heart stopped. She swallowed. "Marry?"

McCalpin's sincerity was real. Throughout her childhood, he'd never been cruel to her. Nor had he ever teased her unmercifully when they were younger. Many would not believe it, but he'd always gone out of his way to inquire about her life and interests. Even though he was her brother, she considered him a friend.

All three men held unspeakable power over her at this moment. If her parents found out about Portsmouth, or God help her, last night, they'd be devastated. What choice did she have but to ask her brothers to keep her secret? "There's another way. If you don't tell father or mother, we won't have to marry. Somerton won't say a word."

Nick's thunderous gaze was directed at her when he lifted a brow. "You know me well enough by now. I'll not lie if asked."

One of floorboards creaked under Nick's weight, and the sound broke what little peace had existed between the four of them.

"Somerton, you're a dead man." Will's threat was low and deadly. There was no mistaking the venom in his voice.

"I would consider it my good fortune if you decide to do it yourself. It'd be a pleasure to teach you a lesson in manners." Nick kept his gaze locked on Will. If one surly smile was directed his way, he'd punch the reprobate.

Emma stepped in front of him. "Enough," she whispered, her words loud enough to draw Will's attention to her.

Maybe she was wiser than he thought. The ramifications of her trip now involved her whole family.

Emma tilted her chin and faced William. "How did you know I was here?"

If she hadn't been standing so close, Nick would have missed the slight tremble in her voice.

Will adjusted his stance and held out his hand. "McCalpin sent word after hearing from Alex. Once I got the note . . . Emmy—"

She didn't take the hand he offered. "And what?"

"I'm sorry." Her brother's eyes softened. "I informed father."

Her soft gasp hit Nick like a punch to his midsection. As sure as he breathed, all he wanted at that moment was to reassure her they'd weather this storm together. Even if he risked her brothers' wrath, he took her hand and squeezed. When she returned the squeeze, he wanted to sweep her into his arms. Brothers present or not.

Will grimaced. "What was I to do? What if you were hurt? I had no idea what I'd find when I arrived." He sneered at Nick. "It's worse than I imagined."

"Alex sent Nick—" She caught herself before she revealed anymore. "Alex sent Somerton to bring me back."

Will's eyes narrowed in disbelief. "And not me, your own brother?"

"After our last dinner together? I doubt if anyone would have believed you'd be willing to cross the street on my behalf."

A grin tugged at one side of William's mouth. "Ah well, if Mr. Clayton's leopard was on the other side, perhaps I wouldn't have crossed the street for you. But nothing would have kept me away from here and ensuring you were safe." His gaze focused on her, completely ignoring Nick and McCalpin. "Truly, did he—"

"No, Will. He came on behalf of Pembroke. He's been a perfect gentleman."

Nick almost choked on her words.

The only way he could describe the last several days with Emma was enchanting. Even facing her two irate brothers, he would do it all over again. McCalpin and Will were quite concerned with their sister—worried enough to risk violence on her behalf. Their love was a testament to the strength of her family. When William's fury turned to genuine concern, he'd redeemed himself in Nick's eyes. The man truly loved his sister.

As an only child, such emotion was foreign to him, but for the Cavenshams it was an ordinary occurrence. He dropped Emma's hand. The loss of her fingers beneath his signaled the end of their time alone with each other.

He had been quite satisfied with his own company before Portsmouth. Now loneliness stole through him, robbing him of all contentment. At the end of the day, he'd miss her smile, her straightforwardness, the wisps of golden curls that would eventually escape from her hair, her laugh, the perfect dark spot next to her lips that enhanced her creamy skin, and most of all, her intelligence. Simply put, he'd miss everything that made Lady Emma Cavensham spectacular.

The thump inside his chest demanded more of her. "How" was the question. How to have her without ruining both their lives? He was so close to exceeding his father's wealth. It was everything he'd worked for over the last twelve years, but to add the distraction of a wife could be a disaster.

He breathed deep. But he couldn't see returning to his old life.

The trip home would provide some distance, a chance to allow rational thought to return. The morning was slipping away from them. "Shall we depart?"

Emma started to protest, but Nick cut her off with a wave of a hand. "Harry's had the horses ready for over twenty minutes. We'll leave immediately. As you may surmise, we all have much to discuss."

Chapter Fifteen

❧

The carriage creaked in protest as it rolled slightly to the side before straightening on the cobblestone drive. Nick pulled the curtain aside. Their journey would be finished within moments. Lost in her thoughts, Emma had been silent the entire way from Portsmouth. He'd tried to engage her at least ten times with little success. Every question or comment was met with a one-word response.

McCalpin had ridden ahead to prepare the duke for their return. He'd intimated he'd try to forestall any hint of marriage. A sharp pain had twisted inside Nick's chest robbing him of a proper thanks for the marquess's efforts. All he had managed was a nod in acceptance. Will had feigned sleep until they arrived in town. He'd directed Harry drop him off at White's. Clearly he wanted nothing to do with the aftermath of Emma's trip to Portsmouth.

From a distance, Emma's father stood with his feet apart and hands behind his back. The vehicle moved toward the carriage house, and the pain in her eyes grew evident. They only had another few minutes alone. He caressed her face, and she allowed his touch without a quibble. She even leaned slightly toward him as if seeking strength.

"Courage, Em," he said. Besides her fortitude, he needed luck to face Langham and walk away intact. In a scenario only a playwright could create, he was about to deliver her home with an elderly groomsman driving and her brother not even bothering to play chaperon on the ride back. Guilt chiseled his conscience when he remembered last night. If he ever considered himself a true gentleman, he should have convinced her to marry him during their trip back. Her brother's presence be damned.

The softness of her skin provided the impetus to blurt the words he should have uttered last night. "Marry me."

Her wide-eyed gaze jerked to his and she stared, speechless. He swallowed the panic threatening to refute the offer.

Before the carriage came to rest, the duke entered in one fluid motion and closed the door. "Puss." The low rumble of his voice filled the space. Langham studied his daughter, not making a move. When her lip trembled, his ducal reserve fled and he swept her in his arms. His hand wrapped around her head, and he tucked her close to his heart. "You're home."

Without letting her go, the duke swung his gaze to Nick. "Have Pitts escort you to my study."

"Papa—" Her voice cracked.

"Hush." The duke brought his mouth to the top of Emma's head. "Your mother is waiting."

Their tender moment caused Nick to look away. Yesterday proved he was a colossal fool. He'd been the one to comfort her until he'd cast her aside. Now, once again, he was an outsider looking in—nothing more than an intruder in their exchange. He had to escape. Thankfully, the duke put his torture to an end. In an instant,

Langham was outside and lent a hand to assist Emma to the back entrance.

She glanced back, her eyes shining with unshed emotion. If his damn heart split in two, it would hurt less than what he was experiencing at seeing her upset. The intense crushing pain was what he'd always tried to avoid. He blew out a breath. He had no place for any of this in his life.

After Emma entered the house, Langham returned to the carriage and delivered a cold stare. "Don't make me wait for you."

"As you wish, Your Grace." For the first time in his life, Nick experienced something tantamount to a noose tied around his neck.

With little ceremony, he followed the duke through the servants' entrance where the ubiquitous Langham family butler, Pitts, waited to escort him to the duke's inner sanctum. When the study door opened, Alex stood in the middle of the room with McCalpin by his side.

"Somerton." Alex extended a glass of whisky.

Nick took the glass and collapsed in a chair facing the fire where Alex and McCalpin stood.

"Tell us before Langham comes in," Alex said with a quick nod.

"I found Emma with Harry tagging along and brought her home." Nick drank the smoky contents in one swallow. The liquid fire burned his throat, but it wasn't enough. He held out the glass for a refill. "McCalpin and Lord William found us. Not surprisingly, William wanted to tear my head off."

After Alex poured another two fingers of the amber spirit, he raised one eyebrow. "Is there a need for a special license?"

An unholy growl emerged from McCalpin, warning Nick to be careful in his answers. He choked on his second swallow and barely managed to keep the contents in his mouth. He slammed his fist against the chair arm. "For God's sake, Pembrooke."

"I should have known the answer is no. You'd never allow yourself to compromise Emma." Alex examined him. "Besides, your head is still attached."

"It was tense for several moments, but Emma explained you sent me." Nick traced the rim of the glass with his finger. Suddenly restless, he stood. "McCalpin, I owe you thanks for verifying it. Still, William wasn't too happy."

McCalpin took a swig from his glass and, with an uncharacteristic appearance of umbrage, regarded Nick.

"That's not a surprise," Alex said.

The lingering pain of her denial to her brothers that nothing important happened in Portsmouth still left a gaping hole inside. "Just now, I asked her to marry me."

All the color drained from Alex's face. "What?"

McCalpin set his drink down on the table. "Why did you do that? I've already talked to my father. Nothing will come of it."

"You found me in her room at the Ruby Crown. It's important I do the right thing. We were preparing—"

"Don't worry about William." Langham's entrance had been silent.

Nick readied his stance for when the duke's fist would meet his nose.

"I just left Emma with Ginny. Perhaps her mother will make sense of this." The duke exhaled his apparent frustration as he made his way to stand beside Alex. "The blame for Portsmouth lies directly with me. She's just so . . . so unsettled." The duke shook his head. "Somerton, you didn't stand a chance when Pembrooke sent you to collect her. She's too damn independent."

Alex handed the duke a glass.

It was time to face Langham and his wrath. He took a deep breath.

The duke downed half the contents and set the glass on the nearby table. With an unholy fire in his eyes, he slowly stalked toward Nick. His right hand shot out, and Nick prepared for the blow. Instead, the duke grabbed him by the shoulder as if thanking him.

"She suffered a dreadful moment or two, but she's safe." Nick returned his stare. "Whatever is necessary to protect your daughter, I'll do." His gut clenched in a tangle of nerves. "If you'll allow, I'd be honored to offer for Lady Emma."

Even though all four of them were of similar height, the duke's presence overtook the room. Nick held what little ground he had while he waited for the duke's verdict.

"I'll consider it." Langham exhaled with a groan, the troubled sound poignant. He released Nick and stepped to the fire. "Pembrooke explained the situation to me. As you may have surmised, she's headstrong and believes in her actions. I've taught her that, but I'm at my wit's end. I should be the one to face the consequences, not you."

The expected relief at the duke's statement was not forthcoming. Instead, a familiar hollowness breached his stalwart demeanor. "She's an intelligent woman who has an uncanny talent to land on her feet. I'm not certain I provided much assistance to her."

The duke rubbed his hand down his face and turned to Nick. "My only complaint—either you or Pembrooke should have told me earlier."

"You have my sincerest apology, but I didn't discover she'd left until it was too late." It was best to accept responsibility and leave Langham Hall as soon as humanly possible.

"Thank you, Somerton." The duke extended his hand for Nick to shake.

"There's no need to thank me." He took the offered hand, but the strength in the duke's grasp wasn't reassuring. "It's the least I could do."

"I'll take my leave." The duke nodded and then finished his drink. "Ring for whatever you need."

"I'll join you." McCalpin started for the door after his father, then hesitated. His attention darted to Nick. "I care for my sister a great deal. You have my gratitude also."

After the footman closed the door behind McCalpin, Nick allowed his body to relax. "At least that's one confrontation I don't have to worry about. Any word leak about our travels to Portsmouth?" Nick didn't bother to hide his bitterness.

"No one outside the immediate family knows anything. The Langham servants are loyal." Alex's face displayed a mischievous interest. "You're wound up tighter than your pocket-watch over Emma's rescue."

The weariness that coursed through Nick's body caused him to speak on impulse. "Nothing happened in Portsmouth."

"Reminds me of Queen Gertrude. 'The gentleman doth protest too much, methinks.'" Alex threw his head back to the ceiling and laughed with delight. "Wait until I tell Claire."

"Sweetheart, tell me what happened." Her mother stroked her fingers through Emma's hair.

Barely aware of the chintz flower design, Emma lay in bed and stared at the canopy. "I think I lost Somerton's friendship." She turned away from her mother's ministrations. "Plus, I've disappointed you and Father."

"Your father will be here shortly, and we'll sort this

out. Somerton may be angry now, but he'll forgive you. He values you also." As her mother slowly blinked, her lashes fanned across her cheeks. "After we arrived at Blanche's, Will sent a note you were missing and asked if we'd come home. My God, when you weren't here, the worry—" Small tears marked the places where her lashes had rested. "You look tired. Did you and Lord Somerton—"

Emma quickly sat up. She forced herself to meet her mother's eyes. "He asked me to marry him."

Her mother's eyes widened. "How did you answer?"

"I didn't," she whispered. The shock of Nick's quickly spoken words still reeled inside her head and collided with all her well-established beliefs. "Father interrupted us."

Her mother raised one eyebrow. "He usually has the most impeccable timing."

Two sharp knocks sounded on the door. Arial answered and opened the door wide to admit her father.

"Will you have a bath prepared for Lady Emma?" her mother asked. The maid left with nary a sound.

Her father strolled purposely into the room. She'd dreaded this moment since leaving Portsmouth—facing her parents. Wary of her father's response, Emma gave her best effort to guard the roll of emotions pressing through her. If she cried, he'd tear the house down.

Her father sat next to her mother. With a slight smile, he gave a gentle pat to Emma's leg. "Puss, remember when you tried to ride my best hunter? Somehow you managed to get a saddle on him and left before anyone was up."

"Oh, Sebastian . . ." Her mother lost the fight to hold back her tears, but a hint of humor lit her eyes. "What a day that was."

The worry wore itself on her parents' faces. Dark circles

had appeared under her father's eyes, and the misery lined her mother's beautiful face.

"Come here, Ginny." Her father drew her mother in his arms. A single tear fell on the side of her mother's cheek, and he kissed it away. "It took all day, but we found you. Titan had thrown you into a stand of bramble bushes." He chuckled. "You somehow tangled yourself into such a state you couldn't move. Scratched, angry, and hissing like a kitten when I found you. Remember?"

Emma nodded. She wanted to prove she could ride with her brothers during the annual autumn hunt. That was the reason her father called her "Puss." She bit her lip and waited. There was more to the story, and she was sure she'd hear it all.

"Your mother and I aged about five years that day. We aged ten years after that Bentham book episode." He studied Emma with an intense look. "Child's play compared to this."

"I'm sorry I've caused you such distress." The ever-present tears burned her eyes. She blinked rapidly in an attempt to keep them at bay. She'd always considered herself the type of woman not to cry, but Portsmouth had made her doubt quite a bit about herself.

Her father examined her. His blue eyes were clear, but much darker than Nick's.

What had happened to her? Every thought circled round to Nick.

"Your mother and I strictly forbade you from interfering in Lord Sykeston's business." He sighed and pulled her mother tighter into his embrace. "You were extremely lucky Somerton found you. Why didn't you come home the next day?"

Emma fidgeted with the coverlet. "Before Lord Somerton awoke and made plans for our return, I left with Harry Johnson and a servant from the inn to visit

Mary Butler, Lena's maid. I asked her to come work for me, but she refused."

Her father shook his head. "Emma—"

"Sebastian, let's discuss this later. Emma needs to rest." Her mother's attention and tender smile made Emma's heart ache.

Her parents rose from the bed, and her mother kissed her forehead. "I'm so relieved you're home, sweetheart."

"Downstairs, Somerton asked me for your hand." Her father's tone was matter-of-fact without any real emotion. "Your mother and I will discuss it."

Inside her chest, the familiar flutter took flight at the mention of Nick. "Is it still my choice?"

"You're tired." Her father leaned over and kissed her good night just like he'd done for years. "Rest."

The hint of his evening beard brushed her cheek. For a moment, his warmth and the familiar smell of sandalwood reminded her of how he'd tuck her into bed when she was a child.

Her recent comfort fled. Nick's offer could change everything between them. But he only asked because he was a gentleman. She could count Claire and Daphne as her best friends, but the rapport she shared with Nick was profound in a different way. She'd experienced so much with him over the last couple of days. If she lost his friendship, she'd never recapture those feelings with any other man.

The door closed, and she fell back onto her pillows. She'd risked everything she'd been brought up to hold dear—her duty to obey her parents, her family's good opinion, and her place in society. Everything rested on the edge of a precipice because of her actions.

Yet she'd do it all over again if it'd bring Aulton to justice. Whatever the outcome of Portsmouth, she deserved it. But her family shouldn't suffer any censure or hint of scandal. If her father took a stand and made her marry, she'd be devastated.

The last glow of the sunset disappeared from the window. Night had fallen, and the warmth of the day was just a remembrance as her thoughts strayed to Nick. For the most part, he treated her as an equal. But marriage went against everything she learned from her experiences. Society saw women as commodities, and men, even ones as honorable as her brothers and Somerton, tried to control women. She swallowed at the thought of Lena's horrible existence in marriage. All of it led to one conclusion—a woman would surrender everything if she married the wrong man.

Worry wove itself through every thought and rattled any hope for peace. For a brief moment, the confession she'd shared with Nick had diminished the sense of loss and guilt she suffered over Lena's death. But like an unrelenting nag or a bad penny, it returned as the new day dawned over Portsmouth.

What did the proper and honorable Lord Somerton think of her integrity now? Pity? Horror? Did either make a difference? Why did he ask her to marry him?

Emma hugged a pillow and closed her eyes.

How could she have him and refuse his proposal?

Chapter Sixteen

Lovely visions of Emma cavorted and frolicked in Nick's mind and body without any relief. He'd seen her two days ago, and sleep had been elusive ever since. He paced the length of his study and ran his hands through his hair in frustration. Langham hadn't made a decision as to Nick's offer, or if he had, he'd deemed Nick unworthy of a response.

After an endless dance with insomnia, he'd spent last night at his desk, back to work on the inventoried cargo of the last two months. It was the only thing that had tamed his thoughts of Emma.

By dawn, his mind had cleared to the extent he had a sense of how to proceed. He'd call on her and again ask for her hand. If she declined, he would put it to rest, no matter the disappointment. His business was too important to ignore and needed his full attention.

Only one thought calmed some of his unease. If his ships' profits continued their steady climb, he would have doubled his money in two years. Nick planned to open up offices on the busy Thames harbor with the Somerton crest displayed prominently. He hoped his father cringed that his heir pursued a career in trade instead of begging forgiveness and learning to manage the Renton duchy. If it fell into a heap from neglect, Nick wouldn't waste a second look.

However, even his business couldn't keep him distracted for long. He took refuge behind his desk and sat. Only one thing could explain his ennui.

Emma.

God, he wished she'd marry someone—anyone—tomorrow and put him out of his misery. He'd have no other alternative except to move on. He rued the days since he followed her to Portsmouth.

The butler interrupted his reverie. "Lord Paul Barstowe to see you on a matter he says is of extreme importance."

Nick stilled, and the familiar nip of rage stole his attention from *Her Folly*'s manifests. "Hamm, tell him I'm not receiving."

"Somerton, I could see you from the window outside." Lord Paul swept inside the study with the force of a blizzard. "I promise not to take up much of your *precious* time."

Society had ostracized other men for far less, but Lord Paul was the prodigal son. The second son of the Duke of Southart was most likely to inherit his father's title as his older brother's health was in rapid decline. He and Nick were similar in build and coloring but that's where their resemblances ended. Lord Paul's talent for scandal and outlandish behavior proved valuable entertainment for the *ton*. Every time Nick thought of him, an overwhelming longing to pound a hole in the wall threatened.

Nick leaned back in his chair as Paul unbuttoned his coat and chose a chair in front of the fire. "It's damned cold this morning. However, I wanted to see if you'd be interested in a ride? I've got a beautiful bay mare outside with the prettiest star on her—"

"Why are you here?" Nick wasted no time on pleasantries.

Paul took his gloves off one finger at a time before he offered an answer. Every nuanced movement coming from the uninvited guest was deliberate. His stern countenance made Nick even more wary than before.

"You should be pleasant. I come with the best intentions."

"Is this about money?" Nick rubbed his face with his hands.

"You're like a badger. One sniff, and you charge out of your hole ready to attack." He examined his well-manicured fingernails. "Yes, this is about money."

Another unopened letter from his father distracted him, but he dismissed the offending missive from his attention. It was as if Renton and Paul had planned to aggravate him in tandem. "You need to leave. My time is valuable. Make an appointment—"

"Your solicitor received a banknote today for five hundred pounds." Paul cleared his throat. "The amount covers the two hundred you paid for my debt at university. At four percent interest compounded semiannually, it equals roughly four hundred pounds. The extra is for your aggravation. I should have given it to you years ago, but I let it fester. I apologize."

"Why are you making amends now?" The man could have made scheduled payments, gotten the money from his father, or spent some of the inheritance he received from his mother long before this.

"Simple. I'm finally taking responsibility for my life." He dipped his chin to his chest and studied the floor. "The physicians don't believe my brother will last through January. I'll not see his final days clouded with worry over me."

"I'd heard he'd taken a turn for the worse," Nick said. "If there's anything I can offer or do on his behalf—"

Paul shook his head. "That's very kind, but there's no need. He has the best doctors in all of England."

If Nick had paid a fortuneteller and they'd predicted this conversation, he'd have demanded his money returned. Never in his life had he considered Lord Paul the type of man to make amends for his misdeeds.

"I'll forward your payment immediately to Renton." With any luck, the old man would likely suffer a paroxysm of shock and stay in bed for a week after receiving the restitution.

Paul walked to the window and stared outside for a moment. "I'll be honest. I have no idea how to mend the rest of the damage I caused. Your break with Renton is because of me. Tell me what you'd have me do or say, and it'll be my first priority tomorrow."

For the millionth time since his father drove away, Nick considered if there was anything that could repair the damage. He always reached the same conclusion. There was nothing to be done. He coughed in a feeble attempt to clear the thickness that threatened to consume him. "This is more than enough for reparation."

Paul's face hardened much like a piece of granite. The gleam in his blue eyes resembled ice. "I have another matter to discuss."

Nick snickered. No doubt, Paul had come for help with money. "If it's a request to invest with me, you'll have to have at least twenty thousand."

"No, thank you." Paul took a deep breath and smiled. "It's about Lady Emma."

A ringing exploded in Nick's head, and he sat at the desk. "Why discuss her with me?"

"I wanted to ask your intentions. I always thought you and Lady Daphne would marry, but lately, it appears you're quite taken with Lady Emma." Devoid of any expression, Paul waited.

"It's true I attended Lady Emory's ball and danced with her." How to explain their relationship without betraying Emma was harder than he anticipated. "I'm not certain how you've come to that conclusion."

"I was at my club yesterday. Aulton was there." Paul drummed his fingers on the table as if debating something. He leaned back in the chair and regarded Nick. "He spread the tale"—he leaned forward, his piercing gaze focused—"you were in Portsmouth together. If you're pursuing her, I'll consider stepping aside. Otherwise, I'm going to visit the Duke of Langham and offer marriage."

Lord Paul's declaration hit him like a punch to the gut. That he'd approach Langham after he publicly broke his engagement to Claire and humiliated her was bold and foolhardy. Thankfully, Pembrooke had saved her that night. But Emma? His Emma? The man had a death wish. Over his dead body would he allow that to happen.

"Close your mouth, Somerton. Shock does nothing for your looks. I understand completely. The truth of her beauty and kindness is undeniable. Simply put, she's delectable." He relaxed in his chair with an irritating half grin. "Her plump lips are red like summer raspberries. Have you ever noticed her bottom lip always looks like a bee stung it? Don't get me started on that beauty spot."

Nick stood with such force he knocked the chair over. "Don't say another word."

"Just as I thought." Lord Paul carefully examined Nick. "You care for her. Fair warning. As the de facto heir to the Duke of Southart, my suit will be considered especially since I was once engaged to Lady Pembrooke before Pembrooke stole her from me."

Nick moved around the desk, and his mind filled with images of pushing the miscreant out the window. At the least, he would tie Lord Paul with ropes and ship him to some far distant port of call. "After what you did to Claire? The duke won't give you the time of day."

"You mean what Pembrooke did to Claire. We shall see," Paul answered with his typical swagger and stood. "But that's neither here nor there." A sly smile slid across his face. "Emma's extraordinary. I hope I never have to extend my congratulations on your nuptials." Paul's low chuckle rumbled like thunder. He straightened his cravat and waistcoat and moved as if he wanted to address Nick again, but hesitated. With a refined gait, he walked to the door, then turned around. "Emma should be married quickly to keep the damage to her reputation to a minimum."

Nick nodded in acknowledgment. "Good day."

Lord Paul closed the door and walked back to the desk. "I can't leave without you knowing all of it. Aulton says you're lovers. He saw you enter her room and not leave. He's commissioned several caricatures for posting all over town. For her sake, don't dally."

Nick waited until the man rode down the street, then pounded his fist against the desk. *Bloody hell.*

"Hamm, have my horse saddled!" His bellow ricocheted around like the opening break of a billiards game.

How was he going to convince her to marry him?

Nick waited for over five hours. There was little doubt the Duke of Langham thought to punish him by making him wait for an audience. Astute, the duke knew such inactivity would drive Nick mad. He hadn't thought to bring any work, so he waited, then waited some more.

Finally, Langham issued the summons. Nick squared his shoulders on the way to the duke's study. His sense of dread multiplied much like field rabbits in the early spring. With the duke's legendary anger, there was little doubt tonight would be one of the longest in his life. It made little difference. He'd protect Emma.

Two somber liveried footmen stood outside the study. Without looking in his direction, they opened the massive double doors simultaneously as he approached. He stepped into a circular atrium to find Pitts waiting there. Another set of floor-to-ceiling double doors led into the inner sanctum of the study.

"My lord, I'll announce you now." Pitts briskly nodded, and Nick followed him into the room. "Your Grace, the Earl of Somerton."

For a butler who loved to boom announcements and roll his *R*s, Pitts kept his uncharacteristically muted.

An ominous sign.

The Duke of Langham stood in front of a great bowed window that faced a trio of fountains at the entrance to Langham Park.

"Pitts, you may leave." The duke addressed the window, but the reflection of his countenance confirmed the anger in his face. "Somerton, come in."

"Your Grace." Nick bowed in greeting.

Langham turned to face him and raised an eyebrow as if trying to decide what manner of a man stood before him.

"Thank you for seeing me. Let me begin by apologizing for any distress I've caused. I presume you've heard the rumors. I'm here to ask for Lady Emma's hand in marriage." He didn't add "again" though the word burned his tongue.

Anger pinched the duke's face, his color high as his eyes flashed. "I should thrash you on the spot."

"You have my deepest apologies. I never meant to dishonor her. She's—" He struggled with his feelings as his words evaporated. How to explain that she made the air he breathed cleaner, the water he drank sweeter, or simply, that she made his dull life shine? How could he explain her magic? He released the fists he hadn't realized he'd clenched. "I want to fix this transgression. I *want* to marry her."

The duke humphed, "Transgression? That's like describing a dike breach as a simple leak. I've worked all afternoon stopping those horrendous caricatures from posting tomorrow."

"Please, Your Grace"—Nick captured Langham's gaze—"I *need* to marry her."

The duke's anger visibly dissipated as he slowly blinked. He walked to his desk and sat down. He pushed a paper in Nick's direction.

Without waiting for an invitation, Nick claimed one of the massive leather chairs in front of the duke's desk and picked up the document. The simple marriage settlement could only be described as very generous. Emma's dowry was worth fifty thousand pounds. The standard terms insured that she and their children would be provided for in case of Nick's demise.

"There's nothing hidden in those clauses," the duke rumbled as he waved his hand at the parchment. "I want Emma happy and secure, and cared for, you understand?"

Nick nodded and took the quill Langham handed him and signed the settlement. Inside, the mass of ice buried in his chest melted. "I want the same for her, too, and I plan to make it my life's mission to see that she never wants for a thing. You have my word your daughter is my first priority. I'm changing the directive of my will. If I pass before Emma, she'll receive my entire fortune. All four hundred thousand pounds. I trust her to make the decisions for our children's future if we're so blessed."

The duke crossed his arms over his chest, than raised one hand so his chin rested between the thumb and forefinger. "The duchess and I failed to help her with her grief. You'll carry that burden. If anyone can help her, I believe it's you."

"Your confidence means a great deal, Your Grace."

With an exhale, the duke continued in a voice eerily calm. "This is how you'll rectify the damage your *transgression's* caused."

Never a good omen if Nick could believe Pembrooke. "I'm at your service," Nick offered.

"Somerton, I do not want to hear one utterance until I finish." The duke's cheeks burned crimson, and his eyes flashed with heat. "You march straight to Doctor's Commons tomorrow and get a special license. Understand?"

Nick nodded his agreement. "I'll be there first thing in the morning."

"Then I want you here posthaste," Langham continued as if Nick were a scribe taking notes for the duke's pleasure. "We'll have the service here."

"I cannot do that." Pinpricks of irritation burst inside head, but he ignored them. This was his due for compromising Emma. "There are several matters I must manage before we marry."

"Such as," the duke drawled clearly displeased.

"Seeing my solicitor about my will and securing my wife's wedding present." That was all the information Langham would receive from Nick. "Plus, my staff needs extra time to make her chambers ready for tomorrow."

The duke's face relaxed and his steel-blue eyes flashed. "I always thought you'd make an admirable son-in-law," he exhaled. "But I never dreamed it would be under these circumstances."

Shameful heat coursed through his veins. "I truly apologize. I never meant to hurt Emma or you and your duchess."

"Believe it or not, I understand your situation." A rueful smile creased the duke's mouth. "Sometimes, if you're lucky, a woman consumes you."

Relief began to course through Nick, and he started to relax. The confrontation had been nonexistent.

"Do you love my daughter?" The duke's cerulean eyes burned straight through Nick's chest to the rusty enclosure that kept his heart safe and protected.

He waited for Langham to examine the deficiency he'd find in the center of that cage. Renowned for his acute perceptions, the duke would surely find every one of Nick's flaws. "Your Grace, I don't have an answer to your question."

"You soon will," the duke muttered under his breath as he straightened his desk. "One more thing." Langham captured his gaze. "I think it best you not say anything to Emma about our meeting. If she catches wind and reacts, *The Midnight Cryer* will make her their lead article, causing even more damage. I rather we keep this quiet."

"Of course, Your Grace."

With a blinding smile, the duke stood and pulled the bell cord to summon a servant. Without addressing Nick, he proceeded to the side table and then poured a glass of Claire's family whisky.

Nick stood ready to take his leave. Immediately, the study door swung open and hearty male laughter spilled into the room. Pembrooke, McCalpin, and William clearly had waited for the summons.

McCalpin extended his hand. "Welcome to the family."

"You're a brave man, Somerton." William slapped him on the back. "She's worth it though."

Not trusting himself to speak, Nick nodded his thanks. He swallowed the overwhelming lump in his throat. He truly was part of a family now.

Alex offered his own congratulations. "I'm happy for you." He stole a glance at the Cavensham men who had gathered around the whisky-filled glasses. "I always knew this was your destiny. You chose well, my friend."

Soon everyone had a glass. The duke's gaze fell to Nick. "I'm delighted to announce that Somerton will soon be an official member of this family. Every day, I find I fall in love with my duchess all over again. I hope you and Emma find the same happiness."

After the resounding *Huzzahs* and *Hear, hear's*, laughs and toasts and stories were passed throughout the gathering.

After midnight, Nick found himself in his study where he poured a fingerful of Claire's family whisky. Lord William had insisted he take a bottle home.

The duke's question of whether he loved Emma had tormented him all evening.

God help both them both if he did.

His inevitable companion, doubt, crept into his thoughts. Emma's marriage expectations were a mystery except that she wanted no part of it.

Their marriage would require he attempt to win her over after the ceremony. Convince her he wanted her as his wife. If that wasn't a recipe for disaster, then he didn't know what was.

He'd never wooed anything in his life, unless he counted his father's old hunting dog. His success at courting had turned out rather poorly. He'd wanted the dog to sleep with him at night, but the mongrel had bit him in the hand after he'd fed her his entire meal one day. It was the last time he had attempted anything along those lines. Now, he had no idea how to behave or what to do.

His creativity was nonexistent, which didn't bode well for his chance to convince Emma that he wanted this marriage.

Chapter Seventeen

Finally, the last of the rain had departed, and the rest of the day lent itself to a leisurely walk about Langham Park. A murmuration of starlings darted back and forth across the trees, maneuvering to find a spot to land for the night. Emma understood their yearning, at home yet still restless. She didn't belong here, but had no place else.

Rumors about her and Nick had been fueled by *The Midnight Cryer*'s daily taunts. Daphne had warned her that Aulton had made a public spectacle of informing the biggest scandalmongers in town that he'd personally seen Nick enter Emma's bedroom in Portsmouth. The increasing gossip and insinuations from society and the talk of her involvement with Nick had ruined her opportunity to bring Aulton to justice. She hadn't even been able to work on the idea of opening her bank. Her parents had dictated she stay confined to Langham Hall.

She reached inside the pocket of her pelisse. The weight of Lena's letter to Audra rested against her fingers. For the first time, the comfort and strength she usually drew from reading the vellum were missing.

Questions kept needling her. Did Lena ever find any enjoyment in her marriage? If she'd had married another man besides Aulton, would Emma's own perceptions of marriage be skewed differently? How could some couples have success like her parents and Claire and Alex while others seemed doomed from the start to share a horrible union?

No matter how much she cared for Nick, she'd be true to herself. His proposal was a weight tied to her heart. She could easily capitulate and make her family happy and relieved. But she might lose the freedom she so desperately valued.

After she finished her walk, she entered Langham Hall to find Pitts patiently waited. "My lady, the duke and duchess would like a word. They're in the study." He quietly added, "Lord Somerton is with them."

He'd finally come. The urge to flee whipped through her something fierce, but she stood rooted, unable to move. Nick had visited Langham Hall yesterday, but hadn't asked to see her. No doubt the reason for his visit had been to address the swirl of rumors with her father.

Today, they'd put his marriage proposal behind them, then determine the best course of action. Her heart lurched with the sudden realization she and Nick would soon find their relationship completely changed. The only question was whether they'd still be friends—friends who enjoyed an easy companionship or people who avoided each other in order to keep the gossip contained. She straightened her shoulders and tilted her chin, ready to face whatever lay ahead of her.

"Thank you, Pitts."

The butler gave a noncommittal smile. "My lady, my assurance means nothing, but I believe everything happens for a reason."

She turned without answering and headed for the

study. Pitts meant well, but if anything, his words made her more uneasy. When she walked through the door, both her parents and Somerton turned at her entrance.

"Lady Emma, won't you sit down?" Her father waved a hand toward a chair next to her mother. His hard gaze branded her cheeks.

He never called her "Lady Emma" unless she was in dire trouble. The fire's crackle turned into a mocking annoyance as it amplified the hell that surely awaited her.

"Emma, I'm flummoxed at where to begin." Her father spoke quite calmly, but the exasperation in his tone colored every word. "God's teeth, these rumors are vicious. Somerton's come to help put this mess behind you both."

Unable to answer, her gaze flew to Nick.

He walked toward her, his eyes warm as if coaxing her to trust him. With an athletic grace, he quickly moved to her side. She tensed when he reached to take her hand in his.

"Lady Emma, please accept my heartfelt apology if I've caught you unawares." He lowered his voice to a whisper as he bent over her hand. "Circumstances require we act."

Her parents were forcing him to marry her.

"Stop!" She stood and backed far away from her parents and Nick. "We can't marry!" Shock kept her from running out of the room. They hadn't even discussed options. Without her even having the opportunity to voice her opinion, they'd decided her future. Their stratagem felt like a betrayal, and it cut deep with a ragged edge.

Her mother answered without hesitation. "Emma, if Lord Somerton hadn't come forward, no telling how deep the damage to your reputation would be. There is only a small window. You should be thanking him. This isn't some adventure that went haywire. This is life."

There was no anger, but she recognized resignation. Her mother was the most astute person she knew, and she'd accepted this fiasco without question.

"You were aware of the consequences when you set off for Portsmouth." Her father's steely voice vibrated with a barely controlled emotion. He ran his hand over his face. "Personally, I'm not all certain I could withstand another of your escapades. Perhaps Somerton can maintain some control."

"Control? This wasn't an adventure or an escapade. My actions were for Lena. Both of you have raised me to be the type of person who is aware of what is right and wrong." It took every ounce of strength not to scream at the frustration that pulsed through her veins. "You've instilled in me a sense of duty. I followed my heart. And now, I'm to be punished?"

"This isn't punishment. This is having a care for your well-being." Her father's sympathetic gaze rested on her. "Puss, you'll not escape this."

Stunned, she fought for something—anything—to say. Her ability to reason her way out of this was disappearing like sand in an hourglass. "Nothing happened in Portsmouth. What about me having the choice?"

Her father humphed and shook his head. "Here's your choice. Somerton or Lord Paul Barstowe. Both have offered for you. Unfortunately, Lord LaTourell withdrew his interest after the barrage of rumors. He had to protect his sisters."

"That's not a choice." She strove for calmness, but it failed miserably. "Lord Paul offered for me? I haven't seen him. . . ." She couldn't remember the last time they'd met at a social gathering. "What did you do? Approach every duke in the kingdom and ask if their sons would agree to marry me?"

"Puss, believe it or not, they approached me." His

voice was gentle, but there was a hardness in the words, one that foretold she'd not escape.

"Enough." Her mother walked to her father's side. "Lord Somerton has secured a special license. The only solution is that you'll marry."

Her heart began to beat in an erratic pattern, one so off-rhythm it was entirely possible she'd faint. She was to marry? Tonight? What about finding her own purpose? The need to pursue all means to see Lena's death avenged?

As importantly, what about Nick? Everyone in the entire *ton* knew he shunned marriage. He refused to attend any type of social event that carried the smallest hint of matrimony.

For heaven's sake, he'd never even attended Almack's. They were both condemned because of Portsmouth.

The need to rebel rose, and she found the strength to fight. "No."

"Oh yes, my love." Her mother's gentle voice didn't soften the message. "The vicar is waiting in your father's study. The ceremony shall take place immediately. Only family will attend. It will be your father and me, Claire and Alex, McCalpin and William."

Emma winced as if a runaway horse were headed straight for her and she couldn't get out of the way.

Her mother addressed Nick. "Lord Somerton, if you prefer, we could wait until morning when your father is available."

Nick answered in a polite but curt manner, the cold radiating from him apparent to all. "Renton will not attend my marriage."

Her mother nodded, and an awkward silence filled the room.

Emma's mind tried to recall everything Claire had divulged about Nick and his father. There was an estrangement, but over what? She couldn't recall, and it made her panic even greater. What kind of a home and family would she have? She had scant details about his past.

"Then allow our family to act as yours before the ceremony. We certainly will be after the fact, Somerton," her father added with a smile of understanding.

The imaginary horse had throttled her. Her own parents favored Nick at this point.

"Mother, please," she begged. "What if I stayed at Falmont or Claire's Edinburgh estate until another scandal erupts? I could miss the entire next Season if need be." She closed her eyes and concentrated on presenting other options. What if Mary needed her help and she wasn't here? The tangle facing her was becoming more knotted as the seconds slipped by.

Somehow, Nick had moved behind her to provide support while her parents commanded her to accept their demand. The warmth from his body wasn't enough to soften what was happening to them.

"Might Lady Emma and I have a few moments together? If you'd allow us to speak privately in the music room, I could explain my intentions. Perhaps alleviate some of her apprehension?" His voice resonated behind her, and her traitorous body hummed in appreciation.

Was nothing in her control anymore?

Both of her parents nodded their agreement. Nick held a strong, steady grasp on her elbow.

At that moment she understood what the little girl in the woods faced when confronted by the wolf. Only the wolf before her was dressed in breeches and a handsome broadcloth coat. The hair was suspect, but Nick's nose looked perfectly normal.

His valet, Whaley, had tried repeatedly to convince Nick to wear other colors besides his normal black and gray.

He typically dismissed the valet's suggestions since he liked to stay hidden. Colors reminded him of peacocks trying to show off in front of peahens. He'd never wanted any part of that spectacle. For once, he was relieved Whaley had an uncanny knack for pushing him to dress with more care to the current fashion. He'd wanted to look his best tonight when he convinced Emma to marry him.

With his navy velvet waistcoat and buff-colored breeches, Nick was ready to face Emma's inquisition. His effort to secure the music room door caused the piano and harp strings to vibrate in an off-key serenade.

Wary and ready to flee, she stood tall with her verdant eyes following his every move. She clasped her arms tightly around her waist either to ward off the cold or, more likely, the realization she would lose this fight.

"Emma." He attempted to take her in his arms. Her scent reminded him of summer and their nights in Portsmouth. "I owe you an explanation and an apology."

"What possessed you to agree to this?" she hissed with indignation as she darted to the window.

She resembled a wounded animal cornered—ready to lash out and attack. He stepped closer. She didn't move a muscle, but a small tic below her left eye betrayed her distress.

"Together, we could have presented a united front." She lifted her chin and boldly stared back. The defiance in her posture and the challenge in her eyes transformed her. She'd always been beautiful to him, but today, she was stunning in her resistance.

The task was his alone to convince her to see reason. "Circumstances took the decision out of our control. I'll not let you suffer from the vicious rumors."

"What circumstances?" Her eyes glistened with the sheen of tears. She swallowed hard and threw words at him with a newfound strength in her voice. "I won't marry you because of Portsmouth."

The bitterness in her voice made him pause. His future and hers depended on the next few moments. He had to make her understand why their marriage was important to him.

He took a deep breath and prayed for a little help. "All my life I've strived to be a man of integrity. To allow you to bear the brunt of any rumor or innuendo goes against everything I am."

She hugged herself tighter and surveyed the room, but it didn't hide the pain in her eyes.

"Emma, it defines me. Without it, I'm nothing. I beg you, don't take that away from me."

"You deserve more than a marriage resulting from your sense of honor," she whispered. "You must see reason. I deserve more, and more importantly, so do you."

"What do you want? Lord Paul?" He waited for her answer. That it would haunt him for the rest of his life made little difference. If she wanted another, he'd do everything in his power to make her happy, but he'd not stand by and witness someone else take her for his bride.

She shook her head.

He breathed a sigh of relief.

"Love? Romance?" His father's words once again carved another scar, another doubt, whether he deserved happiness of his own. For a fleeting moment, the sudden onslaught of pain had him questioning his ability to make her happy.

"I don't know," she muttered. She rubbed her forehead, then locked her gaze with his. "If I *did* want a husband, I'd want a partner who would need and want me in the same manner that I'd need and want him. Someone who would support my work. Someone to help me . . . forget my past mistakes."

"Won't you let me try to be that man?" he coaxed. "Portsmouth isn't the reason I want to marry you. We're well acquainted, better than most couples who've been married for years." In one stealth stride, he closed the distance between them and clasped her arms. "That's justification to marry."

"How do you even know if I'm worthy of your name?" She hiccupped and turned to view her refuge, Langham Park. She trembled as if hit by a blast of arctic air. As natural as breathing, he needed to touch her. He ran his hands up and down her arms trying to ease her discomfort, then gently turned her to face him.

"How do you know if I'm worthy of you?" As soon as he uttered the words, his father's accusation that no one cared for him reared its ugly head. Would it be the same with her? He cast the thought aside as he grappled with convincing her. "You see, I'm not"—he exhaled—"very successful at courting. If I gave you the impression I didn't care, that's not the truth."

She blinked twice in rapid succession then swallowed. The slim column of her neck mimicked the movement.

"Marry me," he pressed gently.

Her gaze dropped to the floor then returned to his. "I care—"

"I care about you." If he could hold her, he'd whisk away all her reservations. "Hear me out," he whispered. "Do you think I take these actions lightly? I had no choice in this matter. Same as you. The consequences of Portsmouth have led to this juncture. Besides your brothers, others saw us together. Aulton is on a vendetta to ruin you. You'll be the one to suffer the hardest from the rumors, not me. Do you think I care so little about your welfare?"

The amount of pain in her eyes, her own self-doubt along with her reservations about him led him to believe he was losing her. He'd not allow that to happen. "Your parents and I couldn't see another solution."

She chewed her lower lip. On a sigh, her resolve crumpled. She dropped her head and her shoulders at the same time.

"I'd never let you go so easily. After everything"—he lowered his voice—"we've shared?"

Her lips pursed together. "I've never seen your home. Do you have any other estates? What do you do in your leisure? What do you eat? A couple to be married should be privy to such information. We need more time than an hour."

"Are you frightened?"

"No, of course not . . . well, maybe a little." The small glimpse of fear on her face dissolved as her lips tilted in a weak smile.

The tension locked inside his chest started to ease. "I'm not happy we're at this point either." Her green eyes reminded him of the lush meadows of his youth, a place and time when his expectations for life were pure and filled with hope. "But only because I would have handled this all so differently."

Even with a grass-stained gown and hair spilling in a haphazard manner about her face, she was lovely this evening. He took a proverbial deep breath and stepped into the unknown. "Come, be my wife. Let's build a life together."

He took her chin in his hand and raised her head. Slowly, he brought his face toward hers and stopped. Her breath teased his lips, beckoning him to close the distance. Her gaze begged for reassurance.

"If you marry me, you'll see our home this evening. I have a house in Cambridge and several warehouses here in London. I own three ships, and I'm not a picky eater. Luckily, I employ a marvelous, but extremely temperamental, chef. In the past, I preferred the color blue. Now, I much prefer green, the same as your eyes. I have a male servant as my de facto housekeeper. My valet is a prima donna, but he'll entertain you, I promise."

"Thank you." The resignation in her voice made him want to allay her fears, but he was at a loss as to how to ease her discomfort. "Sometime will you tell me about your family? I'd like to—"

"Yes, later." An acute surge of disgust rushed his thoughts. He'd not let his father's poisonous words weaken what he was trying to build with her—a chance for a happy marriage and a happy life.

"Would you like to know my greatest secret?" He drew back and placed his hands on her cheeks. His thumbs traced the gentle angles on her face.

"Yes." Her whisper was as soft as swan's-down.

With the slightest touch, he brushed his lips across hers. On a sigh, she opened to let him in. He wouldn't allow her more and drew back.

"It's you. I want you in my bed tonight and all the nights we have together on this earth. I plan to take you places you won't believe." Hoping she could divine his fervent wishes, he took both of her hands in his. The delicacy of her fingers belied the iron will she'd shown him time and again. "I want to travel the continent, perhaps find adventure in America. I want us to have dinner with Mr. Bentham so you can have all your questions answered."

When he chanced a glance at her face, he wished he hadn't made the effort. Her eyes were hooded, and he couldn't determine if this was the Emma from Lady Emory's ball who could slice him in two with a properly placed word, or the befuddled Emma from Portsmouth when he held her in his arms.

He took a step back and dropped her hands. Never had

he felt so ill-prepared and unsure of the outcome of her decision. He ran his hand through his hair. "This is a poor way of expressing my thoughts."

He had only one thing left to share. God help him if it didn't work. "What I want most in this world is you to want me as much as I want you. Do you understand now?"

A surrendering moan escaped under her breath while her eyes flashed. She curled her fingers in his hair. A gentle tug brought him back to her lips. Her rich scent, the fit of her body against his, and her taste left an indelible mark on him, as if she'd imprinted him as hers.

His heart pounded and his blood raced. Every part of him spiraled in a sudden anarchy, ready to fly apart. He pulled her tighter against him, and it was difficult to determine where he ended and she began. This force between them was an eddy that dragged him deeper into an abyss he never wanted to escape.

She broke free on a gasp. Determined not to let her go that easily, he took her lips again while he circled her waist and gathered her flush to his chest. He'd never understood how a man could become lost in a woman—until this moment. For the first time in his life, he felt it. He wanted to stay lost forever and feel her body next to his.

There was no place else he'd rather be.

She pulled away once more, and her eyes searched his so deeply she feared she'd see everything within him— every noble act and every wicked sin.

"That was it," she whispered.

He struggled for control and the ability to understand. "That was what?"

Her chest heaved, and the pink flush on her face intoxicated him. "The kiss."

He'd told her she'd recognize the "kiss" when it

happened. He hadn't planned it, but this kiss, this force between them, was all-encompassing. "Will it do?"

She nodded once, and her eyes never left his. She was as affected as he was.

"Marry me? If you care for me, have mercy. Marry me."

She nodded again, slowly this time. "Yes, I'll marry you."

Her dulcet whisper was forever engraved on his heart, the one he'd so carefully locked away. Her inherent radiance promised a place where he could escape and bask in her glorious light. His darkness gave way to her, like the night to the day.

She had found him and brought him home.

Chapter Eighteen

A knock on Emma's chamber door echoed through the room like a church bell tolling a somber event. Her mother swept into the room ready for battle. "You may leave us, Arial." Her mother waited until the door closed before she allowed her smile to transform into something luminous. "You and I shall chat before the ceremony."

"What if I'm a failure as a wife?" Emma whispered as she plopped into the chair in front of the fire. The words she thought she'd never utter tasted bitter in her mouth. Only her mother would understand her fears. Even though her mother had prepared her for this day—this new life—the thought of leaving home terrified Emma.

Her mother smoothed her dress, and her gentle smile never faltered. "Failure? Sweetheart, let me explain something to you. Your husband-to-be put aside his work and rushed to accommodate your entrance as his wife. He even instructed his solicitors to start enquiries about a new residence in London—one befitting his countess. He'll ensure you're not a failure. You're lucky."

Her mother's words pummeled Emma's insides. "What if he never loves me? I just gave up my freedom for something I don't understand. I'm in uncharted waters and have no idea how to navigate my way through."

"My lovely girl," her mother whispered. "Love comes in many forms, and sometimes it takes a little while before people recognize it in their heart." Her mother's voice grew tender. "Somerton's protecting you in a way that changes his life too. Look at me."

Resorting to an old habit from childhood, she resisted the urge, but finally gave in. Her mother's will was a force to be reckoned with.

Her mother gracefully sat in the velvet chair opposite Emma's seat.

"You know your Somerton better than I knew your father when we married. You've had the opportunity to spend time with him over the years. He's been a constant presence at family gatherings." Her mother pressed her hand over Emma's and squeezed. "Your Somerton is a patient, kind, and thoughtful man. The way he plays with Claire and Alex's children—"

"Mother, I'm not a child like the twins." How could she make him happy, or be a wife he'd be proud of? She wasn't like other women. She had her own dreams of how she wanted to live her life, and none of it entailed the responsibilities expected of an earl's wife.

"It's apparent to your father and me that Somerton has a *tendré* for you. And you for him." Her mother rose and kissed her cheek. "Give this a chance. Go and take your place by your Somerton's side."

"I don't know what to do. How to act." Her breathing grew labored as the reality of her situation settled.

"There's no need to act. Be yourself." Her mother's blue eyes were a constant in Emma's life. Whenever she needed comfort, she always found it in her mother's tender gaze. Her mother released a deep breath. "I need to tell you what happens in the marriage bed. You both have a responsibility to make each other happy. To cherish each other."

Of all the things she expected her mother to say tonight, the topic of lovemaking was not on her list. "Claire explained it to me," Emma said. She studied the fire and snuck a peek at her mother. "Don't worry. I'm prepared."

"That's what I thought." Her mother quirked an eyebrow and regarded her. "You're full of life and that's irresistible. He's under your spell."

"Thank you." Her mother meant to soothe with her kind words, but it was far from the truth. "I don't want to leave you or Father." The confession proved what a coward she was. "I don't want to leave my home."

Her mother nodded in understanding. "I was scared when I married your father." She tilted Emma's chin until she held her gaze. "But he was so gentle and loving to me that within days I knew where my home and heart resided. You understand?"

Emma nodded as she fought against her tears.

"This is a big step for both of us it seems. I'll miss you, too." Her mother's whisper betrayed her own tears as she gathered Emma in her arms and squeezed tight. "Your Nick is a wonderful man. I can only let you go because in my heart I know he'll care for you, and in return, you'll care for him."

"I love you," Emma whispered. "I'm lucky to have you as my mother."

"I love you, too. I'm *so* lucky you're my daughter." Her mother stepped away to wipe Emma's eyes with a handkerchief. "You're beautiful with your tears." Her mother swallowed hard and straightened her shoulders. A duchess through and through, she called out as she glided to the door, "Your father and I will see you downstairs."

The pleasant drone of the vicar buzzed around the salon. The service barely registered as Nick looked at his wife-to-be. Emma had dug in her heels about changing into a more suitable gown. It made little difference to him her dress sported grass stains from her earlier walk. She could wear a horse blanket, and he'd still see every inch of her beauty inside and out.

With an exhale, he released the nervous energy trapped inside his chest. Vaguely, the vicar announced his name, Nicholas Armand Drake St. Mauer, the Earl of Somerton. More importantly, he was marrying Lady Emma Eliza Juliana Cavensham, a woman whose sigh had signaled her resignation. From now on, her fate and her life were irretrievably entwined with his.

Her gaze held his as they stood beside each other. He squeezed her hand to reassure her. She wanted romance and courtship, not some hurried service her parents prayed would forestall the gossips determined to mock her. From this point forward, she was his, and he would see her protected, cherished, and most importantly— happy.

The deep crevice between the vicar's eyebrows warned he grew tired of the service. Nick had allowed his thoughts to wander and repeatedly had to ask the vicar to restate some parts of the vows. Emma seemed to suffer from the same affliction.

The vicar tapped his toe as if calling both of them to attend him. "My lord, the ring?"

"What ring?" He paid little heed to the question as all his focus was dedicated to his lovely bride.

"My lord, we can't continue the ceremony without the

ring." The vicar rolled his eyes and heaved a breath. "Shall I come back later?"

Emma's eyes grew round, and the most mischievous and effervescent smile broke across her face. It took every ounce of resolve not to pick her up and carry her out of the salon, an act declaring to the world she was his.

She made a half turn and faced him with her back to the witnesses, namely her entire family. Her stance ensured they were in their own private world. "We can't marry."

"Pardon?" His mind refused to give credence to her words.

The humor in her eyes glistened like finely cut diamonds. "The church requires you place a ring on my finger to symbolize our union, our partnership. Where's the ring?"

"Exactly. Where's the ring?" The vicar chimed in like an unruly parrot. It wouldn't be a surprise if the man next demanded a plate of seeds.

"A ring," Nick repeated. A war of emotions fought to gain control, but his brain retaliated and demanded an assault head-on. "I need to give you a ring?"

Her seductive scent wrapped around him, but other matters took precedence. How could he have forgotten? The service required he place a ring on her finger.

"Indeed, my lord." The delight in her answer broke a dam within him.

A warning whispered he should proceed with caution. Without a ring, she could walk out the room, out of his life, and no one could stop her. The vicar would probably be the first to escort her so he could finish the rest of his evening in the company of someone who would actually listen to him.

Nick bent his head to hers, but didn't allow her to look away. This was an honest escape if she desired. He didn't even want to contemplate the ensuing loneliness if he let her go. His father's words once again had come home to roost and steal the sliver of happiness he'd found for his future.

For an eternity, her gaze locked with his in a battle of wills. "This is quite a conundrum." As he waited for her verdict, he felt heavy and stiff as if a sudden voracious fever had invaded his body.

Emma glanced at the double doors, then back to him—the most beguiling smile lit her from within.

Her brother, McCalpin, cleared his throat.

Nick glanced over Emma's head. The duke had his head bent to the duchess.

"Emma?" The duke's baritone voice rang through the room.

She didn't waste a glance at her family.

"I've always subscribed to the thought that when you see an opportunity, run with it." The corner of Emma's mouth twitched and drew his attention to the beauty spot adjacent to her naturally red lips. "The way I see it, I have one choice. Wouldn't you agree, my lord?"

She was playing with him like a cat batting its prey before the kill. "My lady, I agree you have a choice. However, the way I see it you have more than one."

She nodded her head and tried to appear sincere as she contemplated his answer. "I hate to disagree, but you're wrong."

Behind him, her family grew restless with agitated murmurs.

"I only have one." She held his gaze.

The simple declaration set off alarm bells.

"What are they doing?" the duke demanded.

"Sebastian, wait." Steel threaded through the duchess's whisper. "Allow them to work this out."

"What are they working out?" Pembrooke asked.

"Lord Somerton and Lady Emma?" the vicar asked, not hiding his growing impatience.

"I do apologize, sir." Emma's gaze never strayed from Nick's as she addressed the vicar. "We won't be much longer, but you, above all, understand the importance of this moment."

"Give him my ring, Alex." Claire's alto voice cascaded toward them.

William finally joined the fray. "She's leaving. Ten-to-one odds she walks out the door."

"*Bloody hell*," growled Pembrooke. "He didn't bring a ring?"

The vicar humphed at Alex's profanity.

Emma lowered her voice. "I will marry you."

Nick strained to hear the soft whisper.

"I could no more leave your side than I could fly across the moon. I gave you my promise."

Inside his chest, every gnarled organ relaxed.

"I'm yours forever." She took his left hand in hers and squeezed. "Give me your signet ring."

Relief pounded through him as he slipped off his seal ring, the one with the lion guarded by a shield, the Earl of Somerton crest. He took her left hand in his and placed it on her finger. The gold was still warm from his body heat. "Have I told you today that you're brilliant?"

"No, but that should be part of your vows. Now, pay attention." Emma returned to her place beside him and faced the vicar.

"You're beautiful, too," he whispered.

Nick didn't waste a glance at anyone. His focus was entirely on his lovely wife. It made little difference the vicar had yet to finish the ceremony. They were married. The simple act of giving her his ring bound them together.

She'd pull him from the mire once again with her

clever solution. He'd suffer through all the loss and humiliation at his father's hands again and again if this was
his reward, a life with Emma.

"I beg you, may we proceed?" the vicar asked. "I
would prefer to arrive home before the morning."

The sun had already set when Emma and Nick started
for Somer House, her *husband's* town house and now her
new home. Soon, the coach slowed to a stop. Nick sprang
from the carriage in one smooth movement.

She placed her hand in his. He rewarded her with a
reassuring squeeze of his fingers as he guided her to the
sidewalk. Her gaze darted to the double entrance doors
that led into his bachelor residence—*former* bachelor
residence. The all-male domain would be demolished as
soon as she and Arial stepped inside.

"Welcome home, Lady Somerton." He brought her
gloved hand to his lips, and she almost missed the wink
from his left eye.

The small gesture caused her heartbeat to stutter. She
bit her lip to stifle a grin but lost the battle.

Nick bent low and whispered in her ear. "What a welcome sight—my wife bestowing one of her dazzling
smiles on me."

She tried to ease some of the tension between them.
"We really didn't have a chance to talk after the wedding.
We were both quiet on the way here."

"We'll have plenty of time later on." Never slowing
his pace, he led her up the steps into the town house.
Two men stood at attention as if guarding the royal
palace.

"Lady Somerton, let me introduce Hamm, our butler.
He served as my father's underbutler until he joined my
household. Mr. Martin acts as my housekeeper."

Emma nodded her acquaintance to her husband's

staff. "Lady Somerton" and "our butler" still buzzed in her head.

Both servants bowed in front of her but neither spoke. Their faces reminded her of an audience watching a magic act. Neither seemed to believe what appeared in front of them.

She'd trained for this moment all her life with the best possible teacher, her mother. She shoved aside her nervousness. "Hamm, thank you for the warm welcome. I'll need your assistance as I become acquainted with Lord Somerton's schedule." She turned to the housekeeper. "Mr. Martin, perhaps tomorrow we could discuss the management of the earl's household, and you could show me the house?"

Mr. Martin nodded. "My lady, anytime you wish to talk I'm available. It's a small staff, and we all help each other."

"Thank you." Before she could ask another question, Nick interrupted.

"Will you have a bath prepared for the countess?" Nick brought Emma's hand to rest on his arm and placed his over hers. "Shall we go up?"

Without a look back, they proceeded up the stairs.

She stopped Nick on the landing. "Shouldn't I meet the rest of the staff?" The situation was confusing enough without the closeness of his body addling her senses. The clean fragrance of soap layered his familiar scent of bay rum and his unique male smell. She could breathe it in all day.

"It will have to wait until tomorrow." His next words left no doubt he was finished with the conversation. "I'll show you to your rooms."

The parchment tucked inside Nick's pocket crinkled when he raised his hand to knock on Emma's door. Would she be pleased with his gift? Within minutes, he'd know the verdict: if her eyes brightened to a brilliant emerald green, then she was happy. He'd worked quickly this morning to get everything arranged for her new endeavor.

Nick had given their staff the evening free. The temperamental cook had demanded the entire day off. Before he went to visit his sister, Mr. Martin, the unofficial housekeeper, had prepared a light dinner with a wonderful vintage champagne for Emma's pleasure. Tonight, Nick would have her in his arms and in his bed. Perhaps then he could get back to his work. His life had to return to normal soon as work was increasing at an alarming rate.

After his brief knock, Emma's maid opened the door, then curtsied. "My lord."

"Good evening, Arial." Nick waited for the invitation to enter Emma's private chambers.

The whole day had turned completely strange. He was lord and master over every square inch of this residence, but within the last several hours, things had changed. Now he must knock on his wife's door, the one next to his, the one that had always stood empty.

His wife's door.

Emma called out, "Come in. I'm ready." When she stood from the dressing table, he truly had entered another world. Dressed in a gorgeous seafoam-green gown trimmed in matching satin ribbon, she reminded him of a present wrapped in silk, for his pleasure to unwrap as soon as he had her alone.

"You may leave us. Enjoy your evening," Nick said while never taking his eyes off Emma. Arial silently slipped out after his command.

Emma tilted her head. "Arial didn't say anything about taking the night off."

In two strides, he stood before her. She smelled of

something pure and beautiful. "In celebration, I've given everyone the evening free. We're by ourselves."

Emma swallowed. Her luminous eyes widened in surprise. "Oh . . ." Innocent as she was, she had no idea how sensuous her voice sounded.

"You"—he tipped up her chin to look at him—"and me. Alone."

He pressed his lips to hers, a sweet start to the evening and one designed to coax her to relax. She tasted like the freshest summer berries. He was desperate to deepen the kiss but wanted to feed her first, so he gently pulled back. Her eyes slowly opened. She looked bewitched and unable to move.

When Emma reached for her kidskin gloves, he grabbed her hand and raised it to his lips. "Nothing is between us this evening. I want to feel your fingers intertwined with mine."

She lowered her eyes, and her hand fluttered in his.

This was not the woman who had tried to seduce him in Portsmouth. Was she frightened of him, frightened of what would happen tonight? He had the perfect solution to dispel her sudden shyness.

"I have something for you." He pulled the paper from the inside pocket of his evening coat. "A wedding gift."

"What is it?"

"Open it."

Her finger broke the seal, and she bent her head. When she finished reading, she lifted her gaze, and the dazzling green of her eyes lit the entire room. "You're giving me a bank?"

"Not a physical bank, but the means and a place of operation. I thought you could start with ten thousand pounds. I have a business acquaintance, Mr. Macalester, who owns a building on the corner of Grosvenor and Bond. He has a small shop for let that would be a perfect location based on your research. Mr. Sedgeworth has serviced my banking needs for years and said he'd be honored to help you get started. He's planning to approach you about investing in it."

The smile that slowly grew across her face proved he'd made the right choice of presents. Suddenly, she stood on tiptoes and pressed a kiss against his cheek. "This is the best gift I've ever received."

Her simple touch was like kindling to his flame. They had all evening to enjoy each other, but at this moment, he wanted to take her in his arms and never let go. "I'm pleased you like it."

She walked to the fireplace, increasing the distance between them. It gave him a perfect vantage point to admire her form. He always thought her striking, but tonight she was radiant.

"I never in my wildest imaginations thought you'd give me this. I expected jewelry."

A rock landed in his chest. In his haste, he hadn't gotten her a wedding ring. His father possessed all of the Renton jewelry the previous duchesses in their family had worn. It would take the devil himself to make Nick ask for anything from his father. "Tomorrow, let me take you shopping for something."

"Please, no. This is brilliant." She came and stood in front of him. "The reason I mentioned jewelry is because Claire always receives some bauble from Pembrooke for special occasions." Emma studied the piece of paper clasped in her hand. "The man has no imagination, but Claire loves him blindly. So, he must have some redeeming qualities."

His answer was a quick nod since her devastating grin left him speechless. Images of a besotted Claire and an even more besotted Alex flashed before him. A jolt of pain pierced his newfound jubilation. It was a waste of time and beyond foolish to want that type of marriage with Emma. It would lead to nothing but disappointment and heartache. It was better to keep this easiness between them and not have grandiose expectations of something deeper.

She fidgeted with the ribbon trim tied around her waist. "I didn't get you a present."

"How could you? There was no time. I don't need—" He soothed his hand over hers, the soft skin enticing him to explore each inch of her. "Actually there is something I want."

She bent her head to hide the most-becoming cherry blush on her cheeks.

"Join me for dinner?"

When she raised her eyes to his, the sparkle was back. She looked like a woman who could rule the world without question. There was only one word to describe her—magnificent.

He led her downstairs and escorted her to an extremely small but cozy room off his study. He used it as a private reading nook. Mr. Martin had built a nice fire that cast a crimson glow around the room, making it pleasant and perfect for a romantic evening.

A table set for two sat before a wall of windows that overlooked a small, secluded courtyard. Various covered dishes and candles of different heights were scattered across the tabletop.

"Oh . . . this is wonderful."

"I'm delighted you're pleased." When Nick had promised himself he'd give Emma romance, he was determined to be a man of his word. He pulled out a chair and helped her sit, then proceeded to pour two glasses of champagne.

"May the adventure of our lifetime together start tonight and never end." His toast earned a look of awe, then a wrinkle of her nose and an affectionate grin. Indeed, marriage had the possibility of fitting into his schedule quite nicely.

"That's lovely." With a coquettish grin, she offered her own. "To my darling husband, may tonight be the first night of many we share as equals in our new adventure."

Before he took the first sip, he nodded hesitantly. "Your toast reminds me of something I learned from a classics tutor. Didn't some philosopher say that a woman becomes a man's superior if she's made his equal?"

"It was credited to Socrates in *Wits Common-Wealth* by Nicholas Ling. That's where I came up with the idea for the toast." Emma lifted her glass and took a sip.

He followed her lead. All the while wondering how he'd keep a step ahead of her if the need ever arose. "Shall we eat?"

He lifted the first cover off the large silver tray in front of them and peered at the congealed mass on the platter. It resembled boiled beef and potatoes covered in some type of sauce. Of all the nights to be at the mercy of his waspish chef, tonight was not the night.

Emma politely picked at her meal. Within minutes, her stomach let out a howl of disgruntlement, and her eyes widened as she placed her hand over her stomach. "I apologize."

Nick stood and extended his hand out to capture hers. "Let's go see what we can find in the kitchen. Bread and jam will be a feast."

If he could kick himself, he would. What a complete flop of a dinner, the first of his married life. It was apparent he had no finesse, but tonight he had planned to woo her. She deserved to have a night of passion and sensual pleasure. It was the least he could do for the lousy dinner he gave her. His father would no doubt be delighted he'd made such a strategic error.

Chapter Nineteen

Nick took her hand in his as they walked to the kitchen. His palm was so large it swallowed hers. Instead of warmth and comfort, his touch set her skin tingling and stoked a tumultuous heat that resided low in her belly. They would make love tonight, and that simple fact twisted every nerve until she felt on edge.

Claire had mentioned the first time there would be pain and a little bleeding. How long would it hurt? How much bleeding? She should have thought this through and asked more questions.

After the champagne toast and the unveiling of the meal, which a scientist would delicately describe as "gray matter," their conversation had grown awkward and stilted once again. She'd done her best to keep it going, but her husband hadn't uttered a peep.

When they reached the kitchen, a block of fresh cheese and a loaf of bread sat on the table. Nick reached into a pine cabinet and fetched two apples. "Do I have your promise not to throw these at me?"

"If you behave." She tried to keep her voice light and honeyed, but a breathy whisper escaped.

He retrieved a cutting knife and placed the items on the table. With a heavy-lidded gaze, Nick bent toward her and brushed his lips across her cheek. "I don't want to behave. Not tonight. Or any night in the foreseeable future."

His eyes devoured her with such intensity she could almost feel his touch invade every corner of her soul. The look sent a rush of heat to her cheeks. Her legs protested having to stand. She grabbed the knife and fumbled with the bread. Before she could retrieve the wayward loaf, his warm hand covered hers.

"Allow me." With his front to her back, he wrapped his arms around her until he held the loaf in one hand and the knife with her hand in the other. His arms brushed against the sides of her breasts. She closed her eyes at the slight touch, every part of her on alert.

The warmth of his solid chest enveloped her. If he touched any other part of her body, she'd combust into flames.

As he cut the bread and the apples, he bent over her until his cheek rested against hers. His freshly shaved skin caressed her as the smell of the fresh baked bread rose to greet them. She couldn't think of food since a riot of sensations had taken control of her turncoat body.

Nick placed a slice of cheese on a piece of bread and brought it to her mouth. "You first."

Somehow, she managed a small bite. The simple act of sharing was so private and intimate that another flush stole across her cheeks.

He took the next bite. When he offered her another, she refused with a headshake. Her mouth and brain warred with each other. As a result, she couldn't form a coherent thought, let alone a word, as she watched him eat.

Nick pushed the food away. In one move, he picked

her up by the waist and sat her on the table facing him. It was the perfect height to study his features.

His lips twitched. "We'll save the apples for later. I intend to be very bad right now."

A frisson of unease caused her to shiver. He caught her chin and wouldn't allow her to look away. His eyes darkened with an intensity that should have given her pause. He moved her legs apart so he could step between them.

"I want to taste you." His hand traced a path from the curve of her heel to the back of her knee.

At his touch, she wrapped her arms around his neck and pushed against him, desperate for more of his heat, more of him. All nervousness forgotten.

Both of them moaned, expressing the need to get closer to the other.

His hands settled low on her hips, and he positioned her until she was flush against his erection. The movement caused a deep growl in his chest. His mouth moved over hers, hungry and powerful. She opened, and he took charge with an incendiary kiss. In response, she pressed harder against him.

He caressed the back of her knees before finding the hem of her dress. At a tortured pace, his hands slowly trailed up her stockings until he stroked the inside of her bare thighs. His lips left hers. Carefully placed kisses brushed against her cheeks until he found the sensitive spot below her ear. "You aren't wearing anything underneath?"

"Except slippers and stockings," she gasped. Disorder reigned throughout her body and thoughts. "Nothing's underneath my dress."

"You're trying to kill me." For a moment, he rested his head on her shoulder before gently biting her earlobe.

"I disagree. There's undeniable beauty hidden beneath here." He brushed his fingers through her nest of curls.

She whimpered at his intimate touch.

Nick lowered himself before her until he rested on his haunches. "Bring up your skirts and watch me." His smoky-dark voice mesmerized her.

She released a breath as her legs trembled at the thought Nick would taste her.

Once again, he trailed his fingers through her curls, then caressed her inner thighs. With his hands gently holding her legs apart, he kissed her *there*. His breath fanned against her skin.

She closed her eyes at his exquisite touch. Anything he wanted to do to her, she'd allow it.

"Watch me," he whispered. His tongue flicked out and separated her folds.

Her breath caught at the delicate breach of his tongue. Such pure, sweet torment.

He smiled, his eyes flashing brighter than a jolt of lightning, and he repeated the movement again. Every nerve fired at his touch. She stroked his hair as he continued to lick her. Her breath grew more and more ragged until she panted.

"Do it again," she pleaded.

When he repeated the movement, she shivered as the sensation built and billowed within her body. She pressed her hips toward his mouth. He licked her again.

"Do you know when you're aroused, your flesh becomes swollen here?" The hunger in his eyes startled her. He wanted this as much as she did. He took her finger and pressed against the wet heat of her center.

His tongue licked her finger and her swollen flesh. She shifted closer and pressed her eyes shut as flashes of light exploded. Heat scattered from her center. Too weak to resist, she gave over to the sensation as it swept through her. She was close—so close.

"Nick—" Her release rolled through every part of her body. Intense, the pleasure controlled every nerve, every part of her being. In response, she clenched her thighs against his shoulders.

He continued to kiss her there while whispering sweet murmurs of how beautiful she was.

When her body floated back under her control, he rose and gently set her skirts over her legs.

The hunger in his eyes, similar to a night predator determined to be satiated, caused her muscles to tighten. She wanted every inch of him over her, around her, and in her. Their bed seemed a mile away.

Breathless, she managed a simple question. "Will you help me undress?"

"Here?" The word didn't hide his whispered shock.

She nodded. "The bed is too far to walk."

"No, we are not consummating our marriage in the kitchen." Within seconds, he swept her in his arms. Startled, Emma laced her hands behind his neck and burrowed deep within his grasp. She tasted his skin as she caressed her lips up and down his jaw. Soon, she would have his naked body next to hers, and she was not going to let him leave the bed anytime soon.

Nick carried her upstairs to her bedroom then kicked the door shut. Gently, he lowered her until her slippers hit the floor. She found herself pressed against the door as he captured her again in a kiss. His arms formed a bracket around her head.

It was difficult determining what was harder—Nick or the door. Emma shivered and pressed her body against his. Without taking his gaze from hers, he gently removed her hairpins. The weight of her chignon fell down her back. Impatient, he ripped the fastenings on the back of her dress. He covered her in kisses—her shoulders, her neck, even the hollow of her throat—as her dress fell to the floor.

She struggled to rid him of the gray coat and navy waistcoat that hid his body. Both of them panted as if they'd run a mile. He pulled off his boots, then with a flick of his wrist, he untied his cravat and lifted his shirt over his head. She sucked in her breath and caressed his chest, all sinew, muscle, and golden skin.

With their fingers entwined, his gaze slowly swept the length of her body. She froze where she stood, acutely aware of his stare. Flames licked her cheeks as she waited.

"You're perfection." He kissed her with a slow innocence. Her emotions and thoughts swirled into a muddled mess. He added to the chaos with his hand cradling one of her breasts, his thumb teasing her nipple. "Every day I'll tell you so."

He never took his eyes from hers as he undressed. Emma felt the loss of his warmth but waited for what was to come. Deliberately slow, he unbuttoned the fall on his breeches and let them fall. She caught her first glimpse of his cock. Its thickness jutted away from his body toward her. The crown glistened with a pearly liquid.

For a moment, she lost the ability to breathe. Broad shoulders, striated muscles, and narrow hips. She'd never seen such a sight. As if drawn to catalog his physical form, she studied every muscle and sinew. How could a man be so beautiful?

Her gaze settled on the engorged thickness of his cock. How would it ever fit? "Is it uncomfortable . . . like that?"

A pure look of satisfaction crossed his face. "If you

had an inkling of how much, you'd run." The deep low whisper pulsed in time with the ache below her belly.

She wanted him to take her and stop this delightful torture. Her trust overshadowed any fear. She moved to the bed and held out her hand for him to join.

He covered her with his body, and his heat surrounded her. His hands, strong and sure, caressed her as they lay on top of the coverlets. Soft and made from the finest linen, the bedclothes were sensuous to the touch. He kissed her again, and she was lost as he ravished her with his tongue.

"Please." She brushed her lips over his. "Hurry."

Slowly, he raised his body onto his elbows. Passion made his eyes heavy, and his mouth appeared ready to plunder every part of her body. "I've patiently waited for this night, and as my reward, I plan to take my time."

She caught his face in her hands and raised her lips to his. He moaned, and the sound caused his chest to vibrate against hers. She gave him every emotion she could in that kiss before she responded, "I've never felt this way— except with you."

She'd never tire of his body, but more importantly, she'd never tire of him. Deliberately, she traced his flat abdomen until she found the course curls that cradled his erection. He placed his own hand over hers and showed her how to touch him.

She never expected the contrast of smooth velvet skin to encircle his hot, rigid length. With a slow and steady caress, she ran her hand up his cock.

He delivered a smile laced with sin. With her finger, she traced the slit at the tip, slick with moisture. "I could kiss you here. Shall we see if you'd like it?"

"Enough." His voice turned smoky in its whispers. He grabbed her by the neck and brought her forward for another scalding kiss while his finger rubbed and circled her clitoris. He nipped at her lips before he took her mouth again. She ached in her want for him. Impatient, she bucked into his hand.

"We can't rush this." The warning in his words was clear.

She trembled and took a breath, signaling she'd let him attend her without interference—at least for a while. She inhaled sharply when one finger inched its way inside. Foreign, yet it felt tight. He nuzzled her neck as he sucked and kissed a tender spot. She sighed, then whimpered as his thumb continued the sweet torment of circling her tender nub. A second finger joined the first.

His whisper was almost a caress against her skin. "How you respond to my touch." The fullness was still there but it didn't overtake the exquisite sensation that was starting to build. She was close to falling again.

He cradled her head, the touch almost unbearable in its tenderness, as he continued his slow, drugging kisses. His eyes were bright with passion.

"I'm going to take you now." His silken voice enveloped her. "This might be painful the first time. I promise this will be the only time I ever hurt you." He waited as if asking for her permission.

She smiled at his words. How could she not? She loved him. She closed her eyes at the shock. She loved him with everything in her being. She'd loved him for so long and never realized it. Finally, she could experience everything that she'd dreaded the emotion would entail. It was perfect because it was Nick. "The only thing I care about is having you."

He guided himself to her entrance and slowly moved inside her. She moved her legs and wrapped them around his waist to find a way to relieve the discomfort. Sweat covered his body from his evident restraint.

"Look at me." He brought her face to his and kissed

her lips gently at first. He nibbled. The distraction made her forget the fullness.

With a swift push of his hips, he entered her completely. She felt a pinch and the pressure of his invasion. By pure instinct, she pushed away from his hard body. He froze above her.

"Sweetheart, don't move. Give me a moment, or I'll not be able to make it good for you."

"I'm fine," she whispered, but tears welled in her eyes.

"I'm so . . . so sorry I hurt you." He kissed tip of her nose and then bent his head as if trying to control himself. "My brave darling." He delivered a slow kiss along her jaw. "You're giving. Passionate." He delivered a similar slow kiss along the other side of her jaw. "Completely exquisite."

With each word and touch, she softened. He kissed her as he slowly withdrew, then entered her again. And again. Each time he withdrew, she whimpered at the sense of loss.

He cradled her his arms and rocked within her. Soon he came to her mouth and kissed her with his tongue mimicking his movements. It didn't take long until she felt the pleasure building once again, attempting to crest. She moaned and moved with him as she was close to coming.

Her center clenched around him as he flooded her with his own release. He groaned her name on a sigh.

Together they held each other as their breaths returned to normal. She felt something wet on her cheeks and realized tears were falling.

His arms around her gave her comfort, and his body cocooned every inch of her in heat. His breath softly fanned her face. "Thank you. I've never experienced anything more beautiful than you."

She had no regrets, none whatsoever, that he made her wait for her wedding night. This was one of life's most perfect moments, and she was happy and content it was with Nick, her husband.

Unlike anything she'd ever experienced, somehow, he had seized all her thoughts and desires, everything she understood about herself, and rearranged them into some creature she didn't recognize.

Nick's breathing slowed. He twisted until he lay on his side facing her with their noses a scant distance apart. His lips touched hers briefly. "You asked about my father."

She scooted close until their bodies aligned, chest to chest, all her attention on his soulful eyes.

"We were never close. At the age of five, I started attending boarding schools. Briefly, I'd go home for school holidays, but he never spent much time with me. My mother died in childbirth, and my father never remarried."

His mouth was set in a determined line, but his eyes were pinched as if sharing this secret cost him in ways she didn't understand. The hurt he allowed her to glimpse made her breath catch. She traced a gentle pattern across his chin hoping the simple touch would ease his pain.

"I never had many friends. However, at Eton, Lord Paul, for whatever reason, took a shine to me. One day, he found a card game and lost. He couldn't cover his debts, and I signed for them on his promise he'd have the funds within the week. I didn't know it at the time, but his reputation was to play deep without ever paying for his previous vowels. When they threatened violence, I helped him."

The husky resonance of his voice drew her focus to his lips. That he was sharing such a confession made her heart heavy. Yet, she recognized it as a precious gift, one she'd cherish forever.

"I asked my father for the funds. He came to school furious, but he paid it. Before he left, he humiliated me in front of some of my classmates by cutting me off. He told me not to come home. From that day forward I swore I'd never set foot on Renton soil again, nor would I ever acknowledge him." He closed his eyes. "I vowed to do whatever it took to exceed his wealth."

For a moment, she thought he wouldn't say anymore. Then, he took her wrist, the one injured, and brought it to his lips.

"In so many words, he informed me I was worthless and no one cared for me." He continued with his lips on her pulse, the vibration of his words tickling her skin. "You tell that to a fifteen-year-old boy, and he'll believe it. However, Pembrooke proved Renton wrong. Alex found me ill one day and gave me assistance. We've been friends ever since."

Diaphanous pieces of her heart broke away as Nick recounted the duke's spiteful scorn. She couldn't fathom the hate her husband had endured. "Have you seen your father since?"

"No. The day I step foot on the ancestral estate will be the day he dies." His gruff voice belied the agony in his turquoise eyes. Under normal circumstances, the heat from his body would distract her, but the plaintive lines about his face told her volumes. The urge to cry out and curse his father for hurting her husband became unbearable.

"That's why Pembrooke, your family, and especially you are so dear to me."

Such a simple admission caused her heart to rip in two. He had no one growing up. He'd suffered through all of it because of a malevolent father who exercised the power to destroy a precious relationship, one that should have been nurtured and protected. She'd give anything to cure the loneliness of his past and ensure nothing would have the power to scar him again.

She brushed a silken strand of his hair away from his eyes, as she wanted his full attention. "What was your mother's name?"

"Laura," he whispered. As if suddenly uncomfortable, he stood and walked to a basin. He made quick work of wetting a toweling. Her attention, the fickle beast it was, focused on the long line of his body. It was a piece of art, a thing of amazing beauty.

When he returned to her side, he took the cloth and gently washed her. He murmured compliments about her toes and nonsensical words of affection about her elbows as he went about the task. Whether he said it or not, he was clear—she was part of his life. What he needed to know was that she belonged to him.

Could she really be that type of woman—one who vowed to make her husband happy and do everything in her power not to see him suffer any heartache? After tonight, she could easily see herself in that role. After what they just shared, she wanted nothing more than to prove she loved him. Whatever it took, he'd never suffer again.

When he finished the task, he washed himself. He came back to their bed and pulled her into his arms. "Someday, tell me one of your secrets," he whispered before capturing her lips with the sweetest fervor.

His breathing grew even and quiet. Cocooned in his arms, she kissed the space above his heart. Perhaps one day she'd tell him why she fought so hard for the things she wanted. However, not now. She'd not ruin what they created tonight.

I love you. She wanted to whisper the words, but if he could hear her, he'd think she said it out of pity.

She really had turned into a different creature.

Leaving a tousled, thoroughly pleasured Emma was the definition of torture. In the morning, Nick had found her curled next to him with his arm as her pillow and her hand resting against his heart. He wanted to shirk every responsibility and stay by her side in the perfect world they'd created. For the first time in years, he wanted to hurry through work so he could spend the day with her.

He untangled the bedclothes and stole one last look. Sound asleep, she lay in the middle of the bed with her golden hair spread like a crown atop her head. The wonder of it all still amazed him. Even the house possessed a different sensibility because of her presence.

With a lightness he'd never felt, he made his way to his study. He settled at his desk with a cup of coffee and a pile of unrelenting bookkeeping that awaited him there.

"I apologize, Lord Somerton, for the intrusion. Congratulations on your marriage." Whaley, his valet, possessed a flair for the dramatic. Better suited for the stage, he was always eager to share his expressive nature. But his grim smile today was completely out of character.

"Thank you. When the countess comes down, I'll introduce you to her."

With his hands clasped behind his back, Whaley nodded. "Let's hope she's a late riser."

"Pardon?" Nick asked.

"You have a visitor, the Earl of Aulton, who insists upon seeing you." Whaley's face twisted in a frown as if presented with an orange waistcoat and a clashing pale violet evening coat.

Nick leaned back in his chair and contemplated his valet. "Did he state his business?"

"Something about offering felicitations." Whaley's nose tilted two inches in the air. "Not someone I'd want our countess to see this morning."

"Send him in." Nick stood and walked around the desk. It made a perfect place to lean as he awaited his visitor.

Aulton swept into the room with a black greatcoat billowing like a ship's sail behind him. It added a certain menace to his swarthy looks. "Lord Somerton, thank you for receiving me. I won't take up much of your time, but I understand there's happy news. Congratulations."

Nick didn't acknowledge his presence or his good wishes. With a blatant ease that hid his fury, Nick pushed away from his desk and approached.

Smaller by half a foot, Aulton faced him with a smile that failed to reach his eyes. If anything, his gaze resembled a dead shark, cold and lifeless. An appropriate comparison for a cold-blooded killer.

With a deep breath, he brought his right fist back in a calculated move, one designed to provide notice of what was about to happen. It was the only opportunity Nick would give the earl to defend himself.

He thrust forward with his fist and cuffed Aulton square in the nose. The force of the punch snapped the man's head back with a sickening crunch of bones and cartilage. Spurts of bright red blood spewed through the air. Soon, rivers of red trailed down Aulton's face, spoiling the snowy-white cravat tied around his neck.

"That's for touching my wife," Nick growled. His right fist throbbed from the impact, but he ignored it. With his left fist, he delivered an uppercut to the tender flesh under Aulton's neck already slick with blood. The punch carried enough momentum that the blackguard lost his balance and fell atop a Chippendale table. The wood split apart with a deafening racket and collapsed into a pile of kindling.

"That's for marking her skin." Nick bent and grasped the greatcoat in two hands and hauled the earl to his feet. By now, the blood oozing from the broken nose had begun to darken. "If you ever, and mark my words, *ever* come near her again, I'll kill you."

Aulton cowered.

"You cringe in absolute fear when someone fights back," Nick taunted, his own blood roaring through his veins. He barely restrained the snarling beast inside his chest that demanded he continue his brutal punishment. With a couple of well-placed strategic hits, Aulton would be mortally wounded. He pulled his fist back, but his conscience roared for him to leave it. Lady Lena's honor wasn't his fight. Nick released him with a push, and Aulton fell again. "Get out of my house."

Stunned, the immoral wretch didn't move. Finally, he retrieved a handkerchief and held it under his nose. The grunts and groans were a twisted macabre melody to Nick's ears as Aulton slowly got to his feet.

The skin beneath the earl's eyes had started to darken from the punch to the face. By morning, both eyes would be black to match his soul. A fitting advertisement that Nick wouldn't tolerate anyone disparaging his wife.

"Let me return the favor. The warning that is. Your little barbarian show is quite an effective amusement. However, I have another party I'd like to invite you to." Aulton swallowed as if in pain and coughed a spray of blood.

"No, thank you," Nick sneered.

"It's too late," Aulton jeered. "Today, my solicitor will serve no less than four different suits against you to your solicitor." He staggered, but caught himself. "You can save yourself the heartache and expense. All you have to do is keep your wife under control. If she says one more word about me or my late countess, I'll keep the suits coming. My nimble-minded barrister believes four hundred thousand pounds for damages could easily be awarded."

"You're insane." Nick took a step forward. "Are you following my wife? How did you discover we'd married?"

He shook his head slowly as if drugged. "The Duke of Langham threatened every printmaker in town. If anyone posted even a hint that you and his daughter were lovers, he promised to take action."

"You've worn out your welcome." It was the only advice Nick would offer the viper.

For once, the man showed some backbone and stood his ground. "You played right into my hand. Why do you think I spread the rumors?"

"Pure vindictiveness, or more likely than not, you're one who constantly likes to stir the pot." Nick purposely hitched one corner of his mouth up in a mocking half grin.

"Au contraire. I wanted her to marry you. Langham was a foe I couldn't manage. Too easy for him to get his way with all his political connections. But you? No one cares, so anything I do comes with a high likelihood of success." He sniffed a wad of semi-congealed blood back into his nose. "Train your wife to keep her mouth quiet. For her own sake, she better not approach Mary Butler again."

The foul warning had come as a surprise. It would have been more in character for Aulton to come around sniffing for some tidbit on Emma's trip to Portsmouth. The bastard knew she'd visited Mary. He might boast of lawsuits, but the innuendoes were the real danger. The underlying threat he'd hurt Emma was thinly veiled.

They both knew Nick meant what he'd promised. If

Aulton approached Emma, Nick would kill him. He tempered his voice. "We can either settle this on a dueling field, or you can get the fuck out of my house."

Aulton regarded him with a burning hatred, then dragged his battered body out of the study. With Emma asleep upstairs, Nick followed to make certain the bastard left the premises.

Chapter Twenty

Emma woke and didn't immediately recognize her surroundings. She reached her hand across the bed, but Nick's side was cold. His scent lingered on the pillows and sheets. With a smile, she drew a deep breath. His scent lingered on her. In a rush, the memories of last night cascaded and pooled into her thoughts.

She wanted to see him after what they shared. It was no small thing that Nick had survived the loneliness of his childhood and had become a man to admire. The tenderness, passion, and breathtaking honesty he'd shown her last night—was it any wonder she'd fallen in love with him? She closed her eyes. Never in her life could she have imagined she'd be this happily married. With a *swoosh*, she fell back and landed on her pillow determined to remember the joy last night brought and the promise of this morning.

She summoned Arial, and within thirty minutes, Emma was soaking in a warm bath, the lavender fragrance scenting the room. Arial then helped her dress and prepared her hair in a simple but elegant design. It was Emma's best hope to contain the unruly curls on her first day as Nick's wife. Unwilling to squander any more of the morning without seeing her husband, Emma made her way downstairs.

Mr. Martin greeted her warmly at the top of the stairs. "My lady, may I say how lovely you look?"

"Thank you." Indeed, she was wearing one of her favorite frocks, the moss-green velvet. The cut of the décolletage didn't reveal much, but the latticework bodice made the dress intriguing. "Where is Lord Somerton?"

Mr. Martin straightened to his full height in such an elegant manner, even Admiral Nelson would've been impressed. "Lord Somerton's routine is one that cannot be disturbed. If you need him for an emergency, you may contact his valet. Only Whaley can interrupt the earl's work."

He shifted to his right so she couldn't easily slip past him. Clearly, he was hiding something and didn't want her on the staircase or in the entry hall.

"Thank you, Mr. Martin. You've been most helpful."

The man had the good grace to bow his acknowledgment, which gave Emma the opportunity to sweep past and start down the steps.

"My lady, please—"

She made it to the landing, then froze. Standing in the entry of her new home, Aulton's gaze flew to hers. His eyes were black and blue, with blood painted on his clothing.

Death personified had come to call, and everything came to a screeching halt as time stood still. Deafening silence surrounded her. Punishing silence. Like the moment before the executioner drops the ax or the gallows are thrust open or the whiz of the guillotine blade falls.

Nick soon stood beside him and drew her attention. "Lady Somerton, perhaps it's best if you return to the upstairs."

Before she could respond, Alton swept his hand in front of his face, taunting her to examine his injuries. "Look at your handiwork. Congratulations, Lady Somerton." The felicitation curdled into uttered words thick and barely articulate.

"My pleasure." She delivered the retort casually, but her eyes never left his. Her heart pounded at lightning speed, causing every nerve ending to grow taut, ready to break. "You dare—"

"*Emma, upstairs, now!*" Nick roared. Fury stained his cheeks with a scarlet color that matched Aulton's bloody shirt.

"Tsk, tsk, my lady. You should be disciplined for your ungodly tendency to speak out of hand."

"Get out, you bloody bastard." Nick took him by the scruff of the neck and threw him outside. The door then closed with a resounding slam.

Behind the door stood a servant she hadn't met. As if he'd practiced this moment, he bowed deep with a perfect execution. "Good morning, Lady Somerton. I apologize for that horrid performance. Allow me to introduce myself. Stoker Whaley, valet extraordinaire, at your service."

Before she could reply, Nick took her arm and snarled at Whaley. "*Not now.* Have the mess cleaned in my study."

Her husband marched her back upstairs straight to her room. The anger in his eyes was somewhat frightening in its savagery. The man who made love to her last night with gentle regard and care had disappeared. In his place stood a stranger ready to explode in a frenzied wrath.

With a firm hand, Nick escorted her into her bedroom. At their entrance, Arial's eyes grew wide, and she immediately stopped unpacking Emma's newly arrived trunks.

"Out," he growled as he led Emma to the small seating area in front of the fireplace.

When Arial's gaze shot to hers, Emma nodded. Loyal to a fault, the maid narrowed her eyes as if displeased with Nick's gruffness. With last night's linen under her arms, she closed the door with a decisive click.

Emma turned to stare at the stranger before her. "What are you doing? Why did you allow Aulton into our house?"

He collapsed in a chair beautifully upholstered in yellow and blue-green chintz, the bright colors in stark contrast to his dangerous mood. When he rubbed his hands over his face, she gasped at his injuries. Raw and red, his scratched knuckles had swelled with ugly bruises.

She rushed to his side. Gently, she took one hand in hers. "What happened?"

He released a breath. His earlier fury had calmed, but the rigid set of his jaw hinted he was still angry. "Aulton showed up out of the blue. What a vain coward. I punched him for hurting you."

After gathering a basin of fresh water and linen toweling, Emma knelt by his side and carefully washed the cuts on both hands. When she finished, his fingers tightened around her hands as if intending to never let go. Her breath caught. If Aulton had carried a weapon, Nick could have faced death. The horror of such a loss flashed before her eyes. Aulton would've stolen another love from her. A deep breath did little to tame the wave of trembling that had erupted.

"Nick . . ." The blatant hunger in his eyes kept her from turning away. He valued her enough that he'd risked his own safety. He didn't fight for his honor or some code only gentlemen abided by—he did it for her.

"I hit him again for marking you." Nick leaned forward and brushed his injured knuckles across her cheeks. The torn skin tickled hers, causing her body to shiver.

He'd fought for her honor without hesitation. Since it was impossible to harness the tumultuous emotions rolling through her, she gently took his injured hand and placed a kiss on his fingers. "Why was he here?"

"He threatened legal action. Apparently, his solicitor will be serving papers on mine today for who knows what." He grimaced as he flexed his fingers, stretching the digits wide apart. "Mr. Odell has been my solicitor since I started business. We should both be present when he comes to discuss our options."

"Where did you learn to fight like that?" she whispered.

"I exercise at Gentleman Jackson's regularly with McCalpin and Pembrooke. They outweigh me, but I'm faster. I've learned to strike first and how to take a punch."

"I've never had anyone fight for me." Her fear of losing him had waned, but her chest and neck heated with the confession, the burn reaching her cheeks. She concentrated on folding the toweling, finding the simple task a needed diversion. "You risked your life for me. I never dreamed you—"

He took her chin in his hands, and she met his gaze. His intense stare, probing in its depth, was naked and totally male. He resembled a tiger ready to devour her. "No one touches what's mine."

"I didn't know I was yours," she whispered the weak protest. "I'm not a possession."

"I possessed you last night." His matter-of-fact tone held a hint of seduction laced with an unmistakable masculine pride. If he had started to pound his chest, she wouldn't have been surprised. "You're mine."

"Well, if I'm yours, then you're mine." She straightened her shoulders in an act of autonomy.

He answered with his familiar gravelly laugh, the one that made every inch of her aware he could bestow great pleasure with a slight touch of his lips or a graze of his hand. How could she become so weak to his every word, every look, every touch? She was turning into a lovesick goose.

With little warning, he hauled her against him as he sat in the chair. Her dress bunched about her legs as her knees straddled his hips. Seductive and slow, his gaze roved over her body. Seemingly entranced, he stared at the expanse of exposed skin on her chest.

His hard gaze set off a firestorm that swept through her and made it difficult to breathe. Unbalanced, she settled her hands over his shoulders.

He whispered, his breath hot against her ear. "Mine."

When she drew back to protest, he claimed her lips with his in a bone-melting kiss. With his tongue, he invaded her mouth as if he planned to conquer every part of her. One hand pressed her back until she was flush against his body, while the other pressed her hips to his groin. He groaned in pleasure, then increased the relentless torment of his tongue, exploring every corner of her mouth. Moaning, he rolled his hips into hers, his thick erection perfectly centered at her sex. Immediately, her swollen flesh pulsated with an awakened need for him to fill her.

With deft hands, he released the buttons on the fall of his breeches and freed his cock. He lifted her dress, shifted her hips, and drove into her sheath. Never breaking from their kiss, he withdrew and thrust again into her by lifting her hips. Quickly learning his rhythm, she moved in concert with him.

He grunted his approval. Her own moans grew in volume as her release was within her grasp. Grinding herself against him, she became aware of the coarse hairs of his groin as his thickness plunged repeatedly into her core.

His movements become more frantic, and she reveled in the power that she'd brought him to this point.

"Come. Now," he demanded, his voice rough with desire.

So lost, she distantly heard herself shout his name as her body and heart shattered into pieces she doubted could ever be reclaimed. With his powerful arms, he held her tight and bucked into her center. Hot, his release flooded her, but he didn't stop his relentless taking—not until they both surrendered.

Slowly, they awoke from the sensual stupor caused by their raw coupling.

"Emma." Her name on his lips sounded like a solemn prayer. Nick took a shuddering breath. Not wanting the moment to end, she nestled closer and placed open-mouthed kisses along the thick tendons in his neck. The musky fragrance of their lovemaking scented the air. She caressed the strong jawline with her lips until she found his mouth. The touch dissolved into a surprisingly gentle kiss.

When they parted, he touched his nose to hers. "I think I just proved who possesses whom."

The unmistakable hint of primal male bravado deepened his already roughened, but thoroughly satisfied voice.

"Indeed." Emma brushed his nose with hers in answer. "I'm the one on top."

As the rich rumble of his laugh filled the room, he lightly fingered a loosened curl on the back of her neck. "You humble me."

"That was not my intent, my lord. I see it as a reminder that you're mine."

"Scary as it seems, yes, I'm yours."

"Nick . . ." She searched his face. Handsome didn't describe him adequately. He was simply the most captivating creature ever to grace the earth. If his face was plain or scarred, it wouldn't change her opinion. His true magnificence came from within. What they'd just shared together, their passion, reminded her of how alive they both were—how integral he'd become in her life. She pressed her eyes shut and gripped his shoulders tight in an effort of stop the emotional cataclysm from consuming her. However, the truth wouldn't quiet. He was so dear to her heart that it caused her breath to catch. "Nick, if I'd lost you—"

"Hush, no talk of that." He stroked her cheek.

The assurance in his touch could only be described as an homage to her. Wonderstruck, she took a breath for fortitude. She never envisioned feeling this way about a man—about a husband.

He turned suddenly serious. "Emma, no more of this crusade on Lena's behalf. Aulton's dangerous. You have to let it be."

She climbed off his lap and straightened her dress. Their passion for each other was a force to be reckoned with, much like ignited gunpowder. But she'd not be deterred from her cause by their lovemaking or the threat Aulton presented. Returning the cloth to the basin, she contemplated an answer that wouldn't start a war between them. Particularly, after what they'd just shared.

She had to convince him her fight wasn't something she could shelve like a half-read book. Her independence and freedom to make her own choices were how she defined herself. If Nick thought himself honorable, she deemed herself stalwart in her drive for justice and the peace it offered.

"I'm your husband. I could say my word is law, but I won't insult either of us. However, you have to be logical about this. If he killed his own wife, what would he do to you?"

"Nothing," she answered with a defiant tilt of her chin.

"Don't be naïve, Emma." He exhaled as if exhausted. "You're more intelligent than that. He threatened you downstairs in front of us both."

Early in life, she'd learned other avenues she could use to soothe those who opposed her. "Nick, I can promise you I'll never approach Aulton about Lena's death." She softened her voice. "You have my word."

"Do as I say," he clipped. "We're already at the center of a firestorm of rumors and innuendoes."

"I won't desert Mary Butler or Lord Sykeston." It wasn't a challenge but a statement. She'd not yield and would see this through to the end. "I must see Sykeston receives Lena's letters, the ones she wrote on her deathbed."

He studied her with narrowed eyes as if trying to divine the truth. He'd known her long enough to expect a straight answer from any question he posed to her. She would always tell him the truth. But he had to ask the right question.

Nick rose from the chair and walked to the door. Before he opened it, he turned in a graceful half circle. Whether he learned such a turn at Gentleman Jackson's, swordplay, or a ballroom made little difference. She could watch him all day, but she had things to accomplish.

"I want you safe. Now, I have a pile of work waiting for me in the study. What are your plans?"

"I believe I'll spend the day establishing my bank," she answered.

Apparently pleased, he smiled.

"May I ask a question?"

He nodded, but his mind was clearly elsewhere, probably already in his study.

"Once you surpass your father's wealth, what will you do?"

He blinked twice.

"How do you want to live your life?" she asked softly. Truly, she didn't want to quarrel. However, after his demand for her acquiescence, these questions needed answers. They were married and forging a life together, and she wanted to learn more about him. "At the end of your life, how will you judge if it was well lived or worthwhile?"

Last night, Nick seemed so certain of his path. He led her to believe he understood hers—the desire to help women and her own need for absolution—evidenced by his gift of the bank and his thoughtfulness when she grieved in Portsmouth.

Now she was uncertain what her path was. The reality hit her with a force of a tidal wave. She was married, and society expected her to obey her husband.

Which begged another question that needed an answer—had he fully examined his own path in life?

With one glance, he let it be known he'd tired of her questions. "I'll see you at dinner." With a bow, he was gone.

Chapter Twenty-one

～♦～

Nick poured three glasses of port from a bottle he'd personally selected on his last trip to Portugal. The remnants of an elaborate meal lay before him. After a day of sitting at his desk, Nick deserved a little reward, particularly when his two brothers-in-law decided to join him and his new bride for dinner—uninvited. He would reciprocate the same courtesy to them on their second day of marriage. Perhaps then they'd understand why it really wasn't a good idea "just to drop in." However, Emma's face had lit up like a chandelier at the sight of her siblings.

All day he'd seen little of his wife. She'd left the house with Arial to start work at her bank, which allowed him to work the day without interruption. Their marriage was working wonderfully, even if they'd been at it for only one day.

Finishing the last bite of a raspberry torte, McCalpin sat on his right. William sat on his left, while Emma sat directly opposite. The table was small, the same one where he and Emma had eaten last night. Still, the distance was too great as he couldn't touch her, which he'd discovered had become a favorite pastime.

Tormented by her nearness and her scent, Nick found the dinner conversation tedious as his attention never left her. She was striking in a dark red satin dress with a black tulle underlay. The deep color accented the creaminess of her skin. But it was her eyes that held him enthralled, completely dazzled by the emerald color.

"Excellent meal. If I have another bite, I'll have to visit the tailor." McCalpin patted his flat abdomen. Though they'd had words in Portsmouth, he was Nick's closest confidant outside of Pembrooke.

William leaned close. "Might we have a word privately?"

Nick waved his hand, and Martin immediately took his leave.

Unable to hide her mirth, Emma caught his gaze, and with the slight tilt of her head, she discreetly pointed toward the buffet.

Acting as a footman, his insufferable valet held a silver platter in lieu of a mirror in front of his face. Keenly concentrating, Whaley adjusted his neckcloth. When he realized he was being watched, he turned his attention to Nick and raised a brow as if challenging him to say something. With a stare, he sent Whaley out the door.

When the door closed, McCalpin addressed Emma. "Father and Mother wanted us to be your first official guests." His face softened in the same brotherly concern Nick had witnessed on countless occasions. The sight never ceased to amaze him that three adults, siblings no less with such differing personalities, could be so close. "Em, I think marriage agrees with you. You're practically glowing."

Emma blushed, and the firelight enhanced her ravishing color.

"Let's talk about the real reason we're here," William offered. "You were threatened by Aulton today. You've got to listen to your husband and leave this alone. Both of us heard that you've been served with four separate suits by Aulton's solicitors."

Emma's attention was locked on Nick. "Is that true? Four?"

"This evening, my solicitor personally accepted the documents and reviewed them. It comes as no surprise they're quite inflammatory." His gut tightened. Aulton would pay for his idiocy. Nothing infuriated Nick more than to waste time on frivolous legal proceedings.

"The suits will be dismissed. He's simply harassing you both." William addressed Emma. "But, no more. Leave Lena's death alone."

"I don't answer to you." Emma leaned forward, her attention solely focused on Nick. "What's Aulton alleging?"

"Slander for one. He alleges you made false statements to Lady Daphne Hallworth at a ball about his treatment of his wife."

Emma's breathing increased in tempo, causing her chest to rise and fall. Worry lined her perfect brow. "What else?"

"Criminal conversation. He alleges you tried to lure his wife to commit adultery while she was alive." Nick didn't glance at William or McCalpin, but kept Emma's eyes trained on him. He didn't want her to be caught unaware and humiliated by hearing such nonsense from others. Even if it was embarrassing to hear the charge in front of her brothers, they were here to support her. "He claims you proposed an affair with her, you, and me, all together."

Her eyes flew open. "I've never heard of such a thing. Do people—" A deep blush colored her cheeks. "That's ridiculous. I did ask her to come to London, but only to escape Aulton's torment," she answered. Her voice never wavered. "That was years ago."

McCalpin continued, "He alleges you tried to steal Mary Butler from his employment. He claims she signed a contract when she arrived at his household with Lena."

William didn't mince any words as he delivered the last insult from Aulton. "He claims you stole personal effects and jewelry belonging to his late wife that are rightfully his."

Emma's gaze darted between her two brothers as if trying to convince them both the truthfulness of her defenses. "Mary Butler gave me personal correspondence from Lena. In her own hand, she directed me to deliver them. That's all. My only dealings with Aulton occurred before my marriage. Why bring an action now? Aulton should sue father, not Somerton. All these supposed events occurred before I married."

"Those are the reasons these matters will be dismissed," McCalpin added briskly. "However, don't engage Aulton. Nothing good will come of it."

"My husband and I are of one mind." She leaned back. Her breathing had eased somewhat, and the normal color of her cheeks had returned. "And the damages?"

"He's seeking a minimum of one hundred thousand pounds," Nick answered.

"One hundred th-thousand pounds for all four?" She placed her napkin on the table and started to fidget with it.

"For each cause of action," McCalpin added.

Emma gasped.

Her oldest brother folded his napkin and studied her. "This is dangerous business, Em. You must listen to Somerton and stay out of this. Do not interfere."

If Aulton were successful with all of the suits, it'd

bankrupt Nick. Even if the bastard was successful with only one, it would damage his business significantly. He'd have to sell a ship to cover the losses, a devastating blow that would hamper his ability to make money.

Nick gripped the handles of his chair as ice invaded his veins. Indeed, he'd stockpile every available resource and attack the bastard with a force he'd never recover from. No one threatened his livelihood, particularly a coward who hid behind solicitors and barristers to do his dirty work.

A gentle hand took his and squeezed. Emma had left her chair to stand beside him. Forced to leave his musings behind, Nick focused on his wife's hand clasped in his. The heat of her touch soothed him, helping his cold anger settle.

"He's insolvent. It's nothing more than a ploy for money," she announced.

William turned toward her. "How would you know?"

"Lena's marriage settlements were matters she shared with me. Under the documents, Aulton couldn't receive her fortune until she reached the age of twenty-five or if a child survived her. He received it a year ago, then lost it in some bad investments." She smiled. "However, these are matters best left to me, and, of course, my husband. Perhaps we can use Aulton's distressed finances to sweep the whole matter under the table." Emma gazed down at him. "You should make him a cash settlement in exchange for his dismissal of the suits."

"I'll not give the bastard a bloody shilling." Not after he'd threatened Emma and placed his filthy hands on her. Not after the audacious arse had come into his home and threatened them both. Whatever it cost, whatever the time requirements, they'd fight Aulton one bloody suit at a time. "We'll hire a barrister."

Emma sighed. The intimate gesture reminded him of

the time he'd offered her comfort in Langham Hall after she'd argued with William. They stood together then and now, united in battle.

The power she held over him provoked an ominous longing he'd do well to tame. With one look, she made him forget all the things he wanted in life. With one touch, she caused a raging hunger that could only be filled by her supple body beneath his.

God, he was lost.

"I'll take my leave and allow you to finish your business," Emma announced. "Thank you for joining us this evening. Tell Mother and Father things are well in hand."

McCalpin stood. "Em, for all our sakes, listen to Somerton."

Will followed suit. "I agree. Don't be obstinate. It doesn't become you."

Defiance made her eyes glimmer in the candlelight. "Neither does delving into others' business become either of you."

Nick escorted Emma to the door and situated his body so her brothers couldn't see her. "Listen to your brothers."

Her eyes flashed in contempt. Before she uttered a word, he silenced her by bringing her wrist to his lips. Like a stroke of a feather, he placed the slightest hint of a kiss against her tender skin. She shivered, and he smiled in triumph. With his tongue, he licked her pulse.

She gasped and her eyes widened.

"Yours or mine?" he whispered.

"W-What?"

"Whose bed shall we sleep in tonight?" He rubbed his lips against her soft skin.

She took a deep breath.

An immediate sense of gratification swelled inside that he could so easily unsettle her. It took an amazing amount of restraint not to kiss her senseless. "There will be very little sleep though, I'd imagine."

The widening of her pupils and the slight flare of her nostrils caused the most acute, but exquisite, erection. The teasing was worth it. He'd entertain her brothers a while longer as he fancied all the wonderful ways he'd pleasure his lovely wife this evening.

"Come find me." Her skirts licked his legs as she turned.

She strolled away with a saunter that caused the most magnificent roll of her hips.

The she-cat had turned the tables on him.

At midnight, Nick finally quit the study somewhat pleased with the amount of work he'd accomplished, yet his guilt made for a miserable companion this evening. He'd not seen Emma since dinner, and he'd promised he'd come to her bed. McCalpin and William had stayed for several hours after she'd left.

He'd not wake her, but he craved the touch of her body next to his. Tomorrow, he'd insist she forget about delivering justice to Aulton. The closer he came to their adjoining bedrooms, the more aware he became of her presence. His body tightened when flashes of silk and creamy skin overwhelmed his thoughts and best intentions to let her sleep.

To wake her at this hour would be beyond selfish. Yet, his restlessness rose the closer he came to her door. He'd never lacked discipline before, but with her under his roof, his willpower had taken a holiday.

A lamp from a hallway table cast a gentle glow against his bedroom door. Even if she wasn't physically beside him, the house seemed warmer and more alive because she resided here. His constant feeling of isolation and the accompanying reclusiveness had diminished—all because of Emma.

He entered his room and found a well-built fire. He plopped into the chair beside the warmth and shed his boots and socks. He stood, removed his coat and waist-coat, and dropped them onto the chair across from his.

"May I help with the rest?"

He glanced to where the honey-silken sound had come from. Like a fantasy, Emma emerged from the darkness. Her golden hair spilled down her back, and she wore an untied dressing gown of moss-green silk trimmed in black satin.

With nothing underneath.

"Thank you for tolerating my brothers. You're too kind to me."

A smile tugged at his lips. "Your brothers are a new definition of purgatory, but it was worth seeing you so happy."

"Also, thank you for my bank. Mr. Macalester's space is perfect, and Mr. Sedgeworth is a genius. I've already received a few customers, women who'd seen the circulars Arial posted this afternoon."

"My pleasure," he offered.

She came to him, and her searching gaze caught his as if demanding he listen to her. He couldn't resist her, not like this. So he did the only reasonable thing a man could do with his wife. He embraced her and drew her close. She pressed her lips to his.

Slowly, she pulled off his shirt to expose his bare skin. As if sampling an exotic treat, she took her time and slid her hands down his chest. Sensitive to her touch, his muscles tightened. She pressed her mouth to one of his nipples, then nipped it. She laved it with her tongue and sucked it into her mouth in response to his sharp inhalation.

She would drive him mad before the morning.

His erection pulsed into her lower body as she explored the hardness of his chest, tracing every line of his body. Slowly, she unbuttoned the fall of his pants and pushed them to the floor. She drew a finger down his abdomen.

"I'm not pursuing Aulton." Her voice trailed to a whisper as her lips pressed tender kisses along his chest.

With strength and speed, he picked her up and placed her in his bed. Emma reached for him, and he covered her with his body. Every drop of blood had congregated in his throbbing erection. With a brush of her finger, she traced a line down his chest, winding her way down to his stomach.

He caught her finger in his hand. "Emma, promise me."

"Anything about Aulton"—she leaned forward, and her lips met his—"but please don't ask me to forget Lena."

He'd waited all night for a taste of her sweet lips, and he'd be damned if he'd let Aulton come between them tonight.

"Say it," he demanded.

"I promise." She sealed her vow with a kiss.

Chapter Twenty-two

In the weeks since she'd been married, Emma had developed a work habit she rarely strayed from. Today was the exception as she'd received an extraordinary summons. Instead of heading to her bank, E. Cavensham Commerce, like every morning except Sunday, Emma made a detour to the Earl of Sykeston's London home. Yesterday, she'd received a note from the earl advising of his arrival in London and stating concisely he'd be pleased if she'd visit. He apologized for the inconvenience and explained that he wasn't making social calls of his own.

He'd kept her waiting for over an hour before he appeared. When his door finally opened, the man who entered bore little likeness to the Lord Sykeston once known as the catch of the Season. With his gaunt frame and long brown hair, he could have been easily mistaken as a street beggar. Only his mahogany-colored eyes resembled the old Jonathan, a man who once took immaculate care of himself.

With an uneven gait, he used a cane for balance. With every step of his left leg, he grimaced in pain.

They had always shared an easy friendship, one developed from the years when he'd escorted both Lena and her to social events. As one of Will's best friends, he'd been a frequent guest at Langham Hall.

Even with all the history between them, the earl now regarded her as if she was a stranger.

"Hello, Jonathan." Emma stood as he came to her side.

"Lady Somerton." Aloof, he briefly bowed and turned to a small table that held assorted bottles of spirits and a few glasses. "May I offer you a refreshment?"

Emma shook her head.

"More for me." He poured a generous three fingers of brandy into a snifter. After a hefty swallow, he returned to her side. Instead of waiting for her to sit first, he plopped into his chair and exhaled as if the effort had drained him.

"It's good to see you." Without Jonathan's invitation, she sat opposite him. "Will sends his regards and promises to stop by soon."

He didn't acknowledge her greeting, but instead, studied her.

"How were you injured?" Never one to be reserved, she went to the heart of the matter.

He responded with a bark of laughter and then rewarded himself with another healthy swig. "You were never afraid to ask what no one else dared."

If Lena were alive, she'd be appalled at the state of her brother. The two siblings had been close, even more so after their parents had fallen ill and passed away within days of each other. For over ten years, Jonathan and Lena had been each other's only family. To see her brother in such a state would have devastated her.

"I made it for three years on those godforsaken battlefields without a mark on me. When I received word about Lena's death, I immediately resigned my commission

and arranged to come home. Alas, I mounted my
horse, and before I could even make it out of camp, a
band of French renegades attacked. My leg was completely mangled by a bullet. The old surgeon assigned to
our unit wanted to amputate, but I told him no. As there's
not much call for a one-legged earl in London, I didn't
much care if I'd lived." He threw his head back and stared
at the ceiling. "So prosaic to discuss death these days."

He wasn't as unaffected as he'd pretended. "I'd have
missed you. And Will, too."

A look of confusion crossed his face. He took another
swig and emptied the glass. "I'm thirsty. Be a dear,
Emma, and refill this for me."

She retrieved his glass and filled it with only a finger
of brandy. Gently, she set it on the table next to him.
When she took her seat, the glass sat empty, completely
drained.

He rested his head on the back of the chair with his
eyes closed. The odors of alcohol and day-old tobacco
surrounded him in a haze of fetor.

"Jonathan?" Emma stood to rouse him. She'd waited
for over three months to see him and wouldn't let him
waste time in a nap. "There are matters that must be discussed."

"Sit down. I'm just resting my eyes." He didn't move.

With a sigh, she did as directed and opened her reticule. She'd tolerate his insufferable behavior as her heart
went out to him. Somewhere under his bitter and cynical persona was the man she once knew. She had to believe it. He was the person Lena had loved above all
others.

"Your sister wrote you and me letters on her deathbed." The pain poured into her, and the hint of hot tears
burned, but she fought back. His mood required she keep

her grief in check. "Mary Butler sent them to me for safe-keeping until you arrived home. I have one addressed to me and your unopened letter. I also have a letter she wrote to Audra, her stillborn child. I want you to read them."

"In my own time," he muttered.

"I went to Portsmouth and talked to Mary. Aulton killed Lena."

He didn't move or open his eyes at her words.

"I read the coroner's inquest findings. Aulton paid him to write Lena had been drinking and fell down the steps. He's threatened Mary and her mother, who just happens to be his housekeeper, by promising to accuse them of stealing if they say a word."

With every passing second, her anger increased. The lack of response was disrespectful to her, but more importantly, to Lena. Silent, he appeared frozen, but when his hand wrapped around the arm of the chair, the knuckles were as white as ocean spray.

"Jonathan, did you hear what I've said?" she whispered.

"Every word." He pushed away from the back of the chair. "Why are you telling me this?"

Infuriated, she bit the inside of her mouth to keep from blistering him with a wealth of words. She imagined grabbing him by the shoulders and shaking until his teeth rattled. At least it'd be some response.

"You have to bring charges against Aulton. You're the only one who has the ability and the authority. This is the best way to see him punished for his crime." She softened her voice. "With your military service, your title, but most importantly, the fact you're Lena's brother, the House of Lords will act, and he'll go to trial. People will listen to *you*. You can seek justice and make Aulton pay for what he's done."

"I can't go against him. I've read the coroner's findings, and it disputes everything you're saying." He picked up the empty glass and examined it as he twisted it in his hand. He held the glass to her again. "No one gives a fuck."

"What is wrong with you?" she asked incredulously. If he hoped to find answers or comfort in the brandy, then the war had damaged his judgment as much as his leg. "I care. Will cares."

"Pardon me, Lady Somerton, if I've offended your tender ears." He waved his hand in the air as a smirk tilted one side of his mouth. "Don't you have some ball or luncheon to attend?"

It was simply easier to ignore the insult than accept the bait. His bloodshot eyes made him appear weary, but his focus seemed to have improved.

"You must pursue the charge of murder. With your influence and my husband and family behind you, we'll see he's punished." Her fists ached from clenching them so long in response to his behavior. "I've done everything I can. I'm married and want to give my full attention to my husband. Please do this for Lena."

"I can't. Do you understand?" Jonathan stood so quickly that he teetered before catching his balance.

With his cane, he limped to the side table and refilled the glass himself. He apparently didn't care for her miserly servings, which, in her opinion, was just as well. The next time, she would have thrown it in his face.

"This is Lena we're talking about." He'd completely changed. The old Jonathan would have already challenged the Earl of Aulton to a duel. Known for his excellent shot, he'd have had Aulton either dead or escaping from England in the dead of night.

"Don't you understand?" he growled.

"No. I wish I did," she offered.

"Must I spell it out for you?" He slammed the glass on the table, tipping one of the decanters.

It twirled for a moment, giving all appearances it would settle upright. Slowly, as if it lost the will to fight, just like Jonathan, it tipped to the floor. The leaded glass smashed against the marble of the fireplace hearth. Pieces of crystal and drops of spirits scattered like a flock of birds flushed from their nests. The strong smoky scent made the room smell like a distillery.

He viewed the mess and shook his head. "I'm about as capable as that decanter. Or what used to be that decanter." He turned and, with an arrogant tip of his chin, stared at her with an air of challenge. "Have you taken a good look at me?"

"What are you saying?" She bit out, not bothering to temper her anger. "My God, you're her brother."

"I'm not the man I once was, Emma. If you haven't noticed, I can barely walk. Stairs are a nightmare."

His flat intonation made her finally see him for what he was—a ghost, one completely consumed by his own self-loathing.

"It's over. Nothing I can say or do will bring her back. Leave it and me alone." He grimaced, but it didn't hide the breathtaking vulnerability in his eyes. He was hurting over more than Lena's death.

Once he'd realized she'd seen his pain, he schooled his features.

"Jonathan," she whispered. She took a step to take his hand and offer comfort. Together they could grieve, or she'd just listen. She'd help him with whatever he needed—except more brandy.

"You need to leave." He turned his back on her. "I have a busy day ahead of me."

"I see." She bit her tongue. She was certain the only things on his agenda were more drinking and self-loathing.

She sorely doubted if Jonathan was capable of accepting anything from anyone at this point.

"Thank you for your time and your stewardship of my sister's letters." His formal tone clearly indicated she was dismissed.

"Jonathan, I know you're hurting. But taking action on her behalf will help—"

"Good day, Lady Somerton. I apologize, but as you can see I'm quite busy."

She picked up her reticle and, by some miracle, made it to the door without crying. No matter how horrid his behavior, she truly cared. She turned once more to engage him in hopes she'd break through the façade he'd erected to protect himself. "Lord Somerton and I would be pleased if you'd come and join us for dinner. I'll send an invitation soon. I'll ask Will and McCalpin to join us."

He didn't even acknowledge her.

Emma fought her tears until she was safely ensconced in her carriage bound for her bank. What she'd found at Jonathan's made her heartsick. She had no earthly idea how to help him. Married to a bottle, he'd be dead in a year, if not sooner.

The war had destroyed Lena's champion, the man her friend had looked up to without reservation. Without Jonathan's involvement, Aulton would go free. Lena's final chance for justice would be extinguished.

He hadn't even spared a glance at the packet of papers. His interest was completely consumed by the brandy.

She leaned her head back against the squab and stared at the ceiling of the coach. Everyone ignored her conviction that Lena's murderer had to meet justice. If she shouted it from the rooftop, it seemed no one would listen.

The indifference around her meant her own chance of redemption was greatly diminished. Still, she could do little else but follow her own path. What other options did she have?

The gems in the earrings were the size of Emma's thumb. When the light hit the sapphires, they seemed to dance. "Miss Lawson, I have a safe where they'll be locked up tight. The man who owns the building has it guarded twenty-four hours a day. His business and residence are located just above our floor."

"Thank you, Lady Somerton. The earrings were a present from my father to my mother. They were left to me when she passed." Miss Lawson's cheeks grew redder as she placed the earrings in a pouch. Without a word, she put it in front of Emma and clasped her hands. "Soon, I'll have access to my trust fund. I hope to repay you sooner, but if wool prices decline, I'll have to wait until I receive my money to repay the loan."

"That's perfectly acceptable, Miss Lawson." The woman's discomfort was apparent. Something deep within Emma buckled to see another woman, one so similar to herself, be in such need she had to use family heirlooms as collateral. She placed her hand over Miss Lawson's and squeezed. "Please call me Emma."

"Only if you call me March." She took a deep breath. "If you hadn't sent a note about your bank, I'm not certain what I'd have done. Mr. Garrard would only offer five pounds, and that was to buy them outright."

Mr. Garrard may be the favorite jeweler of the Prince Regent, but Emma would ensure her entire family knew how the man conducted business, taking advantage of women like March.

"I approached the roofer about making payments for my overdue bill, but I understand it was already paid by you. I'll reimburse you—"

"No, I did it because I wanted to," Emma interrupted.

To have the responsibility for raising her two sisters and brother while managing an estate boggled the mind. She admired March and wanted to lighten the young woman's burdens in whatever way she could.

March tapped her index finger on the counter and pursed her lips. "May I ask a question?" She released a breath.

Emma nodded.

"The family trustee has failed to acknowledge or answer any of my requests for funds. I'd be grateful if you could recommend a solicitor I could engage." She tilted her head and regarded Emma with a look of pure determination.

"My husband employs Mr. Odell. I'll have him contact you as soon as possible," Emma offered.

"Thank you for everything." March held her gaze and nodded. She gathered the thirty-five pounds from the counter and slipped them inside her reticule. "I must go. My brother needs his Latin lesson before the afternoon escapes."

"If you need more, come see me." Emma escorted March to the door.

After they exchanged good-byes, she watched the young woman get into a cart with an older man about her father's age. Even with the money, the woman's stress was high if her pinched mouth and wary eyes were any indication. What made the exchange more poignant was that she and March shared the same age.

"Lady Em—Lady Somerton, I think you made a new admirer today." John Small, the footman, stood sentry over the door. His name was a misnomer, as he was one of the tallest footmen in her father's employment.

"She found a new admirer, too. Miss Lawson's strength will insure she succeeds in helping her family." Emma put the earrings in the safe, and a sense of satisfaction rooted her earlier sadness out the way. This was always what she'd envisioned her bank would provide—a sense of security for woman.

The bell over the door rang, announcing another customer. "Good morning, Lady Somerton."

A well-dressed man entered, followed by an equally well-dressed woman.

The man performed a hurried bow. "Allow me to introduce myself. I'm Lord St. John Howell. I wonder if my sister and I might have a moment of your time as we find we're in desperate need of your assistance."

Chapter Twenty-three

After spending the last several weeks litigating the frivolous claims of Aulton, managing his day-to-day business, and overseeing the refitting of his new acquisition, *Her Splendor*, to his exact specifications, Nick's schedule hadn't allowed much interaction with Emma during the days. Unless he had evening appointments, they spent their nights together.

Aulton's suits were being destroyed little by little. The criminal conversation and the tortious interference with a contract were readily dismissed as there was no basis for either of the suits. The slander and stealing charges remaining had more of a bite to them.

At every opportunity, Aulton's barristers and solicitors waved the coroner's inquest findings in front of Nick's solicitor, Mr. Odell, and the barristers he'd hired. Confident, Odell had stated the slander charge against Emma wouldn't stand. The stealing charge against Mary and Emma had yet to be considered.

"Whaley, where is the countess?" While walking down the stairs, he put on the black wool morning coat over his gray silk waistcoat. He was never one to follow his valet's suggestions that he be properly dressed before leaving his dressing room. Things were more efficient Nick's way.

Whaley stood at the bottom of the steps with Hamm next to him. "My lord, where she is *every* Wednesday, E. Cavensham Commerce," drawled the valet, who relished his saintly duty of keeping his master abreast of the household while alluding Nick was an ignorant fool.

Emma's maid whirled around the corner with a basket of laundry. Nick ignored Whaley for the maid. "Arial, would you enlighten me about the countess's schedule?"

"Certainly, my lord. On Mondays, Lady Somerton attends the Royal Archeological Society meetings. This month the lectures are covering the ancient Mayan ruins of the Americas. Tuesdays, she attends the Historical Guild of Greater London. I'm not really certain her agenda—"

"Thank you." Nick presented his most enchanting smile so Arial wouldn't take offense. "But I was wondering if you could give me an approximate time when she'll return home today?"

Arial shook her head. "That's difficult to predict. The Duke and Duchess of Langham have arrived in town. After Lady Somerton finishes her duties at the bank, she plans to return to Langham Hall for a visit. Sometimes, the duke and duchess host small card parties or intimate gatherings with friends followed by music. If it's one of those nights, she may stay for several hours, but only if you're not home," she added with a sweet smile.

Christ, she'd practically left him by the sound of things. She must have grown weary of him. Already, she had found other amusements to while away her hours. The shock had to be visible on his face.

"My lord, it's all perfectly safe. His Grace insures that

one of his coaches brings her home. Her favorite footman always escorts her inside."

Perfectly safe, his arse. "Hamm, direct the coach readied."

"Yes, my lord," the butler answered.

It didn't escape Nick's notice that Hamm raised his eyebrows and grinned at Arial and Whaley.

The front door opened, and Emma entered with a Langham footman acting as a sentinel.

"My lord, may I have a moment of your time?" With sharp, efficient movements, Emma removed her pelisse and hat, then tore off her gloves. "There's something of extreme urgency we need to discuss."

Nick nodded and held out his arm. With Emma's hand linked around it, he escorted her into his study. He perused the never-ending piles of paper that begged for attention. Another letter from Renton stood front and center on his desk. The man must have wasted a fortune on the amount of paper he'd sent over the last five years.

Emma gingerly ran her palms down her skirt. She straightened her shoulders and met his gaze. Immediately, his earlier tension dissolved as if the tether stretching his entire body finally relaxed.

"Please, sit down. I was coming to see you after having my fill of reviewing the refitting proposals for *Her Splendor*."

She sat on the edge of one of the navy brocade oversize chairs in front of his desk. He stood until she was seated and followed suit by taking the winged leather chair behind his desk.

"It's fortunate I saved you a trip. Something happened at the bank . . . and we should discuss it." She stopped and blinked slowly. Her mouth quivered, but she took a deep breath and regained control. The movements warned that the tumultuous control she held over her

emotions was weak, and a storm was about to be unleashed.

His earlier sense of contentment vanished.

"Tell me." It wasn't a question, but a demand. If
Aulton's minions were hounding his wife, he'd hire five
hundred solicitors and the same amount of barristers to
keep the bastards occupied for years. He'd hire an army
to stand guard outside her bank. All morning he'd kept
his anger at bay over the earl's outrageous actions, but he
was more than ready to let it loose.

"A gentleman stopped by today with his sister. You're
acquainted with him. He told me you were at Eton together." Her voice trailed to a whisper while she twisted
her fingers together. Immediately, every hair on his body
lifted in alert as if electricity had infused the air.

"Who was it?" He leaned his elbows on the desk and
kept his voice even, but little else. A restless fury took
root, whipping his musings into an orderly chaos that was
a familiar companion. What he wouldn't give to have a
sparring partner ready at Gentleman Jackson's for an
intense workout. He needed something to calm the
aggravation that threatened to combust into flames of
anger. If anyone from that miserable school had deemed
to harass or bother her, he'd break every bone in their
body. There was a reason he kept fit. Never again would
he tolerate a mocking word or jab said against him, and
that vow now included his wife.

"Howell, Lord St. John Howell, and his sister, Miss
Blythe Howell," she said.

At the mention of Howell's name, his mind reeled in
protest. He'd never mentioned Howell's cruelty on that
fateful day. That the miscreant dared enter Emma's bank
proved he either was a fool or had a death wish.

He'd made life miserable by gleefully relishing Nick's
humiliation by his father's hand at every opportunity. If

Howell had spent as much time studying as he did making Nick's life a living hell, the blighter would have made top marks.

But Nick attained his revenge. At the end of the term, he had found Howell and beat him to a bloody pulp. Howell's incredulous expression when he'd raised his hand to his face and discovered his nose rearranged had made Nick's wait well worth it. Their paths had never crossed since, and Nick planned to keep it that way.

Emma started to pace, clearly agitated. "He and his sister, Miss Howell, came to ask for a loan. The amount is greater than my reserves. Do you think we could—?"

"No." He grabbed the first thing he could and crushed it. He chanced a glance. The crunch and crackle of the clutched paper was his father's missive. He'd pulverized the wax seal bearing the Renton coat of arms to dust.

Fitting coincidence that his father and Howell were at his mercy.

"Under no circumstances will I help that bastard." Nick was mildly surprised at his matter-of-fact tone. He could have been commenting on the weather. Inside he was seething that Howell had set foot in his wife's bank.

He forced himself to breathe evenly as he leaned back in the chair. He could still hear Howell's laughter peal like a jackal before a kill. The blockades he'd carefully constructed for his own survival would hold against any assault, even if came from his wife. His well-honed resistance would withstand her disapproval and condemnation if need be.

Emma glided to the desk and stood before him with her hands braced against the edge. Her rose scent drifted toward him, encouraging him to lean closer. With Howell in the forefront of his thoughts, he couldn't succumb to her allure or her persuasive powers. Not with this turn of events.

"I know he was intolerably cruel and wicked at school. He told me how he regrets his actions. Please, Nick, they're desperate," she pleaded. "They've been turned away from every other lending institution. If we don't help them, they'll be forced to look at other avenues, moneylenders or—"

"I don't care if they're thrown out in the street and have to find lodgings in Seven Dials. You're not helping them." He pounded the desk so hard the wood creaked in protest. Papers spilled to the floor as if to escape his wrath. "They'll not receive a shilling."

Startled, she stepped away from the desk. The hope in her eyes dimmed. She chewed her lip and studied the view through the window. The miserable fog had lasted all day and made it impossible to see the street from his window. He could practically hear her thoughts whirling into arguments as she stared into nothing.

"Howell doesn't have the money to break his sister's betrothal." The mellow honey in her voice was shaded with a hint of steel. "His sister doesn't wish to marry."

She was relentless when she wanted something, and he would expect nothing less from his wife than a meticulously, artful debate. Her green eyes sparked with the brilliance of perfectly cut emeralds, and her flushed cheeks enticed him beyond all reason. Any other time, he'd throw his work aside and take her in his arms, soothing her worry. Unfortunately, he couldn't—*no, he wouldn't*—yield, not even to her sweet temptation. This was an argument she would lose.

"Why am I not surprised? He was always an extravagant spendthrift." Nick arranged the manifests on his desk. He turned his attention elsewhere as his anger was increasing to a steady boil.

"He was careless and even agrees that he was foolish. Instead of saving, he used every available fund to rebuild his stables. He didn't realize . . ." Once again, she leaned across the desk and put her hand on his, her warm touch urging him, willing him to look at her. "Miss Howell is engaged to the Earl of Aulton. He's anxious to wed her."

"Howell is and always has been a bloody fool," Nick offered.

Emma shook her head. "Regardless, they need our help. His sister's situation is similar to Lena's. At the age of twenty-five, she's to inherit a substantial fortune. Aulton's trying to shore up his depleted accounts. What if he kills her like he did Lena? Once he gets Miss Howell's fortune, who knows what he'll do."

He studied her fingers clasping his fist. Small and perfectly shaped, her hands provided endless comfort when he needed it or maddening sensual bliss when he wanted it. But the tremble in her hands was a sight he didn't want to witness. Nor did he want to see her hurt and desperate. When she entered his study, the stress of Howell's request had already creased her brow with worry.

Bloody hell. This was preposterous. How could he even consider her request or let his guard down? He'd not capitulate to Howell or her.

"Howell . . . they didn't realize Aulton's reputation until it was too late. Aulton demands that Miss Howell marry him within the month. She doesn't have much time."

"Can't she just tell him she refuses? Let Howell clean up his own mess." Nick would press her until she ran out of arguments. "Women break engagements all the time."

Emma exhaled. She shook her head and pressed her fingers over her mouth as if she was trying to keep her steadfastness from escaping. "Miss Howell explained to Aulton she couldn't go through with the marriage and apologized. He laughed in her face and threatened a breach of promise suit. He said he'd spent a fortune preparing for their wedding."

"What about Howell's solicitors? Aren't they bright enough to come up with a settlement of some sort?" He chanced a glance at Emma's face before realizing his error. The glimmer in her eyes mirrored her passions, and it was his greatest weakness. He couldn't look at her again, otherwise, he'd be lost.

"Aulton will allow Miss Howell out of the marriage only if Howell pays his expenses. Aulton claims the amount is ten thousand pounds. However, she must promise not to marry another until he takes a wife. He's trying to save his reputation." She rubbed her arms as if the room had suddenly chilled. "He should realize he doesn't have one to save."

"I'm sorry, but I won't help Howell. I'm afraid he'd never pay it back." Nick stood and scooped one of her hands and raised it to his lips. It allowed him to concentrate on something other than her face. "That's my final word," he whispered as he released her hand. "If you'll excuse me, I have work."

"No." The sharpness in that one word forced him to glance up into her face. Her calm demeanor fell apart in front of his eyes. Emma stepped back and raised her chin in challenge. "This is too important. Miss Howell will face the same circumstances as Lena. With the same result. We can't allow this."

"I can and I will." His tight restraint had frayed and weakened. The final thread snapped. In two steps, he'd rounded the desk and stood before her, the space between them no more than a hand's width. The heat of his anger radiated around them.

"Do you know what will happen to her? What kind of life you'll sentence her to?" Emboldened, she wove every softly spoken word into an immovable conviction. She didn't retreat as her gaze pierced his.

Her skirt brushed against his legs, and the weight anchored him. He couldn't move, but his fury thrashed and twisted inside his chest, bucking and baying to free itself.

"First, it will be a bruise on the arm, perhaps in the shape of a handprint. Next, it'll be a bruise on her face with the excuse she clumsily ran into a door, then a broken arm from falling in the pantry as she reached for a basket." Her chest expanded as she drew a frantic breath. "Finally, she'll trip or fall down the stairs because she misjudged a step. If she's lucky, she'll break her neck. If there's a merciful God, she won't have borne him any children, saving them from the same fate or worse as they see their mother destroyed in front of them."

"It's not my concern." He kept his voice flat, though he was horrified at the life she described. In protest, his stomach roiled. She was manipulating him into doing her bidding.

"Perhaps not." She never blinked. She wouldn't allow his gaze to leave hers, like a battle of wills between two titans. Only she didn't realize that he'd never capitulate— no matter what.

He drew back just an inch, just enough to escape her intense concentration, which seemed to shimmer in waves, each assault more powerful than the next.

Her tricks were deadly wicked. The sheen in her eyes pierced him deeper than a stiletto. His determination bled freely, and when mixed with her agony made a deadly combination that threatened everything he'd worked for over the years. He fisted his hands in an attempt to retain his hard-fought control.

"Don't you see? It *was* my concern. Lena was my concern, and I did nothing." Her voice weakened, and a sob escaped. She clutched her hand to her heart. "She wrote and shared the horror of her life in those very words, and I did nothing."

"Emma, you'll never get the money back."

"*Yes, I will.* Miss Howell promised that once she came into her fortune, she'd pay me back with full interest. Even if she doesn't"—Emma exhaled—"I don't care. I'd be saving her life."

It was an act of kindness on her part when she turned her head. One tear, and he would have surrendered. Never in his life did he want—no, *need*—to offer comfort as he did now. He desperately wanted to take away the anguish that feasted on her conscience.

"Don't," he whispered. Like a magnet he was drawn to her. No matter the cost, he had to comfort her. He moved to take her in his arms. "You're torturing yourself."

She whirled away and sought refuge by the fireplace. The flickering light of the flames shadowed her face as if kissing away her grief.

"Then help me." She faced him, and the fire cast a red halo around her. The soft glow of light seemed to blaze from within her. She looked like an angel, and her words were a plea from her soul.

Her voice called to his heart, the same one he'd so carefully protected for an eternity. The mutinous organ pounded against his ribs trying to break through and reach her.

"If you help Miss Howell, then you help me unlock these chains that have weighed on me since I heard of Lena's death." She closed her eyes and tilted her head to the ceiling as if looking for strength. "Please, for me?"

He didn't answer. Did she have any idea what it would cost him to help the blackguard? It would be akin to self-mutilation. If he gave his soul to the devil, he'd suffer less.

"Do you remember the words you spoke when we married? *If you care for me . . .*" The brittle timbre in her voice exposed her vulnerability. "I'm asking you now, if you feel anything for me, please—"

He cleared his throat in a desperate attempt to release the vise that had cinched it closed. Her pain, so pure and understandable, was palatable. But it didn't diminish the vow he'd made to himself. What kind of a man would he be if he couldn't abide by his own beliefs and truths?

"Don't ask that, Emma. I'm sorry, but no. I promised myself years ago, I'd not have anything to do with Howell." He took a deep breath and released it. He was exhausted, and it was time she accepted his decision. "The answer is no."

She bent her head. In any other person, it would be a sign of defeat, surrender. She shook her head. Then the vivid green of her eyes caught his, and deep down he knew she wouldn't relent. He almost gave thanks in relief. This was the creature he'd married, a beautiful, intelligent woman whose strength couldn't be denied.

"If you don't learn the power of forgiveness, then how can you expect me to forgive myself? How do you expect me to accept what I didn't do for Lena? *My Lena*, who had no family nearby when she needed help. All she had was me." Emma finally succumbed to the tears and gasped as if it was her last. "All the while she was married to that monster."

Determined not to concede, he shook his head and increased the distance between them until he sat at his desk. She was close to breaking down not only her defenses, but his. He couldn't let her change his beliefs. She had the power to strip everything from him, everything he trusted, and then throw it asunder.

"Nick." The sound of her whisper was a gauntlet extended in challenge. "If you continue the path you've chosen, you'll become like your father—empty and alone."

"Emma, don't interfere." If she thought to use his father to turn his decision, she'd made a strategic error. Just the mention of his name doubled Nick's resolve.

"Please, for both our sakes?" She balled her hands into fists as she pleaded.

"You'd betray me like this?" As soon as the words escaped, he regretted it. She stumbled a step. Astonishment colored her pale cheeks.

"Betray you?" The bridled anger in her voice didn't hide her fury as her green eyes clawed him like talons. "All I'm asking for is a loan. How could you compare saving a woman's life as a betrayal to you?"

Determined not to react, he stared purposely at her.

She pursed her lips into a tight line and exhaled. The gesture hopefully meant she'd seen the error of her thoughts. She studied her hands. "I would never, ever betray you. You're . . . my husband. You're mine."

The fervent whisper of her words bespoke the truth. He allowed himself to relax. She wasn't capable of hurting him intentionally or with little regard. He'd accused his own wife of diabolical actions, and it left a sour taste he wasn't sure he'd ever be able to purge from his mouth.

She cleared her throat. "I'll ask Claire or my mother for assistance then."

"Absolutely not. I forbid it. You're my wife and my responsibility." Running his hand through his hair, he continued. "I take care of you. You'll not drag your family into this."

"I don't want to be your responsibility. I want to be your equal, your partner."

"I don't want to argue," he bit out.

"You have a fortune. I mean so little to you that you'd

choose your money over me." The whispered declaration was as sharp as a slap across his face.

He'd allowed her access to his deepest weakness—the hope she'd love him. He couldn't tell her what she meant to him because he was a coward to say what was in his heart. Not after the words he'd uttered. If she denounced him as unworthy, he doubted he'd ever recover. So, he responded the only way he knew how, the only thing he'd allow. "If you'll excuse me?"

"You can make a difference in this woman's life." She left her refuge by the fireplace and stood before him. "I saw you do that with Mary Butler when she was so scared for her mother and you offered to take them in."

She studied him in that inscrutable way she had—the one that could knock a man's legs out from under him. "The question is whether you have the courage to offer it to others. Don't let your father and others dictate your actions. You're a completely different man than them."

The heat of her gaze burned through him, but he ignored it. It was the best choice for both of them. "This isn't like Portsmouth and Mary Butler. It's personal for me like Aulton is personal for you. Howell and my father are lines that will never be crossed." His lips curled into a sneer. "Don't push me, Emma. You'll not like the results."

"I see the results, Nick, and you leave me no choice." With an innate grace, she walked away from him.

Her simple act of leaving gouged the foundation of his beliefs. For a brief instant, he felt the rejection, much like he did when his father left him.

"I'll find another way," she whispered, but the sound flew across the room like a javelin. She opened the door and gave him a final look, the same disappointment as his father's reflected in her gaze. Finally, the door softly clicked close.

Like an ancient Celtic warrioress, she'd made an excellent throw. She'd pierced his heart, and his conscience bled with the words.

How could he have let this happen? All his life he'd desperately wanted to hear that he was loved and valued—words that someone claimed him as their own. When Emma had passionately described her love for Lena, everything within him had stilled. The chance for something so rare and so precious with his wife had been before him, and he'd squandered it. In order to keep from changing his mind and running after her, he stared at the neatly arranged papers on his desk. Instead of relief, a familiar numbness enveloped him, one that he hadn't experienced since that fateful day at Eton.

It was easier this way, so he just . . . sat at his desk and went back to work.

Later, he entered the library. To pass the time, he poured a small glass of Claire's family whisky. The spirit's smoky-peat fragrance matched its taste—bold and fiery. It immediately brought to mind Emma when she'd left his study earlier.

He had to convince her to accept his reasoning. She couldn't expect him to disregard his own values and principles to help Howell. If only Miss Howell had come to Emma without Howell's interference, Nick's decision would be different. However, with that arrogant arse to have asked for the funds, it was out of the question.

Her terse advice to make amends with his father wasn't even to be considered. Nick would rather find the next ship sailing out of London to nowhere than see Renton again.

"My lord, her ladyship will not be joining you this evening," Whaley announced as if he were an obnoxious town crier.

"Where is she?" Nick took another sip.

310   Janna MacGregor

"She's indisposed." The valet shed the persona of Somer House's official proclaimer and addressed Nick directly. "Arial shared our countess is upset over something, but she doesn't know why." His surliness returned with a vengeance. "Do *you*?"

"Have a tray prepared and delivered to my study." He ignored Whaley's latest theatrical performance and downed the remaining whisky in hope it would lessen the pain. "I'll be working the rest of the evening."

He tried to bury the intense sting at the news Emma wouldn't join him. She wanted nothing to do with him, and he'd hurt her enough that she couldn't stand his company.

Just as his father had declared.

He was a fool to even try for anything more or allow such thoughts. Disgusted with his own weakness, so similar to the one he'd experienced years ago in front of his father, he'd turn to the only comfort he could rely on—his work.

He had to stay true to himself. Let Howell go to hell.

Light from the midday sun beamed into the windows of Emma's bank. No matter how much light entered, it didn't diminish the dreariness that seeped into every inch of her office.

Last night, for the first time of their married life, Emma didn't sleep with Nick. Their argument had been too raw. She'd seen the futility of her actions. She shuddered a breath and managed to keep her defiant heart from breaking. But she was losing the battle. She'd fallen in love, kicking and screaming the whole way. At first, their easy companionship had been ideal, but she'd let her guard down. How simple to dismiss all her objections to marriage.

Eventually, as it always does, the truth tore down the walls she'd created stone by stone, brick by brick, until she couldn't ignore it anymore.

She believed she'd carved the perfect marriage for herself, one with a husband who cherished her values and beliefs as much as she did. Never did she think the stark truth of his regard for her would be this blistering. His resolve to view the world in a way that benefited only him was a truth she hadn't wanted to accept. But now she must since he'd made it abundantly clear—he'd never relinquish his own personal vendetta even if it destroyed her. He'd either disregarded her need for absolution or didn't care.

From her own family and her interaction with Jonathan, she'd finally accepted what she didn't want to believe—Lena's death didn't justify any retribution. She couldn't stop asking the same question repeatedly, ad nauseam—if it had been Aulton murdered by his wife, would there have been a different standard of justice? She suspected the answer would ravage her so completely she'd lose herself.

A lone tear escaped and dropped to her desk. As she'd feared, she was stuck in a marriage with a selfish man. Her own husband, the man she loved with her whole being, didn't think her worthy enough to set aside his vows of making money to save a young woman's life. He'd already become the hardened English lord who put his interests above all others.

The bell rang once more.

She took a deep breath. While he didn't care, she did. There was a reason she chose to be at her bank—to help others in their time of need. Whether anyone helped her or not was a question she didn't have the fortitude to examine now.

"Am I interrupting?" Nick stood before her looking

every inch the virile, magnificent man she remembered marrying weeks ago.

The rich rumble of his voice caused her heart to squeeze. With just a couple of words, he'd cut her to the bone and made her vulnerable. She closed her eyes. God, she hated this feeling of powerlessness.

"No, my lord." She blinked, desperate to keep some control so she wouldn't make a fool of herself.

He nodded to John Small and removed his greatcoat. With eyes locked on hers, he prowled toward her, familiar yet dangerous. A fire smoldered in the blue-green depths and singed what little forbearance she'd gathered to shield herself against his allure. She was nothing more than prey at this point.

He took her hand and raised it to his lips. The gesture made her perfidious heart topple in an endless somersault.

He surveyed the room, and his gaze settled on John. "If you'd be so kind as to step outside and keep customers from interrupting us?"

The footman bowed and took his leave.

"Is he here the entire time?" Nick asked.

No matter the reason for his appearance, she could not and would not turn in to some simpering fool. With a nod, she swallowed the sudden flutters that had erupted in her stomach. "My father wants someone with me at all times when I'm working."

"I didn't think. . . ." With a grimace, he stole another glance around the room. "With my investigator, Mr. Macalester, conducting his business above yours, I didn't think there would be a need for a full-time escort. I should thank your father and offer to reimburse him."

"No need. In my opinion, it's too much," she said.

"Arial shared that John is your favorite footman, and he brings you home from your outings."

His outright smile turned him into the man she married, the one who teased and flirted until he got a reaction that pleased them both. This version was so different from the one who denied her request to help Miss Howell.

"I must see if I can be fitted into the Langham livery. I want to be your favorite." He tilted her chin with one hand so her eyes met his, and she prepared for his kiss. He took her by surprise when he trailed his lips against her cheek. "Show me how you conduct your business."

From nowhere, renegade tears started to well in her eyes. That was the depth of her despair. Of all the times for tears, this was not it. She took a deep breath in an attempt to control her unruly emotions. "I hoped you'd ask."

"I've upset my wife." He reached into his pocket, then handed her an embroidered linen. "I can't stand your tears. Each one is as sharp as a knife and takes a sliver of my heart when it falls."

"Don't say such things," she whispered. This time the square had the letter 'N' designed in gold thread with a beautiful scroll design. After she wiped the errant drops away, she attempted another smile. "I'm glad you're here."

His expression collapsed into concern. "Emma"—he cleared his throat—"last night . . ."

She opened the drawer to retrieve Mrs. Jones' prized woodcarving. Last night had been a nightmare, and she didn't want to revisit it, at least not yet. She was still attempting to understand what had happened between them. "Do you have an appointment with Mr. Macalester?"

"No, I'm here for you." Nick took her in his arms and kissed the top of her head as if he were comforting Lady Margaret.

His every move, touch, and word chipped away at her resolve. He made this rift between them appear simple, as if it was a debate over the most appropriate wine to serve with a leg of lamb. It'd take so little to convince herself that he truly cared for her the way she wanted. Was it too much to expect that she was a higher priority than his money and his own past?

"Now, what do you have there?" he asked.

Carefully, pulling back the linen wrap, Emma placed the piece of wood before him. "This is the collateral for the last loan I made yesterday."

"How much was the loan?" A hint of doubt underscored his words.

"Two pounds."

His eyes darted to hers, then returned to the carving. "Are you concerned she'll abscond with the money?"

"Of all my clients, she's the one who will pay the money back early. She works hard as a laundress, takes care of her appearance, and has already made arrangements for additional work to pay me back. Her son's wife is carrying, and she needs a doctor's care. Her family is her whole world." She presented the carving for his inspection. "That world, my lord, is represented here. Her son carved this for her as a present. It's the most valuable possession she owns."

She traced the woodcarving a final time. "There are other things besides money that motivate people. If one looks hard enough, the reasons are always visible."

An elevated eyebrow proved he held little regard for her theory. His response was further proof of his priorities. She'd chosen to ignore them in the past, but not now. She had nothing else to lose.

"My operation is quite simple. I offer funds in exchange for collateral and only collect a simple interest rate." She replaced the carving, then pulled open a drawer with a jewelry case inside. "Most women have a piece of jewelry they offer as security. Some bring items such as silver candlesticks. All of my profits go back to the operation. If I continue at this same rate of success, I plan to open an office in Portsmouth or Edinburgh, maybe even Bath. Women need these opportunities. Perhaps one day I'll have enough monies to start a charity specifically dedicated to women like Lena and Mary and Miss How . . ."

She let her voice fade to nothing. She couldn't contain her sadness or the awkwardness that caused a sudden silence between them. With a deep breath, she squared her shoulders. "I only planned to stay open a half day, and I've still got a lot of bookkeeping to do before I leave." She stood and grasped several items to put away in the vault. "What may I help you with?"

He clasped her hand tightly. "Howell."

Chapter Twenty-four

Emma locked the bank vault in the back of the room and returned to Nick's side. In order to have her undivided attention, he brought her to sit in one of the simple mahogany chairs that faced her escritoire. He pulled the other at an angle so he faced her.

Her face had paled, and the forlorn look in her eyes warned him he had to be careful how he approached this conversation. She appeared to be as fragile as a dried flower pressed between the pages of a book. Guilt coursed through his veins with the knowledge he'd pushed her until she'd flattened into this dull, colorless person who sat before him completely defeated.

"I think it's best you understand why I can't help Howell, and why I don't want you to help him either." Nick rubbed his thumb across her knuckles in a repeated pattern. His need to touch her was more for his benefit, even though her hands were like ice. Proof he was a completely selfish bastard.

She shook her head slowly. "He was a downright loathsome menace who made your life hell. He took advantage of you after your father left." She pulled her hands away and fidgeted with her fingers, the telltale sign she was upset. "What more is there?"

He nodded in agreement. "When I promised myself I'd never lift a hand to help him or his friends, I've lived by that creed. To forget that promise destroys who I am."

She turned away and bit her lip at the same time. When she returned her gaze to his, a glimmer of skepticism resided in her eyes. "This is what you wanted to discuss?"

She leaned back in her chair and clutched her arms around her waist in a protective stance. With her slow deliberate act, she made it clear she was shielding herself from him.

She wanted him gone.

"I didn't care for sleeping alone last night. Did you?" He wanted that simple truth to soften her so she'd talk to him. He'd come to make things right between them so they could go back home and return to the life they were building together.

"Wasn't your bed comfortable?" she asked in a tone suspiciously guileless.

Her inner minx clearly was still itching for a go. A bubble of laughter bounced inside his chest, but he didn't release it.

"Emma, you expect me to give up my commitment so you can help Howell?" He coaxed her gently. "You want me to forego how I've lived my life and how I define myself? Do you want me to give up everything?"

Her eyes brightened, and she leaned forward. "I expected you to help me. I promised to pay you the monies in full." She assessed him with an honesty that unnerved him. "I gave you everything and thought you'd do this for me. Let us help that poor woman."

" 'Everything.' " He repeated the word in an effort to stall as his mind raced to find a response. "Your dowry was generous, but help me understand what you're suggesting by 'everything.' "

She closed her eyes. The wall of defense she'd erected earlier shriveled before his eyes as she exhaled. A cold knot formed in his stomach.

"When I married you, I gave you the most precious thing I had in my possession. It was *everything* I had." Her lips trembled, and she pointed toward the middle of her chest. "I gave you . . . me," she whispered.

His heart constricted at the softly spoken words. His assuredness that he'd convince her he had good reason to deny Howell floundered. A surge of desperation to atone for the hurt she suffered made him reach for her. He'd not let her go until she understood how much he appreciated her precious gift. When he touched her, she drew back much like the day when he'd convinced her to marry him. She was the same wounded soul who had to be coaxed into trusting him. "Emma—"

"Remember when I asked how you knew whether I was worthy of marrying you or not?" The strain in her voice galvanized him to watch her every nuanced move.

He nodded. He had no idea what she was going to say next.

"You see Lena, Miss Howell, and Miss March Lawson, one of my customers, are all women born into nobility." She stared and waited for his acknowledgment.

"And so are you," he answered.

"Exactly, but each one of them is far nobler than me," she answered with a firm nod of her head, the movement of the curls causing her hair to glisten in the sunlight. "Lena futilely tried to survive while day by day she was destroyed by a monster. When Miss Howell stood in this very room, her bleak future didn't rob her of her dignity, an undeniable strength not many have. And poor March struggles daily trying her best to keep her family clothed and fed, not to mention respectable." She drew a breath and held his gaze. "I thought if I could convince my family or Jonathan to care about Lena, then I'd prove to myself that these women mattered in our world. That we all cared for their wellbeing. I stupidly thought such action would push my grief aside. But when everyone turned their back on me for Lena's sake, I realized how hopeless it all was."

"You're being overly critical of yourself."

"What I'm being is realistic. When I discovered I had a chance to save Miss Howell, I came to you." She bit her lip and shook her head. "Of all the people in the world, I thought you cared."

"I care. I value what you do."

"Oh, my God!" She laughed through her tears.

There was no amusement in her voice, and his mind raced as bells bonged in warning. He'd walked straight into a trap.

"I said the same thing to Jonathan, Lena's brother, when he told me to leave him alone. I told him I cared about him and Lena. Then I railed at him for not doing anything about her murder." She dried her tears. "I'm as pitiful as he is because I haven't done anything either."

He stiffened. "Wait, when did you see Sykeston? Didn't I tell you to leave this all alone?"

He became the latest casualty of her steely glare.

"Jonathan asked me to visit the morning that Howell came to see me. You have nothing to worry about. It's over. Jonathan can't muster enough interest to care either." She blinked and lifted one of her perfectly arched eyebrows. A chilly reserve replaced her frosty stare. "I asked Sykeston to take action on Lena's behalf, and he refused."

Bewildered, he had no idea how to respond. But she needed comfort, and he'd be damned if he'd let her suffer anymore. Sykeston's refusal, along with his own denial to help Howell's sister, had driven her to a level of despair far greater than her grief in Portsmouth. He reached for her, and she scooted her chair out of his reach.

"You may not believe this, but I remember every word you've spoken to me. I remember every smile and wink you've sent my way. In Langham Park, when I was banished to Falmont, you said something profound. You teased me, saying you knew I was intelligent even though I read."

He smiled at the memory. She'd been so contrary and utterly charming. He'd fallen in love with her that day. The realization tore down the carefully constructed barriers erected around his heart. He had loved her for years, always from afar, until Portsmouth. He had no idea how it happened, but he was the most fortunate man in all of England.

A pure and breathtaking lightness filled him. His heart skipped a beat before it started to pound, causing the blood to rush to his head. She had no idea how he felt about her and the impact she'd had on his life. He'd not let her leave the bank without knowing exactly what she meant to him. He reached for her hands, and this time, he didn't let her pull away.

By the slump of her shoulders, she had grown even more despondent. "I wish I had never picked up a book in my life. They made me believe and hope I could make a difference . . . but when Lena was murdered . . ."

She looked through the window and then to him as if seeking reassurance. He squeezed her hand in answer.

"I couldn't understand why no one cared. I couldn't accept it, and so I fought for her. But when every door I opened was slammed in my face, I finally discovered the truth. Lena, Miss Howell, March, and all these women—women just like me—women of the same ilk—

they mean nothing in our world. If they mean nothing, then I mean nothing."

"Don't say that. You mean everything to me."

She studied him, and the intensity of her stare cut right through, as if she looked at someone behind him. "If you valued me, it stands to reason that you'd have helped me. At first, I thought your refusal to help was about money, but this goes deeper."

"I care for you." He leaned and pressed a kiss to her lips. Gentle, but sure, he wanted her to know exactly how much she meant to him. "I love you," he whispered.

Her green eyes narrowed with doubt.

"Emma, I think I've loved you since you gave me that kiss in Langham Park in exchange for *Bentham's Essays*." Whether she loved him in return wasn't a question he wanted to examine in their current circumstances. He'd use every power of persuasion to make her understand how special she was and then take her home. Then he planned to give her every pleasure he could think of so she knew how much he loved her.

"I'm not certain the love we share will ever repair what's wrong here. I can't see it any differently at this point." She gently pulled her hands away. "The most important things in my life, I need you to respect. It's the same for you. I should respect the beliefs you have." She bit her lip and winced. "The resolutions you've made in life are in direct conflict with mine. You choose money and the rancor you hold for Howell over my need and desire to aid Miss Howell. By helping her, I defeat Aulton for Lena." With an elegance born from her years as the Duke of Langham's daughter, she stood.

He joined her in standing. "Emma—"

"I can't make you see how important it all is to me, and you've made me doubt if I'm even worth it." With a step back, she rounded the desk. "If you'll excuse me, I have work."

"I'm not leaving until we come to an understanding."

In response, she turned toward the door and gathered her pelisse.

Everything—his heart, his breath, and his life—came to a quiet stop. She was leaving him.

"I don't want to live with the doubt. If you'll excuse me, I'd like to be alone. Will you please lock up when you're finished?" She walked out without sparing a glance at John Small. He fell the accustomed one-step behind her to make their way through the London streets.

Numb, Nick sat there and tried to make sense of what had just happened. Finally, he'd confessed his love to his wife, the woman who'd captured his heart and all his hopes for a happy life.

If he wasn't mistaken, she'd just told him that she loved him in return. Pure elation should be racing through his veins at the thought that Emma felt for him the same as he did for her.

But her parting words haunted him. She didn't believe their love could fix this breach between them. How had something so wonderful and pure spoiled so quickly? The words and emotions were uncanny in their similarity to his father's words that fateful day.

He clenched his fists. Wasn't this the same type of pain he'd protected himself against time after time?

He'd left himself wide open, and she'd taken the opportunity and crushed him.

When would he ever learn?

The clock on the mantle and the study's well-built fire consumed Nick's attention. For the last three hours and three minutes, he'd allowed nothing to interfere with his concentration as he stared at both—except for Emma.

After he locked the door to the bank, he'd come straight to his sanctuary, his study. He loved her, and she wanted nothing to do with him. As he took a sip of brandy, its normal fire failed to offer comfort. His life was a complete shambles, and his father had predicted the result. Nick raised his glass in salute to the fire. What a fitting tribute.

Hamm stepped into the room. "My lord, the Earl of Sykeston is here to see Lady Somerton. Since she's not available, he's asked if you might have a moment."

"Send him in." Why in the devil had he come to see Emma? She'd made their visit sound as if it was a disaster and Sykeston couldn't wait to be rid of her.

Hamm escorted the earl into his study and closed the door.

"Lord Somerton, thank you for seeing me on such late notice." Sykeston held himself much like a military man. Though his uniform was missing, the cut of his clothes indicated a man of precision and good taste. His posture was perfect, and his face was a mask of indifference.

Nick waved a hand at a chair in front of his desk and waited. Sykeston's labored gait jerked and bobbled resulting in his use of a cane to walk, but his bearing indicated a proud man, one who would be offended if Nick offered any help.

Once he reached Nick's side, he slowly lowered himself into the chair. "I apologize I didn't send a note around, but I don't have much time. I have a practice scheduled at Manton's shooting gallery later on."

"Please, it's no inconvenience." Nick took his seat. "Would you care for a drink or other refreshments?"

"No. I'm not drinking, not today." He took a deep breath. "Your wife came to see me about my sister's and niece's deaths. I was quite rude to her." He cleared his throat, clearly uncomfortable. "I came to apologize."

"Indeed, she was quite upset." That was putting it mildly. She'd been distraught at Sykeston's total lack of regard. Much to Nick's dismay, he had added to her devastation by refusing to help Howell.

Simply put, he'd decimated her, and she'd done the same to him.

Sykeston rested his elbows on his legs and studied the floor. When he looked up, pain and grief lined his face. "Emma came to me demanding that the travesty of Lena's death be answered, and I was too lost in myself to see what she was offering me."

"What was she offering?" Nick asked. He envisioned her standing before Sykeston with an unbendable will.

"For at least a couple of days, I could forget my own circumstances. It forced me to find the nerve to consider my sister and everything she suffered." He rubbed his hand across his face. "She married a savage fiend, and I'll never forgive myself for approving the match." The earl was lost in his thoughts until he straightened in his chair. "Will you relay a message to Emma—Lady Somerton—for me?"

Nick nodded.

"I've challenged Aulton in a duel to the death. The idiot picked pistols as his weapon of choice. Hampstead Heath at dawn tomorrow. He'd have a better chance if he'd have picked swords." The coolness with which the earl relayed this message indicated he possessed a supreme confidence. He stood to take his leave.

"If you need a second, I'll stand for you."

Sykeston bobbed his head. "Lord William has agreed, but thank you. If I survive, there will probably be a scandal, something I'm sure you want no part of. So, I must ask why?"

He'd do it for Emma. He'd walk through the bonfires of hell for her—he knew that now. "My wife needs you to succeed. Your sister's death has affected her greatly. Anything I can do to help you, helps her."

"A man with ulterior motives," he jested as if he didn't have a care in the world. "Don't worry, I'll succeed. Anyway, I have matters that need my attention this evening. Please tell Emma I appreciate all she did for Lena, Audra, and me."

"I will." Nick joined him around the other side of the desk. "Good luck."

"Thank you. I'll send word after it's over."

Nick waited until the door closed, then collapsed into his chair. Emma's commitment to justice was finally coming true, but not in the way she'd envisioned it. She'd wanted the earl to bring charges against Aulton, but Sykeston was of another mind. There would be a scandal afterwards, but Lena's memory could be preserved without Aulton having a pulpit to smear his late wife's character and virtue as he sat through a trial.

The revelation began to hum in his blood as he considered Sykeston's words. He said Emma gave him an opportunity to change his life.

Wasn't that what she'd given him?

She supported him in his work, but more importantly, she'd opened his eyes and shown him how he could change his stark existence and make it into a life worth living. She'd taught him how to love and made him truly believe he deserved more than just wealth, a poor substitute for the affection and companionship he'd thirsted for his entire life.

What he wouldn't give to turn back time and say all the things he needed to say, and do the simple acts she'd asked of him. He'd convinced himself his reasons were sound, but the truth demanded he acknowledge his duplicity. To protect himself, he'd become a man who could only see value if it increased his wealth, his power, and his ability to make himself invincible from being hurt.

What good was any of it if he didn't have Emma?

What he believed was worthwhile in life—his so-called honor—had in turn caused him to be the weapon of Emma's deepest hurt. He'd chosen his own wealth, the demon he'd listened to all those years. He'd accepted the shallow and pithy words that nothing mattered except how successful he'd become.

A wrenching ache caused each beat of his heart to intensify until he thought it would burst. It was as if a hammer was striking an anvil inside his chest. His trite words from earlier echoed in his ears. He'd told her he loved her, but he couldn't show her how. Was it any wonder she doubted they'd ever find happiness with each other?

Hamm rushed forward, his cheeks red as fire. "I apologize sir, but you have another visitor who says it's urgent." The butler's voice dropped several octaves.

"Do you have his card?" Nick started walking before Hamm could respond. He didn't have time for another visitor. He had to find Emma and bring her home.

"My lord, he's in the formal salon. Hamm added softly," Next to Lady Somerton's sitting room.

"Of course, I know where the salon is. Do you think I don't know what is in my own household?" Nick scolded. Whaley must be giving Hamm acting lessons. Indeed, his whole staff must think him a loon.

They wouldn't be far off the mark. Nick chuckled for the first time today.

His first priority was Emma. He'd give the visitor five minutes, then he'd go find his wife. Nick threw the double doors open and walked in without breaking stride. A bright fire warmed the room with hospitality.

But when the man turned to face him, Nick's insides turned to ice, the kind that cracks from a sudden deluge of artic cold. He stopped midstride to catch his breath. "*You* are not welcome here."

Chapter Twenty-five

❧

I'm well aware I'm not welcome." The Duke of Renton's face went slack, and he stared down at his hands. "You've made that abundantly clear. Please just give me a moment."

The years had not been kind to the stranger before him. The duke's blond hair had grayed, and the pronounced lines on his face proclaimed he'd lived a hard life. What was most startling was the stoop in his once proud carriage. The man looked like a shell of the imposing duke Nick remembered.

An itch, one of those irritatingly inaccessible prickles, encouraged him to pivot and leave the room. He hadn't suffered such an aggravation in years, not since the last time he saw his father. His own sense of worthiness started to crumble as all the pain and anger crept to the surface. After all these years, his father's presence conjured the familiar bitterness and shame—all spinning into a whirlpool that threatened to drown him in his contempt for the old man standing before him.

No, he'd not succumb to the duke's power to inflict cruelty. This was *his* home. The only solution to remedy the discomfort became obvious. After he grabbed his father by the scruff of the neck and threw the bastard out, he'd order the salon cleaned from top to bottom.

The Duke of Renton waved a hand toward a chair, oblivious to Nick's torment. "Would you mind if I sat? My knees give me fits during this type of weather. Mr. Martin was kind enough to build up the fire on my behalf."

"You must have mistaken me for someone who cares." By design, he attacked first because he intended to cut the old man in two.

"I've waited sixteen years to see you." The duke's eyes were red. "Son, I need—"

"It's time for you to leave. Neither of us has anything to say to the other. Hamm will see you out—"

"When I wake in the morning, my first thought is always how much I regret our last meeting. I treated you horribly." The duke's hushed words were barely audible. He slowly sat in one of the brocade chairs that flanked a matching sofa. "Please?"

The urge to leave increased to such an excruciating degree that Nick's flesh burned as if he'd been thrown into a hellfire made by the devil himself. Perhaps he was in Hades. He couldn't think of anything more miserable than listening to his sire's litany.

The reasonable part of his mind encouraged him to suffer through whatever ridicule and vitriol spewed from the duke's mouth. If Emma were here, she'd insist he bear it for his own sake. Before he could change his mind, Nick sat across from his father and waited without a word.

"Thank you," the duke said, acknowledging Nick's seeming benevolence. "When I left Eton, I almost came back for you. I actually had the coach stop a mile down the road."

The duke's eyes usually held a disapproving gleam whenever he'd bother to glance at Nick. However, today they shimmered in pools of remorse. Nick straightened. He must be imagining things; the duke never experienced such an emotion. His father was too proud to offer an apology. Nick's constant companion through the years, the niggling self-doubt, started to burn a hole through him.

"I made myself ill. Sick from our confrontation and nauseated by the cruelty I inflicted that day. You were my son, the only family I had, and I threw you away like a piece of garbage."

The duke's pain was so raw that Nick actually had to turn away from the intensity and stare at the blazing fire. Before Nick's very eyes, his father who held such power over him crumbled into a weak mass of wrinkles and bones.

The duke didn't bother to wipe the evidence of his contriteness away. "I'm most ashamed of the lies I told you that day. After all these years, I've come to realize that I can't die in peace until I make amends, or at least try. . . ." He clasped his hands before him in a manner similar to Emma's ever-constant fidgeting. "Your mother loved you."

"Pardon?" He couldn't trust he'd heard correctly. His chest tightened to the point he was certain his lungs would explode.

Over the years, he'd let the duke's diatribe of his unworthiness and inability to find someone to care for him steal his happiness. He'd lived in a self-created shell, one designed to protect and keep him isolated. He'd finally found enough courage to let his wife break through, even if she didn't want him now. He'd not retreat into that empty existence again.

"When she was carrying you, we'd lie in bed together.

She'd take my hand and place it on her belly so I could feel you kick. We'd laugh at your antics, and she'd tell me her dreams for the man you'd become. I'd never seen her so happy. Before we'd fall asleep, she'd whisper that she loved us both." The duke shook his head as if the memories were too painful to continue. "I've never enjoyed my life more than when she was with me. She was my sun. My whole world revolved around her."

"If you loved her, why did you deny her feelings for me?" None of it made any sense. This rare glimpse of his parents' life didn't reconcile with his own perception. The man his father described was not the bitter, aloof duke Nick despised.

His father's gaze darted from his hands to Nick's gaze. Pain reflected from the depth of his eyes, but also something more profound. Remorse.

Everything Nick valued in life began to fall into a rubble of doubt. He straightened his shoulders. He'd not forgo the crippling memories because of an old man's apology and rueful offers of explanations.

"I couldn't love the way both you and she deserved. When she passed, my weaknesses were finally exposed. I . . . I was utterly lost. My whole life lay barren before me. The only way to survive my grief was to push all remembrances of her aside. You were the biggest offender. Every day that I saw you, I saw her, and I relived the bitterness of her death all over again." The duke exhaled and appeared to shrink before his eyes, the old bluster replaced by emptiness. "I'm sorry I wasn't a better father . . . and a better man to have raised you."

Nick closed his eyes as the burn of his own tears became too painful. All those years, he thought his father hated him, but in truth, he hated the memory Nick represented. His resentment dissipated somewhat, but in its place a deep sorrow took root for all the things he'd lost as a child. All the security and comfort a parent could've offered—*should've offered*—when he was hurt, all the joy of sharing time and company together, all the moments that could have been created and handed down to his own children. A man incapable of dealing with his own grief had stolen it all from him. His father was weak. How had he not seen it before?

If Nick lost Emma in childbirth, he'd grieve deeply, but he'd take their child and dedicate all his energy to ensuring that Emma's kindness and goodness were remembered. He'd see their child cared and loved for every day as a tribute to her.

God, his lovely Emma. This was what she'd been teaching him. He needed to find his own happiness within himself so he could love her freely. When he hadn't listened to her and had failed to consider her words, he'd lost so many precious moments already in their short time together.

The lesson of such a life sat before him. The duke had lost the opportunity for love and wasted his precious time on this earth. Nick had turned into his father, and the realization made his stomach churn in agony.

"Nicholas, I pushed you away selfishly." The duke's voice had softened. "It was far easier for me to criticize you and drive you away than face the memories you represented. I should've hired the best tutors and kept you at Renton House. My biggest regret is not having you by my side."

Silence stretched between them. The only sound in the room was the shifting and snapping of the wood in the fire. Finally, the duke raised his head.

"The two hundred pounds I brought you at Eton was all I had left after the harvest failed that year. I still had to pay the tenants and make repairs with loans."

"I just sent you five hundred pounds. Are you looking

for more?" Nick hid the shock of his father's confession
with a roll of his head to stretch his neck. It was a way to
relieve the knotted muscles and bide a few minutes to
consider his father's words. Not once did Renton ever
mention financial problems with the estate, nor had Nick
caught a peep of it before or after that fateful day.

The duke shook his head slowly. "No. I mortgaged
some land that year. After a couple of successful harvests
and wise investments, the duchy was flush again in cash.
It took me a while, but I realized my foolish pride got
the best of me that day. I've come to offer . . ." The hard
swallow mimicked a man drowning of thirst after being
discovered in the Sahara. "I chose you that day."

The words made his misery acute. Nick could taste the
desperation of wanting to believe his father, so much so
his own mouth grew thirsty.

"When you wrote to me that those men threatened to
harm you if you didn't pay Lord Paul's debts, I roared in
anger. I could either have saved you from the violence of
those thugs Lord Paul had introduced you to, or I could
have applied it to repairs on the tenants' roofs. I chose
you, but I was furious you forced me to make that decision. I blamed all my loses—physical, emotional, and financial—on you. I grew more and more sullen as time
passed. However, deep in my heart, the only real choice
I had that day was you. Son, you were my last connec-
tion to your mother."

Nick blinked, trying to understand what the man was
confessing. He'd actually shirked his responsibilities to
the duchy for him, the son he detested?

It was unfathomable. His father, the Duke of Renton,
sat before him a broken and humble man asking for forgiveness.

"Perhaps if you had—" Nick drew a deep breath in an
attempt to rein in his own grief.

"It's not something you want to share . . ." The duke blew out a breath and cleared his throat. "I've written in hopes I can make amends. Have you received my letters?"

"Yes, but I've never read them." Nick wouldn't lie to him just to appease his conscience.

The duke slowly nodded as if accepting his due punishment. "I've watched you and your success since you left university. I knew Pembrooke was a major force in your life. I was envious of him, but thankful, too. He's a good man."

"I was fortunate we became friends. I hate to think what would have happened if he hadn't taken an interest in my welfare."

The duke flinched at his words, but Nick wouldn't soften the truth. He wouldn't be the man he was today without Pembrooke's friendship. "I married." The announcement came from nowhere. "The Duke of Langham's daughter, Lady Emma."

The first hint of a smile tugged at his father's lips. "Langham wrote me. It gave me the courage to come and see you. I thought if you refused, perhaps your wife could convince you to meet me." The duke eyes were red and bloodshot. "I met her once when she was a small child. But I remember she was full of life and a true beauty. She'll make a perfect duchess, just like your mother."

Was he actually giving Nick a compliment? For the first time, Nick spied the real man underneath the title and the trappings of the duchy, a man who might be capable of affection.

"She's not here at the moment, or I'd introduce her to you." His voice had lost the jagged edge of his anguish. A weight was lifted from his chest, and he breathed a little easier.

"Perhaps . . . a later time?" The entreaty in the duke's tone couldn't be missed.

If the duke saw him as the last link to his mother, wasn't the duke the same link for him? Could they heal this breach between them with their mutual love for a woman who died thirty years ago?

He had to consider whether he even wanted his father in his life. Yesterday, the answer would have been an adamant "no." When Emma had left him earlier in the day, his "no" would have weakened to a "maybe." Now he wasn't certain of the answer, but he was confident of one thing—Emma would take one look at the lonely and dejected man and urge Nick to forgive him. She'd want him to take this opportunity, take the risk, and try to salvage what was left between him and his father. She'd urge him to take this new beginning and build something positive from their previous mistakes.

"I'm certain my countess would welcome meeting her father-in-law sooner rather than later." With that invitation, Nick's self-doubts shattered. It was hard to fathom, but he'd take this chance to try to find peace with his father. Perhaps it was a way to win his wife back into his arms.

"Thank you, Nicholas. I didn't expect . . . but I'd prayed you'd let me meet her." The look of gratitude in Renton's eyes was hard to mistake. "If there's ever anything I can do for you, I hope you don't hesitate to ask."

In that moment, an epiphany charged through Nick. He knew what he needed to do to show Emma how much she meant to him. He'd prove he loved her beyond all reason.

"Will you meet me at Hampstead Heath tomorrow? The Earl of Sykeston is dueling the Earl of Aulton. They'll fight to the death to achieve satisfaction of their grievance. If you can't, I understand. But I'd ask you not support any retribution in the House of Lords against Sykeston if he's the winner."

"I'll meet you and support the Earl of Sykeston." His father nodded, then grew serious. "Do you love her?"

Everything within him stilled. He loved Emma with a force that required he unapologetically proclaim it to the world. He laughed and let the exuberance of that reality overtake him. "Desperately."

He needed to be by her side and let her know about the duel. He needed to show her how valuable she was, not only to him, but to all the others who depended upon her goodness and her strength.

He'd show her all the people she'd touched and how their lives had changed for the better because of her. He'd show her that she couldn't give up on them. That they all needed her.

But more importantly, he needed her. He couldn't let her give up on him either. But first, there were several matters that he had to attend to in order to have everything ready for tomorrow.

The fateful day promised to be quite busy for him and his lovely, but wildly bewildering, wife.

After she'd walked for hours, Emma found herself at Langham Park. For the first time in her life, the familiar refuge seemed as dissolute as the gaping hole within her heart. There were no squirrels to offer a lecture or dogs to nestle their noses in comfort or cheerful flowers to offer a bit of joy. Just a cold north wind that blew through the empty branches of the trees. It all foretold the truth she'd been unwilling to accept.

Her husband might say he loved her and supported her convictions, but his actions and words the last two days were the new foundations of their marriage.

"May I join you?" Claire's green cloak snapped in the

wind, and tendrils of her auburn hair blew about her face. Her cousin tried to tame the wayward locks, but the wind was too strong.

Emma scooted over, and Claire took the seat beside her. While she surveyed the park, she took Emma's hand in hers. "What's wrong? Don't tell me nothing. I see it in your face."

"I don't know what I'm doing—in my marriage or in my life." A defiant tear slid down her cheek. The cold wind attacked, leaving a trail of wetness stinging her cheek. "Before Lena's death and my marriage, I'd constructed everything in my life to my liking. Now, I have control over nothing." More tears collected in an attack against her composure, their will stronger than hers.

Claire narrowed her eyes as she raked her gaze over Emma. "Does your husband know how you feel?"

"Yes." Emma shuddered before taking a breath. "He doesn't care."

Claire threw her arm around Emma's shoulders and drew her close. Without any space between them, the wind lost its bluster. "I'll share all I've learned so far in marriage." Claire's voice was low and blanketed Emma in a calmness she hadn't experienced in days. "Maybe it will help you find your way."

"I've missed you," Emma said.

"Me, too." Claire took Emma's hand and rubbed it across her cheek. "No one knows better than me how hard marriage is. Remember I was ready to forgo Alex and the idea of a family. I didn't have the strength or desire to carry the weight. But Alex shouldered everything for a while until I was ready to try again and we could work out our differences."

Emma closed her hand over Claire's and squeezed. "I remember how hard it was for you. I thought you were moving to Scotland."

Claire raised her eyebrows. "I know you crave independence in our world and justice for the wrongs that befall women, but marriage can be the vehicle to attain your heart's desires."

Emma snorted. "Lud, Claire, what nonsense." She grew solemn, and her voice wobbled. "I wasn't ready. I don't know if I'll ever be ready. I'm not a woman who makes a dutiful wife. Now? I'm fighting to keep what little I can control in order."

"Do you think Somerton wants someone docile? If he did, he wouldn't have followed you to Portsmouth. Nor would he have accompanied you to Lord Sykeston's house or offered Lena's maid and her mother employment. He wants you." Claire reached up and brushed Emma's hair away from her face. "Do you love him?"

"Yes." Emma gave a hiccup. "I hate it. Everything he does I study to find the exact meaning behind the actions. I'm such a lovesick fool, I make myself cringe." She gave a small laugh. "Who'd have thought that I would be in such a web?"

"Emmy, that's not true." When Emma tried to shake her head, Claire held up her hand. "Let me finish. When you come into the room, he moves toward you, sits next to you, watches you, but more importantly, he's centered when you're with him. Both Alex and I have seen it. Frankly, Alex has been entertained by Somerton's befuddlement for weeks. That night when I found you here next to the bench, Somerton delivered a most appropriate set-down of Alex's behavior toward you and your beliefs."

Emma's breath hitched. Claire deserved the truth. "Aulton is betrothed to a woman who wants to break the engagement and needs money to do so. She's the sister of a man Nick despises. When I asked him to let me lend her the money, he refused."

Claire raised an eyebrow.

"I thought if I could save that woman, it would rid me of my grief." Emma closed her eyes and swallowed the misery that threatened to choke her. "But he chose his money and his past over me."

"Have you talked to him about your feelings?" Claire tucked one of Emma's curls behind an ear and then drew the hood of Emma's cloak about her head.

"For the last two days."

Claire studied the gray landscape. "My advice is to give him a chance to make this right. Remember when I told you that neither of you are good at compromise? Perhaps you both need time to determine how you can bridge these differences between you. He loves you. Nothing you can say could convince me otherwise."

"Oh Claire, you see life as perfect. The truth is sometimes love isn't enough."

Claire blew the breath out of the left side of her mouth. A tell her patience was at an end. "Emma, listen to what I'm saying. You have the ability to have a wonderful and full life filled with love, happiness, family, and anything else you desire. Are you going to let this adventure of a lifetime escape without taking the ride offered? Are you afraid to risk your heart for something truly rare and beautiful? You're not that obtuse, are you? Imagine creating a family with Somerton, along with the unflinching support of the family who's loved you from day one. But most importantly, a husband who adores you. A husband who would do anything for you."

"You don't understand," Emma murmured. "That's not my life."

"He gave you ten thousand pounds and helped you start a thriving business. Most men wouldn't have given their wives the opportunity to discuss such an operation, but Somerton did. He's supporting your beliefs the best way he knows how." Claire's sigh was barely audible. "Emma, find the good in your marriage and work on making the rest of it better."

She shook her head and was about to deny it.

Claire continued, not allowing Emma a word edgewise. "All you have to do is take a chance. Open your heart. He needs you desperately. Somerton is a wonderful, loving man. If it hadn't been for him, I'm not certain Alex and I could have saved our marriage."

The vehement loyalty in her cousin's face was breathtaking. "Really? I never knew he helped you."

Claire nodded. "I won't go into the details, but Somerton encouraged Alex to come to London and make amends. He made the trip with Alex." She took Emma's hand and entwined their fingers. "There's a marvelous journey ahead of you. Marriage with a true partner. It's everything you could want and more. You'll never have it if you don't try. When has a Cavensham not taken a risk?"

"Perhaps it's too late." In so many words, she'd told him their marriage would never work. But how could she give up on the man she loved beyond all reason?

"If there's love, it's never too late. Give him a chance." Claire let go of her hand and stood.

Emma followed suit and kissed Claire on the cheek. "Thank you. I'll go home and see my husband."

Claire tucked her arm around Emma's and led her back to Langham Hall. "I always knew you were brilliant."

After leaving Claire, Emma returned home and waited for Nick in her bedroom. She'd sent Arial to bed and waited some more. When he never came home that night, deep inside, she feared her words had caused a chasm between them that would never heal. Unable to sleep, she'd sat in a chair and guarded her window, willing Nick to return. As the first wisps of dawn broke, a soft knock at her door drew her attention away from her watch. "Come in."

Nick stepped inside and closed the door. Not moving or saying a word, his gaze affixed to hers. Every word she'd wanted to say escaped when he entered the bedroom. He looked tired, and his face was drawn.

"Good morning, love," he whispered.

The endearment caused her heart to miss a beat. "Good morning."

He slowly walked to her as if wary he'd frighten her away. When he reached her side, he pressed his lips against her cheek. She swallowed and kissed his in return. If only they could go back to last week, they wouldn't have to face the harsh realities of the day.

"You're wearing your gown from yesterday," he said.

Too afraid to break the strange peacefulness between them, she could only nod her head.

"You didn't sleep either?" He rested on his haunches and faced her. His black morning coat fell away to reveal a dark gray waistcoat that fit his body like a second skin. The immaculate mathematical knot of his neckcloth emphasized the breadth of his neck and shoulders. Lean and powerful, he resembled a lion ready to strike and protect what was his. And she was his.

She shook her head. "I couldn't until I spoke with you." She trailed her finger down the sharp angles of his jaw. His hand covered hers, anchoring it to his cheek. "I must apologize."

His brows drew together. "Why?"

She swallowed and forced herself to hold his gaze. "I allowed . . . my obsession with Lena to come between us. You've shown your support for me over and over the short time we've been married." She studied his long fingers pressed against hers, the inherent strength harnessed as he tenderly touched her. "You deserve better. If you'd find it in your heart to give me another chance—"

"Yes, always." His hand tightened over hers, the touch comforting. "I understand your grief. It mirrored my own in so many ways. Together, we'll help each other heal. Whatever you give me is enough—"

"No." Her eyes anchored his, willing him to understand. "You have all of me—my heart and my commitment. Let me prove it to you."

He caressed her with his gaze. She closed her eyes and leaned her forehead against his. More intimate than a kiss, their touch was a pledge between them.

"Sweetheart, we don't have much time," Nick whispered. His lips swept across hers. "We need to leave."

"Where?" Her voice croaked with the resonance of a bullfrog.

"I'm taking you to a duel. Now, hurry."

Her eyes flew open in disbelief. "What?"

"Sykeston is meeting Aulton at Hampstead Heath at first light. You're going to witness Lena's final justice."

"When did Jonathan challenge him?" Every thought churned into a tempest as she struggled with what Nick was saying.

"Yesterday." Nick took her hands in his and helped her rise.

"Was he sober?" she asked.

"He appeared perfectly fine." He led her to the dressing table. He twisted her braided hair into a knot, but his large fingers fumbled with the hairpins.

"Let me do this." Emma quickly pinned the mass of hair into place. "What weapon did Aulton chose?"

"Pistols. Sykeston told me yesterday afternoon."

She stood and straightened her gown. He evaluated her and nodded his approval.

"Perfect. I'll tell you everything in the carriage." With her hand in his, he led her downstairs. At the foot of the stairs stood Arial, Whaley, and Hamm.

"Good morning, my lady." Arial greeted her with a smile and a beautiful black velvet cloak trimmed in gray cording. "His lordship bought this for you yesterday."

The elegance of the cloak stole her breath as Arial held it for her. The rich fabric shimmered as the light caught the nap of the fabric. She allowed Arial to slip it around her shoulders. The finishing touch, a diamond button, served to secure it about her person.

"It was striking in the shop's window, and immediately I thought of you," he whispered.

His gaze devoured her, and she lost her ability to form a coherent thought. When Arial straightened the hem, Emma concentrated on the simple action and forced herself to breathe.

With a trademark flourish, Whaley held Nick's black greatcoat. "My lord."

Hamm swept open the door as if they were going to opening night at the opera.

Nick held out his hand for her to take. "Are you ready?"

At the sound of his voice, she lifted her head. Nervous, Emma again smoothed her hand across the luxurious velvet, the beauty of the garment belied the inherent strength of the fabric. It reminded her that her husband's handsome exterior covered an unwavering fortitude. Before her eyes stood a man who promised her a life she so wanted—a future they would build together based upon the love and care they had for each other. The man she had doubted, her husband, was the reason for the resurgence of her hope. He was taking her to see justice done and to find her long-awaited absolution—a hope and dream she believed dead.

"Thank you for this." She swept her hand down the cloak. Last night's misgivings diminished as this indefinable moment grew in importance. "Thank you for this morning."

He didn't acknowledge her thanks, but the satisfaction in his visage was unmistakable. He took her hand and helped her into the carriage. Within seconds, they were barreling north through town with their destination, the Hampstead Heath dueling grounds, less than a half hour away.

Nick sat across from her in the rear-facing seat. When she started to speak, he held up his hand. "You have a thousand or more questions, but let me start. Sykeston came to our home in hopes he'd be able to offer his thanks to you personally for the letters. After he read them, he wasted little time in finding Aulton at White's. Yesterday morning, Sykeston issued the challenge in front of practically the whole club. Aulton had no choice but to accept."

He leaned toward her with his legs framing hers. His warmth penetrated the thick velvet cloak, but it wasn't enough, and she moved closer. She shut out all distractions except for him.

"Why are you taking me there?" Her blood surged to where they touched; his massive thighs dominated hers in size.

Tilting her chin, his caress commanded she pay attention. There was no need as his compelling eyes held her mesmerized.

"From the first time I saw you hell-bent to retrieve the Bentham book, I wanted you." Brushing his knuckles against her cheek, he continued. "Never in my life had I seen such vitality in another. I tried to banish such thoughts and concentrate on my work. But, time and again, we'd meet. My need, my want, my longing grew until I couldn't deny it."

Her body threatened to combust from the heat in his eyes. The honesty in his expression locked her in place.

"Yesterday, after I met with Sykeston, I had another visitor waiting for me. My father."

Involuntarily, she moved toward him to offer comfort. It had to have been a shock for him. She searched his face for any sign of unease, but found nothing but earnestness. "I wish I would have been there for you."

"Actually, I think it was best you weren't as it forced us to confront the pain we'd inflicted on each other." His admission caused a tightening of his lips. "It was the first honest conversation we've ever shared."

"What did he say?" A heaviness centered in her chest at the thought his father had hurt him again.

"He apologized. He readily admitted how wrong he was all those years."

The dawn light seemed to fill his eyes with an energy that made them luminous. She stared, unable to say a word.

"He confessed more, Emma." Her name on his lips resonated like a vow. "His whole life was centered on my mother. When he lost her, it destroyed him." He grimaced as he hesitated. Sadness crept into his handsome face, and her heart stuttered in protest. "He couldn't love any-one else without her. He didn't know how . . . which left me . . . alone."

She squeezed his hand in reassurance, hoping he'd feel the love she had for him. Hearing a parent say they didn't have room in their heart for you would level her. But Nick didn't falter, proving his own strength was astonishing.

"I'm so sorry," she whispered thickly.

In silence, he sat consumed by his thoughts. He shook

his head as if awaking from a bad dream. "I realized all the while he was confessing his own emptiness and sorrow, that you were correct. I couldn't love you the way you deserved unless I became whole myself. The wounds I carried inside never healed. I became an expert at ignoring the pain."

An unrestrained anguish ripped through her at the thought she'd caused him additional distress at her demands. "Nick—"

"Shh, listen." His fingers touched her lips. "I'm not perfect by any stretch of the imagination, but I'm changing. I've taken steps to do what's right." He took a deep breath before slowly releasing it. The lines around his eyes relaxed, and his unhappiness seemed to diminish. "I met Howell last night with a loan to repay Aulton. It makes little difference if Aulton survives or not. I don't want some heir crawling through his rotten woodwork, waving the settlement agreements with some obscure contingency that demands Miss Howell's hand in marriage or payment of the twenty thousand pounds. She's free of him, Emma."

The shock of his statement caught her off guard, and she simply stared.

"I'm not completely reformed." A rakish smile tugged his lips. "Howell has to pay me back at a healthy rate of interest, and I'm holding his best racehorse as collateral."

Her pulse leapt wildly at the news. He'd done what she'd asked of him. He'd committed to her and believed in her. She hurtled herself into his arms, raised her lips to his, and sealed this moment between them forever. She loved him with a vibrancy that would never dim, and she had little doubt it would grow bolder and stronger each day they shared with each other.

"You're filling the empty spaces within my heart, Emma. Never doubt that."

The carriage came to a sudden halt. The movement caused her to pitch backward, but Nick held her tight in his embrace, not letting her fall. He swept her into his arms and deposited her in his lap. After a brief swipe of his lips against hers, he turned his attention to the carriage window.

The dawn cast a pink glow that covered the empty field before them. A low patch of early morning fog still clung to the ground, refusing to release it. The cloudy wisps resembled lost souls created in the past during other desperate duels.

A group of men nervously milled around a figure she immediately recognized as Jonathan by his halting gait. She reached for the door, but Nick grabbed her hand.

"We stay inside. Sykeston knows you're coming. Aulton doesn't. It's safer for you. No one needs to know you're here. Do I have your agreement?" The silkiness in his voice didn't hide the resolution in his request.

With a nod, she trained her gaze on the men next to Jonathan. The remaining slips of fog were burning away. The sun would rise within minutes, and the day would begin with bloodstains painting the ground.

"Isn't it illegal to duel to the death?" She narrowed her eyes in a desperate attempt to recognize their faces. "Who are those men? Is that my father?"

"Those men are the ones who care deeply that justice is attained for Lady Lena." He drew near, his cheek touching hers as he pointed toward the men to the far west. "Next to Sykeston is William. He's acting as the earl's second. Next to him is McCalpin. Pembroke is talking with the Duke of Langham and the Duke of Renton. All three as members of the House of Lords will insure that Sykeston isn't tried for his actions today."

Her body stiffened in shock. "Your father is here too?"

He drew her closer. "They're all here because Lena

matters and you matter. You're a fiercely determined woman who they admire and want to support."

"Did you do this—" Her voice broke when she understood all that her husband had accomplished last night.

He nodded. "I spent last night meeting with your family and convinced them they had to be here today in a show of support for you."

All the men in her life stood together to defend Lena's honor. Her husband had given her the proof that her pursuit to help Lena and other women was important. Proof that women like her were valued.

Her heart swelled, stealing her breath. She tried to wrestle with the unruly beast, but it was pointless. She had no control over it anymore. She'd given it to Nick. "I love you," she whispered.

A tear streamed down her face. With the slightest touch, Nick kissed it away. "I'll love you until the end of my days and beyond."

She closed her eyes in a desperate attempt to gain control over the trembling inside. He kissed her hand and then her wrist.

There was more to say, but the battle between the two men had started. William met with Aulton's second to inspect the pistols. With solemn respect between the parties, the seconds delivered the pistols to the duelists who stood back-to-back to each other. One of the other men presiding over the deadly drama waved a white silk tie, indicating it was time to start.

Aulton and Jonathan started their death march until approximately forty feet separated them. Emma had counted twenty paces apiece.

The two combatants turned and stared at each other. Each raised his weapon. The air thickened as if to slow their motions. Time stood still. Silence blanketed the area. The birds ceased their chatter, the wind quieted, and the only sound that broke the dead air was the simultaneous cock of the pistols.

As if desperate to flee the upcoming massacre, a host of sparrows shot straight into the sky. A red silk cloth dropped to the ground. Two cracks from the respective pistols broke the stillness, the reverberations of the gunfire echoing through the field.

She hadn't realized it, but she'd grabbed Nick's hand and squeezed, all the while watching this macabre ritual of honor play out. She clenched her eyes and prayed. *Let it be over. Let Lena and Jonathan be free.* If there truly was justice in the world, Aulton would be dead.

She never saw herself as bloodthirsty, but today proved there were dark depths about her own soul she didn't even recognize. She accepted them as if an old friend had visited. She may go to hell, but she wanted Aulton *dead*.

She opened her eyes. One of the surgeons ran from the side to attend Aulton, who'd fallen to the ground. Jonathan stood tall without a mark on him. She battled the urge to recoil from the horrific scene on the field.

Aulton's surgeon shook his head as he examined the body that lay on the ground. As a modicum of respect, he placed Aulton's greatcoat over his body.

All her grief and sorrow escaped with a shuddering breath, closing her throat and robbing her of speech. Emma closed her eyes and fell against Nick. He cradled her in his arms and rocked. He whispered words of comfort, but she couldn't concentrate on anything as she wept for her friend and the horror she witnessed today.

It was finished. Lena was truly free now.

Chapter Twenty-six

In the hurried minutes after Aulton's death, Nick helped Emma out of the carriage. Her father and the Duke of Renton had come to inquire after her.

"Puss, it's over," her father whispered as he bent to kiss her cheek. "I want you to meet—"

"My father," Nick offered. "The Duke of Renton."

The duke took her hand and raised it to his lips, and she was struck by how much her husband favored his father.

Distraught, she couldn't answer as a numbness infused her body. Nick stood close with his arms wrapped around her waist as if he'd not let her go. Never had she been more thankful for the intensity of his support as she had in the aftermath of the duel. The heaviness in her limbs and the ache in her chest made it impossible to think of anything else.

She'd expected an onslaught of remorse would weaken her, and the view of Aulton's lifeless body on the field might destroy her. Remarkably, the satisfaction of his ultimate punishment created a slow catharsis. After all the months, it was finally over.

Jonathan waited until Aulton's body was removed before he carefully made his way over to her. He bent low to her ear. "Thank you, Emma. Because of you, I have my satisfaction." He stood back, and his brown eyes gleamed. "Mary Butler and her mother are at my home in Portsmouth."

All she could do was nod.

William, who stood by her side, brought her into his embrace. "Em, it's a good day for all of us. Because of you, I have my friend back."

Her reckless tears returned with such force she had trouble seeing. William kissed her cheek, then immediately returned her to Nick, who encircled her with the steel bands of his arms. Once again, the turbulence in her world calmed.

McCalpin pressed a kiss to her cheek, and for a brief moment, she left the safety of Nick's arms for a hug. He pulled her tight. "I'd do anything for you, Em."

Her brother released her and turned his attention to Jonathan and Will. While they conversed, Alex took her hand and squeezed. "Emma, we love you," he whispered.

She looked into his gray eyes, the ones that reminded her of a spring storm, and squeezed his hand in answer. She loved them all, the wonderful men in her life.

Finally, after what had seemed like hours, she and Nick left the bloody field for home. Numb, she sat on Nick's lap as he cradled her in his arms and murmured soothing words until they arrived home. When the coach stopped, he swept her into his arms and carried her up to his room. After a click of the lock, he gently deposited her on his bed.

His attention never left hers as he undressed her, then he followed suit and closed the curtains around the massive bedframe. He joined her in bed and pulled her tight against him. There was no greater shelter from the horror of the day than his body wrapped around hers. Desperate, she took full advantage of his strength. As she cried for all she'd lost, the full extent of her stubbornly held sorrow became a flood she couldn't control. Nor did she want to.

In his infinite love and grace, Nick gave her refuge, and she let her grief go as he rocked her in his arms. There were no words, but her heart knew he had done it all for her. With one last shuddering sob, she finally released a last good bye to Lena.

Captive in his arms, she found the peace to heal and drifted off into a slumber she didn't even know she needed.

Emma opened her eyes and found Nick studying her with such tenderness it stole her breath.

"How are you?" His fingers brushed away a curl that had fallen in her eyes.

"Exhausted, but happy." Without a hint as to what she should say or do, she simply stared at him. In that singular moment, she understood with an abrupt clarity everything required of her. "Nick, I never—"

"Let me." He pressed his finger to her lips. "There's so much I have to say."

His teeth grazed her lower lip, seeking her touch, showing her a vulnerability she'd rarely seen in him before.

"Yesterday started out to be the worst day of my life. I thought I'd lost you because I couldn't see what I was doing to myself. My selfish need to prove that I was better than my father and Howell almost cost me everything—you."

With his words, a new fervor hit her full force. She loved him with everything she possessed.

"I couldn't let that happen. I wouldn't let you go so easily." The honesty in his eyes opened a place deep inside her heart. "Em, I said I loved you yesterday," he whispered. "But I truly didn't understand what it meant until you left the bank. I sat stunned with no thought as to how I could win you back. Before, I thought if I protected my heart, I'd be happy. But you showed me what an empty life that was. I didn't want to be the person who experienced love only on my terms. I realized I'd miss all the glorious wonders it offered. You made me understand that if I wanted to be a man who could love, I had to learn that in turn, I deserved love."

He stole a kiss in that moment. It was a fleeting touch, but one filled with such heartfelt emotion, she took an involuntary gasp.

"In matters of the heart, I've learned there are no rules. You have to trust your instincts and be prepared for the fall." His hand cupped her cheek. "I'm finally ready."

Once again, her incredible husband surprised her.

"I'm finally ready to give you everything—all my faults, weaknesses, wealth, my body, and my heart. Because then you have everything that I am. Do with it what you will, but all of it is yours." He took a deep breath and smiled. "You made me understand what it is that makes a life worthwhile. Give me a chance, and I'll make our life worthwhile together."

"I love you," she whispered. He stroked her face with his fingers, and his gaze softened like a caress. "When I believed all was lost, you proved differently. You've taught me that marriage to you is the greatest gift I've ever received." She swallowed the tears and took a deep breath for fortitude. "You've given me everything I ever desired in life—a man who saw the true me and still loved me for it. I don't know how I got so lucky."

He eased closer and gathered her in his arms. His mouth took hers in a kiss of devotion and intimacy that allowed their hearts to meld together, each strengthening the other.

They'd experienced passion and romance together. But, now, with each heart bared to the other, the promise of a life filled with love and joy was before them.

Any lingering shadows that surrounded them would be swept away forever in the light of their love. She was determined to make him happy and give him the life he deserved.

"Love me," Emma whispered.

Nick covered her, the warmth of his body more comforting than she'd remembered.

"Always," he answered.

He trailed his hands in a gentle path from her hip to her breast. The touch ignited a searing path of yearning in its wake.

"Nick," she murmured.

"Hmm?" He sucked her nipple into his mouth.

She arched into his touch, desperate to have more of him. "I never answered your question yesterday."

His tongue circled the taut tip, and she whimpered. With his hard body keeping her anchored, he drew back and regarded her.

"Yesterday, you asked how I slept the night before." She pressed a kiss to his chin and whispered, "I don't like sleeping alone either."

His eyes glimmered with such brilliance that it reminded her of the ocean beset by sunlight. "As your husband, I can promise you that'll never happen again," he whispered as he kissed the side of her mouth.

"Never?"

"Ever," he whispered. "I need your brightness beside me. My life before you was a solitary existence. I was a nomad trying to find a place to belong. Then you appeared. A brilliant star in the night sky. I followed your path and you brought me home."

Epilogue

Three months later
Langham Park

The snow that now blanketed the ground had made a surprise appearance last night. A welcomed guest, the frost's influence could be felt as far as the eye could see. It magnified the peaceful quiet of the park while the brilliant white created a canvas too beautiful to disturb. Even the squirrels had surrendered their ritual scampering dances to protect the serenity of the landscape.

Emma studied the letter from Miss March Lawson in hopes she'd misread what her friend had related. The words stung like a kiss from the winter wind. She glanced about the park trying to make sense of how such a thing could have happened.

The scrunch of footsteps meeting the fresh layer of snow drew her attention to the pathway. Her husband's long stride cut the distance between them. She tilted her lips at the sight. With his gray greatcoat and tall black beaver hat, his fine figure commanded her attention. She'd never tire of the sight.

"Lady Somerton, imagine finding you here at our special bench?" He took his hat and hit it against his thigh to remove the thin layer of flakes that had fallen on the fur when he passed under an overhanging tree branch. He dipped close and pressed his lips to hers. "Hmm, fresh-air kisses taste the best."

Though the air was cold, it wasn't uncomfortable, but the heat from his body permeated her black velvet cloak.

"Come sit for a moment and take in the beauty." She patted the seat.

Nick slid beside her and pulled her close.

"What?" The intense look on his face was somewhat disconcerting. "Do I have jam on my chin?"

With his gaze never leaving hers, he shook his head. "I'm taking in the beauty." He leaned close and stole another kiss. "The beauty of my wife."

"Stop." Her cheeks heated with his words. "You're going to start something, and we need to go in soon."

He caressed the back of her neck. Before his lips touched hers again, he whispered, "Then let's go inside."

His sinfully rich voice could make bees leave their hives on a day like today. She certainly didn't have any greater willpower against his allure.

"I received a letter from March. I'd asked her to help me in the management of the bank, but she declined." Emma clutched the letter tight. She couldn't believe what she'd read. "What's your opinion of fratricide?"

Nick laughed and pulled her close. "What's William done this time?"

She shook her head. "Amazingly, it's McCalpin. March informs me she can't help with the bank. She must work on her brother's estate, at least until the sheep are sheared. Do you know why?"

Nick played with a loose curl that had escaped from her simple chignon. "No, tell me."

She took a deep breath. No good could come from her anger, but how she wanted to lock her brother in a room and give him a piece of her mind. Her good opinion of him had transformed into a scathing contempt for his imperious lack of regard. "McCalpin is the new trustee of her family's trusts and has completely ignored her requests for funds."

Nick diverted his attention away from the errant curl and devoted it solely to her. "I'll talk to him and get this straightened out."

"No." She waved the letter through the air as if it were a saber. "We'll both talk to him. The woman turned twenty-five. She's entitled to those funds. Does he have any idea how hard her life is?"

"Easy, love," he soothed. "I agree. We'll handle it together."

It was one of the many reasons she loved him. He treated her as an equal partner. He asked her opinion on his business and their investments, and even helped her with her own bank.

"Let's ask Daphne if she'll help at the bank. She's always had a mind for numbers," he offered.

"Excellent idea," she said. He was absolutely the perfect husband for her.

He gave a satisfied sigh. "I need to get you inside. I don't want you or the baby to get chilled."

"I don't want to go in. It's too beautiful," she protested.

"Have you thought of names?" he asked. He left her side and crouched before her. The loss of his warmth was forgotten when she gazed into the heat of his turquoise eyes.

She kissed the tip of his perfect nose. "I thought if we have a girl, we could call her Laura Lena. I think it's a beautiful—"

He swept her into a kiss that possessed every inch of her. A small flutter in her stomach intensified until she trembled from her head to her toes. It didn't stop even when he drew back to examine her.

"What a wonderful way to remember my mother and your friend." The passion in his voice could have melted every snowflake in the park. "That's a perfect name."

"I'm happy you like the idea." Her eyes watered. Having a baby had turned her into a watering pot.

"I'll escort you inside. The duchess wants to see you." He pulled her to her feet and clasped an arm around her waist. Slowly, they walked back to Langham Hall with Nick's tight grip insuring she'd not slip or slide along the entire way.

"I hope the baby is a girl." He caressed her ears with his lips. "Daring, brave, unpredictable, gorgeous, and filled with love. Just like her mother."

With a scrunch of her nose, she stopped and turned in his arms. "I'd like to have a girl, too. Next time, shall we try for a boy?" The mischief in his eyes told her he'd enjoy the "trying" part quite a bit.

"It'd be my pleasure." With his fingers lingering against the tender skin behind her ear, he brushed a curl back. "Perhaps our position determines whether it's a girl or—"

"Hush, you rogue," she whispered. "It doesn't work that way."

"We won't know unless we make the attempt." He waggled his eyebrows as he led her inside Langham Hall.

Emma's entire family, including Nick's father, had gathered in the blue salon. A blazing fire in the massive fireplace insured the room was warm. Too warm, in her opinion, so she took a position close to the massive windows that overlooked her park. She leaned against her husband, and he bent down to kiss her on the cheek. His arms encircled her, and his hands rested on her stomach. "I love you." He caressed her ears with his lips.

She'd never tire of those words. It still gave her the

same thrill as it did the first time he said them. "I love you."

Her father interrupted the festivities as he raised his glass in the air. "Everyone gather round. It's time to toast our guest of honor this evening."

She tilted her head to question her father's choice of words.

"Puss, it's not you or Somerton. It's the baby," the duke laughed.

Nick laughed even louder. Her father didn't need the encouragement. He'd try to hold the stage for hours if he thought everyone would stay.

"We're honored this evening to have the Duke of Renton join in this most happy occasion," her father said. He stepped aside so Renton could take the floor.

Renton cleared his throat, his unease apparent. "May I start the evening by thanking you all for welcoming me into your home and into your family. This means—" Renton cleared his throat again. "To my son and his darling wife. Somerton, you've grown into one of the most honorable men I know. I'm proud of you and all you've accomplished. Thank you for allowing me to share in this celebration. An old man can die happy."

Nick nodded his agreement and squeezed Emma's hand.

There was still a lot of mending left between the two men. Today, they appeared somewhat comfortable with each other. Emma sighed. This was her husband's family. He truly wasn't alone anymore.

Renton continued, "To the Countess of Somerton, my darling Emma." He delivered a warm smile to her. "When I met you, I realized you'd make my son happy and be the perfect mother for my grandchildren, and last but not least, the perfect daughter for me."

Emma smiled through her tears. It had to be the baby causing all these emotions to tumble out of her control.

"And the perfect, bold wife." Nick didn't help when he bent down and whispered in her ear, "Lucky me."

Author's Note

The English philosopher Jeremy Bentham, who lived from 1748–1832, was a prolific writer. However, he never wrote a book entitled *Bentham's Essays*. It's my personal creation. Mr. Bentham was a fascinating individual. Besides being called the father of Utilitarianism, he's credited as the spiritual founder of the University College of London. Many people know Mr. Bentham because his preserved body, fully dressed in his own clothing, rests in a wooden cabinet at the end of the South Cloisters of the main building of UCL.

What caught my attention about Mr. Bentham was his forward thinking views on women, sexuality, and individual rights. In *The Works of Jeremy Bentham, Vol. 2 (Judicial Procedure, Anarchical Fallacies, works on Taxation)*, he calls women "the best half of the human species." Mr. Bentham was highly critical of an English wife's lack of standing in society and in the institution of marriage. Years before the publication of Mary Wollstonecraft's *Vindication of the Rights of Women*, Mr. Bentham wrote and argued for divorce and equal political power for women.

He never married though he wanted to on several occasions. His ideas of feminism would be whole-heartedly embraced by Lady Emma Cavensham. Is it any wonder she spent so much time and effort to find *Bentham's Essays*?